DEATH
AT THE
CROSSROADS

A Camelia Belmont Mystery

PJ Donison

Death At The Crossroads
A Camelia Belmont Mystery

ISBN: 978-1-7780387-2-3
First Edition, May 2024
Cover Design: https://100covers.com/

Thank you for purchasing my book!

Get updates and information on

new releases, deals, discounts, and more

when you join my mailing list.

https://pjdonison.com/

Already a subscriber? Thanks so much!

pjdonison

26 Letters, Rearranged

DEATH
AT THE
CROSSROADS

Book 2
Camelia Belmont Mystery Series

For in the long run, either through a lie, or through truth, people were bound to give themselves away.
Agatha Christie

Do we loathe our masters behind a facade of love - or do we love them behind a facade of loathing?
Aravind Adiga

DEAD END

SATURDAY, MARCH 19, 11:49 PM

Kaitlyn Fischer loosely gripped the steering wheel with one hand, shifting gears with the other, as she sped to Aaron Anders' home in Paradise Valley. Her belly was taut with anticipation of the night ahead.

Just minutes ago, when she flashed him the keys, Aaron gave her a sly nod and secretive smile, playing it cool in front of everyone at the annual AndersLaw firm party. But she knew what it meant. She wouldn't have to sneak out on her dumbass husband for much longer. They'd come to the crossroads of their affair, and Aaron had chosen her.

The only thing holding them back now was his wife, but Death was already gunning for the current Mrs. Anders. It was only a matter of time. Especially if—as Kaitlyn suspected—Aaron was actually going to follow through with the Sheridan Gambit, like she'd suggested.

But no matter how it came about, she was ready. Ready to take her place at Aaron Anders' side in the privileged legal empire he'd created. Ready to flaunt her role as mistress of that fabulous hillside compound instead of hiding out at his downtown condo. With one of the country's top litigators under her spell, everything she'd ever dreamed of—wealth, power, prestige—would fall around her shoulders like a queen's mantle. She was made for that life.

Kaitlyn glanced up to the clear, black sky above the glow of the city, where a tiny star winked at her from the bowl of a buttery crescent moon.

A good omen.

Even though it was Saturday night, the more respectable Paradise Valley residents were already safely tucked behind their security gates while she raced down the hill, top down, wind whipping her hair against her face. Buzzed on French wine, she downshifted the vintage baby blue Triumph, slowing for the yellow traffic signal in the empty intersection ahead.

The lights flashed to green.

Another good omen.

She smiled as she upshifted to third, accelerating, feeling the little lurch of forward momentum as she approached the intersection.

A burst of light on her left.

Headlights loomed.

Too fast. Too close.

She braced herself against the seat, her foot jammed on the brake.

Too late.

Chunks of glass fell around her as the truck hit the driver-side door.

Metal screeched as pain knifed through her shoulder.

She gripped the steering wheel, but the car was out of her control.

In a tiny, slow motion sliver of time she registered the traffic lights.

Green. All green.

The dump truck folded the Triumph around the light post on the northwest corner, crushing her into the steering wheel. The impact sent gravel flying all over the intersection.

Kaitlyn's mouth filled with the coppery tang of blood.

Her cell phone was ringing, the sound drifting further and further away.

SATURDAY, MARCH 20, 12:23 AM

Detective Sergeant Jose "Moony" Luna mapped out the accident scene in his head as he gathered up bits of paper fluttering around the intersection.

Car headed south. Truck headed west. Driver side impact. Passenger side crushed against the light pole.

Damn shame, too. Looks like a sweet old TR4.

Nothing here to warrant putting pants on for, but it was Paradise Valley Police Department protocol to be called out on a fatality. Even just a routine car accident. He swiped a calloused hand across gritty eyes to focus on the deceased, cataloguing identifiers in his notebook.

Blond hair, red dress, and a blood soaked mess.

Not much else to go on. He stepped around to the driver's side and peered into the wreckage—yep, they were for sure gonna need dental records.

Moony crossed himself and muttered a quick Hail Mary.

Shuffling through the papers in his hand, he found the car registration. Suzanne Anders. He let out a low whistle.

"Shit, man. Who's gonna do the death knock?" he said, to no one in particular. "No way am I gonna be the one to tell Aaron Anders his wife just died."

Waylon "Tank" Sherman, freshly promoted to the Criminal Investigations Unit and Moony's new partner, placed another cone in the intersection.

"What's the big deal?"

Moony shook his head. "Anders. *He's* the big deal. AndersLaw? Ever heard of it? The guy is a legendary asshole. So, if you wanna be the one to knock on his door at," he glanced at his watch, "oh-dark-thirty to tell him the missus is scattered all over the intersection, be my guest."

Tank muttered something.

Moony cocked his head and held up his hand. "Hang on. I hear a cell phone. Where is it?"

One of the fire department crew pointed into the wrecked Triumph.

"It's in there somewhere, but it's gonna take a while to get at it."

Moony pulled his wallet out of his hip pocket, licked his thumb, and fished out a ten-dollar bill. He turned to Tank and handed him the money.

"Grab us some coffee," he said. "And find out if they've located the dump truck driver. We need to talk to that guy ASAP."

"There's a lot of desert between these houses." Tank looked up the hill. "Chopper's on its way, but he could be anywhere up there. I'll go grab that coffee now, Boss." Tank took off at a jog.

What I wouldn't give to have that energy again.

Moony turned back to the wreck, assessing the painstaking job ahead of him.

It was going to be a very long night.

1

MS. IRRELEVANT

MONDAY, JANUARY 11

Monday. Uggh. Here we go again.

Camelia Belmont sipped her third cup of coffee while she skimmed her notes. Suzanne Anders, wife of one of the most powerful lawyers in Arizona, was waiting in the conference room, ready to retain. But it wasn't a compliment. She knew what it meant: all the top tier divorce litigators had declined. With good reason.

Back in December, when she'd briefly met with Suzanne to initiate her divorce from the notorious Aaron Anders of AndersLaw fame, Camelia hadn't committed to represent her. She'd only agreed to file the Petition and attend a preliminary hearing right before Christmas vacation, based on the understanding it was a *limited* appearance. Because who in their right mind would want to face off with Anders and his bulldog, Spencer Ashcroft? But then, before the hearing even began, Anders had a heart attack right in the courtroom.

Was that only a month ago?

Now, the hearing had been rescheduled and Suzanne wanted to retain. Camelia headed to the conference room, balancing her coffee along with the file and a fresh pad of paper. She pushed the door open with her hip and dropped the file on the table before settling in.

"Good morning, Suzanne, and happy new year. How was your holiday?"

"It was a mess, no thanks to Aaron. I have *got* to be divorced as soon as possible," Suzanne tapped a coral pink fingernail on the conference table for emphasis, "or my good nature is going out the window. Along with Aaron, if he doesn't watch it."

"That good, huh?" Camelia said.

"I know it's not as easy as it sounds, but I want this over with." Suzanne pressed her fingertips to her temples. "The whole thing just gives me a headache."

"Did something happen over the holidays?" Camelia's mind flickered back to her own sad, stressful holiday: her Auntie Freda's unexpected death, alienating her extended family, and, ultimately, contributing to her cousins' arrest.

"Other than Aaron milking his heart attack for all it was worth, and making me out as some kind of heartless monster?"

"So, he's recovered, I take it?" Camelia asked.

"Rather quickly, if you ask me. He was back at work within days. And if the kids weren't on his side to begin with, they are now. I'm the mean old mommy thrashing dear daddy for a divorce when he *almost died* of a heart attack." Suzanne rolled her eyes. "Of course, Aaron's saying the stress of the divorce led to the heart attack. It's complete bullshit, but they bought it."

From what Camelia knew of Anders, it wasn't a surprise he would use his heart attack to get their adult children on his side. The timing couldn't have been better. Not that he'd *planned* the heart attack, but it was sure as hell convenient.

"I'm sorry. That has to be frustrating." Camelia paused as she recalled Aaron's purple-tinged face, but that wasn't all she'd noticed that day in Court. "I have to ask, does Aaron have a history of drug use?"

"What?" Suzanne laughed.

"I'm serious. I saw the Narcan box on the stretcher when the medics were wheeling him out of the courtroom, Narcan is only used for—"

"I know what it's used for. I spent 25 years in healthcare. But I don't think . . . I mean, Aaron?" Suzanne shook her head. "He's way too uptight for that kind of thing."

"Just the same, if Aaron's using your money for his addiction, it gives us leverage," Camelia said.

Suzanne's perfectly arched eyebrows shot up. "Addicted? Aaron? Not unless it's old Scotch and Viagra."

"His face had the purple tinge, a classic sign of fentanyl overdose. And then there's the heart attack. Opioids increase the risk of cardiovascular events. That, along with the Narcan package, makes me think we should subpoena his medical records. If we can prove he's using something, it gives you the upper hand." Camelia would need to press any advantage she could get.

Suzanne shook her head again, more adamantly. "There's no way Aaron is using fentanyl or anything like that. He's done a line of coke now and then, just like everyone else down at the courthouse, but that's not what drives him. It would be completely out of character."

"If you say so." Camelia shrugged. "But based on who we're dealing with, your divorce won't be a slam dunk, so any little bit of leverage would help. Even with a bargaining chip, you're in for a long, hard battle. Are you up for it?"

"I . . . um." She twisted a tissue in her hand, her clear blue eyes welling with the promise of tears.

Camelia let the silence expand, pressing against the teak paneled walls and floor-to-ceiling windows. The hush deepened. Usually, given an expectant opening and a bit of time, truth came gushing out like blood from a bone-deep cut. All of Suzanne's sins and faults, everything Camelia could imagine—and many things she had never dreamed of—would eventually come to light if she could just hold out.

But just when she thought Suzanne was ready to reveal the dirt beneath the veneer, Camelia watched her prospective client rein it back in, blinking back shiny tears, pulling down the shades on her vulnerability.

Suzanne gave Camelia a knowing smile. "I know who I'm up against. The real question is, are you ready for the fallout if you serve him with those discovery requests? Because if you go after Aaron's medical records based on a suspicion of drug abuse, he'll completely flip out."

Camelia didn't bother to soften the edge in her voice, hoping it would make Suzanne think twice about retaining. "Probably, but that's *his* problem, no matter who represents you. My problem—if you want to call it that—is to get you the best settlement possible. Assuming you're willing to let me run the case the way I see fit." Camelia flipped to a page in her file. "I see Tina Halston referred you. If I may ask, why are you here instead of Sherman Wright or one of the other big firms?"

Suzanne took a deep breath. "Don't take this the wrong way, but *no one* will touch my case, thanks to Aaron. I called Tina for a referral because we're friendly and I've known her for years. She thought we'd be a good fit because guys like Aaron don't intimidate you, and you don't have a problem taking down powerful men with bad attitudes." Suzanne smiled and leaned back in her chair.

It was true. Camelia did relish bringing men like Anders to heel. But she wasn't keen on what came with it: testosterone-fueled posturing and an avalanche of paper. Because that's what lawyers like him did. And Anders didn't just have money to burn, he had an entire firm at his beck and call. He would drown Camelia in legal bullshit. But Suzanne wanted to retain and, despite all the downsides, even knowing she was the last choice, Camelia was going to take the case. All because it could be the tipping point to make partner. And, with any luck, she'd get to dish out a bit of comeuppance to the Almighty Anders.

"So, I'm Ms. Irrelevant?" Camelia laughed.

"Of course you're not irrelevant!" Suzanne protested. "I need your help."

"That's football talk for the final draft pick." Camelia smirked and tapped her pen on her legal pad.

"Oh," Suzanne laughed in response. "I get it. So, are *you* up for a long, hard battle?"

"I'm not intimidated by old warhorses like your husband. But he doesn't need to know that," Camelia said. "Seriously, though, my job is to get you divorced as efficiently as possible. And that means finding common ground, getting some basic cooperation and concessions from your husband and his attorney. There's no reason we can't settle this. But if Spencer Ashcroft and Aaron Anders can't be reasonable, they'll regret the day they met me."

Suzanne clapped her hands, once, like a punctuation mark. "So, you're in?"

"As long as the partners approve. And I'm sure they will." Camelia took a sip of water.

Suzanne pulled a checkbook out of her handbag. "How much is the retainer?" she asked, pen in mid-air.

"We'll start with fifty thousand, but be prepared to triple that, because I can't imagine Aaron and his attorney will just roll over."

Camelia mentally ticked off the list of what she was actually expecting: stall tactics, discovery games, faux settlement offers, social media campaigns, and emotional warfare with the adult children as hostages. And those were just the underhanded maneuvers she could think of off the top of her head. She knew there would be more, because Aaron Anders was the prominent face of a mid-size firm—forty or so attorneys and a battalion of paralegals—infamous for its scorched earth litigation tactics. His single-minded dedication to destroying his enemies while they bled money made him hard to beat. Anders didn't care whose back he stepped on, as long as he came out on top.

But so what if Aaron Anders was a career litigator who left a trail of broken lives and empty bank accounts in his wake? Or if Suzanne was a rich Paradise Valley empty nester with nothing better to do than shop for designer swag? This was the type of rainmaking case that would get Camelia voted up to partner. Finally! And if she didn't take the case? Her boss would be furious.

Camelia drew a circle on the pad with a bold dot in the center. Aaron Anders was about to become her target.

"There's a reason I ended up here, with you. I'm just sure of it," Suzanne said.

She accepted Camelia's outstretched hand in both of hers, a little hand hug, and swept out on a breeze of expensive perfume and privilege.

Back in her office, Camelia shut the door and slumped in her chair. *Anders is going to make my life hell.*

She tried to hush her doubts with a sip of lukewarm coffee. For a moment, she thought about a little shot of vodka, but it wasn't even noon yet, and a dozen or so messages were flashing on her computer.

Work was the antidote. She would dive in and lose herself. And that's what she *had* to do: stay sober, keep her head down, and bill like a demon, just as her boss, Byron McCaffrey, had demanded after the Anders hearing in December.

Byron had read her the riot act over a rumor spread around town by Aaron's asshole of a lawyer, who claimed Camelia was drunk in the ladies' room the morning of the Anders hearing. That smarmy jerk, Spencer Ashcroft III—as if the world needed three of them— almost got her fired. And all because of a lie. She wasn't drunk. She was hungover. And she'd had another panic attack.

Camelia shook her head. She didn't have time to worry about Ashcroft. It was already the middle of January and the partner vote was just six weeks away. She had to focus on her career. But these days, focus was elusive. After the sudden death of her Auntie Freda over the holidays, Camelia had returned even more ambivalent about her practice than usual. But how she *felt* didn't matter. She didn't have an alternative plan, and she couldn't just up and quit.

So, she had to change. But the only change she could make, *had to make,* was in her own behavior. Otherwise, she would never make partner. Hell, based on that conversation with Byron before Christmas, she might not even keep her job if she didn't turn things around. He'd made no bones about it: making partner depended on a steady stream of billing and total sobriety. What he didn't know is that sobriety required tamping down her runaway anxiety, and that was a *much* bigger dragon.

She snapped the rubber band on her wrist. According to her therapist, it was supposed to help break a bad habit. But Dr. Carlos Chavez hadn't realized the habit was alcohol when he'd offered the rubber band, and Camelia wondered how many times she would have to raise a welt to make the thirst quiet down.

After a late lunch at her desk, Camelia fell into the zone, fully focused on preparing for the Campbell trial the next morning. She didn't realize she'd been at it for a couple of hours when her assistant, Cate Sanchez, lightly knocked on the door as she entered, breaking the spell.

"I've got your case summaries ready for the meeting. Need anything else?" Cate flipped a hank of auburn hair over her shoulder.

Camelia glanced at her phone. She hadn't realized the time. "Did you add the Anders case to the list?"

Cate smiled and waved a sheet of paper. "Yep. And thanks for pulling a fifty k retainer out of her, because we're going to need every penny and then some. This case is going to be intense."

"Don't remind me," Camelia groaned.

"Better get going, or Sonia will mark you tardy for class," Cate quipped, rolling her eyes.

Camelia stood up with a weary sigh. After the case meeting, she was facing at least two more hours of trial prep. It was going to be a late night at the office. Again.

2

SIDE-CAR SONIA

MONDAY, JANUARY 11

Unless you were in Court or with a client on a Monday afternoon at five p.m., the McCaffrey Rhodes & Rodriguez weekly case review meeting was mandatory. Byron's assistant, Sonia Marsh, reviewed new clients first, then everyone gave a brief report on their open cases. Well, everyone except Arturo Rodriguez, who loved the sound of his own voice, so none of his reports were brief.

Sonia tucked a glossy blond curl behind one ear and began the summary, running her manicured index finger down the page as she read off the case names and issues. No one interrupted until she came to Camelia's most recent acquisition.

"Anders, Suzanne, dissolution. Opposing party is Aaron Anders, represented by Spencer Ashcroft." Sonia glanced up at the ripple of murmurs around the table. "Yes, *that* Aaron Anders. She's with Camelia. Or that was the plan."

"She's ready to retain, but . . . I have some concerns. Such as, Anders will strip the hide off me and make life hell while he does it," Camelia said, turning to Byron. Her ally. Her mentor. Or so she'd thought until he'd dressed her down right before Christmas. "I'm not sure it's worth it."

Byron laughed. Unkindly, it seemed to Camelia.

"Oh, for Chrissake, Cam, he's just a guy getting a divorce. And Ashcroft? He's not the best or the brightest, but he's a rotter. And that means abundant billing. You need this case to get your numbers up." Byron sat back, balancing his Montblanc pen between the tips of his fingers, elbows resting on the arms of the leather chair. His smirk dared her to contradict him.

"I appreciate the vote of confidence, but my caseload is already maxed out, and this is guaranteed to be another high conflict divorce."

"You'll manage. You need the billables and the firm could use a good boost of Scottsdale mommies. You know how they are. If we get in with Suzanne Anders' circle, we'll be making bank on high dollar divorces for years. And come on! Don't you want Aaron Anders' scalp on your belt?" Byron smiled, and Camelia wondered why she had never noticed the predator behind the smile—a hungry shark with chum in the water.

She swallowed her humiliation at being called out in front of the others for her billables. "You're right. And I already got the retainer—"

"Fifty thousand," Sonia added, smiling.

"It's a start," Camelia acknowledged, "but it's going to take a lot more than that. Given the resources Anders has at his disposal, can I count on Sonia to help us out, as needed?"

Sonia looked up from her note-taking and glared at Camelia. She had been assisting Byron since he founded the firm, and considered herself above working with anyone whose name wasn't on the door.

"I'm always happy to help Cate out when she can't get her work done." Sonia gave Camelia a cold smile.

The dig was uncalled for, but underscored the long-standing rivalry between Cate and Sonia.

"Great. Now, where were we?" Byron asked.

Sonia went back to her list. "The Williams matter is a simple B and E and should go to one of the new associates, because Camelia's not the only one with a heavy caseload right now, Mac."

Camelia's head snapped up as Sonia abruptly stopped talking.

Mac? Everyone knew better than to use the nickname his wife—and *only* his wife—called him.

Byron dropped his pen on his pad of paper, laughing loudly. The red splotches on Sonia's neck confessed her transgression.

"Yes, the B and E should go to Stafford. Besides, I'll have a new capital case if the wife in that domestic homicide from Cave Creek gets charged." Byron's voice seemed unnaturally loud. He glanced around the conference table. "What else is in the pipeline?"

Holy crap. Is Byron banging her?

Camelia had never entertained the thought until just this second. One look at Byron's face, though, and she instantly knew it was true. He was studying the case list, but his cheeks were flushed. She looked around at the dozen or so attorneys in the room, wondering if anyone else had picked up on it. Trent Rhodes was busying himself with his case binder, avoiding Camelia's eye.

So, Trent knows.

Suddenly, Camelia saw Sonia in a new light: smart, organized, uber professional, always ahead of schedule, and impeccably groomed. Of course, Byron would have a different vantage point: blond hair and blue eyes, like the California girl she used to be;

attractive and youthful, single woman in her 40s, with a great ass and legs; and always at his beck and call. Even when he was in the office working late, night after night.

Sonofabitch.

Camelia glared at the side of Byron's head. He should know better. And she couldn't wait to tell Cate—Sonia's sworn office enemy—this juicy tidbit.

By the time the meeting was over it was after six o'clock—no thanks to Arturo—and Camelia still had a couple of hours of trial prep for the Campbell case. She stopped by the kitchen for an iced tea, then trudged to her office. Cate was already gone for the day, so she couldn't even enjoy a few minutes of office gossip. She dropped her case binder on the desk and plopped into her chair, kicking off her shoes.

The sun was already down, and all that was left of the day was a hazy purple glow on Camelback Mountain. A steady stream of rush hour commuters cut a red and white streak through the valley. She rubbed the back of her neck where that stubborn knot liked to live, and opened Joshua Campbell's file on her computer.

It should be an easy win: two kids, a lucrative real estate investment business up for sale to buy out Campbell's wife, Shelby, and no hard feelings. But that didn't stop Camelia's insides from tightening into a ball of anxiety. Even now, all these years into her practice, she still dreaded trials. She'd learned the hard way how easy it was to screw up an entire case—and someone's life—with one misstep, one wrong word, one missed exhibit. Which was why she over-prepared for even the most innocuous hearing.

She found the place in the list of exhibits where she'd left off, and went back to drafting her trial notes. If she could focus, she'd be done in no time. Then, she could go home, get into her jammies, and pour a glass of wine. But just one. Her New Year's resolution was no hangovers on weekdays, and she was determined to set up enough roadblocks around her drinking to ease back into a socially acceptable limit. Because no fucking way was she going to end up like some of her boozy, burned out colleagues, dragging a long train of whispered rumors and side-eye everywhere they went.

No, things were going too well to blow it now. She'd scored two points on her partner scorecard. She had the Anders case, which would bring in a ton of billing. The Campbell trial was a sure thing, and a happy, influential client like Josh would refer a lot of work. But she'd have to tiptoe around this scandalous revelation about Byron and Sonia, because—if she actually made partner this time around— her fortunes and her reputation would be tied to Byron's.

Even so, maybe today wasn't such a bad day after all.

3

SANDBAGGED

TUESDAY, JANUARY 12

"Good morning! And how are we this fine Tuesday?"

Cheri Chernyak's sing-song greeting, like everything else about her, was over the top. She had a stripper's physique and dressed far too provocatively for a law office receptionist. But Byron was a shrewd business man, and Cheri was catnip to the firm's growing clientele of rich criminals; a sweet treat, fawning over new clients as they forked over fat retainers. Cheri knew how to play the game, but it irked Camelia to no end that Byron exploited her physical advantages.

"Morning, Cheri." Camelia didn't break her stride. Between the lack of sleep and Josh Campbell's trial exhibits marching in formation through her brain, she wasn't up for chitchat.

"Your driver's on his way," Cheri offered.

"Thanks. Just gonna grab my files," Camelia said as she rounded the corner into the hallway.

In her office, she packed the case files into her rolling brief and tucked a couple of fresh legal pads in the outer pocket. She was rifling through her inbox as Cate tapped on the open door.

"Got everything you need for trial?"

"Yep. Just checking to see if opposing counsel sent anything over last minute," Camelia said. "I was expecting his expert's report, but hoping for a settlement offer."

"I already checked mail and email. Nothing from Griffin's office." Cate picked up Camelia's travel mug. "Don't take your coat off. I'll fill this up, then you need to be on your way. The car will be here in five."

Of all the places she longed to be, Court wasn't one of them; but at least she didn't have to drive. Byron had a car service on retainer for shuttling the firm's attorneys to and from Court, a rare luxury that Camelia appreciated.

She snapped her briefcase shut, dragging it behind her as she stepped into the hall, where Cate approached with her coffee.

"Suzanne Anders just called. She wants to meet." Cate made air quotes. "*Urgently*. Said she needs about a half hour. Do you want me to put her off until tomorrow?"

"Nah, that's okay. I'll head right back after trial. Five thirty should work." Camelia hitched a worn designer tote higher on her shoulder. "And remind me to tell you a very juicy little bit of gossip when I get back. See you later."

"That's hardly fair," Cate called after her.

Camelia was almost to the lobby when she heard the elevator door chime. She quickened her pace to catch it. When the doors opened, Byron stepped out, with Sonia on his heels. Was it just coincidence they were arriving at the office together?

"Morning, Belmont. On your way to Court?" Byron nodded at her briefcase.

"Yeah. Campbell trial," Camelia said, as Sonia slid past her.

"Who's opposing again?"

"Blake Griffin. East Valley guy," she said.

Byron nodded in support. "You got this. You'll eat him for lunch. Break a leg!"

Stepping into the elevator, Camelia waited for the doors to close. She didn't feel nearly as confident as Byron. She used the elevator's mirrored walls to smooth her hair and touch up her lipstick. In her navy blue suit, white blouse, spectator pumps, and carefully-messy French twist, she looked like a prime time version of a successful trial attorney. Other than the puffy purple smudges under her eyes. Camelia had been at the office until after nine, then tossed and turned all night—she never slept before a trial—but it didn't matter. She still had to bring her A game.

Some people loved performing in Court. They got their *Law & Order* fix by showing up in expensive suits, an entourage of paralegals and associates toting boxes of exhibits, the whole shebang. In the beginning, Camelia thought she'd love it too. The thrill. The drama. The scripted storytelling that trials require should have been right up her alley. But then she saw how it all *really* worked. What was the saying? You never want to see how the sausage is made.

As the town car pulled up to the Maricopa County Superior Court, her phone dinged. Camelia glanced at a message from Cate.

> Griffin sandbagged you. Courier just delivered the expert witness report. I'm emailing the exhibits now.

Fuck.

Camelia walked as quickly as she could to the Court entrance, taking her place in the attorney security screening queue. As she waited her turn among the dozens of lawyers, a familiar baritone carried over the din.

Blake Griffin.

"So, we're on the fourteenth green. It's hot as hell, and we're all half blind on spiked Arnold Palmers. Damned if Sorensen doesn't chip it in for a birdie. And that's how I lost three hundred bucks to the judge . . ."

Camelia turned and spotted Griffin a few feet behind her in line, laughing too loudly and standing too close to the soon-to-be-ex-Mrs. Campbell.

Pretentious ass.

Camelia gathered her briefcase and tote bag from the security belt and zipped around the corner to the bank of elevators. As she waited, she quickly weighed her options. She could make a fuss, quote Griffin's golf story, and try to get Judge Sorensen to recuse himself for a conflict of interest. But that was a risky game. Judges tended to get prickly when their character was questioned, and Camelia didn't think Griffin's golf game was enough to force a recusal.

Even if she did bring it up, there was no guarantee Judge Sorensen would step down, and that would be even worse. He would be furious with her for questioning his integrity, leaving her no recourse other than filing for Special Action, which was a whole other level of trouble. No, it was best to just let it go and trust that Judge Sorensen still had some neutrality tucked under his robes.

When Camelia arrived at the sixth floor, Joshua Campbell was standing in front of the courtroom doors, talking on his phone. He hung up as she approached.

"Good morning, Counselor. Raring to go?"

"Let's get you divorced!" Camelia said, leading the way into the courtroom. As her client took his seat, she began unpacking her briefcase. "Just give me a minute to get organized."

She lined up two pens, two highlighters, and two pads of Post-its on her left. One legal pad center, one in front of Josh. Bottle of water, top right. A tabbed binder of exhibits, top left. Finally, her scripted notes of the entire hearing on her right. Her name and her client's name were prominent on the cover page because once, when she was still a newbie, Camelia had a panic attack in Court. She couldn't recall her own name, never mind her client's. The judge had thrown her a lifeline while opposing counsel snickered and rolled his eyes. The shame of that moment still stung.

As if her memory could cast a spell, Camelia glanced down: Joshua Andrew Campbell. She repeated his name silently to herself.

"So, ready for cross-examination?" she asked.

"More ready than they are." He nodded in the direction of Griffin and Shelby as they entered the courtroom. "Because I have you in my corner," he said with a wink.

Josh Campbell was a flirty smartass, but he was also a model client. He paid his bill promptly. He did all his homework. He never commented about his personal life on social media. He followed the rules. Right now, he was adjusting his pale pink silk tie, smoothing it over a starched white pinpoint Oxford. The very picture of a successful mid-40s real estate investor.

"I hope so, because Griffin sent over Shelby's vocational report a few minutes ago, and I need a minute to skim."

Camelia glanced over at Respondent's table, where Griffin and Shelby Campbell were whispering, heads together. Griffin glanced up and gave Camelia a knowing smirk.

Asshole.

She took out her iPad and opened the exhibits Cate had sent over. One was their expert witness's curriculum vitae. The other was a painfully long vocational report on Shelby. Camelia clicked through to the last page.

"Shelby Campbell is unable to earn a wage sufficient to sustain the social status and lifestyle she enjoyed throughout this marriage of long duration . . ."

Blah blah blah.

Of course, Griffin delivered it late, hoping to throw her off her game. He was a mediocre attorney who thought he was way smarter than he actually was, so she should have seen this tactic coming. This kind of sleazy move was just one more reason she'd been drinking herself to sleep every night. Well, until lately.

Camelia took a long gulp of water and exhaled, low and slow. Even with a last-minute expert report, Camelia knew Byron was right. She had this case in the bag because the facts were on her side. The bailiff opened the door behind the bench and the clerk stood up as Judge Sorensen entered.

"All rise."

Camelia didn't forget her name, or her client's. She was in the zone as the trial progressed. However, despite repeated objections, she hadn't managed to have the vocational report withheld. But it shouldn't matter. She'd made her arguments without missing a beat, pulling out exhibit after exhibit to drive her point home. Then Judge Sorensen interrupted her.

"Ms. Belmont, there's no need to go on. I think you've made your point that Mrs. Campbell had opportunities to better herself."

She gave herself a silent cheer. She'd just won the case. Campbell beamed at her with his professionally whitened smile.

After closing statements, Judge Sorensen announced he was taking the matter under advisement, and adjourned. Camelia felt triumphant. She high fived Campbell as they stepped out of the courthouse.

"Congratulations, Josh. You did great on the stand. It's never one hundred percent, but I'm pretty sure you won't be paying Shelby a dime."

"You rocked it, Counselor! I have a good feeling about this," he said, grinning widely. "How soon will we have a decree?"

"It might be a few weeks, but I'll call you as soon as it hits my inbox."

Josh Campbell gave her a quick sideways hug. "Talk soon!"

Campbell waved as he walked toward a cherry red Escalade waiting on the curb, his company logo plastered all over it.

Very subtle.

The Phoenix downtown core was jammed with rush hour traffic as Camelia stepped down from the Court complex plaza to the sidewalk, looking for her ride back to the office. It was almost five o'clock, leaving only half an hour before her meeting with Suzanne Anders. Although she'd only just retained yesterday, Suzanne was already demanding short-notice meetings, without explanation. Camelia hoped she could shut this trend down before it became a habit.

The car pulled up and the driver tucked her rolling brief in the trunk as she slid into the back seat. As the town car crawled through the snarl of commuters, Camelia replayed key moments of the trial in her head. Was the judge's question about Shelby's prior employment good or bad for Josh? When she objected to Griffin's expert report, did she state the correct rule? Or did Judge Sorensen deny the objection for some other reason? Based on what Griffin said in the security line, should she have requested that Judge Sorensen recuse himself?

Her doubts were biting at her, nipping away at her confidence. Camelia leaned her head back and exhaled. Had she nailed it or failed it? She wouldn't know until the ruling came out. By the time the town car pulled up in front of the firm's office tower, she was deflated and tired. She just wanted to go home, kick off her shoes, and curl up on the sofa with a book.

And maybe a double martini.

4

SUZANNE'S DEADLY SECRET

LAST YEAR: TUESDAY, NOVEMBER 3

Suzanne Anders parked her vintage baby blue Triumph in front of the oncologist's office, squaring her shoulders as she walked resolutely into the lobby. Her Fendi Baguette and Burberry jacket quietly announced her wealth, but even those talismans of status couldn't protect her today.

She was swiftly ushered into an exam room, a testament not just to the efficiency of Dr. Baum's practice, but also to their long standing friendship. They'd been neighbors for years, and their kids had gone to the exclusive Rancho Solano Prep School together. But seeing him today as a patient, rather than socially, was new. And it scared the hell out of her.

A quick tap and Richard Baum, M.D., entered the room with a practiced smile.

"Suzanne," he said, and held his arms wide. After a brief hug, he sat next to her. "You know I don't like to sugar coat tough news, especially given your background . . ."

"Thanks, Rick." Suzanne gave him a weak smile. *It must be bad.* "I appreciate the courtesy."

"Okay, first, the data." He sighed as he flipped open her chart. "We got the labs back, along with the MRI, and you can see why I'm concerned." Dr. Baum pointed at two grainy blobs on the scan. "There's a mass on your left ovary, here, and on your fallopian tube here. We'll biopsy everything during surgery, of course, but you should know it looks like ovarian cancer."

When Suzanne didn't respond, he continued.

"Now for the strategy to address the data. I'm scheduling your surgery for next week, and we'll know then if it's metastasized, but unfortunately, that's what it looks like. Either way, you'll need to have chemo."

A shimmer of sweat broke out around her hairline and she suddenly felt nauseous. Ovarian cancer was bad enough, but *metastasized?* She knew the statistics.

"I see." Suzanne paused as her hopeful mind looked for an out. But she knew it wasn't a mistake.

He flipped to a new page in the chart. "Now, I'd like to get some history. Have you had any bloating, difficulty eating, or feeling full quickly?"

"A bit, I guess. It's hard to know, exactly," she said.

What did I miss?

"Any abdominal pain? Urgent need to urinate? Fatigue?" His pen hovered over the page.

"Some, yes. Over the summer, I had some intermittent cramps and constipation, but nothing earth-shattering." She cocked her head. "You do know I've experienced pretty much all of these symptoms my entire adult life, at one time or another, right?"

"Yeah, and that's the problem with ovarian cancer. It hides behind all the usual aches and pains. So, let me ask another way. When did you first decide something was wrong?"

"Around Labor Day, I guess. I started feeling fatigued and noticed I'd lost some weight. And I had this sensation in my pelvic region. Heaviness. Two weeks ago, when I went for my annual, my OB/GYN ran bloodwork. And here I am," she said.

"Well, I think it's been with you for a while. It's a sneaky bastard, hard to diagnose. But we'll know soon enough what we're dealing with." Dr. Baum got up to leave and paused at the door. "We're gonna take good care of you, Suzie, I promise."

Despite a sudden impulse to walk out, social graces took over. "Of course, Rick, thank you. I'm sure it will all be fine."

But she wasn't the least bit sure.

Suzanne picked at a loose thread as she went back over every twinge, every headache, every little stabbing pain. When did the bloating start?

When should I have known?

LAST YEAR: FRIDAY, NOVEMBER 13

Ovarian cancer. Stage 4A.

The day after her robotic hysterectomy at Mayo Hospital, Dr. Baum came to Suzanne's private room to break the news in his quiet, bedside voice. As he detailed the treatment plan, she gripped her elbows with white knuckles, willing herself to pay attention, to nod at all the right places. But she knew the odds. That goddamn clump of rogue cells was bound and determined to kill her. Not if, but when.

"And Suzie, I'm going to do everything in my power to make sure you dance at your grandkid's wedding. We'll do *whatever it takes*," Dr. Baum said, his eyes shiny with compassion. "You're my friend first, my patient second. You have my mobile. Consider me on call twenty-four-seven from now on."

"Rick, that's very kind. And yes, of course we're going to fight the good fight. But I do have one favor to ask."

"Name it."

"I know you're bound by the law, but seriously, you can't tell a soul. Not the kids, for sure. And under *no* circumstances are you to tell Aaron, understood?" She stared hard into his hooded brown eyes for emphasis.

"Suze, that's a mistake. You're going to need their support—"

"No, I won't. I have girlfriends for this. I don't want my kids worried sick, hovering over me. And I don't want Aaron distracted from running the firm. He has so much on his plate already. I mean it. You will not say a *word*." Suzanne grabbed his hand. "Shake on it, Rick."

"Jeez, you drive a hard bargain! But yes, I'll keep it close." He gripped her hand in both of his and gave a little squeeze, his dark eyes peering into hers. "Now, are you ready to go sleep in your own bed?"

After signing all the discharge forms, Suzanne took a cab from the Mayo Hospital in North Scottsdale to the hillside compound she shared with Aaron in Paradise Valley, craving her cool, dim bedroom.

She trudged upstairs, gasping at the pain just a simple flight of stairs brought on. Dropping her handbag on the bed, she bolted the door. This was her sanctuary, the place she could cry in private. She needed time to center herself before . . . what? Since Aaron moved into the casita last year, he hadn't set foot in the house. All three of their kids were grown and gone, living their own busy lives. Even Alma Reyes, her fussy, protective housekeeper, had already left for the day.

There was no one to interrupt her ping-ponging thoughts. Loneliness gathered in the space between her ribs. She pushed it away with a deep breath, studying the carpet for answers.

The diagnosis was forcing her to look at her entire life through a new lens. The lens of not much time left. The lens of *how can I pack all my living into one year?*

Suzanne slowly paced the floor, vibrating with the tense energy of a finite life suddenly brought into sharp focus. She rummaged through one of the purses in her closet and found the pack of Marlboro Lights she kept tucked away; a rare, sinful pleasure for days like this.

Alma kept the wine and coffee bar in the sitting area well stocked, so Suzanne grabbed an open bottle of pinot noir and poured a tumbler full before lighting a cigarette. She flung open the sliding glass door to the veranda and carefully settled in one of the chairs overlooking the swimming pool.

Beyond the pool was the casita, where Aaron had been living since that blowup last year over his *femme du jour*. Just days before Christmas, he'd humiliated Suzanne by showing up at El Chorro, a favorite neighborhood haunt, with a curvy brunette. One of Suzanne's girlfriends happened to be there for happy hour, and texted a photo with the message, *Who TF is this?* By the time Aaron got home, Suzanne had changed the key code to the main house and thrown a garbage bag full of suits on the sidewalk. But Aaron refused to leave, compromising by moving into the casita, waiting for her to get over it. They'd been tiptoeing around a fragile truce ever since.

She had no idea how many women there had been since then, but Suzanne stopped caring a good long while ago. She snapped her fingers and pointed at the casita.

"We're done," she declared out loud.

There would be no reconciliation. She didn't have that kind of time. She would divorce Aaron, take her half of everything, and live her last days fast and hard.

And first class all the way.

She walked inside and fished her diary out of her purse. There was so much to organize, to arrange, to schedule. The first step was to hire a first-rate divorce attorney who could settle it all quickly. Assuming she could find someone to take her case.

She scribbled a list of every divorce attorney she knew on a first-name basis. Just as quickly, she scratched through all but one of them. The rest were all in Aaron's circle: golf partners, law school buddies, and a bunch of back slapping cronies. They would never break ranks.

She tapped on the contacts in her phone and called her one and only remaining option, Tina Halston at Sherman Wright. The stylish blond had taken care of a friend's divorce last year—Julia didn't even have to show up in court—and even if she wouldn't personally take the case, Tina knew people.

"I mean, Suze, really, I don't know who would want to go toe to toe with Aaron." Tina didn't sound optimistic. "He's got quite the reputation around town."

"Which is exactly why I need someone like you," Suzanne said.

"Aaron's already conflicted us out. He met with the head of our family division a while back. And even if it wasn't an ethics violation, I know you both personally. No way am I touching your case."

The sonofabitch ran a beauty contest.

Aaron had done the rounds, meeting with all the top divorce litigators in town to make sure Suzanne couldn't hire them.

"Well, you must know *someone*." Suzanne tried to keep her voice neutral, but Tina picked up on her desperation.

"I know a lot of *someones*, but you need a lawyer with some grit. Maybe . . ." She could hear Tina typing. "Try Camelia Belmont. She's not easily cowed by guys like Aaron. Or if she is, she sure as hell doesn't let it show in court."

"Never heard of her. Which firm is she with?" Suzanne scribbled the name in her notebook.

"Do you know Arturo Rodriguez at McCaffrey Rhodes & Rodriguez? She's their senior family law person," Tina said.

"Yes, I've met Artie. He's darling. But is this Belmont person any good?"

"Honestly, she's probably the best you'll get under the circumstances, at least in Maricopa County," Tina said. "It's worth a consult to see if you like her."

"Good point. And hey, thanks," Suzanne said. "I appreciate you, even if you're snubbing me."

"Suze, really, I'm sorry, but even a she-wolf like me has boundaries." Tina laughed. "Hey, will I see you at the Wong's dinner party?"

"Yes, so not a word in front of Aaron. See you then."

Suzanne hung up, huffed a sigh, stubbed out her second cigarette, and took a long swig of wine.

She'd never heard of the attorney Tina mentioned, but she trusted her friend's judgment. Even so, was an associate at a small criminal defense firm qualified to manage this kind of divorce? Didn't a high value marital estate with a lucrative law practice in the mix demand a special skillset?

The powerlessness of her situation came skidding into the room and slapped Suzanne hard in the face. Here she was, the wife of one of the most influential trial attorneys in the southwest—hell, in the whole Western U.S.—and she couldn't even get a partner level attorney to represent her. Without any other options and a ticking time bomb in her belly, she would have to rely on an unknown entity named Camelia Belmont to work out a complex settlement on a short deadline.

As lights winked on across the western hills, angry, heaving sobs burst through Suzanne's veneer of calm control. She let the torrent of bitter tears burn away the final dregs of her life with Aaron.

It was time. It was over.

I just hope it isn't too late.

5

TRUE CONFESSION

TUESDAY, JANUARY 12

Arriving back at the office after the Campbell trial, Camelia dropped her rolling brief and handbag, then headed to the conference room for her meeting with Suzanne Anders. Cate caught up to her in the hall.

"How was the trial?"

"Oh, there you are. I thought you'd left for the day. The trial? I wish I knew." Camelia shrugged. "At first, I was pretty sure it was in the bag. Now, I'm not so sure."

"You always say that after you kick ass in Court," Cate said, handing Camelia a folder. "Here's the Anders file, and tomorrow's schedule is on your chair. Suzanne seems upset, so go easy on her."

"Did she say what's up?"

"No, she just . . . I think she's been crying. Anyway, I've gotta head out," Cate said. "Meeting Dave for happy hour. See you mañana!"

"Hasta la vista," Camelia said and turned toward the conference room.

Camelia couldn't understand why a woman like Suzanne would have married someone like Aaron Anders in the first place, but there's no accounting for love. Or lust. And at this point, why not just coast? She'd been putting up with his shit for more than thirty years, Aaron had already had one heart attack, and he seemed to live pretty fast. How much longer until the Big One left Suzanne a widow?

Maybe she had an impatient man on the side. She wouldn't be the first. But it made representing her harder if Camelia didn't know the truth about what was going on. No matter what it was, Camelia hoped Suzanne would finally confide in her, because there was something off about this sudden rush to get divorced.

She rapped twice and pushed the conference room door open. Suzanne looked up with bloodshot eyes.

"Uh oh. What's happened?" Camelia asked.

"Thanks for seeing me on short notice." Suzanne dabbed at her eyes with a tissue. "It's time for me to 'fess up."

Camelia slipped into the chair opposite Suzanne and pushed her file to one side. She leaned forward on her elbows.

"Tell me everything. And whatever it is, we'll sort it out."

"Not sure there's a way to sort this one." Suzanne twisted the tissue. "There's no nice way to say it. I have ovarian cancer, and it's pretty far along. Not a friendly cancer that will go away quietly."

Jesus, Mary, and Joseph.

Camelia swallowed and looked down at the conference table, overcome with still-fresh sorrow over Greta, her vibrant, adventurous friend from law school. She'd been valiant through it all, but ovarian cancer beat her down to a pale shadow before a brutal, painful end. Like it was about to do to Suzanne. Even though she *looked* perfectly fine, Camelia knew appearances had nothing to do with what was happening at the cellular level. She blinked back tears.

"Oh, Suzanne, I'm *so* sorry. That's quite a blow. How long have you known?" Camelia asked.

"I found out last fall, November 3. A date I'm not likely to ever forget. A week later, I had a hysterectomy," Suzanne said. "I called you soon after."

"Why didn't you tell me then?"

"Oh, you know. Just being a good little soldier, chin up and all that. Really, I was just in denial. Anyway, I started treatment after surgery. And even though things are going as well as can be expected . . ." She drew a ragged breath. "I need to be divorced right away. I don't really know . . . the prognosis is . . . how shall I put it? The statistics are damn grim, frankly."

"You're a lot of things, Suzanne, but you're *not* a statistic." Camelia's mind was whirring. "Who else knows about this?"

"My oncology team, obviously, and my brother. My housekeeper. A couple of close friends. And now you."

Camelia didn't know if she could be so stoic in the face of that diagnosis. "So, you haven't told your kids? Or Aaron?"

"As for Aaron, I won't give that bastard the satisfaction. And I can't tell my kids because they'll tell their father. Or at least Allison will." She gave Camelia a sad smile. "I want to live the rest of my days on my terms, not just be patronized and fussed over."

"You don't think Aaron—" Camelia stopped herself. It was an insensitive question, and speculation about what Aaron would or would not do wasn't useful. But Camelia knew that if he had an inkling of Suzanne's diagnosis, he could drag things out, play the long litigation game, and outlive his wife in order to inherit their entire estate.

"Do I think he'll use this against me if he has half a chance? You can bet on it. And, not that I'm expecting this," Suzanne's voice cracked and fresh tears pooled in her eyes. "But hypothetically, what happens if I die before the divorce is final?"

"The divorce would be dismissed. Aaron would still legally be your spouse and inherit the marital assets." Camelia flinched at the look of horror on Suzanne's face. "But I'll do everything I can to make sure that doesn't happen."

"You have to *promise me* we'll get a decree in the next ninety days," Suzanne's voice had taken on a hard edge.

"Suzanne, I . . . is that how long you think you have?"

"Who knows? But I don't want to spend every last minute of whatever time I have left fighting with Aaron." Suzanne blew her nose. "I know you'll find a way to back Aaron into a corner and get me divorced."

"I appreciate your confidence, but . . ." Camelia glanced at her blank legal pad, looking for hope.

"Promise me you'll do whatever it takes. Because I will *not* go to my grave married to that sonofabitch," Suzanne hissed.

"Without a settlement . . . unless we come up with a miracle, the divorce will take the better part of this year. And that's if everything goes smoothly. There's no way it will be final in less time than that."

"But it's only January!" Suzanne gasped.

"I know," Camelia said quietly, hoping to soften the blow. "But for a divorce like this . . . well, it's still not a lot of time. We have to get busy." Camelia scribbled some notes on her legal pad. "I know you're dealing with a lot, and I'm sorry to do this to you, but it will move things along if you can pitch in, especially on the document review."

"Don't you have paralegals for that?" Suzanne asked.

"Yes, but you know your case better than anyone, and we can't afford to miss even the tiniest detail. Not if we want to get this over with quickly." Camelia stood and tucked the Anders file under her arm. "For now, go home, relax, have a glass of wine. Because you won't have much free time once I start sending over files for review."

After seeing Suzanne to the elevators, Camelia went back to her office and sank into her chair. What Suzanne was asking was nearly impossible even with cooperative clients. But with Aaron Anders on the other side? She could imagine how tickled he would be to find out that all he had to do was dig in his heels and wait it out. But Suzanne deserved better. And Camelia would do whatever it took to make sure she got her divorce.

What have I got myself into?

She heaved a sigh and opened a new document. She noted everything she'd ever heard about Anders, his career, and his personal life. The one thing she knew for sure: winning was all he cared about. Well, winning and wooing all the pretty young things. That was his weakness: women. Aaron's penchant for the ladies was her best advantage.

She opened the State Bar of Arizona website and reviewed Anders' profile for disciplinary actions, but there was nothing on record. Next, she went to the Superior Court website and searched for cases with Aaron as a party. There were a handful, mostly fee disputes, but it looked like they'd all settled. There was one civil suit pending over a real estate claim that she'd get a copy of later. With nothing else to go on, Camelia did an internet search for *Aaron Anders* and *AndersLaw* to see what might pop up.

In story after story, Aaron's legal victories and philanthropy were lauded. When she clicked on the images tab, Aaron and Suzanne Anders smiled back from a dozen black tie events. They were a striking couple. As she scrolled, they posed with the governor in Arizona Suns jerseys, shook hands with the mayor at a July 4th barbecue fundraiser, and Aaron stood behind the podium at an array of legal conferences and law school classrooms. He was a goddamn local hero, if you believed the press.

Now I really need a drink.

She saved her notes and shut down her computer.

Despite being an unrepentant jerk, Anders seemed to have kept a lid on his indiscretions. There were no bar complaints. No sexual harassment claims. Without an informant, someone on the inside of Anders' circle, she might never break through the walls of secrecy he'd erected around his affairs.

Camelia needed to find one of them—just one—willing to spill her guts and give up the details she needed to nail him on a marital waste claim. Hotel bills and pricey gifts were enough to tarnish any well-buffed image, and that was exactly the type of evidence Anders would pay to keep out of the public record. But how would she find even *one* of those women? It wasn't like Camelia ran in their circle. She couldn't just ring up so-and-so to tap a deep well of Anders gossip. She would have to find another way, but she didn't have a clue what that might be. Not yet, anyway.

As she prepared to leave, Camelia's attention was pulled to lights blinking on in the deep purple shadow of Camelback Mountain. She wondered if she would have any free weekends until this divorce was final.

She already knew the answer. It was a resounding no.

6

LOVE TRIANGLE

FRIDAY, JANUARY 15

Now that Camelia knew about Suzanne's serious health problems, resolving the case had taken on a dark shimmer of urgency. It wasn't just that Camelia had to squeeze a settlement out of a formidable egomaniac, she was facing an impossible timeline.

Her best strategy to move things along quickly was to find an angry, talkative ex-mistress willing to provide a few juicy details. She'd been calling around to her lawyer buddies for days, trying to find someone, *anyone*, willing to rat out Anders. But no one in the notoriously gossipy legal community seemed to have any dirt on Anders or his affairs. Or if they did, they weren't talking. That, by itself, was strange.

They've all closed ranks.

Suzanne said Aaron had moved up from secretaries and paralegals to more challenging prizes these days—junior attorneys—and the credit card statements in the initial disclosures supported that theory. His "entertainment" costs had skyrocketed over the last year. Apparently, the perks of a fling with a man like him—extravagant dinners, fancy hotels, and pretty jewelry—could smooth over a lot of hard feelings. Not to mention how a well-timed phone call to the right people from a successful litigator like Anders could boost a fledgling career.

Maybe that's why none of the exes were pissed off. These were smart, educated young women who no doubt surmised from the get-go they were a temporary fling. Camelia guessed many of them wouldn't be surprised or upset when it ended. They knew him for who he was, and they didn't have time for a high maintenance, full time boyfriend, anyway. Why not enjoy an influential Sugar Daddy while it lasted?

Her phone buzzed.

"Your consult is in the conference room," Cate said.

"Remind me?" Camelia had been so absorbed in what she was doing, she'd completely forgotten about the consultation.

"Christopher Fischer. He's the lawyer that called yesterday. He wants to pick your brain about community property laws. Since he's one of us, you said I could set him first thing this morning as a courtesy."

"Oh right, got it. I'm on my way."

Camelia hung up and grabbed the cosmetic case from her top desk drawer. She freshened up her lipstick and fluffed her hair, then stood and smoothed her trousers before stepping into the hallway. Cate handed her the intake file as she headed to the conference room.

When Camelia pushed the door open, the man looked up from his phone, standing as she entered. Her eyes traveled up. He was well over six feet tall.

"Christopher Fischer? Camelia Belmont. How are you today?"

He briefly clasped her hand in a clammy palm.

"Okay, I guess. Thanks for seeing me on short notice."

"No problem. Professional courtesy has to count for something, right?"

He was still standing.

Camelia gestured to the cream leather chair across from hers. "Do you go by Christopher or Chris?"

As if confused by the question, he paused for a moment.

"Chris is fine," he said, ducking his head as he sat. "Sorry. I'm not usually this distracted. I haven't had much sleep the last few days."

Camelia looked across the table into large, droopy brown eyes ringed with dusky shadows. Fischer was whip thin. Gaunt, almost. He reminded her of a greyhound pup, except not nearly as energetic. He was fidgeting with his water bottle and kept sighing. Loudly. He would not do well on the witness stand.

"So, how can I help you today, Chris? Cate says you want information about community property laws?" Camelia noted the wide gold band on his left hand. "Is this in relation to a divorce? Or something else?"

"I just kinda . . . I'm not even sure where to start."

He swallowed hard, and Camelia watched his prominent Adam's apple bob with the effort. She would need to ease him into it.

"Okay, let's start with some background. When were you married?" she asked.

"July 4th weekend, right after law school graduation. So, almost eight years ago."

"Where did you go to law school?"

"Creighton. In Omaha. We graduated, got married, and moved to Phoenix. I came to clerk at the Supreme Court, and Kaitlyn got a job at Jackson Barr. But now it's all blowing up. All because of . . ." Chris ran a bony hand over his pale face. "We have privilege, right?"

She shouldn't have to counsel a fellow attorney about privileged communications, but he was clearly anxious.

"Yes, per the rules. Even if you never retain my services," Camelia said. "All our conversations fall within attorney client privilege."

"I should know that, right? Sorry, I'm a mess right now, and I'm being extra cautious because this is a career-limiting disclosure." Chris swallowed a long drink of water. "My marriage is blowing up because of Aaron Anders."

Camelia had perfected the art of the impassive, blank face. Or so she hoped. She took a deep breath.

"So, what does Mr. Anders have to do with your marriage?"

As if I can't guess.

"Let me back up. My wife and I are both senior associates at AndersLaw. We've been there almost six years." Chris paused, as if reluctant to go on. "But it turns out, Aaron's been taking *advantage* of the situation."

Jesus Christ. I need to buy a lottery ticket if this pans out.

Camelia had been so focused on hunting down jilted flings, she'd overlooked all the husbands and boyfriends left in Anders' dust.

She quickly ripped through a conflicts checklist in her head. Chris worked for Anders, so that wasn't a problem, because she didn't represent Anders. But what if he knew things about the firm that were prejudicial to Aaron? She needed some time to map out the ethical issues, assuming there were any. For now, though, she needed more details.

"Let me get a bit more background. What kind of law do you practice?" Camelia asked.

"I started out in civil litigation, working directly with Aaron on bigger cases. But I'm not cut out for that kind of pressure, so I got benched. For the past year or so, I've worked on mergers and acquisitions, corporate governance work, that kind of thing," Chris said.

"What makes you think your marriage is blowing up because of Aaron Anders?"

"I don't really know how to say it without embarrassing both of us. It was . . ." Chris shook his head and heaved a sigh. "It's disgusting and demeaning. How much do you need to know?"

"Ooooh. I understand." Camelia nodded slowly. "You caught them in the act, didn't you?"

Chris's face flushed crimson. He looked down at his clasped hands and closed his eyes as he exhaled.

"Last week, I was heading out and decided I'd take Kaitlyn out for a quick bite to eat, because she was working late on trial prep. When I opened the conference room door . . ." Chris drew a ragged breath and blew it out. "When I opened the door, Aaron was there, too. With his hand up Kaitlyn's skirt."

Camelia took a breath. "Do you think she was being forced? Or was it consensual?"

"Kaitlyn was all over him and she sure as hell wasn't protesting. Which is why I don't believe her when she says it's harassment."

Camelia couldn't believe her good fortune.

"Okay, so . . . did you confront them? Have it out right there?"

"I just stood there with my mouth open, like an idiot. That asshole was in no hurry to let go of my wife, either. He walked out smiling like the Cheshire cat." Chris's cheeks were flushed with anger. "I was so shocked I couldn't even speak. I'll give him this: he's got balls."

"What did Kaitlyn have to say for herself?"

"Not much, because I didn't give her a chance. I know better than to argue in the office. The last thing I need is everyone at work knowing all our dirty laundry, so I just turned around and slammed the door damn near off its hinges. Later, when Kaitlyn got home, we had a *very* loud conversation." Fischer grunted a mirthless laugh. "Pretty sure the whole neighborhood heard us."

"It didn't become physical, did it?" Camelia asked.

Chris looked shocked. "What? No! Nothing like that." He swallowed a mouthful of water. "Kaitlyn swore up and down it was all some harebrained scheme to lure Aaron in so she could file a sexual harassment and discrimination claim, get a big settlement, and we could walk away with enough cash to start our own firm. Like we've always talked about." Fischer's face crumpled.

Camelia pushed a box of tissues toward him.

She'd assumed Anders' typical girlfriend was a busy baby lawyer focused on her career. It hadn't occurred to her that Anders would be stupid enough to get involved with an attorney in his own firm. As for that ridiculous claim about blackmailing Anders? Surely Chris wouldn't fall for such a flimsy cover story.

"I really thought we were solid, but . . . ." Chris cleared this throat and pressed a tissue to his eyes before continuing. "Kaitlyn never discussed this so-called plan with me. It came completely out of left field, and I think she's full of shit." He glanced over at Camelia. "Sorry for cussing."

"Oh please, terms of art. And I'm so sorry. This has to be very difficult. But if Kaitlyn plans to commit blackmail or extortion—"

"Right? What kind of person comes up with a stupid plan like that? And to take on AndersLaw? I've seen what happens when you poke the bear." Chris shook his head. "Besides, I'm not buying that cockamamie story of hers."

Who says cockamamie anymore?

"So, how did you leave it with Kaitlyn?"

"I gave her an ultimatum. Knock it off with Anders, quit lying, and find a new job. *Or else.*"

"Or else what?" Camelia prompted.

"Or else I'm gonna file for divorce. I mean, not today, but if she doesn't end it . . ." Chris heaved another heavy sigh.

Camelia took a sip of water and jotted a couple of notes. "Did anything else happen after you caught them? Was there any fallout from Mr. Anders?"

"With me? Nah. I'm laying low. We're at opposite ends of the office, different practice areas, so I hardly ever run into him." Chris gripped his water bottle with a slender, trembling hand. "And I'm trying *not* to run into him, because I . . . that sonofabitch deserves a tune up."

"Yeah, I can understand that, but you're not at risk of harming him, are you?"

His eyes widened. "Nah, I'm not the fighting type. In case you can't tell by looking." He splayed his gangly arms wide, then pulled his elbows in tight, clasping his hands on the conference table. "Besides, Anders has a security guy that would snap me in two."

"Okay, just confirming you're not gonna do anything stupid," she said. "Because you'll derail your career and your divorce pretty quickly if you start throwing punches."

"No, I'm cool. But I figured I better get clear on my situation since things with Kaitlyn look like they're headed south. We don't have kids yet, thank god. But we have a townhouse in Tempe, a vacation home in Oregon, 401(k)s, stuff like that." Chris was back to business. "So, I need to know how all that works in a community property state."

Camelia began reciting the law, interjecting examples when she thought Chris looked confused. When she finished her spiel, she pushed her legal pad aside.

"Is there anything else I can clear up for you?"

"I think I'm good. For now, I'm going to see if she does what I've asked," Chris said. "But it helps to know where I stand."

"An affair doesn't have to be the end, you know. If you think you can work things out with Kaitlyn, I'm happy to give you referrals for marriage counseling. Otherwise . . ." Camelia let the inevitable hang in the air. "Give me a call if you want to start the divorce process. No matter what happens, I recommend you consult with a headhunter to find a good lateral position, because you can't keep working there."

"I know. I've already decided to quit the first week of April. I would just walk out now, but I'm not giving up my quarterly bonus over this mess," Chris said as he rose to leave. "And you should know, I love my wife. If she wants to make it work, I'll do everything I can to save my marriage."

"I think you should," Camelia said. She wondered what Kaitlyn was up to. Was this a one-off or was she aspiring to be the next Mrs. Anders? "But if you can't save your marriage, you need to save yourself."

"Yeah, you're right. And if it comes to that, I'll need that bonus money for legal fees." Chris grinned and stood up. "Thanks for being straight with me. I'll be in touch."

Camelia walked him to the elevators, craning her neck up to look at him as they shook hands. Chris gave a little wave as he entered the elevator.

"You know how to find me," she said.

Camelia paused at Cate's desk to drop off the file with her fresh notes.

"How was he?" Cate asked.

"He's nervous, upset. But get this. He works at AndersLaw and caught his wife messing around with Aaron Anders!"

Cate's eyes widened. "You've got to be kidding! How did we get this lucky?"

"No idea, but I'll take it," Camelia said with a shrug. "Anyway, please call ethics counsel to clarify we don't have a conflict of interest if Chris retains. I don't want any muddy waters. And speaking of Anders, any word on the rest of our discovery requests?"

"Not yet, but the deadline isn't until next week. Do you want me to call Ashcroft's office?"

"If they're not delivered by noon on the deadline, light him up. Suzanne doesn't have time for his shenanigans."

"Will do. Oh, and we found Waldo!" Cate grinned. "Your mom called while you were in with Mr. Fischer."

Camelia laughed. *Where's Waldo* was the code they used for her globe-trotting octogenarian mother, who was always off on an adventure, usually somewhere with no phone or internet.

"Oh no! And I missed her!" Camelia said. "Is she still at Machu Pichu?"

"The reception wasn't great, but I swear she said she was in the mountains with a shaman for an ayahuasca ceremony." Cate shook her head. "Anyway, she said to tell you she's fine and will call again when she's back in Cusco."

Camelia laughed. "I can't believe some of the crazy stuff she gets herself into, but hey, she's having more fun than us!" She shrugged. "And now, back to work."

She had no sooner settled at her desk when Cate popped her head in the doorway.

"Sorry to interrupt but Byron just called from Court and wants you down there pronto. His client needs some divorce advice before the hearing."

"How about no? I'm not hauling my ass all the way downtown for a ten minute conversation."

"Hey, don't kill the messenger!" Cate snapped back.

"Shit, sorry." Camelia immediately regretted taking her frustration out on her assistant. Her own caseload was more than she could handle even without Byron expecting her to rush to his aid whenever he snapped his fingers. And it didn't help that she was feeling out of sorts.

How many days had it been now?

"It's just . . . you know how much we have on our plates already, without dropping everything for one of Byron's darlings."

"He was pretty insistent. Today's darling is that airline pilot up on criminal DUI and indecency charges. I've already called the car service, and they'll be downstairs in about ten minutes. Do you want me to cancel?" Cate moved closer and dropped her voice, speaking softly so nearby staff wouldn't hear. "Personally? I think you should go. The partner vote is—"

"I know, I know. You're right. It's just . . . Okay. Let me stop at the ladies' room, then I'll head out. I should be back within the hour," Camelia said, grabbing her handbag.

She was already on her way to the elevators when Cate caught up to her, a bit breathless.

"We got the ruling on the Campbell divorce." Cate thrust a slim sheaf of papers in Camelia's direction, still warm from the printer.

"Already? That was quick!"

"Thought you'd want to read it right away. It's . . . it's not what you expected, Cam."

"You're just a little ray of sunshine today, huh?" Camelia stuffed the papers in her handbag. "We'll talk about it when I get back, but can you give me the CliffsNotes version?"

"The bottom line is that Sorensen awarded spousal maintenance to Shelby."

"Shit. Okay, please schedule a meeting with Josh right away."

Jesus. What next?

Camelia jabbed the elevator button repeatedly, anxiety eating away at her patience, anger bubbling up around the edges. She needed to be focused on the Campbell ruling and not this pro bono boondoggle for Byron. It didn't seem to matter how well she performed; he didn't treat her as a peer. Hell, most days he acted like she was his assistant. Yes, he was the boss and could pretty much snap his fingers at any one of them. But it seemed to her—the only senior attorney in the firm who also happened to be a woman—that Camelia got a lot more than her share.

Her litmus test: would Byron ask any of the male attorneys to run this kind of errand?

Hell no. And he shouldn't ask me either.

7

WRONG WAY

FRIDAY, JANUARY 15

Camelia buckled in as the driver pulled away from the curb, headed toward the downtown Court. Settling in, she pulled the Campbell ruling from her bag, skimming the first page. She couldn't concentrate, though. Chris Fischer's revelation was burning a trail through her brain. Now that she knew about Mrs. Fischer's workplace tryst, she had the leverage she needed in the Anders case. So, how could she use it—tactfully, skillfully, *carefully*—to bring Anders to heel without blowing attorney client privilege with Chris?

Her phone rang. Byron. Of course.

"Yes?"

"I need you down here now," Byron hissed into the phone. "Didn't Cate tell you?"

"Yes, and I'm in the car. I'll be there in a few minutes." She couldn't quite keep the edge out of her voice. "What's going on?"

"My hearing is in forty five minutes and my client is having a meltdown. I need you to talk him down, because he's not gonna do well on the stand in this state of mind."

"What's the issue?" Camelia asked.

"Senior airline pilot. Got caught in a compromising position with his boy toy co-pilot. Because they were in his car, he was charged with a DUI and public sexual indecency. Long marriage, grown kids, substantial nest egg. The usual. I mean, other than the boyfriend."

"Okay, but substance abuse and infidelity are run-of-the-mill divorce issues. What's got him so upset?"

"He's not an alcoholic, he doesn't want to be outed like this, and he doesn't really want a divorce. But if the wife finds out about the boyfriend . . . it will be messier than it has to be," Byron said.

"If he's convicted, his wife will surely find out. Even if he beats the DUI charge, the airline will probably ground him and send him to rehab."

"Well, if he has to go to rehab, I guess he'll just have to manage the fallout. But that won't be the thing that kills his career. Or his marriage. It's the other charge that will sink him."

"The sexual indecency charge? Jesus Christ, what year is it? I thought cops stopped using that against gay guys a long time ago," Camelia said.

"Who knows what inspired the cop to add the indecency charge," Byron said. "Fucking homophobe."

"If you're not able to get that dropped, he needs to get in front of it." Camelia sighed. "As for coming out and coming clean about the affair, there's not much I can do except hold him while he cries."

"Hey, you're the firm's divorce expert, so just reassure him. I want white glove service on this because Gerson isn't just an airline pilot. He's also a former Navy combat pilot, and all around hero. And,"

Byron continued, "the big takeaway here is, if we handle him right, we'll get *all* the DUIs and divorces for the flight crews, because they all talk. There's a *lot* of that work to go around."

And *that*, Camelia thought, was the real issue. Gerson's hero status wasn't nearly as significant to Byron as the potential work a glowing review from his client would bring to the firm.

"Be a good little rainmaker. Please. And thank you." He hung up.

Camelia dropped her head against the back of the seat and closed her eyes. She breathed slowly in, slowly out, trying to divert the tension from becoming something worse.

It stung that she was never credited for the added value she brought to the firm. The focus was always on her billables, despite times like this, when she was expected to counsel Byron's client *off the clock*. So, this little excursion would cost her at least an hour in lost billable time. Meanwhile, the other associates—all men!—would play eighteen holes of golf and buy a round of drinks, and the next thing you know, they're a partner. Yet here she was, seven years in, and not even close.

Is this really how I want to live the rest of my life?

At the courthouse, Camelia wound her way through the throngs of people and headed toward the café, which doubled as a meeting space for attorneys and their clients. The overly warm room smelled of fried food and disinfectant.

She spotted Byron in a far corner, darted past the lines of people ordering, and zig-zagged between the tables. Byron's client had his back to her, but his shoulders were slumped in the universal posture of regret and shame.

"So, Jim," Camelia began after Byron introduced them. "I understand you have a potential DUI, along with another charge, involving a co-worker, which you think might result in a divorce. Ask me anything." Camelia pulled a legal pad from her tote bag and hovered her pen over the blank page.

Jim Gerson wouldn't look her in the eye.

"It's not just the DUI, although that could get me fired. The bigger problem is my co-pilot, Dan, and that fucking sexual indecency citation. Teresa, my wife . . . well, she suspects . . ." He didn't finish.

Gerson was red from his starched white shirt collar to his receding hairline. His dark eyes were sunken into purple bags and puffy lids. If Camelia was going to get him back on task, she needed him to buck up, to draw on the training that saw him through combat and back again.

Camelia looked at him sharply, and her tone matched.

"She suspects what, exactly, sir?" She dropped in the honorific at the end to remind him of his military days and to show him due respect. Because what she said next was intended to sting. "That you're an alcoholic? That you're having an affair? That you're gay? Or maybe all of the above?"

Her words had the desired effect, snapping him out of his self-pity and back to problem solving. Gerson squared his shoulders and looked Camelia in the eye.

"Okay, okay, yes. Dan is my best friend, and yes, he's also my . . . lover. But I am *not* an alcoholic. I've never been a heavy drinker. It was just bad timing. Two of our crew members got married, and . . . Teresa didn't come because it was a gay wedding. Dan and I went together, as friends. Coworkers." Gerson twisted his wedding ring as the words gushed out. "But then they started the champagne toasts. And then someone opened a bottle of good tequila, and . . . you get the idea. I knew we should have called a cab. Hindsight, right? And I wasn't even driving. We were just in my car, in the parking lot of the wedding hotel. I really don't want to lose my ass over this."

"Jim, one baby step at a time, okay? First, let Byron work his magic. Do *exactly* as he tells you, and he'll manage the DUI. As for the indecency charge, that will no doubt go away." She glanced over at Byron and he nodded. "And *then* we can strategize how to minimize the damage in your divorce. If it even comes to that."

"I'm confident the indecency charge will be dropped automatically. No one wants to prosecute that kind of discriminatory crap," Byron said.

"Look, I want to protect myself, but the truth is, I don't want a divorce. Things are actually okay the way they are. Or at least I think they are."

Camelia turned her gaze to Gerson's weathered but still handsome face. Good old Jim wanted to have his cake and eat it, too.

"Oh, I *see*." She heard the exasperation in her own voice.

"I can't just up and divorce Teresa, because I can't leave her without insurance," Gerson explained. His voice had softened to a near whisper. "Which is what will happen if we divorce. She had breast cancer two years ago and is still doing follow ups. She's not insurable."

"Well, that's awfully kind, even if it's not exactly honest. You can keep her on your insurance if you legally separate. Her spousal benefits through the airline remain intact all the way up to a divorce decree." Camelia tucked her notepad into her bag, readying to leave. "And, from my position, I think Mrs. Gerson should have a say in what happens next."

"I'm not sure what I would even tell her," Gerson shook his head. "What a mess."

"Jim, *look at me*. One mess at a time. If anyone brings up your indiscretion with Dan, it was all a misunderstanding. Your strategy is to focus entirely on giving your best in Court today. Then, once the DUI is managed and the other charge dismissed, you'll have a better idea of what you're facing." Camelia pulled out her card case. "Consider marriage counseling, and we can nail down your narrative when the time comes. Here's my card." She rose to leave. "And Jim, don't worry about the DUI. Byron's the best."

Camelia gave Byron a quick smile and briskly turned to walk outside, where the car service was circling the block.

What a colossal waste of time.

On the way back to the office, Camelia pulled out the Campbell ruling and began to read. Everything looked fine—and fair—until she got to the section about spousal maintenance.

In a divorce like the Campbells', there were assets to divide: a lucrative real estate business, a couple of houses, investment accounts, and cash. What she'd expected, and what the case law supported, was for Shelby Campbell to receive *either* spousal maintenance *or* half the business. Not both. But Judge Sorensen had opined that in the current situation, Shelby was entitled to half the business value when it sold, *plus* $10,000 per month in interim spousal maintenance until then. But selling the business could take months, years even.

Interim support wasn't uncommon, and she could have argued against it if she'd thought it had legs. But Blake Griffin hadn't even requested interim support in the Petition; his entire argument was for long term support. Camelia had been so fervently defending against long term support, she hadn't thought it was necessary to bring up interim support, based on the pleadings. But it was an oversight nonetheless. And Josh was going to be *furious*.

Could Judge Sorensen's friendship with opposing counsel have played against her? All she knew about was one golf game, which could be nothing more than name-dropping bluster on the part of Blake Griffin to impress his client. She couldn't *prove* a conflict of interest, and to infer anything of the sort would amount to slander. Besides, Sorensen probably thought he'd handed Josh a win when he denied long term support.

Camelia didn't know how she was going to deliver this news to Josh Campbell, or explain how her confident assessment was so off the mark. All she could do was immediately file a Motion for Reconsideration—which would undoubtedly be denied—followed by an appeal.

She blew out a long exhale and closed her eyes.

I should have seen this coming, so why didn't I?

Seconds later, the car stopped. She opened her eyes and saw they had arrived at the office. Now, all she had to do was face the rest of the day.

Back in her office, Camelia looked around for something, anything, to distract herself. She opened her drawer and pulled out her trusty copper flask and shook it. Again.

Still empty.

And what the hell was she doing with an empty flask that only reminded her of what she was craving? She snapped the band on her wrist and tossed the flask in the drawer.

She buzzed Cate.

"Were you able to reach Josh to set a post-decree debrief? I was going to call him, but I really don't want to have this kind of conversation over the phone," Camelia said. "And the sooner the better. If there's a conflict on my calendar, clear it."

"I'll call him now," Cate said, and hung up.

The meeting with Chris Fischer, followed by the rushed meeting with Byron and his client, on top of this bad ruling in the Campbell case had left Camelia twitchy and tense. She really wanted a calming swig of *something*. She looked at the clock on her computer. It was only 2:45 p.m.

She had a long, dry afternoon ahead of her unless she could cop something out of the kitchen without being noticed. She sauntered in and casually refilled her water bottle.

There was an open bottle of wine in the fridge, but who knows how long that had been there. She opened the freezer and there, behind the Lean Cuisine and ice cream sandwiches, was a nearly empty bottle of Absolut. Camelia wrapped it in a paper towel and rushed from the room, cradling the icy vodka bottle against her ribs.

She entered the restroom and quickly locked herself in a stall. How many days sober now?

Does it even matter?

Yes, it mattered! She had to stay dry in order to focus on her cases, ramp up her billing, and be the partner material Byron was looking for. And, more importantly, she had to actually be in control of herself, her life. Being sober was important. It was the right thing.

And yet . . .

She lifted the frosty bottle to her mouth, pouring the viscous fluid down her throat. It left a cold burn in its wake. She closed her eyes. Waited for it. That warmth. That comfort. It was just what she needed to quell the panic nipping at her psyche. It was the tonic that would let her get back to work. She was already calmer.

Just one more swig.

She filled her mouth with the icy liquid and swallowed.

So little left in the bottle, might as well finish it.

And she did.

Whew. That might have been too much, after all.

Camelia listened for a moment to make sure she was alone, then exited the stall. She shoved the empty bottle way down in the garbage can by the door and covered it with paper towels.

As she washed her hands, she looked up to see her reflection staring back at her with a grimace. Her face was flushed from the alcohol and she looked disheveled. Frouzy, even.

What the fuck did I just do?

She rinsed her mouth, and patted her cheeks and neck with damp hands.

Chin up, now. Time to start over. One more time.

8

PAPER TIGERS

TUESDAY, JANUARY 26

Suzanne was stirring the pot of chicken tortilla soup her housekeeper, Alma, had prepared for lunch when the security phone rang from the front gate. She dropped the wooden spoon on the counter and shuffled across the kitchen in a pair of fluffy slippers.

Today, even walking slowly hurt. At first, the effects of chemo had been minimal, but now she was always achy and felt like she had the flu. With her medical background, she'd known what to expect, but knowing was not the same as living through it.

"I have a delivery for Suzanne Anders from Camelia Belmont," a man said in a bored voice.

She buzzed him through and watched the delivery van pull up the driveway. She'd been expecting the documents. Camelia had served

Aaron with a broad discovery request, and now Suzanne was about to be inundated with an avalanche of paper, compliments of her husband.

The driver, a young man in a khaki uniform and matching ball cap, opened the back doors of the van and pulled out a dolly, the tires bouncing on the driveway as he let it drop the last few inches. As he began stacking file boxes on the dolly, Suzanne recalled Camelia's warning. She hadn't really believed Aaron would treat her—and their divorce— like just another lawsuit to be won, but she should have seen it coming.

She directed the delivery driver to the study where he stacked the boxes along the wall. The spacious room used to be Aaron's sanctuary from their busy family and a constant parade of play dates. But that was years ago. For the past thirteen months, since they'd hammered out their tense truce, the main house was Suzanne's domain and Aaron kept to the casita.

Her heart sank as the stack of boxes grew.

She remembered Aaron bragging about his scorched earth tactics. *First, we bury them in irrelevant paper.* For Aaron, winning was *only* thing that mattered, and she'd been naïve in thinking he wouldn't turn his predatory skillset against her. But if that sonofabitch thought he could get away with using his courtroom tactics on her, he'd better think again.

With a dozen file boxes stacked against the wall, the room seemed to pulse with tension. What was she going to find in those boxes?

Probably a lot of hotel bills and boozy lunches.

Camelia had been right when she'd pointed out the advantage Suzanne had over staff paralegals. *You know your own case better than anyone.* If she wanted a quick divorce, she would have to deal with all of it—including Aaron's underhanded tactics—head on. That seemed to be a theme lately, facing the worst of the worst. But if she could deal with cancer and all its challenges, she could damn sure deal with Aaron.

Her stomach gurgled. She would do her homework, as promised. But first, she needed sustenance. Suzanne returned to the kitchen and ladled out a bowl of Alma's rich, brothy soup. She perched on a stool at the kitchen island and mindlessly scrolled through social media while she ate.

Like

Love

Wow

Laugh

Angry

She didn't really care about any of it, especially now, but she needed the distraction. Her phone rang.

Camelia Belmont.

Speak of the devil.

"Hi Cam, I was just thinking about you."

"I guess that means the initial discovery was delivered?" Camelia said.

"Yeah, I've got a big pile of boxes in my study." Suzanne pushed aside her half-eaten bowl of soup and grabbed her water bottle, walking into the study as Camelia talked.

"I just need you to sit down with a highlighter and some Post-it notes, and flag anything that looks odd or potentially like marital waste. Jewelry purchases, travel, meals, hotels, whatever Aaron spent that didn't include a known client or you. I realize that's hard to pin down, but do your best." Camelia paused. "And . . . I don't want to be insensitive, but look at the HR files for issues with former employees . . . women employees. Just to see—"

"Ah, yes. Anyone who got a payoff."

"Exactly. We can use that type of information as leverage," Camelia paused, then asked. "Aside from all this, how are you doing?"

"Me? Oh, I'm okay. Just feeling a little run down from the chemo. I'll get busy on this today and maybe finish it up over the weekend?"

"Pace yourself. What you got today is about a third of what we'll eventually have to review. We're still waiting for the rest of the firm financials and Aaron's personal financials," Camelia said.

"You mean there's more?" Suzanne imagined the room stacked to the ceiling with file boxes.

"I know," Camelia sighed in a way that Suzanne recognized as commiseration. "It's tedious. And per your request, we didn't subpoena his medical records. I still think that's a mistake, but for now, let's see if we can find a little treasure in what we have. I'll be in touch next week."

"Got it. I'll do my homework!"

Suzanne hung up and leaned against the door jamb, suddenly tired. It was a *lot* of paper.

Heaving a sigh, she sat down and slipped the lid off the first box. The chemical odor of paper and ink hit her in the face. She used to have an iron gut—you had to in healthcare—but the chemo had put her sense of smell on overdrive, and lately everything made her nauseous. She walked over to the French doors and swung them open to the covered patio. A warm afternoon breeze ran into the room and ruffled some loose papers on Aaron's desk.

My desk.

She took a sip of water and returned to the stack of boxes.

Goddamn you Aaron!

If he could've just kept his pants zipped, she wouldn't have to go through all this. Her husband was selfish. And greedy. And, as she was now discovering, he was also a petty, vindictive asshole. Had he always been like this? Well, no. At least not at first.

Suzanne's mind flashed back to a younger Aaron, before law school, before that summer he spent clerking at Sullivan Greenberg in Los Angeles. He was majoring in political science, while Suzanne did nursing practicums at Planned Parenthood. Aaron was the one who brought up marriage and kids, not Suzanne. She'd been planning a gap year in Europe before starting her Master's program, but she'd already fallen under his spell. People thought they were an odd match, but the Aaron she knew was affectionate and gentle. She remembered stargazing out in the desert late at night, his fingers interlaced with hers, the salty taste of his neck on her lips.

There was more to it than just youthful lust, though. They had dreamt up a future together and made detailed plans to turn those dreams into a shared reality.

While Suzanne worked on her Master's in public health, Aaron was in law school. She knew now, in hindsight, that's when the shift happened. After that summer clerkship at Sullivan Greenberg— which he still claimed was the most pivotal three months of his life— something snapped into place in Aaron's mind, and his behavior took on a ruthless, sarcastic quality. His litigator bones hardened, and the tender shoots of their dreams were mowed down by Aaron's ambitious new plans.

Suzanne sighed at the memory of a Thanksgiving dinner during the George W. Bush years with her liberal Jewish family. A red-faced Aaron rammed his index finger into the dining table repeatedly, defending the post-9/11 invasion of Iraq, as her father quietly poured another martini and her mother silently glared at her. Her parents were both gone now, and Suzanne was glad her father wasn't alive to collect his I-told-you-so.

She turned back to the open box. Being a litigator's wife had taught her enough about the process to know every piece of paper had to be thoroughly reviewed.

No stone unturned.

Suzanne lifted a binder out of the first box and began reviewing credit card statements. At first, she had to peer closely at each transaction to decipher what they meant, but soon enough she was able to quickly skim through the statements, easily spotting the anomalies. She dutifully marked anything that might interest Camelia, but there wasn't much here to incriminate him. Aaron must have another credit card somewhere. One he used for his flings. She made a note to Camelia to pull his credit report.

To give herself a break from the tedium of the credit card statements, Suzanne moved on to HR records. She read the summary page at the front of the first binder: AndersLaw had 42 attorneys on payroll, of whom five—including Aaron—were senior partners, another nine junior equity partners, along with 76 staff, and one contractor: Dov Saminski of International Umbrella. Suzanne didn't know much about the company, so she googled them. Their website was bland, riddled with corporate buzzwords. They provided "organizational security services to government agencies and multinational corporations". Whatever that meant.

Who was AndersLaw representing that would require that kind of security service? Sure, there had been some law firm shootings over the past few years—even a couple of lawyers they knew personally had been victims—but Suzanne thought Aaron was being overly dramatic.

Why would AndersLaw need this level of protection?

Suzanne had a lot of questions but no one to ask, so she went back to the file box and pulled out the binder labeled *Contractors*. She flipped it open to see a black and white photo of Dov Saminski, the firm's Chief Security Officer.

He looks so young.

The next tab held his contract, and she began to skim the document, noting Dov had been with the firm almost five years. Had it really been that long? It seemed like she barely knew him, even though they'd spent hundreds of hours together.

While Aaron was working the room at a seemingly never-ending parade of society events and legal conferences, Dov and Suzanne bonded over their shared Jewish heritage, including a love of crisp latkes and dry martinis. He was unlike anyone she'd ever known, and she found that intriguing. She ran her mind's eye over him, smiling to herself. Dov was compact, solid, with grey-blue eyes and glints of silver in his close cropped hair. His shirts were tailored to accommodate thick, muscled shoulders, and he always smelled like he'd just walked out of the forest. Dov was handsome, in a rough, gung-ho kind of way, and if circumstances had been different . . . well, Suzanne might have enjoyed a quiet life with a man like him.

But what exactly did *like him* mean? She realized she didn't know much about the capable, watchful man who took care of Aaron's security needs. Her curiosity was piqued, so she flipped to the tab with his resume.

Dov was born in Chicago, then joined the Navy at nineteen. After six years on active duty—four of those in the SEALs—Dov finished a Bachelor's degree in Information and Cybersecurity. He bounced around for a few years until he joined International Umbrella. There were no details about his assignments prior to AndersLaw.

The memory of a gala dinner party they'd attended at a legal conference in Los Angeles a few years ago flashed into her mind. It had been the usual predictable event: chit-chat with the other wives, bland banquet food, and too much cheap wine. Then, late in the evening, a young woman in a tight blue dress walked right up to Suzanne—far too close—and began shouting in her face. She was very drunk.

"What's it like being a dried up old baby factory? He doesn't even care about you, so why not just let Aaron go, you fucking bi—"

Dov swooped in, cutting the tirade short. He tucked his arm around the woman's waist and dragged her out of the ballroom as she sobbed. The room had gone silent as every head swiveled in Suzanne's direction. She was still trembling when Dov returned a few minutes later.

"I'll come back for Aaron, but we should leave *now*," he said, taking Suzanne by the elbow, steering her out of the room on a river of whispers.

On the way back to the hotel, Dov reassured her that Blue Dress was just a crazy girl with a fixation on Aaron. Suzanne knew the truth was far more tawdry and the encounter had shaken her. But, despite her suspicion that Dov was just protecting Aaron from being exposed for the cheating bastard he was, she was grateful for the escape from all those accusing eyes. From that point on, Dov was much more than his job title, at least to Suzanne. He was an ally, a solid shelter from the fallout of Aaron's lifestyle.

She flipped back to the service contract. His official title was Chief Security Officer. When she saw the compensation—$175,000—it seemed out of proportion for the size of the firm, but then, Suzanne wasn't exactly sure what a CSO did. She knew Dov took care of their electronics: updating firewalls, managing security cameras, reminding everyone to update passwords, scanning the office for recording devices, that kind of thing. He also escorted Aaron and Suzanne to and from all those events and parties they attended, and he drove Aaron to all his hearings and meetings.

What else is he doing to earn this kind of paycheck?

She flagged the file with a lime green Post-it and scribbled a note:

Saminski contract - threats to AA?

The light in the study shifted to a hazy golden glow as the sun slipped behind the western hills. Looking up from the desk, Suzanne realized she'd been at it for hours. Placing Dov's file back in the box, she stood up to stretch, her back aching from sitting for so long.

Beyond the French doors to the veranda, the sun slid away, and a chill entered the room on the evening breeze. As she went to shut the doors, the motion light came on in the driveway below her.

Surely Aaron isn't home this early?

Suzanne stepped back into the shadows and watched. A few seconds later, a late model Lexus sports car pulled up in front of the casita and parked.

Suzanne grabbed her phone out of her pocket, ready to dial 911, but paused. Whoever it was had the gate code and, for all she knew, someone was dropping Aaron off. Instead, a lanky blond in a grey skirt suit stepped out of the car. Alone. Suzanne snapped a pic with her phone, but in the dim light it came out grainy.

Who the hell is she?

The woman glanced around before swinging a large tote onto her shoulder and heading to the front door of the guest house. Whoever she was, she obviously had the gate code, the door code, *and* Aaron's permission. This was a first.

A light came on in the casita. Suzanne's heart thumped in her chest. She waited. And waited. Finally, she dashed inside, grabbed a blanket and a glass of wine, and settled into a chair in the shadows to wait and watch. It seemed like an eternity before the lights at the casita went out and the woman emerged. In the glow of the landscape lighting, Suzanne could see she was no longer wearing the suit—she was in workout gear, now—and her long hair was up in a ponytail. The woman looked up at the house. Suzanne could swear she felt the woman's eyes on her, even though she was cloaked in darkness. She watched as the bright yellow Lexus wound its way down the driveway, and a white hot rage gripped her by the throat.

Not in my house.

The guest house was Aaron's domain, but their Paradise Valley enclave was strictly off limits to Aaron's flings. It was nonnegotiable. Their lawyers had put it in writing and he'd readily agreed. As far as she knew, he'd never broken the agreement. Until now.

So, who was this tart, showing up like she owned the place? She seemed to know *exactly* what she was doing, so maybe this wasn't the first time she'd been to the casita. And what the hell was so important that Aaron would breach their agreement? None of it made any sense.

Suzanne picked up her phone and tapped on Aaron's contact, but paused before calling. She was tempted to give him an earful, but she knew he'd talk circles around her, and end up making her feel foolish.

She whirled on her heel, slamming the door behind her, and stood in front of the stack of file boxes, anger solidifying her resolve. Her voice came out in a growl.

"Aaron, if it's a war you want, I'm just the one to deliver it."

9

HOME INVASION

TUESDAY, JANUARY 26

Camelia's direct line started ringing just after seven p.m. She hesitated at the thought of which client might be calling, but gave in on the third ring.

"Cam, it's Suzanne. Sorry to bother you so late, but something weird just happened."

"I can barely hear you. Why are you whispering?" Camelia asked.

Suzanne cleared her throat. "Sorry. I'm just . . . is this better?"

"Much. What's going on?"

"I'm at the casita and—"

"What? *Why?* If Aaron finds out, well, you know who you're divorcing. Expect some backlash."

"I, um . . ." Suzanne paused.

Camelia hated this part of her practice. Clients didn't always take signed agreements, statutes, or even Court orders seriously, and then couldn't understand why the judge was throwing the book at them. Suzanne had agreed the casita was for Aaron's use only, at least until the divorce was final, so why was she there, whispering into the phone?

"Okay, start at the top," Camelia said. "And please don't tell me he's trying to seduce you."

"Oh god no, nothing like that," Suzanne said. "And it might be nothing, but—"

"If it's nothing, you wouldn't be calling me. Are you okay?"

"I'm fine. I'm *furious*, but I'm fine." Suzanne heaved a sigh. "I just watched some blond pull into the driveway in a bright yellow Lexus and go into the casita. And what she left behind is just . . . odd."

"What do you mean?" Camelia pulled her legal pad closer and started taking notes. "Aaron had some woman over?"

"No, Aaron wasn't with her. But she sure seemed to know her way around."

"Where is she now?" Camelia asked.

"She's long gone, but she was here for a quite a while, maybe half an hour or so, then took off," Suzanne said.

"Could she be an assistant?"

"It absolutely wasn't Darla. And Aaron's not even home. Which is even more strange, because whoever it is, he gave her the gate code and the entry code for the guest house. If Aaron gave her that kind of access, she must be pretty damned important."

"Do you know her?"

"I don't remember meeting her," Suzanne said. "But there was something about her that screamed lawyer. I looked at the firm directory online, and I'm pretty sure she's a senior associate named Kaitlyn Fischer."

Camelia tried to mask her sharp intake of breath. She made a note for Cate; she'd need ethics counsel to sort out whether she should— or could—tell Chris Fischer this little tidbit.

"You said she left something behind?"

"Yeah, a file. And a pair of underwear," Suzanne said. "Seems awfully brazen, if you ask me."

"Did you call Aaron to ask him about it?"

"No, I did not." Suzanne huffed. "He knows the damn rules."

"So, you decided to break in?"

"Hey, she was on *my* property. And she didn't just drop something off. As I said, she was here for quite a while. And when she came back outside, she was wearing different clothes. I decided to see for myself what was going on," Suzanne said. "Then I get down here, and can you believe it? Mrs. Fischer helped herself to a shower."

Camelia gasped. "She what?"

"Yep. She took a *shower*. Weird, huh? So, I decided to see what else the little tart was up to. I found the folder on his desk and . . . it's strange."

"Suzanne, hang on," Camelia said. Her voice softened. "I doubt Aaron would be reckless enough to keep anything important or secret at the casita. But if you think there's something you need to *investigate*, like a *break in* on the property . . ."

When Suzanne chuckled, Camelia knew she'd understood.

"I *did* witness a break and enter. It would make me feel so much *safer* if you could drop by. You know how the *police* are. It's not an *emergency*, so they'll just take their sweet time."

"Give me fifteen minutes."

Camelia hung up and closed the file on her desk. She really just wanted to go home, kick off her shoes, and have a glass of wine. But whatever Suzanne had found might be important, and she needed to see for herself. She picked up her mobile phone to text Leon.

Stopping at client's in PV.
Won't be long. xo

As she hurriedly packed up her bag, Camelia glanced at the time. It was almost seven thirty. With any luck, this would be a non-event and she'd be home by eight, eight-thirty at the latest.

Twelve hour day. Again.

The Anders' hacienda style house was tucked up against the west-facing slope of a rocky hill, with the main house at the highest point of the property. Terraced flagstone walkways led down to the pool and, beyond that, the casita. Camelia parked in the crescent drive near the main house, inhaling deeply as she exited her car. She never got tired of the scent of the desert. She stood for a moment, letting her eyes adjust. There wasn't even a faint glow left on the horizon, but amber puddles lit the paths leading up to the house and down to the guest house.

She threw her purse over her shoulder and headed left, toward the casita, her heels tapping loudly on the flagstone walk. As she approached, she inspected the heavy Spanish style door for a security camera. The last thing she needed was to be caught on video by Aaron Anders. She was still looking for a tell-tale red light when the door swung open.

"Thanks for coming." Suzanne beckoned Camelia inside.

"Suzanne, before we go any further," Camelia glanced around, "are we going to show up on your security cameras?"

"He broke our agreement, so as far as I'm concerned, all bets are off." Suzanne's cheeks were flushed with anger. "I *dare* Aaron to make a fuss about it."

"That's fine for *you*, but—"

"Don't worry. The camera system is controlled in the main house, and I turned it off before you got here. So, you're in the clear. But he'll know I was here, and I hope it drives him nuts." Suzanne rolled her eyes and huffed an exasperated sigh. "Follow me."

Camelia followed Suzanne down a wide hall and turned into the first doorway on the left. The large study was lined with light oak bookshelves packed with legal tomes, and Mission style furniture upholstered in cognac leather.

Very manly man.

On the desktop was a brown pocket folder, typical of law offices everywhere.

"Is this what you found?" Camelia said, pointing to the folder.

Fear was wriggling around in Camelia's belly. Suzanne was breaking a written agreement, enforceable by the Court. Camelia was now privy to that violation and yet, here she was, spurring Suzanne on, even though neither of them had any right to be here.

"Yes. That little bitch had the nerve to come in here and just make herself at home. Like I told you, she took a shower and then left her wet towel on the bed, which will *infuriate* Aaron." Suzanne smirked. "And that's why I left it where it was."

"Suzanne, I get it. This is a really crappy situation." Camelia would figure out how to use Kaitlyn Fischer's visit to the casita to her advantage later. For now, learning more about this mysterious file was the urgent task at hand. This might be her only opportunity to get a peek at it, and the last thing she needed was Anders walking in on them. "But we need to focus for a minute. Why would this file be so important to Aaron that he had it delivered to his home?"

"Beats me. It's some kind of electronic device," Suzanne said. "And there's a thumb drive and some paperwork in the file as well. Receipts, a manual . . ."

"But Aaron would have *asked* that this be delivered, right?"

"I doubt it. Since he started the firm, not *once* has anyone from the office come to the house when Aaron wasn't here," Suzanne said. "He's extremely picky about client confidentiality and, in case you missed it, he's a total control freak. Then," Suzanne continued, "after that scandal with that estate planning firm? He became obsessed."

"What scandal?" Camelia rifled through her memory.

"Remember? Five or six years ago? A disgruntled office manager at—Wilson, Williams, something like that—tossed all the closed files in the dumpster behind the building, and a sanitation worker picked up several hundred client Social Security numbers?"

"Oh yeah. We all got a sternly worded notice from the State Bar about file retention and destruction policies," Camelia said.

"Yeah, well, that's when Aaron hired a Chief Security Officer and came up with a strict procedure. No one is supposed to carry a paper file out of the office unless they're headed to Court. He sure as hell wouldn't leave a client file in the casita, and he would *never* give *anyone* the house codes," Suzanne said, emphatically. "This is all *very* suspicious."

"So what's in the file?"

"I have no idea. Here," Suzanne said, plucking a padded envelope from the folder. She handed it to Camelia. "You tell me."

Camelia pulled the device from the shipping envelope, squinting at the writing on the bottom.

"Sheridan Electronics. I don't have a clue." She set the device on the desk and picked up the file. "This could be privileged client information and, if so, neither of us has any business looking at it. If it pertains to the divorce, we'll do a formal discovery request. If not . . . let's just keep it between us, okay?"

Suzanne nodded as Camelia flipped the folder open.

"These docs are Bates stamped as exhibits," Camelia said. She flipped through the papers, separated by colored slip sheets.

"Right, but why would he need those delivered here?"

"No idea. Credit card statement." Camelia flipped back to the first page. "The only charge is for some kind of traffic light thing. That must be what this doohickey is."

"Well, it's probably for one of their cases," Suzanne said. "Sometimes Aaron recreates a scenario for the jury, and when he does, he orders all kinds of crazy junk. One time he brought an entire 50-gallon drum of motor oil to Court and dumped it in a kiddie pool to make his point. This is nothing to do with us."

"Wait. Let's make sure." Camelia flipped to the next sheaf of papers. "There's a warranty, user's manual, a receipt for whatever this thing is, and a flash drive. And what's this?"

Camelia pulled out a handwritten note on an AndersLaw notepad.

A ~ Sheridan Gambit research for your review. XX K

She handed the note to Suzanne. "Any idea what this is about?"

"Good grief. Who knows? And really? Kiss kiss? Is she twelve?"

"Yeah, that's kind of embarrassing," Camelia conceded. "But it looks like this is for a case that has nothing to do with your divorce."

"You're right. But why the hell would she take a shower?" Suzanne shook her head in disbelief. She beckoned Camelia to follow her. "Come here a second. You have to see this."

Camelia followed her across the hall to a spacious bedroom looking out onto a courtyard. Suzanne flipped on the lights and pointed at the floor where a hot pink thong was abandoned on the rug.

"She left her damned underwear! It's like she's marking her territory. So, maybe she's comfortable showering here because it's not the first time. Maybe that bastard's been sneaking her in right under my nose all along. I mean, who knows? Maybe they—"

"Suzanne!" Camelia could see the signs of a meltdown coming. "We don't have any evidence of that, and imagining those scenarios will only drive you crazy. We know Aaron's been having affairs, so that's nothing new. It's really shitty behavior, but it's not against the law. Let's focus on what's in front of us."

Camelia snapped a couple of photos with her phone, then turned and walked back to the office, as Suzanne trailed behind her.

"Okay, your security camera footage will prove someone was here. Most likely Kaitlyn Fischer. So, aside from Aaron possibly breaking the no visitors clause—"

"What do you mean *possibly*? She was here!" Suzanne's voice pitched up.

"Yes, but technically she was not Aaron's *guest*, because Aaron wasn't even here. A guest requires a host. If I were his attorney, I would argue there was no breach of the agreement." Camelia turned toward the door. "And the file is unrelated, irrelevant to your divorce, so I can't see a reason to pursue it."

"Maybe not, but there's someone who can tell us for sure. Dov Saminski, Aaron's Chief Security Officer. I reviewed his HR file today and flagged it for you to look at. Honestly, I think he's a fixer of some sort." Suzanne pushed her hair behind her ears. "I bet he knows all kinds of secret stuff, including all the women Aaron's been sleeping around with. If I can just get him to talk."

"A fixer?" Camelia was curious about why Suzanne used that word. "Why on earth would Aaron need someone like that?"

"I don't know," Suzanne shrugged. "Like I said, he's paranoid. Lawyer shootings, computer hacks, corporate espionage . . . all that stuff just sends him into orbit. And, if Dov knows everything about the firm and Aaron's professional life, he'll damn sure know the personal stuff, too."

"Hmm. So, is this Saminski guy someone I should depose?"

"Well, he works for Aaron. Not sure you'll get much out of him, but you can try," Suzanne said.

Camelia didn't bother explaining that's what depositions were for as she arranged the items on the desk. "And I will. But right now, I'm gonna take some pics, in case this comes up later." She finished taking photos and dropped her phone in her handbag, then scooped up the paperwork, flash drive, and device, placing them all back in the folder. "Okay, how about we skedaddle before Aaron gets home?"

"Good idea," Suzanne said, walking down the hall toward the front door. "Because he does *not* want to hear what I have to say right now."

Suzanne locked the door behind Camelia. As they walked up the broad, terraced steps toward the main house, she couldn't help but notice Suzanne struggling for breath.

"Are you doing okay? I mean, health wise?"

"Yeah, it's just the chemo. I don't have as much stamina as I used to. Among other things. But considering the alternative, I'm fine." Suzanne's eyes were hidden in the shadows. "Hey, look at that." She pointed up and Camelia followed her finger to a fat full moon rising over Camelback Mountain.

"One of the best things about living in the desert, isn't it? These great, clear skies," Camelia said. "Okay, I'm going to take off—"

"Can I offer you a glass of wine? It's the least I can do."

Camelia pulled her coat closer as the night air settled around her neck.

"I'd love to, but Leon's holding dinner. Rain check?" Camelia opened her car door before she could change her mind.

"Of course, any time. And thanks again for coming by. I'll get the rest of these documents reviewed in the next couple of days," Suzanne said.

Camelia cranked up the heat in her car as she idled down the driveway, suddenly feeling more cheerful.

I did it!

She felt a rush of accomplishment at having turned down the offer of wine. Maybe she could do this sober thing after all. All she had to do was refuse the next glass of wine. And the next.

As she approached the gate, it was already sliding open. She thought Suzanne had opened it remotely until she realized there was a car waiting on the other side.

Camelia drove through the gate as the black Porsche Panamera drove slowly past, the driver side window down. Aaron glared at her, his mouth a grim line that tightened even more when Camelia waved at him as she rolled by.

Maybe not today, but you'll get yours, asshole.

She paused at the approach to the street and pulled out her phone to text Suzanne.

Heads up! Aaron's home.

"Anybody home?" Camelia called into the silent house. Nothing.

She kicked off her shoes, walked to the back of the house, and changed into yoga pants and a sweatshirt. When she came back into the kitchen, she saw the note stuck to the fridge.

Walking the boys. Dinner's in the oven.

How long until Leon returned? She had no way to know. Their dog walks were usually 45 minutes, but she didn't know when he'd left. She glanced at the note again.

Fuck it. I deserve a reward.

Camelia jerked open the freezer and wrapped her hand around the icy neck of a bottle of vodka. She was just pulling it out of the freezer when she heard the back door bang open and frantic panting as their two rescue mutts, Calvin and Caesar, raced to the kitchen. She shoved the bottle back and slammed the freezer door.

What the hell was I thinking?

"Are these my good boys? Where's your daddy? Who wants a treat?" Camelia devolved into baby talk.

"Daddy's right here and I could use a treat, too," Leon said. He pulled Camelia into his arms. "Long day, huh?"

"You have no idea, babe. Let's get our dinner and I can tell you all about it," she said.

"Glass of wine?" Leon asked.

Camelia paused. "I think I'll just have a Perrier, but you go ahead."

Was that so hard?

Actually, yes. It was the hardest thing she'd done all day.

And it would be the hardest thing she would do tomorrow.

And the day after that.

10

HEAD ON

TUESDAY, JANUARY 26

Arriving at his Paradise Valley enclave just as Camelia Belmont drove through the gate raised the hackles on the back of Aaron Anders' neck. Something must have put Suzanne into quite a tizzy if she'd called her lawyer out at this hour. Then again, a bottom feeder like Belmont was probably used to making house calls with distraught divorcees.

He had that tingling sensation as he walked through the casita, flicking on lights on his way to the kitchen. Something was off, as if someone had been there. He could swear he caught a whiff of Suzanne's perfume. Was he losing his mind, or . . .

She wouldn't dare.

If she'd been here, snooping around, he'd rain hell down on her and Belmont for breaking their agreement. But he was smug in the knowledge that she'd found nothing. He wasn't so careless as to leave anything incriminating laying around in the casita.

He dropped his briefcase and wallet on the kitchen island and walked back to his bedroom to change. When he flipped on the light, he reared back. A towel had been tossed on the bed and a hot pink thong was on the floor.

What the fuck?

That sure as hell wasn't Suzanne's underwear.

That stupid little bitch.

Kaitlyn had broken his cardinal rule.

But why the hell would she come here, to his house? How the fuck would she even get in? And why would she take a shower?

As he shed his suit for a pair of joggers and a well-worn Diamondbacks sweatshirt, Aaron's mind rifled through all the ways Kaitlyn could have gained access to the guest house. He had never given her or anyone else the gate code or the key code for the house.

Did Suzanne let her in?

He huffed a laugh at the very thought of it. Suzanne would *never* allow a stranger onto the property, let alone a pretty young woman, and he'd happily conceded that condition when they made their agreement. Life was simpler if his wife and girlfriends weren't within striking distance of each other.

So how did Kaitlyn manage it, then? And, more importantly, *why?*

He walked back to the kitchen and grabbed his briefcase on the way to the study. As he entered the room, he smelled Suzanne's perfume again. It was unsettling, like her ghost was lingering. When he turned on the desk lamp, he immediately saw the file on his desk and a cold wave rolled over him. Was that . . .?

Aaron picked up the file and dumped the contents on his desk. Client exhibits from the Sheridan trial: a traffic preemption device, flash drive, and accompanying paperwork. And a note from Kaitlyn on a firm notepad.

A ~ Sheridan Gambit research for your review. XX K

He crushed the note in his fist. How could she be so reckless? So goddamn stupid?

And showing up here, at the Paradise Valley house? Not only was it a violation of the agreement he'd made with Suzanne, it was bad form, tacky.

He desperately wanted to call Kaitlyn right then and there, give her a piece of his mind. But a phone call wouldn't be nearly as satisfying as watching her grovel for forgiveness.

He texted her instead.

> Dinner tomorrow Lion's Den @ 6.
> I'll pick up Thai.

WEDNESDAY, JANUARY 27

Fueled by the clandestine meeting with Suzanne the night before, Camelia arrived at the office the next morning eager to dig into the Anders case. Besides the bombshell of Kaitlyn Fischer's bold intrusion at the Anders' Paradise Valley estate, this whole idea of a fixer at AndersLaw was intriguing.

If anyone would know about that kind of guy, it was Byron. But before she ran to him with questions, Camelia needed to lay the groundwork. Starting with a deposition date.

Sipping a fresh coffee, she flipped open the file, took a deep breath, and dialed AndersLaw. She didn't expect to get anything of substance out of this Saminski guy, but at least she could get a feel for him while she scheduled his deposition.

She tapped her pen on a legal pad in time to the Eagles as she sat on hold.

Lyin' Eyes. That's appropriate.

"Saminski, how can I help you?"

His voice was low and resonant, exactly as Camelia had imagined.

"Camelia Belmont here. I represent Suzanne Anders in their divorce, and we're gathering information for the business valuation. I was wondering if I could pick your brain a bit? Informally?"

"I think that might be a waste of your time, Miss Belmont. Even if I didn't have a nondisclosure agreement, I deal with security, not the business end. You should call the firm's accountants."

"The accountants are already working with the business valuators. This is for context. Such as, are there any threats to the financial health of the firm, any unhappy associates, you know . . . the kind of stuff you manage?" Camelia could already tell Saminski would be a challenging witness. "I mean, I assume you manage those issues, right?"

Saminski sighed. "I'll have to clear it with Mr. Anders. If he says I should talk to you, I will."

"I can always issue a subpoena for your deposition if that would make it easier for you," Camelia said.

"What would be easier is to be left out of the personal business of my employer. But you do what you need to do," Saminski said.

She wondered just how much Saminski was involved in Aaron's personal business, how much he knew. *Who* he knew.

"I only want to talk about your job. Risk analysis, threat assessment, that kind of thing. So we can logically value the practice. No *personal* revelations necessary. Let's go ahead and schedule your deposition while I have you on the phone." Camelia gave Saminski a few dates as he consulted his calendar.

"Okay, pencil me in for Tuesday the 16th. I don't expect Mr. Anders to approve your request, but someone will let you know either way," Saminski said.

"Well, it's not really a *request*, Mr. Saminski. You can expect a copy of the subpoena in the next few days," Camelia said.

"Okay, I guess I'll see you soon, then," Saminski said before hanging up.

Camelia had expected more pushback, confrontation, even. But Dov Saminski had been polite, if not exactly cooperative. She went back to her draft of deposition questions and began to reorganize them. If she could just get Saminski to the table, maybe she could pull some dirt out of him. People slipped up all the time in depositions. They got comfortable, started rambling, went off script. So, how could she stack the questions to lull a guy like Saminski into telling her more than he intended to reveal? And what did he know, if anything, about that piece of equipment Kaitlyn Fischer left at the casita?

She opened the photo library on her phone and swiped until she found the six images she'd taken. The receipt for the device read Sheridan Electronic Imports. Camelia opened a browser and typed in Sheridan Electronics and the company website popped up. It looked to be a successful local company that provided "traffic management solutions" to cities and emergency responders. Seemed like a big *so what*.

She copied the case number off the file folder into her search bar. The first case up was from the Court of Appeals: *Arizona Emergency Services, Inc. v. Sheridan Electronics Imports*. When she opened the appellate decision, her eyes went first to the attorneys on the case: Aaron Anders and Christopher Fischer on behalf of Sheridan Electronics Imports. Interesting that those two had been working so closely at one point. Had it been Anders' interest in Kaitlyn that scuttled Chris's rise in the firm?

Camelia skimmed the facts of the case. A few years ago, Sheridan won the bid with Arizona Emergency Services, the purchasing arm of the emergency departments for Maricopa County fire, police, and ambulance. They all used this brand of device to override traffic lights when responding to an emergency call.

But Arizona Emergency Services had sued Sheridan, claiming the devices were faulty. Their expert testified that a bug caused a delay, a stutter in changing the signal. Meaning two vehicles could both have green lights at the same time. In the case they'd brought, the plaintiffs claimed an ambulance and city bus collided in a busy intersection in Central Phoenix. The ambulance had been using Sheridan's preemption device. And two people died.

Anders and Fischer successfully defended Sheridan's company from the product liability and wrongful death suit. As Camelia read the opinion, it dawned on her that Anders had won on procedure, legal technicalities, and sharp arguments. The issue of the faulty device—whether it was or wasn't—got lost in the procedural weeds.

Last night at the casita, Suzanne said Aaron often used props to illustrate a point in the courtroom. If what the plaintiffs in the lawsuit said was true, the device at the Anders casita was more than just a harmless trial exhibit. But what use would Anders have for a faulty preemption device? And why had Kaitlyn delivered it to the casita?

Camelia glanced at her phone. Time to switch gears. She needed to prepare for her meeting with Josh Campbell in the morning to discuss the ruling. But just thinking about that $10,000 per month spousal maintenance award made her belly roll into a knot and her cheeks burn with shame.

How did I misread that outcome so badly?

At least she had a good rapport with Josh Campbell. Even so, she knew he was going to be upset—angry, even—and who could blame him? She hoped he would take the news in stride, like he'd done with other setbacks throughout the divorce. Regardless, she had to be prepared with counter-arguments and strategies. Camelia jotted down the major points from the award of spousal maintenance Judge Sorensen had ordered—a completely opposite result than she'd predicted—then began drafting ideas on how to craft an appeal.

She felt pretty good about their chances, but Josh would need some convincing. Never mind Byron. Given that Josh Campbell was a wealthy, influential business man and one of Byron's golf buddies, her boss would consider the ruling an outright failure. And if Byron didn't see a clear path to victory, he wouldn't risk Camelia losing on appeal, because that would open Josh up to paying Shelby's legal fees. Which would be an even bigger blow. Either way, she was screwed.

Bye bye partner vote.

If Griffin hadn't blindsided her with that expert vocational report on the morning of trial, she'd have been better prepared to argue against it. And had she known the direction the case was headed, she could have made a fuss over that golf game Griffin was bragging about. Too late now. And why the hell did she make that reckless promise to her client? Well, not a *real* promise, but she'd been far too cocky in her assessment of the risks.

If there's ever a day to fall off the wagon, this is it.

As she drafted notes for her meeting with Josh Campbell, her phone buzzed.

"Ashcroft is on line six. He wants to talk to you about Saminski's deposition subpoena," Cate said.

"Wow. That didn't take long. I just got off the phone with Saminski a half hour ago!"

Camelia pushed the blinking light on her phone set.

"Spencer, my man, how can I help you today?" Camelia tried to sound collegial.

"Well, Camelia, I'd say you've already helped my day immensely by pissing off my client enough that he's willing to pay me to talk to you," Ashcroft said.

Camelia could picture his malicious grin through the phone.

"Always happy to be of service. So, what's got Mr. Anders' knickers in a twist today?"

"It's a short list, but you're at the top. Actually, the top *two* on the shit list."

"Well, this is quite an honor, Spence. How did I get so lucky!"

"First, Mrs. Anders showed up on the security cameras entering Aaron's home last night," Ashcroft said. "And then you were leaving the property when Aaron got home. Naughty, naughty, Camelia. It's enough to get you suspended if he decides to make a bar complaint."

Camelia's words lodged in her throat. She took a slow sip of water. Do not freak out. Suzanne said she'd turned the cameras off. Was she mistaken?

Who was monitoring those cameras?

"Well, I'm glad you brought that up, because it sure looks like Aaron breached the parties' agreement when he granted that woman friend of his access to the casita. Mrs. Kaitlyn Fischer ring a bell? Made herself quite at home, from what I hear. And yes, I visited my client last night. What of it?"

There was a long pause on the other end of the phone. She'd hit a nerve. Even Spencer would have to concede that Aaron bringing his flings onto the property violated the Anders' signed agreement.

"Well, I guess we'll call that a *draw*," he said, his voice oily with sarcasm. "But then there's the not insignificant matter of Dov Saminski. You know a deposition isn't gonna fly with Aaron."

"But Spence, it's not up to Aaron. When Saminski suggested he was not at liberty to discuss firm business due to an NDA, I simply offered that a subpoena might make the process easier. But how does that concern you? You don't represent Mr. Saminski, do you?"

Camelia's neck was tightening into a series of knots, and her head was beginning to pound. She just had to be cool and get off the phone as soon as possible, so she could warn Suzanne about being found out.

And a stiff drink wouldn't hurt either.

"No, I don't represent Saminski. We have a corporate attorney for that," Ashcroft said. "And you'll be hearing from him about this deposition. But do we really have to go through all this? You and I both know you won't get a word out of Saminski, so why bother? Aren't you just wasting time and money? Or do you need to churn the bill this month?"

She took a deep breath. Camelia knew better than to get into an unscripted sparring match with Spencer Blusterbutt. She wouldn't give him the satisfaction of taking the bait, even though it was so tempting.

"Well, Spence, this has been delightful, but I have to run. Be a dear and put all your various complaints in a letter, would you? I'll be sure to get back to you right away," Camelia said.

"So you really are churning the bill, huh?" Ashcroft laughed. "The letter is already drafted and on its way. I'll need an answer by Monday. And stay the hell away from Aaron's house and his employees, understood?"

"I'm just the hired help, Spence. As are you. Let's remember that, shall we?" Camelia hung up and dropped her head into her hands.

Fuuuuuuuccccckkkkk.

She didn't know if there were cameras outside, inside, or both, and even though Suzanne said she'd turned them off, she seemed pretty blasé about it. Easy for her to be nonchalant, because even if the judge came down on her, it would likely be nothing more than a stern word. And the security footage of Kaitlyn entering the casita would be all the evidence needed to prove Aaron's breach of their agreement, so it would mitigate any fallout to Suzanne.

Camelia, on the other hand, could be facing serious repercussions.

If it got back to Byron that she'd accompanied a client in breaking a binding agreement—which he'd find out if Anders filed a bar complaint—Byron wouldn't stop to ask *why* she was on the premises, and he wouldn't care that she was responding to her client's request. No, he would probably fire her on the spot.

She snapped the rubber band on her wrist and thought about the martini she'd be enjoying as soon as she got home.

Can't come soon enough.

11

ROUGH ROAD AHEAD

WEDNESDAY, JANUARY 27

Aaron was at his downtown condo finishing up a bowl of tom yum soup at the kitchen island when Kaitlyn came rushing in, breathless, her cheeks pink with exertion.

"You're late, so I started without you," he said, watching her compose herself.

She stepped up beside him, nuzzling his neck. "Sorry, Ace. One of those days."

Good lord. He really wished she would stop calling him Ace. It was embarrassing and demeaning.

She turned to the takeout containers on the counter. "Thanks for picking up dinner. I'm starving." She snapped a pair of chopsticks, opened a box of noodles, and scooped up a mouthful.

"Dig in before it all gets cold." He slurped a spoonful of broth.

She leaned against him, running her hand down his thigh. "The soup might be cold, but I've got something that's always hot."

"Yeah? You mean like these?" Aaron pulled the pink thong out of his pocket, dangling it on his index finger.

Kaitlyn grinned as she snatched it away. "Maybe."

He glared at her. *"How the hell did you get into my house?"*

She stepped back at the snarl of anger under his accusation.

"What do you mean?" She retorted, a note of defiance in her voice.

"I came home to find your underwear on the floor, a wet towel on the bed, and that fucking client file *in my study*." He gestured at an AndersLaw tote bag at the end of the counter. "How the hell did you get in?"

She stepped to the other side of the island, jerking the refrigerator door open. She pulled out a bottle of water and turned back to face Aaron.

"Oh *please*. I'm not *stupid*," Kaitlyn said.

"Kitty, you're a goddamn idiot if you think you can play games with me. How did you get past the gate and into my house?"

"Duh." She tapped his mobile phone on the counter in front of him. "Face ID. I got the codes off your phone when you nodded off after our little smash yesterday, Ace. Next question?"

And now he understood why Dov was so adamant that none of the attorneys enable the face recognition feature on their phones. But Aaron had done it anyway, because it was easier than constantly entering his password. He *never* should have let his guard down.

"What made you think it was a good idea to go to my house and leave that file on my desk with your stupid note? Never mind dropping a trail of laundry behind you." He shook his head, his mouth a taut line. "What the fuck are you playing at?"

"Oh, I'm not playing, Ace. I'm dead serious. In case you missed it, I'm trying to help you climb out of your crappy marriage with a dollar left in your pocket. As for the underwear, well, I know what you like." She crossed her arms and shifted her weight to one hip. "And I needed a shower and you know very well why. I couldn't exactly go home smelling like a stag in rut."

His hand *itched* to slap her. Just once, but hard. So hard she would snap out of whatever delusion she was under.

"Don't be a smartass. You have no idea what kind of shit you've stirred up. Suzanne was home, you know. And she saw you, because guess who was leaving the property when I got home last night? *Her attorney*. So, congratulations. You've made a mess that I'll have to clean up, and I still don't know why. What is your deal?"

"My *deal*? My *deal* is that we're in love—"

Aaron's head snapped up at the pronouncement. Good lord. What the hell had he ever done to make her think that?

"And the only thing stopping us from being together, from making it *official*, is Suzanne. I just want to help you be free of her, once and for all."

Making it official?

He knew damn well he'd never said a word about marriage. But now, knowing what was spinning around in that cunning mind of hers, he'd have to watch his step. Because if she really thought he was in love with her, and would eventually marry her . . . holy shit. He could readily imagine the fallout when he broke it off. Kaitlyn would turn venomous as a viper.

"And I will be." Aaron softened his voice to sound more conciliatory. "We're in the middle of a divorce, for Chrissake. It will take a bit of time, but—"

"But why bother with all that? The time, the energy, the expense. Especially given your heart attack. And what if you lose? I know, I know." Kaitlyn held up her hand to stop him from responding. "It's unthinkable for you, the unbeatable Aaron Anders. But all it takes is one feminist judge to change everything, and suddenly you're down to half your salary for the rest of your life."

She seemed to think he'd never weighed the odds. "Believe me, I've considered—"

"Did you even read my notes? On the flash drive? I've literally done all the legwork for you. It's actually super simple. No one's the wiser and you keep *everything* you've earned." Kaitlyn took a swig of water. "The odds are a lot better than they will be at trial. At least consider it. I mean, the Sheridan Gambit—"

Why did she keep on about this? Was she trying to set him up?

"Why do you insist on calling it that?"

He had to keep his temper in check. Because if Kaitlyn felt rejected, she could easily hand Suzanne all the ammo she'd need to make their divorce very uncomfortable. And expensive. Not to mention what Kaitlyn could do to his image, his reputation, his personal capital.

Kaitlyn shrugged. "Didn't you see that show, *The Queen's Gambit*? It was so good. And it's easier to say than *traffic light preemption device*." She flipped her hair over her shoulder as if she was way ahead of him. "Plus, it's cool."

"No, it's not *cool*. The word gambit means sacrificing a pawn. Who's the pawn in this scenario? Because it's not me, and it's not Suzanne. You get that right?" Aaron shook his head in disbelief. "Seriously, it's a *very* dumb and *very* dangerous idea. You listen to too many true crime podcasts if you think this is even remotely feasible."

Kaitlyn's voice softened. "Won't you just consider it? Talk it through? Like I said, I've done the research, sorted all the details for you. We have the device, so why not use it? It's literally undetectable, but you're just gonna let it get buried in the dead case files, when you could be a happy widow in no time."

"It's *widower*, but okay. For the sake of argument, if I wanted to do such a thing—which I adamantly *do not*—why would I bother fiddling around with that stupid device?" Aaron slipped into deposition mode. He cocked his head and paused, waiting for his words to sink in. "Couldn't I simply arrange a hit and run? Wouldn't that be easier?"

Kaitlyn gave him a sly grin. "So you *have* thought about it. To answer your question, Professor, the reason is plausible deniability. To create confusion about the cause of the accident, to create reasonable doubt. Crim Law 101. If there are any suspicions, they won't stick."

He wondered if she was recording their conversation. It would be just like her to do something like that as insurance, to ensure that once he was free of Suzanne, he'd be forced to marry her. She was in for a serious wake up call. She wasn't going to stitch him up that easily.

Let her play this for the jury.

Aaron slapped the counter. "*Stop it.* I'm serious. Consider who you're talking to, Kaitlyn. I'm a respected attorney, an officer of the Court, a successful business owner, I sit on half a dozen boards, and I'm the father of three great kids. Yes, I happen to be going through a divorce, and yes, I am thoroughly pissed off about it. But I will not *ever*—by my own hand or anyone else's—harm the mother of my children. It's not up for debate. If you mention it again, I'll be forced to report you to the police. Do you understand?"

Damn, I'm good.

Kaitlyn nodded as angry pink splotches arose on her neck.

Aaron stood up and rounded the island to stand in front of her. He gripped her shoulders and she dropped her head to his chest, wrapping her arms around him. He pulled her close.

"Okay, okay. I just wanted to . . . you needed inspiration. And I thought if you came home and saw the solution all laid out, ready to execute . . ." She rolled her eyes. "But never mind. I won't bring it up again. Happy?"

She was pouting now, an errant child who wouldn't admit her wrongdoing, and it made him even more furious.

"Kitty, you know what would make me happy? If you could just be a bit more patient and a lot less pushy."

He could feel the angina coming on, the tightness, the pressure, the ripple of pain in his chest, kicking his shoulder blade. How could he have been so careless? Why did he let this crazy bitch get so close? Anger pulsed through his body, his heartbeat hammering in his ears.

Breathe. Let her go.

He gave her a peck on the forehead, released her, and walked to the wall of windows. He shoved his fists in his pockets to quell the violent tremble, the urge to hurt her.

"Look, I really need the divorce to go smoothly for all the reasons you know and a couple I won't go into, but I'm relying on your help. That means no missteps, okay? So put that goddamn exhibit back in the closed case files where it belongs first thing in the morning. And Kit, you can't *ever* show up at the house again. Understood?"

"Fine. But when that bitch has half your kingdom in her back pocket, don't say I didn't try to help you."

Aaron turned in time to see Kaitlyn shoving her thong in the AndersLaw tote and grabbing her handbag as she headed for the door.

"Good lord, does this have to be a whole *thing*? There will be plenty of time for us when the divorce is final."

"Damn right there will be," she tossed over her shoulder as she walked out the door.

Was that a promise? Or a threat?

Either way, he'd have to be very cautious. He couldn't let Kaitlyn know he was purposefully drawing out the divorce to make Suzanne so uncomfortable she'd fold and settle for way less than half. And he sure as hell couldn't dump Kaitlyn now, and risk her running to Suzanne with incriminating details about his habits. He was going to have to weigh each step carefully, because a quick, clean breakup was looking less and less likely. He realized now—way too late—that if Kaitlyn decided to make trouble for him, he was well and truly fucked.

Kaitlyn fumed over Aaron's stubborn refusal to consider the easy way out of his marriage all the way to the Tempe townhouse she shared with her husband. That arrogant sonofabitch. After everything she'd done for him. *To him*. If he thought he was going to finagle his way out of marrying her when this was all over, he'd better think again. She wasn't just some fling to be tossed aside when he got bored. He was damned sure going to put a ring on it or there would be hell to pay.

As she pulled into the garage, Kaitlyn braced herself. Until Aaron made their relationship official, she had to keep things civil with Chris. And it would make life a lot easier if he wasn't constantly watching her every move. She stepped into the house, quietly closing the back door. Chris was home, no doubt playing video games, as usual. She just wanted a long, hot shower before she had to face him.

She'd barely made it to the bedroom when she heard Chris coming down the hall. She threw her briefcase and the AndersLaw tote bag on the floor of the closet as she turned to face him.

"Hey, you're home early." He gave her a puzzled look. "Everything okay?"

She kicked off her shoes.

"Yeah, why wouldn't it be?" She asked, peeling off her suit jacket.

"No reason." He half turned, then lifted his chin at the tote bag. "What's in the bag?"

She followed his gaze. "Oh, nothing. Just an exhibit I'm returning to the file tomorrow."

Chris whistled. "You better not let Office Bee catch you with a file outside the office!"

"Don't be such a Nervous Nellie."

"Hey, it's your ass, not mine." Chris shrugged.

"Did you eat?" She stepped out of her slacks and laid them on the bed.

"Not yet. I was gonna order Indian after my game with Jeff," he said. "Want something?"

"Sure, I'll have the samosas and chicken pakora. But take your time, I'm gonna have a shower." Kaitlyn walked into the bathroom and closed the door.

As steam filled the room, she tied up her hair and stepped under the pulsing jets of water.

She replayed the argument with Aaron as she washed the day's stress off her shoulders. Had he really been angry with *her*, or was it something else? Ever since his heart attack in December, he'd seemed . . . old. More fatigued. More impatient. Maybe he was just tired.

Not tired of her, obviously, because she knew he loved her, even if he hadn't come right out and said it. Yet. And maybe she shouldn't have dropped the M word, since the topic of marriage hadn't come up before, either. But that was just his way. With Aaron, it was all about actions. Like the way he was with her in bed. And then there was that darling Tiffany lock pendant he'd given her for Christmas. Everyone knew what *that* stood for.

But he seemed stressed, distracted. She considered that Aaron was probably dealing with more than he let on. Which was all the more reason he should follow her lead and take care of his wife now, rather than waiting around. It could take *years* for Suzanne to agree to a settlement. But Aaron was old school, a principled man who liked to take the high road, act honorably.

When it suits him.

She rinsed away the soap along with her silly worries. Every couple had tiffs and disagreements. Theirs, tonight, was just another test of their commitment, nothing more. She shouldn't have left so abruptly. She should have stayed, had some make up sex, smoothed his ruffled feathers. Tomorrow. She would make it all up to him tomorrow.

As for Chris, she would go easy on him tonight. Enjoy dinner together. Maybe watch a movie. Let him think their relationship was settling back into what it had once been: boring, safe, and way too predictable. Because sparring with Chris all the time was exhausting, and Kaitlyn needed to conserve her energy for her next husband: Aaron Anders.

12

BREAKDOWN LANE

THURSDAY, JANUARY 28

The next morning, as Kaitlyn prepared to leave for the office, she fished her thong out of the AndersLaw tote bag and tossed it in the laundry. But as she picked up the bag, it felt light. She pried open the folder and found only paper and the empty padded envelope which had held the traffic light device. Her flash drive wasn't there either.

Her heart fluttered in a moment of panic. When she'd picked up the bag at the condo last night, she hadn't actually checked to see whether the flash drive was there or not, and she hadn't looked in the envelope to verify the device was inside, either. She'd been so angry she didn't even notice the weight of the bag.

Surely, the device and drive had been in the bag when she left Aaron's. Or were they? Maybe Aaron just wanted her to *think* she was returning the device to the client file. Did that clever bastard intend to implement the Sheridan Gambit after all? Was he going to follow her detailed notes and hire that Berto guy to use the device, despite his Citizen of the Year speech?

Kaitlyn smiled to herself. That would be perfect, actually.

Plausible deniability. Damn. He's good.

Then another thought came to her. What if she was wrong? What if it was Chris who had taken it? When she came out of the shower, he was still online, gaming with Jeff, oblivious as usual. But he could have snooped in the bag while she was in the shower. Then again, why would he? Even if he read her notes on the flash drive, they wouldn't make any sense to him. And what possible use would Chris have for the device when he didn't know the truth about it?

Either way, not her problem. And even though the folder no longer contained the device, she would put it back in the Sheridan file, as promised, and never bring it up again.

She didn't have to. The seed had been planted.

Camelia pressed the elevator button. Again. For the sixth time. It was going to be a shitty day and she was in no mood for it. Last night she'd slammed two martinis—or was it three?—obsessing over being caught at Aaron Anders' guest house with Suzanne. If those security cameras weren't turned off, she'd just handed Anders all the ammo he needed to file a bar complaint. Her only defense, and a weak one at that, was Kaitlyn Fischer's presence at the casita.

On top of the Anders mess, she'd lost sleep worrying over what to say to Josh to cover her own ass, without simultaneously slandering Judge Sorensen. She hadn't even completed her prep for this morning's meeting with Josh Campbell, but it was early. She still had more than an hour to finish up before their 9:00 a.m. appointment.

So Camelia was already cranky when the elevator doors opened and who but Josh Campbell was sitting in the lobby. She considered doing a quick about-face and getting right back in the elevator, but it was too late. Josh was already on his feet, coming toward her. She broke into a smile as she pulled the glass door open.

"Good morning, Josh. I wasn't expecting you this early. Cheri will take you to the conference room while I get settled." She flashed her most engaging smile.

"I've already been here twenty minutes and I'm not going to sit around waiting for you any longer than I already have."

Campbell's tone was menacing and his hard smile held no warmth. She recoiled at the riptide of tension flowing around him.

Cheri had kept her head down—typing away as if a nasty scene wasn't kicking off in front of her—but now she glanced up, briefly catching Camelia's eye. She silently mouthed, "Security?"

Camelia gave her a slight shake of the head. Josh was upset, but she was sure he would calm down once they started talking.

"Okay, let's just step into the conference room . . ." Camelia stretched her arm out ahead of her, inviting Campbell to lead the way to the main conference room, a glass cube right off the lobby. She might be paranoid, but she didn't want to end up trapped with Campbell in any of the back conference rooms, where the walls were solid and she couldn't wave down help if she needed it.

Calm down. Why would I need help?

But Camelia knew the answer to that question. Campbell was more than just a little upset. The charming client she thought she knew so well was now a furious stranger towering over her. She could feel the rage rolling off him in thick waves. All her old programming perked right up. It was the survival chant, repeated by women everywhere.

Don't over-react. Don't cause a scene. Stay calm. Smile.

Cate approached holding two thick file folders and tapped on the glass door.

"One second, Josh," Camelia said in her most neutral voice. "Let me just get your file."

He glared at her, but didn't respond. Camelia took a few steps down the hall, out of earshot. Cate handed Camelia his file.

"I tried to reach you on your mobile, but it went to voice mail. He was waiting by the door when Cheri got here this morning, and he's been ranting ever since. He thinks you're to blame for the judge's ruling. I don't think he's . . . he's acting really weird, Cam. What do you want me to do?" Cate whispered. "Should I call security?"

So. Camelia wasn't imagining it. Both Cheri and Cate could feel it, too. The man sitting in that conference room was on the verge of going into a tailspin. But calling security? She could just hear Byron now, the derision in his voice as he mocked them for overreacting. And it would be Camelia who would pay the price for their caution. If Byron had doubts about her abilities before, acting like a *hysterical female* with a high profile client would lower her stock even more in his eyes. No, she could handle Josh Campbell, even if he was mad as hell. She squared her shoulders and faced Cate.

"Oh, come on now. Josh is rightfully pissed off, but he isn't the first, nor will he be the last client to blame me for a bad ruling. I can't go back in there without caffeine, but I don't want to keep him waiting. Can you—"

"I'll be right back with coffee," Cate said, speedwalking down the hall.

As she entered the conference room, Camelia ignored the way her insides were jangling. Yes, that was one of her trauma responses, as Dr. Chavez had repeatedly pointed out. But this *wasn't* traumatic. This was just a difficult conversation with an angry client. Surely, she reassured herself, she could handle a little *mantrum* from Josh. After all, they'd worked so well together until now.

Campbell was facing the windows looking out over Camelback Mountain and he turned to face her as she entered the room.

"Pretty nice view for a bunch of incompetent shysters," he said. "You told me I could expect an award of *zero* alimony. Instead, I'm ordered to pay ten grand a month. How the fuck did you fuck up my fucking case so fucking bad, Counselor?"

Camelia sat down, flipped open the file, and pulled out her notes. "I know the ruling isn't what we expected, but our best option—"

"Sorry to interrupt," Cate said as she walked in with Camelia's cup of coffee and two bottles of water. "If you need anything, just buzz me," she said.

"Thanks, Cate." Camelia took a scalding gulp of coffee, hoping the caffeine would wash away the fuzzy after effects of the martinis she'd had last night. "As I was saying, we have grounds for an appeal. I've outlined a strategy, which we can discuss in more detail when you're ready. But first, if you have questions, Josh, I'm happy to answer them." Camelia hoped he didn't notice the strain in her voice. She gripped her pen and took a deep breath.

Steady now.

Camelia had never seen anything other than the gregarious, flirty, upbeat side of Josh Campbell, but his ex-wife, Shelby, had always maintained that he had a mean streak, and had verbally abused her throughout their marriage. Camelia had doubted her claims, but Campbell's behavior today was proving the truth in Shelby's story.

"Appeal to who?" Campbell plopped down in the chair across from her. "Don't you think the next judge will see the same evidence and hear your same shitty arguments and rule *exactly* the same way?"

"There's only so much I can do at this point. I have to work within the Court system to make this right. Other than that—"

Josh jerked to his feet and paced in front of the wall of windows. "Oh, I see. Other than doing even *more* work and billing me even *more* money, your hands are tied, right? So, you get paid when you totally screw up my case, and then you get paid to unscrew it? What a fucking racket," Campbell said, his arms flailing about for emphasis. "Here's an idea. How about if *you* pay Shelby ten grand a month? Because it seems to me that's your duty. To make me whole. To make it right. Or maybe I should just take a pound of flesh instead," he said, in a low growl.

Camelia's armpits tingled as adrenaline shot through her system. The threat was vague—whose pound of flesh? Shelby's? Hers?—but it was a threat nonetheless.

Campbell turned on his heel and slammed the conference room door open, rattling the glass walls. Camelia jumped up to follow him out, desperate to keep him from making a scene in front of the other attorneys and staff, who would start arriving any minute.

"Josh, please, can we just talk this through?" Camelia pleaded to his back.

Campbell stopped, paused.

"I think I'm done talking." He pushed his suit jacket aside and turned to face her.

The leather holster on his hip demanded her immediate, undivided attention.

Time crawled in slow motion as he popped the snap on the safety strap.

Her eyes were riveted to his right hand.

Out of the corner of her eye, she saw Cheri rise from her chair, turning her back to them as she scooped up a stack of correspondence.

Camelia said, loudly, clearly, and as calmly as she could muster, "Cheri, please go to the kitchen. Mr. Campbell has a gun."

13

Emergency Exit

Thursday, January 28

Josh Campbell's face was flushed pink and the collar of his blue dress shirt was dark with sweat. His eyes were locked on Camelia as she turned away from the reception desk to face him.

She knew she should be scared, and she was. But the fear was miles away, while a quiet rage was plowing through her veins.

He wouldn't fucking dare.

Her mind, usually crowded with thoughts, was remarkably quiet. Time seemed to expand, shuffling along at a reluctant pace. She was beginning to shiver, chilled by the reminder of how close she was standing to the line between life and death, but this was no time for existential angst. Her weapons training—weekend stints for six years in the National Guard, then private defense training every year since—seemed to report for duty, all on its own. She could tell by the clumsy way he was handling that Glock 17, he didn't know what he was doing. She had to *manage* this sonofabitch before he hurt someone.

Fucking amateur.

She spoke in a firm voice, holding Campbell's attention with a steady gaze. "Josh, Cheri's going to take her filing to the back office now, to give us a little privacy." Camelia glanced up at the receptionist just long enough to give a quick nod. As if released from a spell, Cheri bolted to safety.

"Now," Camelia said, turning back to Campbell. "I don't know what on earth made you decide to show up with a gun this morning, but there's no good reason for it, Josh."

He laughed a mirthless huk huk huk and bowed his head, shaking it from side to side.

Josh licked his lips. "It sure as hell got your attention, though, didn't it?"

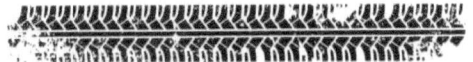

When they heard the shouting, the few early bird staff—Cate, two legal assistants, and one file clerk—congregated in the hallway behind the lobby like panicked horses. When Cate heard Camelia loudly pronounce that Josh Campbell had a gun, she tried to remember the details of the firm's active shooter protocol, but the only thing she could think of was the firm's safe room.

"Get to the kitchen, now," she hissed.

She didn't have to remind them. The other three women were already sprinting to the kitchen as Cheri came running down the hall.

Cate brought up the rear, turning the deadbolt on the steel door. Now, with only the sound of the refrigerator humming in the background, Cate looked around at the other four women. They stared at her with shocked faces, clutching their phones.

The file clerk started crying. "I gotta call my mom," she said, fumbling with her phone. "First, shooters at school, and now at work? This is so fucked."

"Hey, calm down. No one can hurt us in here." Cate nodded at the heavy door. "This is a safe room. Call your mom and let her know you're okay." She gripped the girl's shoulder, then looked at the others. "We are *all* going to be okay."

Cate tapped the screen of her own phone. When it connected, she spoke over the man answering. "Cate Sanchez, McCaffrey law firm, 24th floor. Call the cops. There's a client with a gun in our lobby!" It all came out in a rush. "And don't let anyone else come upstairs!"

"Who else is in the office with you?"

"Five of us in the kitchen and one of the attorneys, Camelia Belmont, is in the lobby with the client. Joshua Campbell. Tell the cops he's armed and out of his mind. He could start shooting at any minute."

As Cate hung up, the file clerk sobbed into her phone a few feet away.

Poor kid.

"Okay, ladies, *focus*. We need to start calling people to keep them from coming to the office," Cate said. She turned to walk away, then stopped and looked back. "Cheri, you have Byron's cell. Call him first. I'll be right back with a roster."

Cate poked her head out of the kitchen door. She could once again hear Josh's raised voice. Fear squeezed down on her throat until she could barely breathe. She scurried to Sonia's desk and grabbed the firm directory from her bulletin board. Rushing back into the kitchen, she locked the door, and turned to the expectant faces staring at her.

"Here," Cate said as she tore the directory pages free of their staple. She handed a page to each of them. "Just start calling. The last thing we need is anyone else walking in on this."

Camelia glanced at the elevators through the bulletproof glass walls of the firm lobby. The glass was a necessary precaution these days, but no damn protection at all when the shooter was already inside the office. The only things barring her escape were those glass walls, the wide landing in front of the elevator, and the man in front of her with a gun.

She took a sip of her now-tepid coffee to soothe her dry throat. "Okay, Josh. You have my attention. Which you've *always* had, by the way. What exactly do you want me to do?"

"No guarantees. Right? That's what you said." Campbell wiped a trickle of sweat from his forehead with the back of his hand, his eyes glittering with anger. "I'm fucked either way. Either you're gonna take all my money, or my ex will, or the goddamn Saudis will. Because the system is rigged against guys like me. Guys who have the *audacity* to make a good living. I can't win." He was gesturing recklessly with the gun in his hand as he spoke.

"Wait, why would Saudis take your money?"

"It doesn't matter now. The bottom line is, guys like me—white, successful, straight Christian men—*cannot win*. And all because of assholes like you and my ex-wife, and that pussy-whipped judge. Meanwhile, Shelby's life goes on like nothing ever happened. She'll be living it up while I foot the bill. Thanks to you."

Josh was waving the handgun around like a conductor's baton as his rage barreled down on her. Camelia realized she was quickly becoming his proxy for all that was wrong in his world.

At least he wasn't pointing the gun at her.

Yet.

But that didn't mean he wouldn't, eventually.

She had to decide: stay or run.

What if he panicked and shot her?

Or followed her?

And where could she go, anyway?

Her breath was coming fast and shallow, now.

Even if she got past Josh, then what? Wait for an elevator? Try to outrun him down 24 flights of stairs in her kitten heels?

There's no way out.

Cate stepped away, toward the windows, to make her own calls as the others migrated to the corners of the kitchen.

You read about this shit every day in the news.

From the window, she could see rush hour traffic backing up in the intersection below as police cars arrived. How could everything look so normal when, just a few yards away . . .

Cate shook her head.

Stay focused.

"Jason? Cate Sanchez, Camelia's assistant. I don't have time to explain, but please do not come up to the office. Stay downstairs until I call you back."

As she began to dial another coworker, she had a disturbing, forbidden thought.

What if he shoots Camelia?

What if . . .

All their lives were in danger now, because of one more unhinged man with a handgun. Cate knew he could turn on the rest of them, just like he'd turned on Camelia. Anger began to take root as Cate dialed her husband, Dave.

"Hey, babe, listen. We're having a situation here . . ."

14

No Way Out

Thursday, January 28

There was no way out. All Camelia could do was try to keep Josh Campbell talking, to defuse his protracted rage, to calm his desperate mind.

"You know, Josh. You're right." Camelia tried to keep her voice steady, her eyes carefully tracking the man pacing in front of her. "The system is rigged and I'm as sick of it as you are. But good luck changing anything. I'm just following the rules while you're stuck in the middle hoping for a fair shake. Which you didn't get."

She was carefully pacing her words and her breath.

Slowly. Slowly.

"Don't fucking patronize me." Josh's eyes were bloodshot slits. "I'm sick of hearing about how this is everyone's fault but yours. You're starting to sound a lot like Shelby."

"Speaking of Shelby . . . aren't you supposed to pick Grace and Levi up from school in a few hours?" Camelia had no idea what his parenting schedule was, but she had a fifty-fifty chance. "You have them through the weekend, don't you?"

At the mention of his children, the wind seemed to go out of Campbell. His shoulders fell, the gun hanging loose at his side as he shuffled over and collapsed into a chair by the window. He rested the gun on his thigh.

"I'm supposed to have fifty-fifty time. Instead, I'm just . . ." he stared at the gun as if he couldn't remember why he had it. "My kids don't even want me around. Shelby's already turned *my own children* against me. There's no happy ending for a guy like me and nothing I can do to change it."

"Well, one thing you can do is put that gun away. You've scared everyone half to death, Josh." Camelia nodded at the gun in his hand as she sank into the chair across from him.

Anxiety was spiraling up from her belly. Camelia slowed her breathing.

Goddammit. Not now. Not now. Not now.

A panic attack would probably get her killed.

"Yeah? Well, I'm scared too," Josh said. For a moment, he looked like he was going to cry. "I kinda . . . look, the business isn't worth a fraction of the valuation amount. It looks like it's worth ten mil on paper, but it's not. Not really."

"What are you talking about?" Camelia said.

Did he just admit to fraud and perjury?

"I didn't do anything *illegal*. Just a few creative appraisals to get the valuation to come in high. Because that way I could sell the business at a premium."

Josh licked his lips and reached for his water bottle.

Camelia wondered for a moment if Josh was on something, or if it was just the adrenaline making him so thirsty.

"But Shelby's entitled to half the proceeds of the sale, whatever the amount, so how does that help you?" Camelia asked.

"It was my escape hatch. I sell, I give her half of *something*, and we're done. But if I have to shell out ten thousand every month based on my *anticipated income*? Yeah, that's not gonna fly. The money's not there."

"Christ, Josh. If I had known—"

"If you had *known*, the business wouldn't be valued high enough to get me out of debt. And that was the *only* upside of the divorce." He was speaking more quietly, with a resigned undertone to his voice. "It's been a lean year. Plus, I'm in deep with those Saudi investors and when the deal crashed . . . Shelby found out. It's what started this whole downward spiral. She blamed me, even though it's not my fault the zoning assholes clamped down on water rights for foreign investors. She figured she'd get out while there was still something left in the bank."

"What the hell are you talking about, Josh? I'm not following."

"Jesus. Try to keep up. I put together a land parcel for a group of investors. Saudis who want Arizona alfalfa for their cattle. But when the deal went south, they lost their earnest money. And it was a *lot* of money." His chest heaved as he took a deep breath. "I even waived my advisor fees, but they want *all* their money back. I don't have that kind of cash, so they're out for blood. Bottom line: I won't be paying Shelby. I'll die first. They'll see to that."

"If they're that dangerous, shouldn't you report them?" Camelia asked.

Josh huffed a bitter *ha ha*. "And who exactly would I report them to? A fine law firm like this?" Josh waved the gun around, as if pointing out the design details in the lobby. "The cops? I'm as good as dead, so I might as well—"

"Might as well *what*? Go out in a blaze of glory?" Camelia's voice was soft and forgiving as a prayer. "Josh, tell me what the hell you got yourself into so I can help you."

He sighed. "I didn't get myself into anything. Not intentionally. But here we are."

A surreal calm descended upon her. If there was a round in the chamber—and she had no way of knowing for sure—Josh could kill her with one twitch of his finger. But his anger seemed to be fizzling out. Camelia saw her opening.

"Whatever trouble you're in, that gun won't solve it. If you hurt someone, I guarantee your children will never have another day of peace. Do you know what the kids at school will say about them? The names they'll be called? It will dog them the rest of their lives. Is that *really* the legacy you want to leave for them?"

Josh turned away, seeming to consider his children's future. But as Camelia stared at his back, she saw a flicker of movement. Beyond Josh, past the elevator vestibule, through the window into the stairwell. Black helmet.

Oh no no no. Not the cops! Not now!

Josh turned back to face her, a hard gleam in his eye. She tried to keep her eyes on him as her peripheral vision picked up two uniforms coming through the side door of the office. It opened into the hallway behind the reception desk. From there, the cops were just steps away from the lobby. Anticipating the worst, she dug her heels into the carpet and pushed her chair back a couple of feet.

Josh returned to the chair across from her and sank into it. He was only six or eight feet away, his back to the elevators now, eyes boring into Camelia's.

"So, am I just supposed to sit around and wait to be taken out by some Saudi hit man?" Josh hissed. "Or by one of those trigger happy cops?" He tipped his head toward the stairwell.

He'd seen them, too. He tightened his grip on the gun, reached over with his left hand, and pulled the slide back. Now there was a round in the chamber. Even if the safety was on, pulling the trigger would override it. It was a known feature of the Glock. And if he didn't drop that gun *immediately*, this would be Joshua Campbell's grand finale.

Death by cop.

"I'm begging you, Josh. Please, *please* put the gun on the floor." Camelia motioned with her hand, palm down. "Those cops won't hesitate, so *please* don't give them the satisfaction."

"I don't intend to give them, or Shelby, or you another fucking thing."

In one swift, deliberate movement, he lifted the gun to his chin.

The only word she could muster—"No!"—was strangled in her throat.

The gunshot deafened her.

Camelia clapped her hands over her ears and pressed her head onto her knees.

Blood and bone and brain splattered against the bulletproof glass wall in a near perfect circle.

She heard herself screaming as if from far away.

Cate had just begun telling Dave what was going on when she heard the shot. "Oh fuck. Oh no. Oh god . . ."

"Cate, was that a gunshot?" her husband asked.

She started shaking, her teeth were chattering, and she felt nauseous. She grasped the back of a chair and fell into it, blowing out short breaths. The office landlines lit up, all ringing at once.

"Cate! Say something! Where are you? Are you safe?"

"Y-y-yes, for now," Cate said. "We're in the kitchen."

"I'll be right there," Dave said.

She blew out a long exhale as tears poured down her face. "Yes, please come. And babe, this is *not* my day to die. I love you."

Cate hung up and dialed security. "We just heard a gunshot—"

"Yes, ma'am. SWAT are on scene. Stay where you are until they've given us the all clear, okay?" She could hear shouting in the background. "Just hold on. Stay on the line, okay?"

As the other four women stared at her, Cate put her phone on speaker. They could hear faint shouting through the reinforced concrete walls of the kitchen. Minutes passed. Cate chewed a hangnail. Finally, the security officer came back on the line.

"Ma'am, you're all clear. The situation is contained. You're all safe now."

"What about Camelia?" Cate glanced up to see Cheri's hands clasped in prayer.

"Miss Belmont is fine. She's being checked out right now. The police asked that all of you stay in the kitchen. They're going to send a deputy back to see you in just a minute, okay?"

"Yep, got it." Cate hung up and swiped the tears off her cheeks as she turned to the others. "Oh my god. She's okay."

The collective groans and sighs quickly turned into cheers and hugs.

Cate tapped on the contacts on her phone and found Leon's mobile. As the phone rang, she muttered, "Pick up, pick up, pick up."

"Hey Cate, what's up?" Leon said.

"First, don't freak out. Camelia's fine. But there's been a shooting. You need to get down here right now."

Camelia observed her hands quivering on the conference table. A medic had swabbed them for gunpowder residue, but all she wanted to do now was scrub them raw.

"I think that's it for now, but we'll be in touch to schedule your formal statement." The officer, a petite woman with a dark pixie haircut, flipped her notebook shut.

As she stood up, Camelia staggered under a sudden onset of vertigo.

"You sure you're okay?" the officer asked. "We can take you to ER to get checked out."

"No, thanks. I'll be fine," she said.

But she was just reciting the words. Time had passed in a blur. She didn't even know how long she'd been here. She'd been checked over by paramedics while a cop asked her questions. Forensics took her fingerprints and DNA. They swabbed her hands and clothes. The medics washed her up a bit. Then, she was interviewed again.

Still wrapped in an ambulance blanket, Camelia stepped out of the conference room into the back hallway. She glanced up to see Cheri, Cate, two other legal assistants, and that poor teenage file clerk huddled near Cate's cubicle. When they saw her, the little group burst into applause and cheers as Cate slammed into her with open arms.

"Cam! Thank god, you're okay," Cate said through her tears.

Cheri plowed into her from the side. "You saved my life, girl."

Camelia's ears, still ringing from the close-range gunshot, could barely make out the flurry of muffled voices.

So brave.

So calm.

A goddamn hero.

All those faces staring at her, hands touching her, patting her arms, her back. It unspooled something inside her, and Camelia felt herself drifting, as if she was miles away. She pulled away.

"I have to . . ." Camelia paused as she pushed through the group to her office. "Call Leon."

"He's already on his way. I'll bring you a cup of tea," Cate said, and shut Camelia's door.

Camelia sank to her knees beside her desk, letting the blanket drift to the floor. She dragged her garbage can to her chest and vomited up a thin, burning stream of bile and coffee.

What the hell just happened?

She pulled open her desk drawer and rifled around for her flask. Her fingers locked around the cool metal and she shook. Empty.

She stood up and wiped her mouth with a tissue before staggering to the windows to close the blinds. A migraine had already stabbed its way into her brain as she fell onto the white leather sofa tucked into the alcove near the windows. She kicked off her shoes and pulled her knees in tight, rolling the scratchy blanket around her.

Josh's hand, moving that gun so smoothly. Then the blast, loud enough to make her fillings ring. The coppery, metallic smell of blood. Shards of bone and brain forming a halo on the glass wall behind Josh's lolling head. His foggy eyes staring at the ceiling. The sensory images were playing on a loop in her head.

STOP!

She had to focus. Tamp down the panic. What time was it? Couldn't even be ten, yet. The tremors started deep inside her belly. Where the hell was that tea? No, she needed a tall shot of vodka. Maybe a whole bottle. She just had to get home. Grab a bottle and curl up on the couch in front of the TV with the dogs. Anything to keep from seeing Josh Campbell staring at her from a pool of viscous red. She shuddered.

A light tap on the door and Cate entered, holding a steaming mug of tea.

"I added honey for the shock. Leon's on his way." Cate placed the mug of tea on the end table. "What else can I do for you?"

"Fucking Josh. For Chrissake. Why would he . . .," Camelia was suddenly so tired she couldn't focus. "Shouldn't you go home?"

Cate let out a little laugh. "You don't need to worry about *me*. The lobby's a crime scene until further notice, so we're all leaving as soon as Leon gets here. Are you *sure* you're alright?"

Camelia took a sip of tea.

"I'll be okay," she said.

When I've had a tall glass of very cold vodka.

15

REST AREA AHEAD

THURSDAY, JANUARY 28

Leon arrived to an active crime scene. He paused outside the elevators, not sure if he should wade into the sea of police and crime scene investigators crammed into the lobby. Even though Cate had tried to prepare him, his stomach rolled and his palms began to sweat at the sight of blood and brain tissue on the firm's glass lobby wall just a few feet away. As he scanned the area, a deputy approached.

"Sir, can I help you?" she said.

"Hi, yeah, my wife . . . they called," he fumbled, realizing he was more freaked out than he'd realized. He took a deep breath and shoved his hands in his jacket pockets to keep them from shaking. "My wife is Camelia Belmont. Cate Sanchez called and said there was a shooting—not Cam, someone else—and I needed to get down here."

"Mr. Belmont, your wife is safe. Paramedics confirmed she wasn't injured. She's pretty shook up, though," the deputy said as she ushered Leon across the elevator lobby, through an unmarked door. "Let's go around here to the side door."

He hadn't even known the additional exit existed, but as he glanced around, he realized it wasn't much of an escape hatch. It opened right onto the elevator vestibule, in full view of anyone in the firm's lobby. He would need to have a chat with Byron about firm security after this was over.

"Do you know where to go from here?"

"Yes, thanks," Leon answered as he walked toward the clump of women huddled outside Camelia's office.

As soon as he caught her eye, Cate quickly stepped forward and put her arm through Leon's, steering him out of earshot of the others gathered in the hall.

"I'm so glad you're here. She's in shock. I tried to get the paramedics to sedate her, but they wouldn't. Not without knowing what she takes for . . . you know, stress," she said, in a low voice.

"Yeah, of course." Leon ignored the implied question about Camelia's anxiety medication. "Cate, what the fuck happened?"

"God, Leon. It's a nightmare. One of Cam's clients showed up at seven thirty this morning demanding to see her about the ruling in his case. She tried to talk him down, but he was beyond reasoning with." Cate hugged her elbows. "He was ranting like a lunatic."

"Jesus Christ. You could have all been killed." Leon ran his hands through his hair.

"I know. I don't know how she did it, but Cam kept him in the lobby, talking. We hid out in the kitchen and called security and . . . Cam just kept talking to him." Cate paused, shaking her head.

"Anyway, the SWAT guys were on the scene when he . . . they were too late."

He saw a shudder run through Cate's body.

"So the cops didn't shoot him?"

"No." Cate shook her head. "He beat them to it. And Leon, Camelia was *right there*. She has blood and . . . stuff in her hair," Cate's voice broke as the tears threaded down her cheeks. She dabbed a tissue at her eyes.

"Jesus fucking Christ. Okay, I gotta get her home. She's in her office?" Leon asked.

Cate nodded and flicked away the tears. "Yeah, I took her some tea for the shock. But I'm not even sure she can walk, so I had the security guys bring that up." Cate nodded at the wheelchair parked outside Camelia's office.

"Thank you for thinking of that," Leon said. "Now, I'm gonna get her outta here. And you can let Byron know she won't be back for a while."

"Already managed. He closed the firm the rest of this week and all of next," Cate said. "And Leon, make her stay away. It'll take a while to replace the carpet and chairs and . . . she doesn't need the reminder."

"Agreed." Leon nodded toward the others. "What's everyone still doing here?"

"Just waiting for you."

"Okay, let's get going." Leon turned toward Camelia's office, pushing the wheelchair ahead of him through the door.

When Leon entered, he half expected to see Camelia at her desk, tapping away on the keyboard, as usual. But his wife was on the loveseat, arms curled around her knees, huddled under a blanket, staring into space. He shut the door behind him.

"Cam? Honey?"

She didn't react when he said her name, so Leon went to her side, squeezed onto the small sofa, and wrapped an arm around her shoulders. Her whole body was shaking.

"Babe, let's go home, okay?" Leon whispered. "Cate brought up a wheelchair, so just let me take care of everything."

He stood and held out a hand. She didn't speak, but Camelia scooted to the edge of the seat. As she pulled the blanket close around her shoulders, her head turned to one side. Leon tried not to look too closely at the dark substance matted in her hair. As he lifted her to her feet, she staggered for a moment, then straightened.

"I can walk," she said in a flat voice.

"I know you can. But just for today, act like you're not invincible. For the sake of the mortals outside." He gave her a tender smile. "No need to be a hero anymore."

She nodded as she sat in the wheelchair.

Leon grabbed Camelia's coat, briefcase, and handbag off her chair.

"I've got all your stuff," Leon said as he moved to open her office door. "And how about if you cover your head for now? There's nothing out there you need to see and I sure as hell don't want any reporters getting photos of you for the five o'clock news."

After Camelia showered, she pulled on fleece pajamas and perched on the end of the bed, toweling her hair. Caesar and Calvin, sensing her distress, plastered their furry bodies to each side of her.

Leon handed Camelia her phone. "I think you should call Dr. Chavez."

"Yeah, I guess so," she said. "Not sure what to tell him, though."

"Just tell him what happened and let him take it from there." Leon rubbed Caesar's ears. "He's a pro. He'll know what to do."

Camelia swiped through her phone and called Dr. Chavez' office. "Yeah, I'll hold," she said.

"Let me talk to him when you're done, okay?" Leon said. "I want to make sure I'm following doctor's orders, too."

"Sure," Camelia responded. "Just give me a few minutes."

Leon nodded as he slipped out of the bedroom and pulled the door closed. He was flipping channels in the family room when, about twenty minutes later, he heard Camelia call him.

When he entered the bedroom again, she was under the covers, her eyes red and swollen with tears. Silently, she held out her phone.

"Hey, Carlos, Leon here."

"Hi Leon, how are you holding up?" Dr. Chavez asked.

Leon stepped into the hall and pulled the bedroom door shut on his way back to the family room.

"I'm a lot better off than Cam. What a goddamn mess," Leon said.

"It is an absolute nightmare, and don't underestimate the vicarious trauma you've just been through, too. How are you feeling?"

"Well, right now, I feel like a pretty lucky guy. But I'm a little shaky, if I'm being honest. And I'm worried about Cam. Worried this is gonna set off an avalanche of anxiety and, and . . . I don't even know what else." Leon took a deep breath. His hands were trembling.

"I've called in a prescription to help her get past these first few days, so if you can pick that up," Dr. Chavez said. "And I've scheduled her in tomorrow for some trauma intervention."

"I appreciate it. But I'm concerned about . . . the first thing she did when she got home was take a shower. The second thing was have a double vodka, neat."

Dr. Chavez paused. "And from your perspective, that's a worry? I mean, I hate to say it, but I kinda want a drink right now, too."

"Right? But I mean . . . you're the expert. Is this the kind of thing that can throw someone like her into the abyss?"

"Leon, I hate to break it to you, but any of us can fall into addiction in response to trauma. It's a way of numbing the pain. And there's nothing you can do to change that, other than be there for her," Dr. Chavez said. "She needs compassion, support, rest, and active recovery."

"What does that mean, *active recovery?*" Leon asked.

"Take her out for regular walks and hikes, anything to get her outside, get her heart rate up, and burn off the cortisol. She needs to stay off social media and her work email, and she shouldn't watch the news," Dr. Chavez said. "And maybe screen her calls? The last thing she needs is to be bombarded by ghouls and looky-loos."

"Got it. And thanks for everything. This is way above my pay grade," Leon said with a dry laugh.

"Don't even get me started. I've been doing this forever and it still feels like it's beyond *all* our pay grades. It makes me *furious* because Josh Campbell is just one more in a long line of people who would still be alive if he hadn't had easy access to a handgun. I'll get off my soapbox now, but god*dammit.*" Dr. Chavez heaved a sigh. "Okay, you've got my number so feel free to call or text any time. And don't forget to take care of yourself, too."

"I'm doing my best," Leon said. "Thanks again."

A few hours later when Leon tiptoed into the bedroom, Camelia was curled up under the covers, the dogs sprawled beside her. Leon sat on the bench at the end of the bed and watched them all sleeping, but not for long.

A head lifted. A tail thumped.

Camelia bolted upright. "What's going on?"

"Hey, hey. You're safe. I'm just checking on you." Leon held her feet through the duvet.

"What time is it?"

"Just after five. Cate and Dave had your favorites from Pizza Heaven delivered, so there's plenty to eat if you're hungry. And I was going to take Calvin and Caesar for a spin around the block, but they won't leave your side," he said, smiling.

She yawned. "How about if we all go? I need to stretch my legs," Camelia said, reaching out to scratch the furry heads staring at her. "Right boys? Wanna go for a walk?"

The two dogs leapt from the bed and began prancing around Leon's legs.

"Oh, you've done it now! Calvin, Caesar, go get your leashes!" Leon clapped his hands at the dogs, then leaned down and kissed Camelia's forehead. "Ready when you are."

As they began their walk, dusk deepened to night. Camelia was silent, but Leon could tell her mind was working overtime.

"So, how are you feeling?" he asked.

"I don't know. Kinda numbed out," she said.

"What did Dr. Chavez say?"

"Not much. I did most of the talking. He just basically said to stay off my phone, go for a walk, and sleep as much as I can. I'm seeing him tomorrow for some trauma work," Camelia said.

"I picked up your script, so you can start taking that tonight," Leon said. "But Cam, are you *okay*?"

"I think so, but it hasn't really sunk in, I guess. Rough day at work, for sure."

"No kidding. I would say you've had an epically shitty day, but that would be the understatement of the century," Leon said, glancing at Camelia in the glow of a streetlight. She looked haggard.

"Today set a new low bar, even for me," Camelia said with a sardonic chuckle.

If he waited to speak up, she would have time to put her shields back up. He knew he couldn't out-argue her and the thing is, he didn't want to. He just wanted her to be safe and, clearly, the office wasn't secure. If he had his way, she'd never go back.

"The thing is, Cam, you've been having a lot of rough days, and that's just the ones I know about. And now this? It scared the living shit out of me and, if I'm honest, I really don't want you going back there. And before you say it, I know, I know—"

"Well, the odds are—"

"I don't give a shit about the odds. I'm worried about the effect this kind of thing has. Long term," Leon said.

"Well, I can't just *not* go back. I'm attorney of record on dozens of cases," she said, quietly. "It's a whole process."

"Okay, so maybe you have to go back and make a list for Cate. But why would you even *want* to go back after this? It's not healthy. And it's not safe. Obviously." Leon paused as the dogs sniffed a particularly interesting tree trunk. "I just think it's time to consider doing something else. Some other kind of law. Or hell, flip burgers, it doesn't matter. Anything other than being in the crosshairs of some lunatic who's upset because he didn't get his way."

"Jesus, Leon. I can't even think about that right now. Do you have any idea how much paperwork is involved in a workplace shooting? The forms, the reports, and I'm sure there will be some kind of investigation. And then there are all my other clients . . ." Camelia looked at Leon and shrugged. "There's no way I can leave Suzanne Anders high and dry."

"Okay, okay. I get it. You're too important to quit," Leon huffed, and immediately regretted it.

Shit. Did I just say that?

"Are you fucking kidding me right now?" Camelia snapped. "In case you've forgotten, I'm the breadwinner at the moment."

"Cam, I didn't mean it like that. I just mean . . . no one is indispensable. You could have been *killed* today. I appreciate you carrying the financial load right now, but no job is worth losing your life over. My vote, if I get one, is for you to find another way to practice law. Maybe corporate?"

Camelia laughed. "You get half a vote, remember? And since most of my experience is in family law, I don't exactly fit the corporate counsel mold." She glanced at Leon. "Honey, I know this scared you. It scared me, too. And makes me so angry. Fucking men with their fucking guns! But changing my practice area would be an ordeal. And I've been a divorce attorney so long, I don't even know what else I could do."

"Well, that's not exactly true. After Auntie Freda's services, you mentioned investigative work. Remember?" Leon said.

"Yeah, I remember. But Byron isn't mentoring me and it just seems out of reach right now, with everything else going on."

"Everything is out of reach unless you plan for it. Don't rule it out. Because the other problem with the kind of work you're doing is the stress. Do you think I don't know how it affects you? How you try to drown it in a martini glass?" Leon said softly. "Not that I blame you, but it's not good for you, babe."

Camelia kept walking, her head down, watching the sidewalk. Leon knew he'd pressed too hard, too soon. His timing was off. But he was terrified of losing her. That fucking idiot could have killed her.

She heaved a sigh into the dry, cool night air.

"I know you're right. Just . . ." Camelia turned to Leon. "Can we come back to this in a couple of weeks? I'm too exhausted to think straight."

"Of course. And I'm sorry for being the overbearing husband. Let's go home and jump in bed. I'll make popcorn and we can watch a cheesy movie. How's that sound?"

"Best offer I've had all day."

They turned the corner and headed back to the house, Caesar and Calvin eagerly tugging on their leashes. It hadn't gone as well as he'd hoped, but Leon knew he'd given her something to think about. All he could do now was encourage Camelia to disentangle herself from the complicated career she'd so carefully crafted.

And try to keep her out of the liquor cabinet.

16

AFTERBURN

THURSDAY, FEBRUARY 4

Byron's face—all piercing eyes and dashing smile—was everywhere. He was the media darling of the week, and right now he was holding forth on CNN while Camelia was supposed to be doing self-care, whatever the hell that meant. She was propped up in bed, flipping channels, nursing a cup of lemon ginger tea topped up with a shot of vodka, trying to distract herself. No such luck. Josh Campbell's suicide had whipped the media into a frenzy.

Byron had promised to shield her from the media swarm, but she knew it wasn't out of altruism. Still, even though it might be self-serving on his part, she was relieved. The last thing Camelia needed right now was a close-up camera shot. And Byron loved the attention. It seemed like he was booked on every talk show, including

Good Morning America and *The Daily Show*, and he didn't disappoint. He spoke eloquently and concisely on the universal corporate concern of gun violence in the workplace.

She noticed Byron was also quick to mention that he was following best practices: he'd closed the office for a few days and hired a trauma counselor for the staff. He even managed to name the mental health and gun control charities he'd donated to in Josh Campbell's name. Byron being Byron, he also slipped in a little dig at Judge Sorensen. Something about the *foreseeable effect of a non-precedential decision creating havoc in the lives of ordinary citizens*. Most of the people watching wouldn't even know what that meant, but Sorensen would, and that's what Byron was counting on. She knew he was just deflecting liability from the firm; still, he was *sort of* defending her from blame, too. It was, after all, Sorensen's orders that pushed Josh Campbell over the edge. Meanwhile Byron's face—and the firm name—were front and center for the curious masses.

Camelia flipped to a local channel and was stunned to see Shelby Campbell's doe-eyed smile on the screen. She turned up the volume.

". . . and this tragedy brought my family to its knees. I simply couldn't have survived without the support of all of your prayers," Shelby paused and smiled at the camera. "Especially considering *how* and *why* my husband died."

Oh really, Shelby?

She was astutely playing up the role of the aggrieved widow, but just wait until she found out about the actual value of Josh's business. Hell hath no fury . . .

Camelia clicked off the television. She sipped her spiked tea through a thumping caffeine-withdrawal headache. *No stimulants right now*, Dr. Chavez had warned.

Her phone dinged. She picked it up to see *The Boss* on her home screen and wondered what was so urgent that Byron was taking time out of his press rounds to call her.

"Hey Byron," she said. Even to her own ears, her voice sounded listless.

"Hey Belmont, thought I'd check in and see how you're doing," Byron said.

"I'm okay, thanks," she said.

And it was true. The exact details of Campbell's suicide seemed fuzzy and far away, so—for now, at least—she was fine.

"That's a relief. I was worried this would . . . it's traumatic, Cam."

"I'm taking care of myself. Doing some PTSD work with my therapist. How are you, Mr. Morning Show?"

Byron chuckled. "No such thing as bad publicity, right? And I'm just trying to get a handle on things, what with the . . . disruption." He paused and Camelia could hear his inhale. "I wanted to give you a heads up. The annual firm retreat is coming up fast, but given all that's happened, I don't think it's the right time for a big, flashy party," Byron said. His voice sounded strained.

"Yeah, bad timing. It might seem callous," Camelia said.

"Exactly. I'm postponing the retreat, including the partner vote, until September. Which is good news, because it gives you . . . gives us all time to recover from this tragedy and re-evaluate our priorities."

So. He was offering what *looked* like a reprieve, but she could read the subtext. They were not going to approve Camelia for partner, but Byron didn't want to make the announcement right on the heels of Josh Campbell's suicide. It wouldn't play well among the other attorneys and staff. She had to wonder if the suicide had derailed her, or if it was that dumb rumor Ashcroft had spread, or maybe it was Maureen Hallman's *almost* baseless accusations about her being drunk at mediation last year.

"Sounds like a reasonable approach," she replied. "And just so you know, I'll be back in the office next week with everyone else."

Because that's what partner candidates did. They bounced back.

"Hey, take as much time as you need, Cam. You've had a hell of a shock," Byron replied.

"Yeah, but sitting around the house isn't doing me any good. I need to be busy."

"In that case, expect a hero's welcome. I know I've already said it, but you demonstrated enormous grace under pressure." Byron cleared his throat. "I'm extremely grateful. It could have been . . . well, anyway . . ."

Just not quite grateful enough to make me partner.

"Thanks, but I only did what anyone else would have done."

"I'm not so sure about that, Cam. Anyway, take care and I'll see you whenever you're ready."

She hung up and dropped her phone on the nightstand as she pulled the blanket up over her head.

It was almost noon. She should get up and do something, anything, but she was exhausted by the mere thought of moving.

Her inner cynic was gaining ground. Why bother getting out of bed today? Or any day? When a random person could just walk in and start shooting, what difference did it make? None of it mattered one whit in the scheme of the universe.

MONDAY, FEBRUARY 8

When she stepped into the elevator the following Monday, her first day back, Camelia's heart started to pound out a list of reasons she shouldn't be here.

As the carriage slowed for the 24th floor, her palms began to sweat.

Her breath quickened.

As the doors slid open, she had a moment of vertigo.

A sheen of sweat broke through every pore as she stepped into the marble hallway.

With a trembling hand, she passed her key card over the sensor and pulled on the firm's heavy glass door as it buzzed. The vague disinfectant smell of the hallway gave way to the smell of new carpet.

Of course there would be new carpet.

She glanced to her right, where . . . nothing was out of place.

There were no overturned chairs. No blood smeared glass. No Josh Campbell, his foggy eyes staring at the ceiling.

"Welcome back," Cheri said, as she stepped from behind the reception desk, coming toward Camelia with open arms. "I'm so glad you're okay."

Camelia tried to wave her off, but it was too late. Cheri was on her, crushing her in a full body hug, towering over her in four-inch heels.

Camelia burst into tears.

Oh god. This is not how this is supposed to go.

"It's okay hon," Cheri said, thumping her back. "You're gonna be fine."

"Thanks, yeah. I'm okay, just . . ." Camelia pulled back from Cheri's arms. "Kinda hit me when I walked in. But, yes, I'm fine."

Cheri grabbed Camelia's briefcase and looped her arm around her shoulders. "Let's go get you a cuppa coffee. Cate's been on pins and needles waiting for you this morning," she said.

Camelia pushed her sunglasses on top of her head and pressed her fingertips to her eyes.

"Coffee sounds like just what the doctor ordered," she said as she reached to take her briefcase back. "But we've all got work to do, right? So, no more fussing. Really. I'm okay."

"That's exactly what every superhero says." Cheri grinned and squeezed Camelia's shoulder. "If you need *anything*, just buzz me, 'kay?"

Camelia gave her a little smile as she turned the corner into the back hallway. Cate's head was bent over her desk. Camelia felt a surge of gratitude for her calm, sensible paralegal. Cate had proved her mettle in the way she managed the other staff and made urgent phone calls while Josh Campbell held them all hostage. Camelia's heart swelled as her eyes misted over again.

"Happy Monday," Camelia said in a low voice.

Cate swiveled in her chair.

"Fancy seeing you here. Shouldn't you be . . . recovering? Or working for the FBI as a hostage negotiator or something like that?" She grinned.

"Not 'til I get my coffee, at least." Camelia stepped into her office to drop her briefcase and coat, and was surprised to see half a dozen bouquets of flowers. She turned back to Cate. "What's all this about?"

"Oh, haven't you heard? You're kind of a big deal. You've got a stack of messages from clients checking in on you, but they can wait." Cate pointed at a tall arrangement of bird-of-paradise. "That one's from Suzanne. The sunflowers are from Nina Garry. And the others are from Dr. Moray, the Arizona Women Lawyers Association, Blake Griffin, if you can believe it, and the Gerbera daisies are from me and Cheri and the others."

"Because you know they're my favorite. Thank you, Cate. All it took was one messy shoot out." She laughed. "Seriously, thank you so much. It wasn't necessary, but I love them." Camelia held up her coffee mug. "Be right back."

She walked down the hall to the kitchen, nodding at some of the other early birds as she passed. The kitchen was empty, thank god, so she grabbed her coffee and speed-walked back to her office before she was waylaid. The last thing she wanted was to talk about all of it again. She waved Cate into her office.

"Bring a notepad," she said.

Cate shut the door behind her and sat down opposite Camelia, pad on her lap, pen in hand.

"First off, thank you for being calm and logical during the whole fiasco. The others all said you were amazing," Camelia said.

"I didn't really do anything."

"Yes, you *did* do something. You kept yourself and four other women safe *and* you called for help *and* you stopped anyone else from barging in while Josh Campbell was waving his gun around," Camelia said. "So that's a lot, actually."

"Okay, well, thanks."

"And second, this is *strictly* confidential until we all get the email. Byron is postponing the firm retreat, which means they're putting off the partner vote." Camelia sipped her coffee. "So, I don't know for sure, but I'm guessing they're not voting me in as a partner."

Why am I not more upset about this?

"After what you've been through?" A flush of indignation colored Cate's cheeks. "He oughtta make you partner just for showing up today!"

"Well, Byron would tell you that making partner is a financial decision, first and foremost." Camelia wondered who else knew about his pre-Christmas ultimatum and what the hallway gossip was saying about her these days. "Whatever the reason, I don't think I'm making partner this year."

"But you won't know for sure until September, right?" Cate asked.

"Yeah, but it's only six months out. So, between now and then we have to buckle down if I'm going to have any chance at all."

"Yep. I get it," Cate said. She flipped her hair over her shoulder and clicked her pen. "Fire away."

"Let's get rolling on the Saminski deposition."

Cate took notes as Camelia listed out a half dozen tasks to complete in the Anders case before moving on to their other cases. As Camelia finished speaking, Cate clipped her pen to her notepad and stood up.

"Okay, I'm getting another cup of coffee before I dig into the Anders list. I should be done before lunchtime," Cate said.

"I have enough to keep me busy, too," Camelia said. "And that's a good thing."

"It's not too late to cancel the depo, if you're not up to it," Cate said.

Camelia looked up from her notepad. "I know. But it's never going to be a good time to depose the Chief Security Officer for AndersLaw, so I might as well get it over with."

"I just want to make sure you're not overdoing it. It seems so sudden to be back at work. Like nothing ever happened."

"Yeah, but that's how it is, isn't it? Whether we like it or not, life goes on." Camelia took a sip of her coffee. "And speaking of such things, Josh Campbell's funeral is on Thursday."

"Please tell me we don't have to go," Cate said.

"God, no. But the firm should send flowers. Can you ask Cheri to arrange that?" Camelia asked.

"She'll be happy to help. You saved her life, after all!" Cate said.

"Well, that's a bit of an exaggeration," Camelia said. "Cheri was never his target. Collateral damage, maybe, but he wouldn't have hurt her on purpose."

Cate raised an eyebrow and pursed her lips.

"Okay, I don't *think* he would have hurt her. Anyway, stop hovering. I have work to do and I'm fine." Camelia shooed Cate out with a few waves of her hand.

"Okay, okay. I'll leave you to it," Cate said as she pulled the door closed behind her.

Camelia had to fill out a 12-page form for the professional liability insurer and then write a statement of facts—a timeline of everything that happened between her and Josh Campbell from the time the case began—for the malpractice attorneys. Because, sure as hell, as soon as Shelby Campbell found out the true worth of the business, she would be filing a complaint with the State Bar. And even though he was deceased, now that Camelia knew about Josh's perjury, she was obligated to correct the Court record. Shelby and her lawyer would never believe Camelia wasn't in on it from the beginning. And who could blame them?

Camelia stood and crossed to the door, turning the lock.

She walked to the wall of windows and watched a trio of puffy clouds chase each other across the deep blue winter sky. The trembling started in her hands. Then her breath quickened. Before she could get to her handbag to dig out a Klonopin, the panic was on her, in her, squeezing down on her throat, slamming her head against the wall.

Really. I'm fine.

All I need is another Klonopin and a martini.

17

STEEP GRADE

TUESDAY, FEBRUARY 16

Therapy helped. Klonopin helped more. But Camelia still felt as if she was walking through wet cement, weighed down by the ghost of Josh Campbell.

As she got in the elevator for the ride to the 24th floor, her heart banged out the usual warning. Even though all trace of Campbell's horrific suicide had been scrubbed away, she was still haunted by the last tense moments of his life every time she stepped into the firm lobby. Maybe Leon was right. Maybe it was time to move on. But not today.

Deep breaths. Deep breaths.

She needed to get her shit together, and quickly, if she was going to get anything out of Dov Saminski. The deposition was in a few hours and, even though she'd read his HR file and grilled Suzanne for whatever personal insights she might have, Camelia still felt unprepared. The scraps of information she'd managed to gather only made him more of an enigma, and his job description didn't help.

Camelia stepped out of the elevator with a shudder. When she entered the lobby, Cheri's head popped up from her computer.

"Good morning, Camelia," Cheri said, smiling. "Cate wants to see you first thing about the deposition today."

"Uh oh. That doesn't sound good," Camelia said.

"She'll fill you in, but sounds like the depo is canceled."

Sonofabitch.

Camelia wondered what Saminski knew that Aaron didn't want her to find out. Or was it just another power play? Either way, Ashcroft was crazy if he thought she'd agree to postpone the deposition. He'd have to go through the judge, because—with Suzanne's lifespan shrinking by the day—Camelia sure as hell wouldn't be granting that request. Besides, if there was anything Saminski could reveal that would help her case, she needed to find out as soon as possible.

As Camelia approached Cate's desk, her assistant turned and waved, her other hand holding the phone to her ear.

"Yes, we'll figure it out. Camelia will call you in about a half hour," Cate said, pausing as the other person talked. She mouthed *Suzanne* at Camelia. "Okay, thank you. Sit tight, and we'll get right back to you."

Cate hung up, shaking her head.

"Tell me everything, but follow me, because I have to drop this load," Camelia said, nodding at her handbag and briefcase. "And sweet Jesus, I need a coffee. Is there a size bigger than venti?"

"I think after venti, it's a quart. Which sounds like just about enough," Cate said. She followed Camelia into her office. "Ashcroft left a message early this morning. Anders wants to cancel the depo and he says Suzanne agreed, so I was just on the phone with her to confirm."

"Are you fucking kidding me?" Camelia asked.

"I wish I was. Suzanne sounded pretty miserable. I told her you'd call her back."

"I heard. Did she actually agree to *cancel* the depo entirely?"

"Sounds like she agreed to postpone the depo *for now*, but keep the appointment time. Ashcroft and Mr. Anders want to use the time for a four-way," Cate said. "Not sure if you want to agree to that?"

Camelia motioned for Cate to follow her as she walked to the kitchen for coffee. "Well, if Suzanne already agreed to postpone, not sure I can walk it back. As for the four-way meeting, we don't even have the biz val. Those two assholes are trying to bulldoze us."

"Oh, you know it. They just want to bully Suzanne into settlement," Cate said. "And that Ashcroft. What a jerk. He *literally* mansplained how to file a Notice of Canceling Deposition with the Court. Like I've never done *that* before."

Camelia stirred cream into her coffee and blew into the cup before taking a sip. "Okay, let me call Suzanne before you file anything, though. I can't wait to hear how Anders convinced her to cancel Saminski's depo."

Back in her office, Camelia scanned the morning's messages noting that a voice mail had come in from Suzanne the previous night at 11:47 p.m., followed by an email from Ashcroft at 6:13 a.m. Anders had been busy. She dialed Suzanne's number.

"Camelia —" The phone had barely rung before Suzanne picked up.

"Suzanne, what's going on?"

"Oh god, it's just Aaron being *very* Aaron. I don't know what he's up to, but he's fawning over me, insisting we reconcile and change our ways. Blah blah blah," Suzanne said. "I have no idea what inspired the sudden interest in his marriage."

Camelia didn't know what Aaron's ploy was, but surely Suzanne wasn't falling for it.

"And is that what *you* want?" she asked.

"Good god, no! But I also don't want a War of the Roses. I told him I'd meet, but only to hash out a settlement, because that's *all* I'm interested in." Suzanne sighed heavily into the phone. "My clock is ticking, Cam. I'm worried that I won't have that many good months ahead of me, and I sure as hell don't want to spend every last minute fighting with Aaron."

"I understand completely. And I'm happy to meet, but I'm zero percent prepared for a four-way settlement conference, especially since we don't have the business valuation yet. My best strategy— our *only* strategy—is to listen, take notes, and respond when we've had a chance to evaluate their offer," Camelia said. "Not that we'd get a word in, anyway, with that much hot air in the room."

Suzanne chuckled. "No kidding. And we can always reschedule Dov's deposition for another day, right?"

"Sure, of course," Camelia said. "But Suzanne, does Aaron know? About your diagnosis?"

"Not from me," she said. "Rick Baum has privacy laws and a promise hanging over his head, so I don't think he'd blab."

"Hmm. I just wonder why Aaron's having such a change of heart. Seems a little suspect, that's all. Anyway, see you in a bit," Camelia said and hung up.

Of course he knew. He must. Otherwise, why the sudden reversal? No, this was just another strategy to delay the divorce. And even after decades of marriage, Suzanne still seemed naïve to his tactics. If he managed to convince her to reconcile, or just continue on as they were, Anders could wait it out. Because if Suzanne died while they were still legally married, he would be a rich widower. And oh, how that would play with the ladies.

"Cheri, is Aaron Anders here yet?" Camelia asked, leaning over the speakerphone. "We were supposed to meet at ten!"

"No, he hasn't arrived, but Mr. Ashcroft is here. He said Mr. Anders is on his way."

"Okay, please let Mr. Ashcroft know I'm cancelling the meeting at 10:30 sharp and notifying the judge if his client isn't here."

"Got it."

Camelia turned back to Suzanne. "Is he always this rude?"

Suzanne rolled her eyes. "In order for Aaron to be rude, your time would have to matter to him. And it doesn't. This is just Aaron Time. *His* schedule is the only thing that matters."

Camelia knew better. This was all intentional on Anders' part. He was upping the ante. Putting the pressure on. Setting them all on edge, so he could breeze in and take over. There was nothing accidental about it.

"Well, he'll be on Belmont Time in about ten minutes. While we wait, let's finish reviewing this background report," she said, and began flipping through the pages of a thin binder. "According to our research team, Aaron was recently involved in a couple of legal actions. One is a fee dispute, so that's probably not useful. But the other is something to do with a land development deal. Do you know anything about that?"

"I didn't know about the fee dispute. It's not unusual though. The firm settles those all the time. But," Suzanne paused for a moment. "I knew there was a land deal that folded recently. Aaron was really pissed off about it because he lost our investment when it fell through. I don't think it was a devastating amount of money, he's more cautious than that. But for Aaron . . . losing *anything* just burns him up."

Land deal gone south. All the money lost. It sounded familiar, a lot like that Saudi investment mess Josh Campbell killed himself over. But it couldn't be. Phoenix was the fifth largest city in the country, so there were probably dozens of land deals going on at any given time.

"Okay, I'll make a note to ask Ashcroft for the details," Camelia said.

"I'm sorry I'm not much help. I used to know everything about the firm—and Aaron—but he . . ." Suzanne grimaced, as if recalling something painful. "Aaron stopped telling me the day-to-day stuff about a decade ago. That's when I knew he was having affairs. He didn't need to cry on my shoulder anymore, and he damn sure didn't want me to have any dirty details I could use against him."

Suzanne's clenched fists belied her calm demeanor. As if she'd noticed Camelia staring at her hands, Suzanne untangled her fingers and wrapped them around her coffee cup.

"Got it," Camelia said, jotting a note. "We'll take a look—"

Cate interrupted with a tap as she opened the conference room door. "Mr. Anders is here. Can I send him in?" She seemed agitated.

Camelia looked at her phone. It was 10:28. "He's *just* under the wire. Everything okay?" Camelia asked.

"Yeah, his attorney's just been bending my ear a bit. So, should I bring them back?" Cate asked.

"Yes, by all means. Let's not keep our guests waiting." Camelia rolled her eyes.

What the hell was Ashcroft talking to Cate about?

Camelia took a deep breath and tamped down her impatience as the men's voices grew louder, signaling their approach.

Unlike most clients, Aaron Anders didn't follow his attorney to the conference room; Ashcroft followed him. Camelia had no doubt it was a metaphor for their professional relationship. Anders stopped in the doorway, pausing to allow his presence to fill the open door.

He was trim and tan, with just a hint of jowl and belly flab belying his otherwise fit image. Camelia could see he was in his element. He was a performer, a dramatic actor taking the stage to deliver his lines. She was confident he'd have rehearsed carefully, planning his zingers in advance.

But how did he have the time? Thinking of her own overburdened calendar, Camelia knew she would never have the luxury of plotting every move so thoroughly. Maybe that was the real difference between a guy like Anders and her. She didn't have wads of time on her hands to craft clever retorts and stinging barbs. She was too busy playing catchup every day. Or drinking it all away every night. But when you didn't have a conscience to distract you, it was probably a whole lot easier to focus on crushing your foes.

She knew that even though she was hopelessly out-gunned by Anders, all she had to do was wait for an opening, and strike fast and hard. Camelia stood up and presented Anders with her best bitch face.

Game on.

18

POWER PLAY

TUESDAY, FEBRUARY 16

"Forgive me, for being late, ladies." Anders paused in the doorway, commanding their attention. "I had an urgent call with Judge Walden in District Court on one of our federal cases, and had to manage that before heading over. I do apologize." He bowed his head a notch and pressed his hands together before name dropping. "Do you know Bob Walden, Cam?"

"It's Cam*elia*, and yes. He's in my Inn of Court. We had dinner together a couple of weeks ago," she replied, with a silent *so there*. "But since we're starting so late—"

"We're here now, and ready to put all this nonsense to bed," Spencer Ashcroft said, pushing past Anders. "This won't take long."

While Ashcroft stowed his briefcase and coat, Aaron quickly claimed the chair opposite Camelia. He leaned in, elbows on the table, hands loosely clasped, in a posture of friendly conversation.

"How *are* you, Camelia? You had quite a scare, didn't you?"

"I'm fine, thanks," Camelia said.

Don't think for a minute you can chat me up.

"What a terrible situation. You're lucky you escaped with your life. These things don't always have a happy ending," he said.

"Not sure I would call suicide a happy ending," Camelia said. "Can we get started?"

"Well, not for poor old Josh . . ." Anders stopped. "Anyway, yes, let's jump in."

Why would he refer to Joshua Campbell as Josh?

"We're ready to hear your proposal," Camelia said, flipping open her file. "That's why you wanted to meet, right?"

Ashcroft and Anders exchanged a look.

"You don't really know me, Cam, and I can't help but feel we got off to a rough start. Even though I don't want any part of this silly divorce business, I'm relieved Suzanne chose to work with someone sensible, like you, and not one of those *crazy litigator types*." Aaron twirled his finger at his temple, clearly making fun of himself. He laughed at his own joke. "But seriously, I'm so glad we're sitting down to talk this through. Suzanne has been very upset with me, and no doubt I've earned a bit of her wrath. But I've seen the error of my ways, my love." He winked at Suzanne, baring brilliant white canines.

"Oh god, Aaron, please." Suzanne rolled her eyes. "Stop laying it on."

"Alright, then. If you don't want romance, let's be practical." Anders turned to Camelia. "Suzanne and I both have a lot to lose if we divorce. Mostly Suzanne." He turned his gaze back to his wife, only this time he wasn't smiling. "Isn't that right, darling? Don't you have *everything* to lose if we split up? I mean, at your age. Who would have you *now*?" Aaron said in the same light, friendly tone of voice.

He may as well have said *pass the sugar*. Camelia felt a wave of indignation rise up from her center.

He's got some nerve.

Suzanne's lips tightened and her nostrils flared. "Don't be such an ass. We're here *at your request* to talk about dividing assets. Let's stay on topic, shall we?"

Aaron rolled his eyes at Camelia, as if they were allies. "You see what I have to put up with? Suzanne can be a little touchy. But hey, she has a right to be angry because, I'm ashamed to admit, I may have been indiscreet. But that's all *firmly* in the past." He cocked his head at Suzanne. "I'm guessing my lovely bride didn't tell you about her own little indiscretions, did she?"

"And how many *indiscretions* have you had in the past decade? Do you really want to score that game? Try to focus. This is about you and me and nothing else, so don't change the subject."

Suzanne's cheeks were flushed. The firm's research team had reported Suzanne's short-lived affair with a doctor more than a decade ago. Since then, nothing.

"I'm sure it was quite a blow to your ego to find out Suzanne had strayed to greener pastures, and with a *doctor*, no less," Camelia purred. "But, as you said, that's all in the past now, isn't it?"

She was calm—soothing, even—turning his own argument against him with a carefully cultivated, threatening undertone. She could play Aaron's game.

"So," she didn't wait for his response. "Now that we've hung all that laundry out to dry, let's talk about the real business at hand. Your divorce. We're close to finishing discovery, other than a valuation on your business, which we'll need in order to come up with a settlement number," Camelia stopped to make a quick note on her legal pad. Looking back up, she turned her gaze to Ashcroft. "I was thinking we could use Leslie Koenig. I called her office, and they can have a preliminary valuation done as early as mid-March. Once we have the valuation, we can hammer out a deal. Isn't that what you would do, Spencer?" Camelia gave Ashcroft an ingratiating smile.

Aaron answered for him. "Surely you can do better than that, Counselor. That's just a boilerplate divorce plan, good enough for people who actually need to be divorced. Which isn't our situation," Aaron said, turning to Suzanne. "Look at us. We're getting old. Well, *I'm* getting old. And I can't bear to think of you out on your own, alone. Especially—"

"Oh please," Suzanne interjected, speaking over Aaron. She turned to Camelia. "He doesn't mean a word of it."

"We need each other, Suzie Q." Aaron turned back to Camelia. "Suzanne needs my money, and I need Suzanne's emotional support, a companion in life. Our kids are grownups, but they still need their parents. Now more than ever, with our first grandchild on the way. Isn't that right, Suzie?" Aaron faced his wife with an expression demonstrating what sincerity would look like if he were capable of ordinary human emotions.

"What do you mean *a grandchild on the way*?" Suzanne looked shocked at the news.

"Didn't Allison tell you? Oh, I guess not," Aaron said with a shrug. "You two have never been that close."

Camelia didn't want to get waylaid by Aaron one-upping Suzanne in the Parenting Competition, so she breezed past his cruel, targeted revelation.

"Aaron, Arizona is a no-fault state. Suzanne wants a divorce and she'll have it, with or without your cooperation. We're doing you a favor here. You know the risks. If we can settle everything, your private information stays private. But if we go to trial, you know full well that everything—and I mean *everything*, Aaron—is public record. It could ruin your reputation in the community," Camelia paused, feeling triumphant as she saw the little flicker of anger run across his face. "Not to mention the risk of having your business competitors lined up in the courtroom to hear testimony about the firm's finances. That could be devastating. But I'm sure you and Spencer have already considered all that." She nodded at opposing counsel, who was glaring at her. Camelia smiled back at him.

"Oh, come now. None of that is necessary. I think marriage counseling will make a big difference. Won't you at least give it a try before we go any further with this divorce nonsense, Suze?" Aaron wheedled.

"*Now* you want to go to counseling? I begged you for *years* to go. You're a decade late," Suzanne said with a weary voice.

"But sweetheart, I had no *idea* you were so unhappy until *now*. All I ask is one day with Dr. Bachman. You've met Tony at the Club, haven't you? We can schedule one of those intensives with him next week," Anders said, his voice softening. "Won't you at least *try* to save our marriage? Or do I have to tell the kids you're leaving me, without a shred of mercy, even after I forgave you for that fling with *their pediatrician*?" Aaron's sugar-coated words held an underhanded threat.

"You bastard." Suzanne's face crumpled.

"Think about our beautiful children. What kind of role model are we, if we just give up at the first sign of trouble? And our future grandchildren?" Aaron reached for Suzanne across the table, but she dropped her hands to her lap. "How do we explain to the littles that Gigi and Papa are divorced? That *they* weren't worth staying married for, even after my *devastating* heart attack?"

Suzanne stared vacantly at the table and nodded her head. Camelia sensed she was witnessing a replay of decades of this kind of manipulation.

"Fine, I'll go to counseling." She ignored Aaron's outstretched hand. "But be prepared to get an earful."

"Well, I guess that settles it, then," Ashcroft said, smiling triumphantly at Camelia. He flipped open a folder and pulled out a few sheets of paper, which he slid across the table. "I took the liberty of anticipating today's outcome. This is a Stipulation to Withdraw the Petition."

Not so fast, Blusterbutt.

"That's a liberty you needn't have taken, Spencer. No one said anything about withdrawing the Petition. I thought we were here to negotiate a settlement. But if there's no offer on the table . . ." Camelia tucked her legal pad into her file folder.

"I made an offer and Suzanne accepted," Aaron said. "We're going to counseling. The divorce is a no-go."

"That will be up to Suzanne to decide *after* counseling. But I can see we're done for today." Camelia stood. "Lovely to see you boys, as always."

"I'll just leave this with you, then. You can file it when Mr. and Mrs. Anders reconcile." Ashcroft stood up, snapped his briefcase shut, and walked to the door.

Aaron took his time. He moved around the table and leaned into Suzanne as she stood, giving her a sideways hug. He whispered something in her ear. Suzanne grabbed her handbag and started toward the door.

"Excuse me."

Camelia moved to the door and held it open as Suzanne rushed out, with Aaron in her wake. As Anders approached, he swiveled and pushed the door shut on Ashcroft's back.

He leaned in, threateningly close, his expression murderous. Camelia immediately tensed and stepped back, a surge of adrenaline hitting her system as Anders' body heat and the musky scent of his cologne invaded her personal space. She could feel the anger pulsing off him and it startled her. Her fingertips tingled.

"Withdraw the fucking Petition *today*, cut Suzanne loose, and go back to your bullshit divorce cases. We're *all done here* in case you missed it," Anders growled. "And no dawdling, *Cammie*, or I'll have to call your boss and give him an earful about you prowling around my house at all hours. Am I *clear?*"

Camelia wasn't prepared for the way her body reacted to the venom in his voice.

Had the trauma of Josh Campbell's violent death flipped a switch? Because, out of the options—fight, flight, freeze, or fawn—the fight response was new. A flush of rage rolled through her body. Her stomach quivered, and she felt a noise, something primal, almost a growl, coming from her throat. She laughed to cover it up.

"God, you're such a drama queen, just like *everyone* said you'd be." Camelia reached past him, jerked the door open and sneered at Ashcroft. "For the record, your client initiated that little *ex parte* conversation, not me. I'd appreciate it if you'd keep your dog on a shorter leash in the future."

Despite her flash of bravado, the dark scowl Anders gave her as he turned away made the hair on her arms stand up.

Was she ever going to have a day that didn't make her need a drink?

19

PARENT TRAP

THURSDAY, FEBRUARY 18

Two days had passed since the tense meeting with Aaron Anders and Spencer Ashcroft, but Camelia still hadn't heard from Suzanne despite her promise to call the next day. Concerned, Camelia finally dialed Suzanne's number.

"Hi Camelia, I was gonna call you later." Suzanne sounded tired. "I've just been feeling a little down. Between the chemo and Aaron, I'm just worn out."

"That's a double whammy, for sure!" Camelia said. "I can call some other time if you need to rest. I was just concerned because you left before we could debrief."

"Sorry, I just needed to get out of there, get some air between me and Aaron before I lost my cool," Suzanne said. "But I've been considering everything Aaron said, including the offer of counseling."

"Suzanne, time is not on your side right now, but if you want to reconcile—" Camelia began.

"I have no intention of reconciling, and I don't want to waste my precious time. I just . . . he knows all the buttons to push. And, as usual, I caved in to Aaron's bullying. He's got the kids convinced I'm a horrible bitch for not welcoming him home with open arms after his heart attack," Suzanne said. "And then threatening to tell the kids about my stupid fling with their pediatrician if I didn't toe the line? He knows how to get his way."

"You're in a tough situation, that's for sure. But if you don't want to reconcile, there's no need to waste your time on counseling."

Suzanne sighed. "It's only one day . . ."

"Well, yeah, if you do an intensive. But it will take until next week to get an appointment, so it's really a week, or more." Camelia waited for Suzanne's response as she pulled the straw out of her iced tea and pretended to smoke it.

Weird how the craving hits sometimes, even after all these years.

"I know," Suzanne sighed. "But I have to think about my children. I don't want to alienate them. Especially not with a grandchild on the way. So I'll play along for now, but there's no way I'm withdrawing the Petition."

"Do you want me to notify Spencer that counseling is off the table?"

"No, Aaron needs to *think* I'm considering reconciliation so he'll get off my back until I can figure out how to give the kids my side of the story," Suzanne said.

After Suzanne said goodbye, Camelia slammed the handset in the cradle and dropped her head into her hands.

"Goddammit!"

Camelia had seen this scenario play out in dozens of cases. Anders was going to do whatever it took to derail the divorce, because anything would be cheaper than buying his wife out of her community interest in AndersLaw. She hoped Anders' ploys wouldn't work this time, because Suzanne's life was too short to squander, even if he didn't know it yet.

"Everything okay in here?" Cate asked as she pushed the door open. "I thought I heard you punishing your phone." She laughed.

"Ugh. I'm just frustrated with the Anders case. Poor Suzanne. Aaron is going to rake her over the coals any way he can." Camelia shook her head. "Today, he's peddling reconciliation. Who knows what he'll be demanding next week?"

"I'm sure he'll think of something. But right now, you need to be across the street. Lunch with Nina Garry, remember?"

"Crap, yes." Camelia stood and pulled on her suit jacket. "If she calls, tell her I'm on my way."

"Will do," Cate said. "And no matter what, do not—I repeat, *do not*—accept a pro bono assignment. We're up to our asses in alligators and you won't make partner on free advice."

"Aye, aye, Captain," Camelia said as she wheeled away, speed walking down the hall.

Lunch was hanger steak on a bed of rocket—one of her favorites—but all Camelia could think about was the glass of pinot grigio her colleague, Nina Garry, was sipping as she talked. Camelia slipped her hands to her lap and snapped the rubber band against her left wrist, repeatedly. She couldn't tell if it was having a positive effect, but it felt good to punish herself for wanting a drink.

"When I heard it was your office, Cam, it knocked the wind out of me. Are you sure you're okay?" Nina took another sip of wine.

"I'm as okay as anyone would be, you know? It's all just so bizarre. The kind of thing you read about in the news. But I'm getting counseling for it," Camelia said as she took another bite of steak. "And thank you for the beautiful flowers. It's the kind of thing that makes a girl wonder about alternative career choices, though."

Nina set her fork down and leaned forward, lowering her voice. "We're *always* hiring," Nina said. "I know you love asylum work, and you're good at it. It's something to think about."

Camelia was a long-term volunteer for a refugee and vulnerable immigrants defense program, and Nina Garry was the organization's pro bono coordinator. Their frequent interactions had led to a decade-long friendship grounded in wine-soaked lunches and an exchange of favors.

"I appreciate it, but we can't afford the pay cut right now. Leon's business is barely off the ground, so . . ." Camelia said.

"I get it. But money isn't everything, and it's not a one-time offer. If you . . . *when* you get fed up, all you have to do is call me, and you'll have a desk the next day. In the meantime, how can you use this fucking awful tragic event to your advantage?" Nina asked.

"I don't think there's an upside. Byron did the media rounds, thank god. Then he postponed the firm retreat and partner vote to the fall, which I'm interpreting as a signal that I'm not making partner this round."

"Why do you think that? Maybe he just didn't think the timing for a retreat was right?"

"Maybe. But he made a point of calling me directly to let me know there wouldn't be a vote. I think it was his way of letting me down easy. And maybe he'll reconsider and put my name on the ballot for the fall meeting, but I'm not holding my breath," Camelia said. She dabbed her mouth with the thick, black napkin, and took a long drink of water, wishing it was something stronger.

Nina's phone dinged "Shit," she said as she turned the phone face up. "I didn't realize the time. I have to wrap up, Cam. Sorry, I have a meeting in a half hour."

After settling the bill, the two women exchanged a brief hug and went their separate ways. Camelia walked across the street, back to her office, considering Nina's offer.

As she counted her breaths and the floors going up in the elevator, Camelia thought, again, about whether the lure of partnership was worth the aggravation. Maybe she should consider the non-profit route Nina was offering. But the paycheck! Ugh. It would be a quarter of what she was earning now. Or maybe she should seriously consider Leon's suggestion to go out on her own.

The elevator stopped and Camelia gripped her handbag.

Deep breath. Deep breath.

Cheri looked up when she entered the lobby.

"Good afternoon, Cam. I hope you had a nice lunch?"

"Yes, thanks."

"Just a heads up. Alex Anders called and asked if you could meet immediately. I checked with Cate and she said you were free, so I set him for 1:45. I hope that's okay?" Cheri said.

"Alex *Anders*?" she asked. "Suzanne Anders' son?"

"Yes. He wants to talk about his parents' divorce," Cheri said.

Camelia groaned inwardly. The last thing she wanted was an impromptu meeting with a client's kid, but it was too late to call it off now.

"There isn't much I can tell him, but sure, I can meet with him," Camelia said.

"Good thing, because he's in the east conference room with his two sisters," Cheri said, as she glanced at her computer. "They showed up a few minutes ago. You've got about ten minutes to spare."

"Ooohkay. On my way," Camelia said as she walked through to the back office. She strode quickly to Cate's desk.

"What the hell's going on with the Anders kids?" Camelia said, pushing the door to her office open.

"Oh, hey, I texted you, but I think your phone's off."

Camelia pulled her phone out of her handbag. "Shit, yes, it's on mute. Sorry. I forgot to turn it back on after lunch."

"Alex called after you left to meet Nina. He said they—him and the two girls—want to talk to you about the divorce. Urgently," Cate said. "I told him you couldn't discuss anything privileged, but they want to meet anyway."

"Weird. I don't want to alienate them, but I'm not sure how Suzanne will feel about it," Camelia said. She chewed her lip.

"Do you want me to call her?" Cate offered.

"No. Let's hear them out, first, then I'll fill her in. But it would be best if you're in the room, just so there's no illusion of confidentiality. Can you take notes?" Camelia asked.

"Sure, just let me save this document." Cate tapped on her keyboard.

Camelia hung her handbag and jacket on the back of the door and grabbed her water bottle before nodding to Cate to follow her. She silently repeated the Anders' children's names as she headed to the conference room, cementing them in her mind. And it wasn't lost on her that they were all A names. Aaron's influence clearly extended to baby naming.

When she opened the door, three dark blond heads swiveled her direction. There was no mistaking their relationship, each of them a striking amalgamation of their parents' genes.

After a round of handshakes and introductions, Camelia took a seat across from the Anders siblings. Cate slipped into the chair beside her, flipping her legal pad to a fresh page as she did so.

Camelia gestured at Cate. "This is my paralegal, Cate Sanchez, who'll be taking notes. I'll answer any general questions you have, but other than that, I'm not sure how I can help you today." Camelia watched as three sets of clear blue eyes—their mother's eyes—bored into her. "And I want to give you fair warning that I can't discuss anything related to your parents' divorce other than what's in the public record. And," she added, "I will be reporting your visit to Suzanne."

As their heads nodded in unison, they exchanged a glance between them before Alex, the eldest, spoke.

"You don't have to tell us anything, and we don't want to compromise your ethics. We just want to give you some insights that might help you counsel our mother to call this whole thing off," Alex said as he leaned forward on his elbows, shortening the distance between them. Camelia recognized it as a move inherited from his father. "Look, Dad's devastated by all this and we are too. For Chrissake, they've been together more than thirty years! He's not perfect, by a long stretch, but neither is Mom. The point is, Dad's not a monster, and he really wants to reconcile."

"So I hear. What does your mother want?" Camelia asked.

Allison, the middle child, shifted in her chair. "Mom's not thinking straight right now. And I get it. She's super pissed at Dad because he had an affair, but it's done. He just wants to put their lives back together before he retires," she said, sipping a Jamba Juice. "Neither of them should be starting over at this point and . . . it's just sad and sort of pathetic. They should be together. Especially given Dad's heart attack."

"I know it must sound like we don't trust our mother's judgment." Alex unzipped his hoodie. He was dressed more like a tech startup CEO than a newly-minted radiologist. "And I guess it's true in the sense that we don't think she really meant to get *divorced*. Mom just wanted to make a point. To get Dad's attention."

"Exactly. And she pushed the right button because Mom *definitely* has Dad's attention," Allison said.

"Right?" Avery nodded at Allison, then turned back to Camelia. "Dad is truly gutted. And Mom is rightfully angry about the affair, but Dad is *trying* to make it up to her. He even offered to go to marriage counseling." Avery was just reciting her father's narrative. "Hell, the cost of the business valuation *alone* is going to be north of forty grand, and that's before you and Spencer start racking up legal fees. I haven't passed the bar yet, but even I know you can wipe out a marital estate in no time if the fight is furious enough."

There it is. The darlings are safeguarding their future inheritance.

"What can you tell me about the affair your father had?" Camelia asked.

"Nothing, really. Dad just said she was an attorney at the firm, things got out of hand when they were working on a big trial, and it ended immediately after. He was pretty sheepish about the whole thing and, obviously, we did *not* want details," Alex said.

"I see. Do you know her name?"

Avery flicked a long strand of highlighted hair over her shoulder. "We didn't ask, and what does it matter?" she retorted, one expertly groomed brow rising on the last word.

"Just want to square up what you're telling me with what your father has said, that's all," Camelia said.

Avery shrugged.

"So, circling back to the whole purpose of our visit," Alex said, leaning back in his chair, "can we count on you to talk to Mom about reconciling?"

Alex was handsome: lean and muscular, with dark blond hair and a scruff of beard. But he really was his father's son, including the entitled expectations of a man accustomed to getting his way.

Cate paused in her note-taking.

Camelia slowly shook her head. "No. You can't count on me to talk to your mother about *anything*, because I don't work for you. But I will report the content of this meeting to your mother. Because I have a duty to my client." Camelia looked at each of them in turn. "But I *will not* recommend *either* divorce *or* reconciliation. That's Suzanne's decision. Not mine. Or yours."

Avery smirked. "Spencer said that's what you would say."

"Well, Spencer was right. There's a first time for everything," Camelia chuckled. "You can quote me on that."

"You may not like Spencer, but he's just looking out for Dad. Just like you *think* you're protecting Mom." Camelia didn't miss the implication of Alex's wording, but he went on, seemingly oblivious to the insult. "The thing is, neither of them needs protection. They really just need to lay down their swords and stop bickering. Which Dad is one hundred percent willing to do."

Number One Son really is his father's child.

"Especially because their first grandchild is on the way," Allison said, placing her hand on a small mound of belly. "It may sound selfish, but I want my parents together for this event. I want our kids, all our kids, to have Gigi and Papa time, without having to favor one over the other. Because I'm not going to play that stupid game. It's both or none."

"I heard you were expecting. Congratulations, Allison." Camelia wondered how a woman with a bodyfat percentage roughly equivalent to her own shoe size even managed to get pregnant.

"Thanks, but it's hard to enjoy the experience while Mom is tearing the family apart with this divorce BS." Allison rubbed her temples. "It just gives me a headache."

It was a harsh—and misguided—condemnation of Suzanne, when Aaron was the one sampling all the goodies at the office.

"It sounds like you're all feeling the strain of the divorce," Camelia said.

Or, more accurately, Aaron was making sure they felt it.

Allison huffed a sigh. "Yeah, we are. But mostly Dad."

Oh, child, if you only knew.

"He's just sick over this," Allison said. "Like, Dad's already had a heart attack, so it's not a stretch to say this is life and death for him. I know you're not in the sympathy business, but don't you realize what this is doing to our family?"

"I'm not sure your father's heart attack was directly caused by the divorce," Camelia said. It was tempting, but she wouldn't be the one to tell them about the Narcan box on Anders' gurney as the medics wheeled him out of the courtroom back in December. "But yes, divorce is stressful. I'm happy to share referrals for family therapists to help you all cope and adjust."

"That's not really the point," Avery said.

"You're right. The point is, your father wants a reconciliation, but he's not interested in any adjustment to the status quo. Is there anything else you'd like me to know?" Camelia asked.

The three exchanged looks, then Alex stood. The other two followed suit.

"That's it for now. We've taken more than enough of your time, Camelia. And we really appreciate it," Avery said as she passed a slip of paper across the table. "This is our contact information. Feel free to reach out any time."

Back in her office, Camelia checked her email and voice messages. Nothing that couldn't wait. It was only mid-afternoon, but she was bone tired. She stood up and walked to the bank of windows facing Camelback Mountain, watching the shadows lengthen. She had to let it go. All of it. Suzanne's family drama, Aaron Anders' conniving ways, Josh Campbell's tragic death, her angst over walking into the lobby every day, all of it.

Que sera, sera.

She had her own life to worry about. Like missing out on making partner. She could feel the past seven years of her career at McCaffrey Rhodes & Rodriguez unraveling. It was the natural result if she wasn't promoted. If she wasn't moving up, there was nowhere else to go except out the front door. And she hesitated to make the comparison, but it was staring right at her. Byron was a lot like Aaron Anders. Not as cruel, not as cunning, but every bit as money hungry and self-centered. Not to mention—as she'd recently discovered—also sleeping with an employee. And, like Anders, Byron was just arrogant enough to expect all of them to politely look away, to shield him from embarrassment, to cover his tracks.

Why would I want to be a partner with a guy like that?

20

DETOUR

FRIDAY, FEBRUARY 19

Camelia was at her desk, going through a stack of mail, when Cate tapped on the door and bustled in, holding yet *another* armful.

"This was just hand delivered," she said, passing a manila envelope to Camelia. "And you're not gonna like it."

"Great. What now?" Camelia slipped the sheaf of paper out of the envelope and began flipping through the pages.

"It's Ashcroft. *Again.* Notice of an Emergency Hearing." Cate began sorting the new mail between Camelia's inboxes: periodicals, correspondence, pleadings. "They've set it for Tuesday afternoon."

"For Chrissake. He's already delayed Saminski's deposition and is pushing Suzanne to withdraw the Petition," Camelia said. "What is he after this time?"

"Two things. They want to transfer the case to conciliation, and Mr. Anders wants an order that Suzanne can't change her estate plan, if you can believe that," Cate said.

"That bastard." Camelia threw the papers on the desk. "He knows."

"Sure seems like it, doesn't it? Otherwise, why would he even think about something like her will?" Cate said.

Camelia chewed her lip. "Insurance policies are covered in the preliminary injunction, so even if Suzanne changed her beneficiaries prior to the divorce being final, he could challenge it. But as for the rest of her estate, she's free to make a new will naming anyone she wants as beneficiaries. This is a preemptive strike. I can't believe they would stoop this low. But then again, strategically, it makes perfect sense."

"What a jerk," Cate said.

"Okay, we don't have much prep time. Please call Suzanne and get her in here on Monday to go over her testimony. I need her estate plan and life insurance policy—the whole policy, front to back—including beneficiary clauses and death benefit." Camelia flipped to the last page of the Emergency Petition. "And get the new associate, Ken whatshisname, to do the legal research, with cites, as to why Suzanne is entitled to control her portion of the marital estate, including her life insurance."

"When do you want it?" Cate asked.

"No later than Monday 8 a.m.—"

"Cam, it's Friday. You want him working over the weekend?"

Camelia looked up at Cate, eyebrows raised.

"Okay, Monday, 8 a.m. it is," Cate said.

"I'll need to meet with Suzanne Monday afternoon to go over her testimony." Camelia tapped the documents with her pen.

"I'll get started and let you know what time Suzanne will be here," Cate said, tucking the envelope under her arm. "And I don't want to nag, but it's almost three o'clock. Aren't you supposed to be—"

"Shit shit shit. Yes, thank you, and I'm running for the elevator now," Camelia said, bolting out of her chair.

She grabbed her coat and handbag from the hook on the back of the door and half ran to the elevator. Dr. Chavez would wait for her, and she would pay for the hour whether she was there or not. But today, she really wanted . . . no, *needed* to be there.

"Sorry I'm late," Camelia panted as she entered Dr. Chavez's sanctuary.

"You're here now," he said as he shut the door behind her. "Everything okay?"

"Oh, yeah. Just a hectic day," she replied. "But I didn't want to miss my appointment because the anxiety . . . it's awful, Carlos. Every time I ride the goddamn elevator, I think I'm gonna have a heart attack."

"That has to be really difficult. Is there any alternative entrance you could use, so you don't have to relive that trauma every day?" Chavez scribbled a note as he talked. "Or is there some other solution, at least in the short term, until we get you past the worst of it?"

"Yeah, I have an idea. How about if I just quit?" Camelia surprised herself as the words leapt from her mouth. She gave a nervous laugh. "I won't be making partner this year. And that was my line in the sand. No partner, no Camelia cleaning up all the divorces for Byron's shady clients."

"What makes you think your opportunity to make partner is no longer viable?" He shifted forward in his chair and tilted his head. "Has something happened?"

"I guess I forgot to mention it because, oh, some guy *blew his head off in my face*," Camelia rolled her eyes. "Byron called off the firm retreat. Which is when they vote in new partners. And he made a point of calling me directly about it, so it sure seems like he was giving me a heads up."

Carlos propped his chin on templed fingers. "I guess that's one interpretation. Or maybe he just didn't think it was good timing to hold a retreat right after a tragic event."

"Well, sure. But the way I read it is that Byron knew it would be really shitty optics to deny me a place on the partner ballot after all I'd been through with Josh Campbell. I think he's delaying the vote so when my name is *not* on the ballot in the fall, it won't be awkward. Six months from now, no one will even remember what happened."

"So he can save face."

"Exactly. And soothe his guilty conscience by not slapping me down just a couple of weeks after I washed my client's grey matter out of my hair," Camelia said, taking a sip of water.

Dr. Chavez studied the note pad in his lap for a moment. He took a deep breath as he looked up. "I'm sorry you have to carry that awful image. I think it's a good place to start today, so settle in, and let's begin."

Camelia picked up a buzzer in each hand, closed her eyes, and leaned back into the pillows. Carlos was a skilled and experienced practitioner of EMDR—Eye Movement Desensitization and Reprocessing therapy—to treat trauma. The bad part was reliving the experience. The good part was the relief when the symptoms abated.

"Ready when you are." Camelia gripped the buzzers, waiting for Dr. Chavez' instructions.

"Start by telling me where you feel the trauma in your body . . ."

MONDAY, FEBRUARY 22

Aaron Anders pushed back his chair and stood as Spencer Ashcroft came into the conference room for their early morning meeting. After a quick grip of hands, Ashcroft flipped open his file and shuffled through a few pages of notes.

"So, we'll need to hammer home the community ownership of the life ins—"

"Yeah, I get it Spence. Not my first rodeo," Anders barked. "But there's something I need you to do, and I want it done today. We need a subpoena for Suzanne's medical records."

"For what purpose?" Ashcroft asked. "And do you really want to open that up? Because you know Belmont will demand tit for tat. She'll subpoena your records, too."

"Let her try. Here's why I need Suzanne's records. I happened to play a round of golf with Rick Baum yesterday." Aaron recalled the dramatically sad expression on Rick's face. "That's *Doctor* Rick Baum, oncologist. And poor old Rick just can't hold his Bloody Marys all that well. Before you know it, he says he's recently seen Suzanne."

"Okay, saw her where?" Ashcroft asked.

"I asked him the same thing. That's when he got flustered. If you put two and two together, the only place *Doctor* Baum would have seen my wife in the past couple of weeks was at his office. Get it? She's sick, Spence." Anders chuckled. "My fucking wife has cancer. Can you believe it?"

"Is it serious?"

"Based on the look on Rick's face, I'm guessing it is. But that's why I need her medical records. I want to know *exactly* what's going on. Because if it's bad . . . well, that changes things." Aaron's mind was already going over the ways he could use this latest bit of information against Suzanne and that uppity lawyer of hers.

"So, I take it the counseling intensive didn't work out?" Ashcroft asked.

Aaron laughed. "I was interested to know whether Suzanne would agree, how far I could get, but she pulled the plug. So yeah, turns out reconciliation is a no-go."

"Well, you didn't really expect her to change her mind, did you?" Ashcroft pointed out.

"No. I knew reconciliation was a long shot because she refuses to be sensible. For an educated feminist, she has some pretty prudish notions about marriage. But this diagnosis changes everything."

Goddammit.

It suddenly occurred to him that when the kids found out about Suzanne's cancer, they would rush to take her side like good little ducklings. But he could turn that to his advantage, too. He could raise his concerns about chemo brain and Suzanne's diminished capacity to manage her financial affairs.

"It doesn't have to—"

"Spence, all you have to do is stall. Time will do the rest. Because there's really no reason for a dying woman to get a divorce, is there? There's sure as hell no reason for a dying woman to change the beneficiary of her will and life insurance policies—which is me, by the way—especially when they're community property and subject to the preliminary injunction."

Ashcroft took a deep breath. "Well, obviously, Suzanne will never agree to release her medical records, and for good reason. And if we subpoena her records, Judge Bailey might become sympathetic to her. He might even expedite the divorce."

"Then we need to cast doubt on Suzanne's mental state," Aaron said. "Once we have her medical records, I'm sure we can find sources and citations to show that she has diminished capacity, at the very least."

"I'll file a Motion to Compel Subpoena, but no guarantee it will be granted," Spencer said.

"Go hard on this, Spence," Aaron said. "Because if you can stall the divorce long enough to keep me on as Suzanne's beneficiary, there's a bonus in it for you."

"Aaron, you know I can't—"

"Can't what? Accept a gift from a grateful client?" Aaron laughed. "Would you really turn down a hundred thousand cash just for doing your job *slowly*?"

Ashcroft paused.

"That's what I like about you, Spencer. You're practical." Aaron smiled. "Just dig in your heels and stall this divorce for as long as it takes Suzanne to die. Based on how maudlin Rick was on Sunday, it won't be long."

Ashcroft looked shocked. "Jesus, Aaron. That's pretty fucking cold."

"Hey, I'm not the one who filed for divorce. She started it. She should have reconciled when I gave her the chance."

Ashcroft hesitated, but only for a minute. "Strategically, it's an easy request. There are a hundred ways to slow down a divorce."

"That's the spirit, Spence."

"I expect we'll get pushback from Belmont. She's not exactly one of *us*."

"Oh, come on now. You're superior to Belmont in absolutely every way other than youth. You don't have a problem with lady lawyers, do you?" Aaron grinned.

"Only the ones like Belmont. She's not like the old guard. Those broads get it. They know how to take a little good-natured ribbing now and then, and they step aside when necessary *for the good of the order*. Not so with bitches like Belmont," Ashcroft said. "I'm not a fan of her type."

"I get it. But this is your chance to put her in her place," Aaron replied. "She may be a good decade younger than us, but she's a burnout. I mean, Christ, her client blew his brains out right in the damn lobby. And now, she's trying to fast track a divorce, when all we have to do is wait it out."

"Well, I don't like to underestimate my opponents, but this little chickadee is way out of her depth," Ashcroft said.

Finally, Ashcroft was catching on. Aaron felt his superiority settle around his shoulders like a shimmering cloak. He smiled at the thought of putting Camelia in her place. She was so uppity. So persistent. He was looking forward to crushing her under his heel, and Suzanne right along with her.

"I think we're all set, then. I'll see you at the hearing," Aaron said, and stood up.

21

MEN AT WORK

MONDAY, FEBRUARY 22

"Good morning! Where are we with Suzanne Anders? What time is she coming in?" Camelia asked as she walked through to her office. "Do we have the research from the baby lawyer?"

"Good morning to you, too! How much coffee have you had?" Cate asked.

"Just about enough!"

Cate stood and walked into Camelia's office with her with a notepad.

"Suzanne will be here around one. You're meeting in the west conference room," Cate said. "She sent over her will and the life insurance policy, and it's on your desk. The associate, Ken, emailed the brief and it's in your inbox. I think you're all ready to go other than reviewing the research and going over testimony with Suzanne."

"I'm going to get coffee," Camelia rose as she spoke, "before I read through all this. And I'm not taking any calls this morning unless it's related to the Anders case."

"I'll let Cheri know. And Cam, while you're meeting with Suzanne this afternoon," Cate's voice dropped, "I'm archiving the Campbell file to send to the professional liability carrier. Is there anything in the file you want to redact?"

Camelia stopped and turned back to Cate. "I haven't really thought about it. I mean, did you see anything that falls under work product privilege?"

"No, but there's an email . . ." Cate paused.

"And?"

"In the email you say there's no way Judge Sorensen would ever order him to pay spousal when Mrs. Campbell was getting half the equity in the business. Josh responded something like you better be right because his life was on the line," Cate said, her forehead furrowed.

How could I have let that slip?

Camelia slowly shook her head. "Oh my god! That's not good." She couldn't believe she'd made such a ridiculous promise, or that she'd glossed over Josh's vague threat as nothing other than a turn of phrase. Had she been zoned out on Klonopin when she responded? Or had she just come back from a boozy lunch? Or both? This is exactly why she had to get a handle on herself. "The thing is, that's not work product so, as much as I'd like to redact it, that email has to stay in the file." Camelia heaved a sigh. "Byron's gonna rip me a new one."

"Yeah, I think that's pretty much guaranteed," Cate said.

How was she going to spin this? Byron would be furious and, for once, she didn't blame him. It was a rookie mistake to promise an outcome, *any* outcome, to a client and Camelia knew better.

Shit!

This was not a distraction she could afford, especially when she should be focusing on the Anders case. Suzanne would be here in less than an hour, and Camelia still had to review the insurance policy before she arrived.

"Okay, don't send the Campbell file over until I've had a chance to warn Byron. I mean, it doesn't make us *liable*, but it sure as shit doesn't help matters. Goddammit."

"Okay, go get a coffee and we'll deal with the Campbell file after your meeting," Cate said as she bustled off to her desk.

Camelia had just finished eating lunch at her desk while skimming the dry, tangled up language of the insurance policy when her phone buzzed. Suzanne had arrived.

Cate handed her the file as she headed to the conference room. She entered to find Suzanne pacing, flushed, and angry.

"Camelia, what the hell is all this about?" she demanded. "Do they not have *anything* better to do?"

"If I may be blunt, this is about your husband running out your clock while trying to profit off your death. They've moved to transfer your case to Conciliation Court—"

"And what is that?" Suzanne interrupted.

"It's basically marriage counseling by the Court."

"I guess since I called off that so-called marriage counseling intensive, he's trying to have the Court order it? *Ha!*" Suzanne crossed her arms. "Good luck with that."

"The problem is, if they transfer your case to Conciliation, it has the effect of putting the divorce on hold until the assigned counselor determines there's no possibility of reconciliation," Camelia said.

"Okay, that's total bullshit. I don't care if Judge Bailey orders it, I'm not going," Suzanne said, her mouth pulled into a tight, grim line. "And what's this about my estate plan?"

"Aaron wants to remain as beneficiary of both your will and life insurance pending entry of the decree, and he's arguing you can't make any changes because of the Preliminary Injunction. We have to convince the judge he's wrong," Camelia said. "And it's not a slam-dunk, because the insurance policy was purchased during marriage, the divorce is not final, and who knows if Judge Bailey will interpret your will as being contrary to the Injunction."

"There's no way I'm keeping Aaron as my beneficiary on *anything*. That money is for my children. All he'll do is blow it on another car, another condo, another . . . whatever we're calling his flings these days." Suzanne's eyes glittered with rage. "I will never sign off on that."

"I think we're safe on the will. But as for the life insurance, if the judge orders you to keep Aaron as beneficiary, the insurance company will have to obey, pending appeal. So, I have to make sure it's never ordered," Camelia said.

"Talk about whiplash. Last week he was my one and only, and now he's out for blood. Why he's pushing so hard?"

"Suzanne, he *must* know about your condition. Someone has to have told him. Who's the leak?" Camelia asked.

"I have no idea, but believe me, when I find out, there'll be hell to pay. The only people that know are a very small circle, and I've sworn everyone to secrecy. My kids don't even know yet," she said.

"Speaking of your kids, they stopped by to visit me," Camelia said. "They're worried you're being hasty. It's time to talk to them, Suzanne."

"What the hell? They came to see you?"

"Yes, Thursday afternoon, unannounced. I'm sorry, I should have told you sooner, but Friday blew up in my face with this Emergency Motion." Camelia shook her head. "Anyway, they told me how hard this is on Aaron and that they don't believe you really mean to divorce him, but just wanted his attention."

"Oh god. They're just repeating Aaron's little fairy tale."

"I didn't tell them anything, of course," Camelia said. "Besides, it's better coming from you, rather than me or, god forbid, Aaron."

"I know, I know. And I'm working on it," she said. "But scheduling time with three working adults is quite the challenge."

"I suppose it would be." Camelia shifted back to the topic of Suzanne's diagnosis. "Is your housekeeper in touch with Aaron at all? Maybe she let something slip?"

"Alma? Well, she cleans the casita, but Aaron's never had much interaction with our staff." Suzanne seemed to be pondering the potential rats. "Of all of them, the most likely is Rick Baum, because he and Aaron play golf now and then. But he's bound by HIPAA. Would he really break the law?"

"Suzanne, people break the law every single day without batting an eye. Maybe he let something slip accidentally, or he may have even thought he was doing you both a favor." Camelia took a deep breath. "See what you can find out, but right now, we have to focus on the hearing. We don't have much time to prepare—"

"And that's another thing! How on earth did he get a hearing on such short notice?"

"Because he filed it as an emergency. The judge has no choice but to set it as soon as his docket allows. It's only an hour, which isn't much time to tell your story, so let's tighten up your testimony." Camelia pulled a folder from the file on the table and flipped it open. "I'll start with questions about your will."

Camelia volleyed questions at Suzanne. At first, she was too chatty, offering up too much information that Ashcroft could use against her, and it would eat up their time. But after Camelia corrected her a couple of times, Suzanne caught on, and answered the rest of the questions succinctly, smartly, with just the right amount of detail. She would be a great witness. They were just finishing up when Cate tapped on the door.

"Camelia, may I have a minute?"

"Sorry, I'll be right back." Camelia said as she rose and joined Cate at the door.

"What's going on?" She asked after Cate pulled the conference room door shut.

"You were right, Cam. They know." Cate handed her a sheaf of papers. "Ashcroft's office just delivered this Motion to Compel Disclosure, along with a subpoena. How did they find out?"

Camelia skimmed the document in her hands.

Ashcroft was demanding disclosure of Suzanne's medical records. Not all of them, though. Just the medical records from Dr. Rick Baum's office.

"Sonofabitch," Camelia whispered.

TUESDAY, FEBRUARY 23

Camelia paused outside the courtroom door and nodded a bit of encouragement to Suzanne, even as she braced herself for the blustery rants she could expect from Spencer Dearborn Ashcroft III. Despite being to-the-manor-born and Harvard educated, Spencer was the disappointing conclusion to four generations of renowned lawyers. The DNA in his line seemed to be degrading, if Spencer was any proof at all. And he was a preening jerk.

Camelia would have enjoyed wiping that leering grin off his smug face even if he hadn't spread all those vicious rumors about her being drunk in Court last December. Although strategically, maybe it wasn't such a bad thing that he'd got an eyeful of her on the ladies' room floor after Anders' heart attack. He no doubt believed he had the upper hand. She'd show him. How delicious it would be to take him down a notch or two.

"Okay, take a deep breath." Even though it was meant for Suzanne, who'd clung to her side like a shadow since they'd entered the building, Camelia took a deep breath of her own before continuing. "The hearing will be recorded, so I'll give you a notepad and pen to write notes. No whispering, because those microphones are very sensitive. And if you need a break, just let me know, and I'll request it, okay?"

Suzanne nodded. "Got it." She blew out a long exhale. "Let's get this over with."

Camelia admired her grit. After learning that Aaron was asking the Court to issue a subpoena for her medical records, she'd called him a few choice names, but then went right back to preparing for the hearing. Despite all she was going through, Suzanne had an enviable amount of focus and fortitude.

Camelia pushed the heavy wood door open, and stepped aside to allow Suzanne to enter, scanning the room as she fell in behind her client. Ashcroft was leaning against the clerk's desk chatting her up, while Anders slouched at the Respondent's table, absorbed in his mobile phone. When they heard Camelia and Suzanne enter, both men turned.

"Why, look who's here!" Ashcroft exclaimed. "Aaron, we might as well pack our bags and go, because one word from these two beauties and the judge will be wrapped around their little pinkies!" He winked at Aaron.

"Good afternoon, ladies," Aaron said as he stood. He approached Suzanne first. "Hello, my love. How are you feeling?"

"I'd feel fantastic if you weren't still my husband," Suzanne said as she turned toward the Petitioner's table. "So, let's see if we can remedy that today."

"Oh dear. Someone's grumpy! And Camelia? I hope you're recovering from your traumatic experience. Spencer tells me you tend to get courtroom jitters, but you'll be fine today, I'm sure." Anders gave Camelia an insincere smile.

Camelia felt her face flush as she glared at Ashcroft, then glanced back at Anders. "I'll be just fine, Aaron, but isn't it *you* we should be worried about? As I recall, the last time we were here, they wheeled you out on a gurney."

Anders' eyes narrowed. "Touché."

"All rise," the bailiff called out, and the four of them stood at attention, waiting for the judge to appear.

After they'd made their appearances, Suzanne glanced at her phone, then furiously scribbled on the fresh notepad and pushed it in front of Camelia.

The leak was Dr. Baum, my oncologist. I'm going to kill him.

22

OVERHEARD

TUESDAY, FEBRUARY 23

"I need to use the washroom." Suzanne's face was pale as she pushed back her chair and rushed out of the courtroom.

The realization that her oncologist and lifelong friend, Rick Baum, had betrayed her confidence, along with her husband's devious moves to capitalize on her condition, had clearly shaken Suzanne. Camelia didn't blame her. She was still fuming over Ashcroft and Anders' shitty tactics herself. When the hearing ended, they had immediately walked out, smiling broadly, leaving Camelia the last one in the courtroom.

As she methodically packed up her briefcase, all the work looming in the case began spooling out in her mind. She might as well get started on the list of upcoming tasks to hand off to Cate when she got back to the office. Phone in hand, Camelia said, "Siri, voice memo," and she began to dictate. "Draft Motion to Seal . . ."

Stepping through the vestibule separating the courtroom from the hall, Camelia pushed the heavy door open with her hip. The hallway was deserted except for the two men facing the wall of windows looking down on Madison Street, their backs to the doors.

Anders and Ashcroft obviously had no idea Camelia was behind them, because they kept talking, heads bent toward each other. She quietly stepped back into the courtroom vestibule as their voices rose in frustration.

"What do you want me to do? It's not like I can just shut the case down," Ashcroft said.

"You don't have to do a fucking thing except stall. Just hold them off. Because you're not getting your fat bonus until I get Suzanne's life insurance," Anders replied.

"I'll do what I can, Aaron, but . . ."

Camelia wasn't shocked at the sentiment, but she couldn't believe they would say it out loud, so matter-of-fact. She burst noisily into the hall, making sure they both heard her. At least Ashcroft had the good sense to turn red and cough, as if that would make up for what Anders had just demanded. Stifling the impulse to confront them—and possibly punch Anders in the face—Camelia shot them both a glare before walking away.

As Camelia entered the bathroom, Suzanne emerged from a stall, looking drawn and tired.

"Are you okay?" Camelia asked.

Suzanne washed her hands and briefly preened in front of the mirror.

"Not yet," she said, tapping powder over her nose. "But I will be. Right after I rip Rick Baum a new asshole. Can you believe it? He got drunk after a round of golf with Aaron and it slipped out that he'd seen me. At his office."

"How did you find out?"

"When I asked around—you know, had anyone heard anything lately—a close friend just texted back that one of the senior partner's wives, Carol Preston, was gossiping at the Club about me being sick. Turns out her husband, Chuck Preston, was in their foursome. Rick blabbed and, of course, Chuck told Carol. So," Suzanne took a deep breath. "The gloves are off. I want to know *exactly* what caused Aaron's heart attack. I know you've wanted to do this since it happened, so yes, subpoena his medical records. *Immediately*. I'll send over a list of his doctors when I get home."

Camelia nodded as she started to put her phone away. It was only then she realized it was still recording. Had it caught the conversation between Anders and Ashcroft? She couldn't very well check now, and risk Suzanne hearing what Anders had said. It was too brutal. But, as soon as she was alone, Camelia would replay the voice note. And, if she had a record of what Anders had said, then she'd have to decide what to do about it.

When she got back to the office, Camelia shut her door and put in her earbuds. She replayed the recording. It was muffled, but audible. She turned up the volume and felt her anger rising as she listened to what Anders had said. His voice held no compassion or sympathy for Suzanne. He also didn't have an ounce of respect for the ethical rules or his attorney, either, because that bonus Anders offered could end up costing Ashcroft his career. Bottom line: Anders had no soul.

Although it disgusted Camelia, she wasn't all that surprised. The tactic was completely on brand for Aaron Anders. And that slimeball Ashcroft was all too happy to oblige. At the moment, her dilemma was whether or not to report what she'd overheard to the State Bar, because Anders mentioned a bonus, which was strictly *verboten* in family law. But she sensed it might be best to wait. A bar complaint could work in Anders' favor. He might even try to get her kicked off the case, which would further delay the divorce. Camelia couldn't risk it, so she decided to make a memo to the file and pursue the matter after the divorce was final. But if things got out of hand before then, this was something meaty to hang over Ashcroft's head.

WEDNESDAY, FEBRUARY 24

The next morning, knowing she had a list of follow up actions to pursue, Camelia pulled up the Court's online video recording of the Anders hearing. Fast forwarding, she couldn't help but replay some of the arguments again.

"I'd ask that the Court rule on our motion to compel medical records of Suzanne Anders," Ashcroft had said.

She watched herself explode out of her chair. "*Objection*, your honor. First off, I just received counsel's motion and I have the right to respond. Second, my client's medical records have nothing to do with the divorce, no matter what Mr. Ashcroft may argue. Ms. Anders' health is not relevant. Third, in the event you decide to grant this motion, the medical records are privileged and should be filed under seal, for *in camera* review only, if at all. These are all points I will include in my response," Camelia responded.

"So noted," Judge Bailey said. "Mr. Ashcroft, I will rule on the issue of medical records upon receipt of Ms. Belmont's response. No reply will be necessary."

Ashcroft then argued that Suzanne's physical health was relevant because it went to the issue of her estate plan, life insurance, and spousal maintenance. And that led him to his real point: Suzanne should be forbidden from altering her estate beneficiaries until the divorce was final. He called Anders to the stand as a witness.

"Mr. Anders, do you have reason to believe your wife is ill?" Ashcroft asked.

"Objection, speculation. Mr. Anders is not a doctor and doesn't have the expertise to diagnose anyone's illness," Camelia said.

"Your honor, Mr. Anders has the right to provide testimony as to information he received regarding Mrs. Anders' health status," Ashcroft said.

"Overruled. Mr. Anders, you may answer," Judge Bailey said.

"Yes, I believe she is gravely ill with cancer, based on remarks made by her oncologist—"

"OBJECTION! Your honor, this is pure hearsay and is not admissible under the Rules of Evidence," Camelia said, a bit more vehemently than she'd intended.

"Judge, we are not under strict compliance," Ashcroft said. "Which means the hearsay rule is not applicable."

"As you well know, Ms. Belmont, if you want strict compliance with the rules of evidence, it's incumbent on you to file a Rule 2(A) notice with the Court," Judge Bailey said.

"But your honor, this was an emergency hearing. We only had a couple of days' notice—" Camelia said.

"Well, then, you had a couple of days, Counsel. I know the rule says you have to file forty-five days in advance, but you could have brought it with you today," the judge said.

Camelia cringed all over again as she watched the recording. She fast forwarded to the end of the hearing.

"It is only proper, and pursuant to statute, that Mr. Anders remain as primary beneficiary on all of Mrs. Anders' accounts, including her life insurance," Ashcroft said, in his community theatre voice. "In the event of Mrs. Anders' untimely death, such a large sum of money should not be left to their three children. Who better to manage the funds on their behalf than their father, an experienced attorney and businessman? Having funded these assets with his income, Mr. Anders is the rightful owner of the accounts and life insurance benefits, after all."

What a crock of shit.

When Ashcroft was finished, Camelia had the last word. "Your honor, my esteemed colleague has made a *lot* of unfounded allegations today. Ms. Anders is sitting right here, and you can see for yourself she's perfectly capable of managing her own affairs. The parties' adult children are all educated professionals who can presumably manage their own inheritance, *when the time comes*. But that is not today. Ms. Anders has a right to bequeath *her own property* to beneficiaries as she sees fit," Camelia said stabbing the podium with her index finger. "She's doing everything possible to be divorced. But, until then, we would like an order granting her permission to manage her portion of the marital estate as she pleases. And that includes her life insurance."

Camelia closed the video player and typed a list of tasks for Cate.

- Subpoena Anders' medical records – Suzanne to provide list of physicians.
- Draft Response to Motion to Compel Subpoena of Medical Records.
- Draft Motion to Seal Medical Records.

Now, she had a million other things to do, and a new client consult in just a few minutes.

As if she'd read her mind, Cate appeared in the doorway with a slim folder.

"Your consult is in the conference room. He's a bit early," Cate said as she placed the file on the corner of Camelia's desk.

"Let me just send you this action list, and I'll be right there."

"I'm fetching his iced tea, so you've got time," Cate said as she walked away.

Camelia emailed the list and had already stood up when Cate ducked her head back into her office.

"Hang on, Camelia. Byron's on the phone. Says it's urgent."

"Just tell him I'm in a meeting . . ."

"You know how he is. He said it will take two minutes. I'll let the client know you'll be right there."

It seemed like everything was an emergency where Byron was concerned. Camelia closed her office door and picked up the phone.

"Hey, Byron, I'm just walking into a meeting with a client. What's up?"

"Won't take a minute, but you're gonna want to hear this. I'm down at the courthouse, just walked out of my hearing, and who do I see but Aaron Anders." Byron paused, a car door slammed, and all the ambient traffic noise went silent. "He's holding a press conference in front of the courthouse right this minute, announcing that he just set up a charitable trust funded by the firm's deferred comp and pension funds. Says it's for cancer research in his wife's name. Did you know about this?"

Camelia gasped. How could he . . . if Anders was suddenly tucking all the firm's liquid assets into a charitable trust, why? What was the sudden interest in making those funds unavailable, other than screwing Suzanne every way he could think of?

"No . . . this is news to me." Camelia realized that today—more than usual—she was out of her depth. "Did he say anything else? Anything specific?"

"I don't think so, but you'll be able to get a copy of the press release from his office or any of the local news stations. They were pretty much all there," Byron said. "Gotta go." He hung up.

Was there an offensive strategy to counter this tactic? Not that she could think of off the top of her head. Camelia felt sick to her stomach, this morning's coffee burning its way through her intestines.

Knowing Anders, he would just park the money in the charity, then pay himself a fat annuity and management fees. If he set it up right, the charity would never see a penny and he'd have a sweet tax shelter. She would have to talk to Artie—Arturo Rodriguez, the third name on the firm's door, and their estates and trusts expert—because she didn't understand all the complicated rules around a charitable trust. This was why it was so risky to leave the firm to start her own practice. There were so many aspects of the law she didn't know. And if she were on her own, who would she call on to interpret this kind of information for her?

Camelia buzzed Cate.

"Can you come here a sec, please?"

Cate came in with a steno pad and perched on one of the chairs facing Camelia's desk. "What's up?"

"Byron says Anders just announced a charitable trust in a press conference, funded with the firm's deferred compensation or something like that. Suzanne is going to lose her shit. And rightfully so," Camelia said, pressing her fingertips to her temples. "And I can't think of a single rebuttal."

"Isn't setting up a charity a good thing?" Cate asked.

"It would be, except half of his investment in the charity is Suzanne's money." Camelia drummed her nails on the desk top. "He's playing at something here, but I'm not sure what."

"Do you want me to get her on the phone?"

"Yeah, let her know I need to talk to her as soon as I'm done my meeting, and she should not take any calls from Aaron." Camelia took a swig of lukewarm coffee. "Scratch that. She shouldn't talk to *anyone* until she talks to me."

"Got it."

"Look online for the press release. We need to know what kind of charitable trust it is, then send that info to Arturo." Camelia scribbled a note to herself. "I need to know everything there is to know about that type of trust and how to break it. You can give him the bones of the situation, and let him know I'll need an opinion letter for the file."

Cate stood and turned to leave. "Will do. Now you'd best get on with your consult."

Camelia's mind was swirling as she headed to the conference room. None of this felt right. Even though Aaron and Suzanne Anders' divorce should be just a run of the mill high net worth case, it was morphing into a legal Hydra. She knew Aaron would have worked out a way to make the charitable trust fall within the confines of the law, and that meant months of delay while trying to get the Court to release Suzanne's community portion of the money used to fund it.

What would that asshole come up with next?

Camelia was almost afraid to ask.

23

HOPE & CHARITY

WEDNESDAY, FEBRUARY 24

It was turning out to be a much busier morning than expected. After Byron's call, Camelia met with her new client, then returned to her office to frantically read up on charitable trusts while she waited for Suzanne.

"Suzanne's just leaving her doctor's office. She'll be here in ten," Cate said from the doorway to Camelia's office. "And I know you probably don't want to hear this, but the coroner wants to know when they're getting your statement on Josh Campbell. I told them next week?"

"Shitshitshit. I totally forgot about it." Camelia dropped her head into her fingertips and blew out a sigh. "I'm almost finished. It's just . . . the last part is a lot harder than I thought it would be."

"If you want, I can write out what I know, then you can edit and flesh it out. Might be easier on you."

"It's always easier when you do it for me." Camelia shook her head and rolled her eyes. "And I'd like to take you up your very kind offer, because I'm just avoiding it."

"I'm on it. Suzanne will be here right away. Small conference room, okay?"

"You're a lifesaver," Camelia nodded. "And yes, I'll be right there."

"I'll pull the Anders file." Cate pulled her door closed.

As she waited for Suzanne, a text message popped up. Fiona and Mandy, two of her closest friends, wanted to get together.

Wanna meet up for happy hour on Friday?

Fuck sobriety.

I'm in. 6:30?

A few minutes later, her phone dinged again. Fiona, confirming happy hour. As Camelia stared at the message—three martini emojis and a thumbs up—she was already regretting opening the door to a boozy evening. But she could always stop at just one, couldn't she?

Can't I?

She grabbed her notepad, pen, and water bottle and headed to the conference room. Cate was already ushering Suzanne Anders down the hall, and Camelia smiled at Cate's bedside manner, the way she leaned in, listening intently.

I'm going to need her when I leave.

She shook her head. Where did that come from? Camelia lengthened her stride to catch up.

"Hi Suzanne! Thanks for stopping by on such short notice. How are you today?"

"Until you tell me otherwise, it's a good day!" Suzanne smiled. "How about you? How's your day?"

"It's family law, so it's too soon to tell," Camelia quipped as she propped the door open for Suzanne to pass.

Suzanne slid into one of the conference chairs and accepted the bottle of water Camelia handed her.

"Sorry for just barging in like this, but Cate said you needed to see me straight away and I was literally just up the street at a doctor's appointment." Suzanne tucked her hair behind her ears. "Did you get the ruling?"

Camelia took a deep breath. "No, we don't have the ruling yet, but another issue's come up. My boss happened to see Aaron holding a press conference at the courthouse today. Do you know anything about that?"

"No. Should I?" Suzanne's voice sounded cautious. "He holds press conferences about his cases all the time."

"This wasn't about a case. He was announcing a private charitable trust for cancer research. In your name." Camelia could feel the charge of the words electrifying the air. "Funded by the firm's deferred compensation and pension funds."

Suzanne's eyes widened and she let out a sharp gasp. "You have got to be kidding me. That son of a bitch," she whispered.

"Right now, I'm trying to figure out how to stop this trust from being funded, since a chunk of it's your money," Camelia said.

"How is that even legal? He knows damn well I won't be able to get my hands on the money if it's tied up in a trust. Wow. This is low, even for Aaron. Can't we stop him? What about the preliminary injunction?" Suzanne's voice was stretched thin.

"The injunction allows Aaron to do all manner of things in the quote, normal course of operating the firm. But this? This is way out of bounds. I'm going to have Arturo, our estates and trusts attorney, give me an opinion letter on it, and we're trying to get a copy of the trust." Camelia scratched out another note on her legal pad. "One thing I'm sure of, trusts can be very tricky to undo. So, do I have your permission to file an Emergency Petition to block funding of the trust pending entry of a decree?"

"Of course! Do whatever you need to." Suzanne pressed her hands to her face. "I just can't believe . . ." She choked on a sob.

Camelia slid a box of tissues across the table.

"I'm sorry to be the bearer of such rotten news."

Suzanne blew her nose and looked at Camelia with red-rimmed eyes.

"He will *never* let me have my money. Even without seeing my medical records, Aaron knows I have cancer, no thanks to Rick Baum."

Camelia scribbled a note on her legal pad. "We can—and *will*—address Dr. Baum's outrageous breach of client confidentiality and violation of HIPAA laws—"

"Oh, I've already taken care of that. I fired him and hired a new naturopathic oncologist teamed with Mayo Clinic. That's who I was just with. She's a much better fit for me anyway. Then I called one of my former colleagues, who now sits on the medical examiner's board. Trust me, Rick will regret his actions for a long time to come." Suzanne took a sip of water and a deep breath. "But Aaron . . . he knows I'm trying to secure my share of our assets before I die, so he's found yet another way to rip me off. You have no idea how determined he can be."

"Oh, I think I've got a pretty good idea. But I don't want you to worry about this, Suzanne. Leave it with me. Maybe, for once, he won't get away with just doing whatever the hell he wants."

But just because she was reassuring Suzanne didn't mean Camelia wasn't worried. She had no idea how to fix this mess. And it got messier every day. Aaron was pulling out all his dirty tricks and, so far, everything he'd done was perfectly legal. In fact, Aaron would come off as a magnanimous benefactor whose heart was broken by his beloved wife's illness. Unless Camelia could somehow expose his cruel intentions.

"I hope you're right, but it's Aaron so . . ." Suzanne shook her head.

"Suzanne, have you talked to your kids yet?" Camelia asked, hoping to change the subject. "If they don't know already, they're bound to find out any minute."

"I know. We leave Friday morning. I've booked a cabin in Sedona for a couple of days. Just the four of us. We used to go hiking up there all the time when they were little." Suzanne's eyes filled with tears again. "I want to enjoy my babies *alone* one more time before I have to say goodbye."

"I'm so sorry," Camelia gulped. She could feel her own eyes stinging with tears. How would she handle it if she had to share this kind of news? "If there's anything I can do—"

"You're doing it! And, no thanks to Aaron, there's a *lot* for you to manage."

Camelia realized the truth of Suzanne's comment. "So, when will you be back?"

"Oh, we're just going for the weekend, and I had to really wrangle to get that. I convinced them I needed to spend time with them one on one before I decided whether or not to divorce Daddy." Suzanne rolled her eyes.

"Okay," Camelia said, relieved Suzanne wouldn't be out of town for long. "I won't be in touch unless it's urgent, but you can call me any time."

"Cam, this is not how I want my story to end. With me in the ground and Aaron living it up on my kids' money," Suzanne sniffed.

"If I have any say in it, that will *not* be the end of your story. I'll do everything I can stop him."

But how could she even make that promise when her adversary held all the cards?

Just days ago, Aaron Anders had been confident his new-found philanthropic values would put an end to Suzanne's money grab. With most of their retirement money tied up in a charitable trust, it would be safe from an immediate payout. And based on her diagnosis, Suzanne would be dead before she could get the trust dissolved. Meanwhile, as trustee, he could pay himself a tidy management fee and there was nothing anyone could do about it.

But even after he'd explained how this was protection for them, too, the senior partners were still nipping at his heels. Instead of seeing the logic in shielding the funds from a future divorce that *any* of them could face, their panties were in a bunch and they were frothing at the mouth. Especially Jim Frost. God, that guy was as much a pain in the ass as his dumb bitch of a wife.

Their reaction had Aaron worried, though. Maybe he'd overstepped. The last thing he needed was a shareholder suit, and that's exactly what Eric Bass had threatened before storming out of Aaron's office.

"You may proceed as you wish with your portion of the deferred comp, *obviously*," Eric said in his Southern Kentucky drawl. "But I'm warnin' you, Aaron. Leave the rest of our funds alone. Your divorce ain't our dog fight."

"Jesus, Eric. Do you honestly think I would do anything to risk our assets?" Aaron argued. "This is for *everyone's* benefit. Because even though your marriage might be bulletproof, what about Chuck? And Jim? This will protect them, most of all."

"So you say, and that may very well be true. But we prefer to invest our retirement funds as individuals. The way *we* determine is best." Eric leaned forward. "Forgive my bluntness, but it seems necessary on this occasion, my friend. Back down, or you'll be served with a shareholder suit. And that's goin' to hurt everyone involved. Mostly you."

Aaron noticed the hard lines around Eric's mouth. Even though his Southern drawl and courtly manners softened the delivery, this wasn't an idle threat.

Eric stood and made for the door. He paused and turned back to Aaron. "And for the love of god, stop flaunting your affairs. Consider this our final word," he said, and flung the door open.

Aaron's mind roiled with worst case scenarios. He had to admit, he hadn't expected pushback from the partners. In the past, they'd always lined up behind him, no matter how bold his schemes. But Eric was no longer the trailblazing attorney he'd once been. He was getting old—hell, they all were—but age had made Eric more fiscally conservative, more protective of his nest egg. And that made Eric a dangerous opponent. One Aaron did not want to cross. Not now. He wasn't up for a war on yet another front.

He slumped in his chair and stared at the mottled backs of his hands. In a paralyzing moment of clarity, he realized his observations of Eric's advancing age were hitting close to home. Even though he'd kept himself in pretty good shape and had the help of one of the top cosmetic surgeons in Scottsdale—his pecs would *never* sag—there was no hiding the history written on the backs of his hands. A cold wave of anxiety rolled over him.

Suzanne might be the one dying, but Aaron wouldn't be far behind. The day was coming, sooner than he wanted to admit, that he would have to stop practicing law before he turned into the forgetful fossil at the end of the hall. And if he was going to live well—for the next, what, twenty years if he was lucky?—he needed the entire estate. Not just the tattered half Suzanne would leave him in a divorce.

With the weight of this reckoning pulling him down to earth, Aaron couldn't help but think that maybe Kaitlyn was right, after all. Maybe he *should* take matters in hand. Maybe the Sheridan Gambit, as she so stupidly called it, wasn't such a crappy idea after all.

If Suzanne was out of the way now—or at least *soon*, before she got her hands on half his money—well, that would solve everything. He could keep his financial estate intact and, with no need to follow through on that charitable trust, the partners would back off. But if he was going to make a move, he'd have to do it soon, before Camelia Belmont made any more trouble for him.

Aaron abruptly stood up and marched down the hall to Conference Room 3. The closed file boxes were stacked along the back wall. He scanned the labels until he saw *Sheridan Exhibits*. He rifled through a couple of boxes before he found the folder Kaitlyn had delivered to the casita.

He grabbed the folder and lifted out the padded envelope containing the traffic preemption device. It was too light. He pressed the sides of the envelope and felt . . . nothing. When he opened the envelope, he caught his breath.

Empty.

That sneaky little bitch.

24

SCOUT'S HONOR

FRIDAY, FEBRUARY 26

Everyone knew the conference rooms were rigged with video cameras. It was even in their employment agreement. Chris Fischer had been stewing over that fact ever since he'd walked in on Anders and Kaitlyn. Why would they take the risk? Or was the risk part of the fun? Anyone with access to the security video—and Chris didn't even know who all had that authority—would get an eyeful of Kaitlyn. He needed to be the *only* one controlling that image; otherwise, it was worthless.

When he got it in his head to steal the video from the office surveillance system, he knew he would need the technical skill to swap the drive and the right tools for the job. Most important, he would need to access the server without anyone else finding out. But he didn't know how to accomplish any of that stuff. However, he *did* know how to plan, problem solve, and overcome obstacles by capitalizing on opportunities.

Chris's colleagues teasingly called him Johnny Hayseed, Country Bumpkin, and even Hicktopher sometimes. It was all part of law firm hazing, and it didn't bother him, because they weren't entirely wrong. But there was another side to this North Dakota farm boy they knew nothing about. He was an Eagle Scout, hunter, marksman. His skills extended far beyond how to use a compass and light a fire. But for this, Chris would need all the skills he'd learned as a Scout, and then some. He was about to break a lot of rules, but it would be worth it because, when he was done, Kaitlyn would regret ever having screwed him over.

Or would she?

Chris wanted to believe Kaitlyn wasn't as cold hearted as she'd seemed the past few weeks, and he considered whether he should bring up marriage counseling one more time. Would she agree? Laugh it off? Just ignore him? More likely, she would gaslight him: deny everything, seduce him, try to convince him it was all in his head. And based on how she'd been acting lately, his wife would go right back to screwing Anders the minute he turned his back.

No, Chris knew the marriage was over. He'd known the minute he swung open that conference room door, even if it took a while to admit it. That's why he was about to do something he'd never expected of himself. The video footage was Chris's ace in the hole. She couldn't deny her adultery when it was all right there. And if he visited a bit of sweet revenge on that asshole Anders at the same time? Well, that was just gravy.

Determined not to screw it up, Chris went over the broad outline of his plan again, concentrating on filling in the fine details. But unlike mergers and corporate deals, Chris didn't know the first thing about servers or data drives or security camera backup systems or, hell, any of it. So, he turned to YouTube, source of all knowledge.

He'd considered how to get to the files containing the security footage of Anders and Kaitlyn together, but Chris didn't know jack about the firm's system and he was clearly no tech geek. After watching a few videos that went right over his head, Chris realized he needed to come up with another way to accomplish his goal. A way to convince—or, better still, trick—someone into getting that footage for him.

He knew who to go to: Office Bee. Yeah, some people called her Office Bitch, but Chris had always gotten along well with Janice. And she was exactly the kind of person he needed right now: a busy little bee who knew *everything* that went on in the firm. Which is why, right before five o'clock, he'd nonchalantly dropped by her office to probe for intel.

"Hey Janice," Chris said as he rapped on her door. "Got a minute?"

Office Bee looked up and took off her reading glasses, dropping them on the desk. She glanced at the clock on her computer monitor before turning back to Chris.

"It'll have to be quick. I had no idea it was this late. How can I help?"

"I'm in a bit of a bind, and didn't know who else to ask. I had a meeting a while back with the guy from Sunnyside Solar." His heart rate ticked up a notch. "I have arbitration on Monday, so I want to review the meeting over the weekend. I was wondering where to find the video file."

"Well, hon, if you need access to security footage, you'll have to ask Dov Saminski. As Chief Security Officer, he manages all that. Even *I'm* not allowed to help you there," she'd rolled her eyes.

"We keep the footage from all the cameras, though, right? I'm assuming—"

"Of course, we do. For ninety days. I gotta tell you though, I'm against all this Big Brother video surveillance crap. But then again, after what happened to that lawyer at McCaffrey Rhodes & Rodriguez, who knows? Maybe it's for the best."

Chris blanched at the reference. He'd heard about the incident at Camelia Belmont's office; the threat of violence that hung over everyone these days.

"Yeah, that was pretty awful. But we just have coverage in the conference rooms—"

"The conference rooms *and* the front lobby all have cameras, five in total. And don't think Saminski didn't push for a camera in every office. But I put my foot down. That's an HR bomb just waiting to explode, if you ask me." She huffed a disapproving sigh. "Anyway, that's not your problem, is it Christopher? *Your* problem is how to get that video file of your meeting without letting the whole office know you can't read your own notes. Because that's what this is about, right?"

Chris felt his face flush. "Hey, my handwriting's not that—"

"Don't kid yourself, hon. You shoulda been a doctor," she laughed as she began shutting down her computer. "But if you want to view that video, you need to talk to Dov."

"Sounds like he's the expert."

"If you say so," Office Bee sighed then dropped the volume of her voice. "Personally, I think Saminski's focused on the wrong stuff."

"Really? How so?"

"What I mean is . . . here's an example, he's all uptight about the server room and wants it locked 24-7. But I pushed back, because that would be a real pain in the patootie for me. I need that space for office supplies because you lawyers never seem to get tired of making binders." She laughed and winked. "If the door's locked all the time, guess who'll have to come running every time Baby Lawyer can't find his keys? Well, I won that round. But then, on the other hand, he lets the security video just overwrite itself every three months. How's that gonna help us out later? I mean, some of our cases go on for *years*. You never know what you're gonna need 'til you need it." She shook her head.

"If the files are backed up to the cloud, then it wouldn't matt—"

"Oh no, not AndersLaw. I'll never get that past the boss. He's terrified of getting hacked!" Janice smoothed her sleek bun. "We've got cloud backup for some stuff, but none of our client data, bookkeeping, or even work product are in the cloud. It's all in that little room, right there, on three computers." She pointed at the server room.

"Really? Is that safe?" Chris couldn't believe they didn't have a more secure system in place.

"Hell no, it's not safe," Janice whispered. "But do you think I can get Mr. Anders to cough up $30k a month for a cloud-based practice management system? Also, hell no."

Chris whistled. "Whoa. I had no idea it cost that much."

"That doesn't even count the new equipment we'd need on site," Janice said. "But I came up with a workaround and—"

Chris had to get Janice to stop talking, or they'd still be here by the time Saminski came by to lock up.

"Anders is lucky to have you guarding the henhouse, you clever little fox!" He grinned. "But hey, I know you need to get going, so it sounds like I just need to catch up with Saminski and have him look up the video file."

It couldn't be that easy.

"Oh, honey, don't even *think* about going to him without your ducks in a row. You need to give him the details. Otherwise, it's like looking for a needle in a haystack, especially if it was a busy day of back-to-back meetings. There's no *way* Saminski's gonna waste his precious time hunting through all the files like I would. But if you have the date and time, along with the conference room number, he should be able to hand it over in about 10 seconds, flat."

Chris paused. "Do you know when he'll be in the office? That guy doesn't exactly keep regular hours, and I need the video pronto."

Janice was shoving things in her purse and stood to put on her coat. "He's always here Wednesday mornings to meet with Mr. Anders, and I know he stops by most nights between nine and ten to make sure we're all locked up." She flung her purse over her shoulder. "Now, I gotta run."

Chris walked back to his office and slid into his chair. How would he get Saminski to help him without raising a ton of red flags? It sounded like Dov could assist with a *legitimate* request, but how far could Chris push his luck with a not-so-legitimate motive? Since even this Eagle Scout was apparently just too dumb to figure out how to disassemble a computer and put it back together in under five minutes, he didn't have a choice. Saminski was his best . . . no, his *only* option.

But he couldn't just outright ask for the footage of Anders with Kaitlyn, because he sure as hell didn't want Saminski seeing Kaitlyn like *that*. And if Saminski's job was to protect Anders, he would no doubt delete the file the minute he figured out what was going on.

No matter how awkward it might be, Chris needed to just suck it up, wait around as late as it took, and ask Saminski for the footage of his meeting with Sunnyside Solar. That meeting had taken place earlier in the day, in the same conference room. But Chris knew how to play up his naïve reputation. If he could get Saminski to show him how to access the footage from his meeting, he should be able to find the file path of the footage he was *really* after.

Once Saminski showed him how to . . . wait. Why would Saminski show him anything? If Office Bee wasn't allowed to access the security server, what made Chris think Saminski would just hand it over? Surely the Chief Security Officer would be a lot more careful than that. Since there was no way to predict Saminski's reaction, Chris would just have to improvise, play it by ear. And capitalize on any opportunities that came along.

Time to Scout up!

As he waited for the last of his coworkers to straggle out of the office, Chris's mind drifted to increasingly elaborate revenge fantasies for his adulterous wife and arrogant boss.

Kaitlyn would be ruined, of course. She'd have a hard time finding another job once word got around. But Anders was another matter. While exposing their affair might embarrass Anders for a few days, it wouldn't do any permanent damage. For that matter, it would probably elevate his status in certain circles. It sure as hell wouldn't ruin his career. But having worked closely with Anders on a few cases, Chris knew the one thing dear to his boss's heart: money.

He needed to figure out a way to hit Anders where it would hurt, but how? How would Chris—a lowly corporate transactions associate, not even a partner—ever get an opportunity to bring Anders down? Unless he could figure out some way of hobbling the firm's cash flow, some kind of untraceable espionage, Anders' wealth and influence was virtually untouchable. At least by Chris. He had no power in this equation. And the firm was pretty much bullet proof. AndersLaw was profitable, highly visible in the legal community and, frankly, a desirable . . .

There it is.

AndersLaw was a perfect, fat little piggy, ready for market. This was Chris's area of expertise: mergers and acquisitions. But who would have the money or the balls to try to buy out Aaron Anders?

It was getting late and most everyone had left, which is why raised voices surprised him. Chris pulled his door open to better hear what was going on, and overheard Jim Frost's strident words coming from David Weisman's office around the corner. Why were the two senior partners going at it?

Chris nonchalantly walked down the hall with a file in hand. He could hear them clearly as he lingered, out of sight, at the junction of hallways.

"I know you're pissed, Jim, but what the hell can we do about it?" Weisman said. "We don't have a majority, and without it, we're screwed."

"Well, I, for one, am not going to sit around and wait for the screwing. I'm not ready to retire just yet, but if I don't get my money out of the deferred comp now, I might not ever see it again." Jim muttered something Chris couldn't pick out.

Chris's mind was still gnawing on the juicy idea of corporate sabotage, a way to slip the rug out from under Anders when he realized the solution was right in front of him. All it would take was one timely rumor. And *now* was that time. Companies much bigger than AndersLaw had folded over less and Chris had seen it play out a dozen times in his role as a corporate transaction attorney. He straightened up and rounded the corner.

"Hey, how's it going?" Chris said, smiling. "Everything okay?"

"Yeah, we're fine, and you?" Frost's response was curt, dismissive. "Kind of a late night for you transaction types, isn't it?"

"Yeah, arbitration on Monday. I was just on my way to make some copies," Chris waved the file folder in his hand, "Sorry, but I couldn't help but overhear. So, it's true?"

Frost and Weisman exchanged a look. Those two were thick as thieves, and Chris could see they were about to clam up.

"What's true?" Frost asked.

"Look, firm business is above my pay grade. I'm only asking because I heard a rumor," Chris said, leaning closer.

Just one tiny fib, an unverified, but completely plausible lie.

Frost and Weisman bent their heads forward. "What kind of rumor?" Weisman asked.

"I don't want to piss anyone off, so don't worry, I'm keeping this close," Chris glanced around. "But if the firm is being sold . . . Look, I just want to make sure I've got a job lined up if I'm not part of the deal."

Weisman looked at Frost, then back at Chris.

"Who told you the firm is being sold?" Weisman said.

"I was at Durant's the other night and overheard some chitchat. Some folks from Sherman Wright, I think. And I know what that means for associates like me." Chris looked from one to the next. "I'll probably be out on my ass, but I'd rather stay on if it's an option."

"Chris, those kinds of rumors are always floating around," Weisman said. "I wouldn't put much stock in it."

"Okay, well, I hope that's the case," Chris nodded. "Because I'm sure Mrs. Anders would jump at the chance to cash out. You know, with the divorce and all."

"You think Sherman Wright approached *Suzanne* about a buyout?" Chris could tell Frost's wheels were already turning.

"Oh, no, I have no idea who they're talking to. I thought it would be you guys. But since you haven't heard . . ." He shrugged. "You're right, it's probably just gossip. Forget I said anything," Chris said as he turned and headed back to his office. "Have a good evening!"

Chris walked back to his office, smiling to himself. Frost and Weisman had chomped down on that hook faster than he'd expected. The grin on his face broadened when he heard Frost and Weisman arguing as they headed out of the office.

Chris was methodical, the type to plot out every step of his life, but he was beginning to see how useful spontaneity could be. And now that he'd stirred up a little shit for the partners to consider, all he had to do was wait for Saminski to arrive.

It was almost nine when Jeff Petronelli, his best friend, stopped by his office.

"You still here? Thought you'd be getting some me time since the womenfolk are all at Andrea's baby shower," Jeff said. "I'm heading out for some ribs and brew if you wanna join me."

"Love to man, but I've got an arbitration hearing coming up on Monday," Chris pointed at a fat file on his desk. "Thought I'd get up to speed tonight so I don't have to work over the weekend."

"You know how I can tell you don't have kids? Because you don't want to work weekends!" Jeff laughed at his own joke. "Trust me, Saturday is sometimes my favorite work day."

Chris laughed in response, but saw an opening for the next step in his plan. "How about happy hour next week?"

"I'll have to check with Rach, but it should be fine. Anyway, I'm outta here. See ya Monday!"

"Set the alarm on your way out, Jeff," Chris called out.

"Yes, Mommy," Jeff called back.

Now, where the hell is Saminski?

25

LITTLE WHITE LIES

FRIDAY, FEBRUARY 26

About a half hour after Jeff Petronelli left the office, Chris heard the staccato beeps of the code being entered and the short bingbing tone that meant the alarm was off. It had to be Saminski.

Finally.

Chris got up and headed to the lobby, calling out as he approached so he wouldn't startle him. "Hello? Dov?"

Saminski was in the mailroom alcove just off the lobby, thumbing through a pile of envelopes.

"Oh hey, Fischer," Saminski said. "You're working late tonight."

"Yeah, waiting for you, actually," Chris said.

"Oh yeah? Why's that?" Saminski put the envelopes back in his mailbox and turned to face Chris. "Something going on?"

"No, nothing like that. I just . . ." Chris paused and swallowed. Why did Saminski make him so nervous? It was like he could see right through you with those steely grey eyes. "I need a favor, and Janice said to talk to you."

"I'm on a bit of a tight schedule right now." Saminski looked at his watch. "Mr. Anders is at an event this evening, so I need to get back as soon as I've done my rounds. Can it wait until tomorrow?"

"Um . . . not really. I wouldn't be asking if I wasn't in the shit on one of my cases," Chris said.

"Okay, I'll stop by your office on the way out," Saminski said as he walked away. He called back over his shoulder, "But no promises. I can't keep Mr. Anders waiting."

As soon as he sat down at his desk, Chris opened the arbitration case file on his computer. He had to look busy, as if he was focused on work while he waited for the other man's return. But just as he'd done with Frost and Weisman, Chris had to seize the moment. And maybe, if Saminski was in a hurry to get back to Anders, he might be a little more lax about how he turned over that video. Maybe Saminski would even be careless enough to let Chris watch when he accessed the file. But even if Chris watched, would he remember what he'd seen?

An idea came to him in a flash of brilliance. Chris put his phone on silent mode.

I'm on a roll tonight!

A few minutes later, Dov stopped in his doorway.

"So, what do you need help with?"

"I was just trying to decipher these meeting notes for my arbitration hearing on Monday, and they're a mess. I can barely read my own writing." Chris waved a couple of pages of scribbled notes before tossing them back on his desk.

"Sorry. I'm a bit rusty on my courtroom tactics," Saminski said with a grin.

So, he had a sense of humor! Maybe he wasn't such a badass after all.

Chris laughed in return. "Yeah, but you can help me with the meeting. They're all recorded, right? The meetings in the conference rooms? Because if I can watch the video, I'll know what these notes say."

Saminski hesitated before answering, as if he wasn't sure he should admit it. "Well, yeah, the meetings are recorded. But only for security purposes. And we don't keep the files indefinitely."

Chris sighed. "The meeting was just a few weeks ago, so it should still be there, right?"

"If it was within ninety days, the file will still be there," Saminski said, propping his hands on his hips. "And I can help you with that, but like I said, I'm working an event and need to get back."

Chris groaned. "Can you just tell me how to get to the file? Is it on the server?" Chris moved his mouse around and clicked on the directory. "You can just show me the file path and I can look it up from there."

"You're not authorized access to the security server, but if you give me the date and time, I can pull the file for you on Monday," Saminski said.

Chris scrambled for something, anything, to push Saminski to help him.

"Please, man. Monday's too late. I'm begging you! I'm already behind on this case and was hoping to get caught up over the weekend, because the arbitration starts Monday morning. And my client is . . . well, demanding is putting it mildly." Chris shook his head. "I need to study up so I'll be ready." Chris employed his most hangdog look. "I know you need to get back, but you can truthfully tell Anders it was my fault you were held up."

Saminski looked at his watch again. "Okay, but I gotta make it quick. If I can sit at your computer . . ." He nodded at Chris's desk.

Chris stood up and moved to the side as he picked up his phone from the desk.

"It's all yours."

But he stayed behind the desk, hovering near Saminski, swiping the camera on his phone to video as the other man sat down. Chris trained the camera on the keyboard as Dov began to type, recording the keystrokes over Dov's shoulder, praying he wouldn't get caught.

"Date?"

Chris picked up the notes on his desk and peered at the top of one of the pages. "Here we go. January 9, 11 a.m."

"Which conference room?" Saminski asked.

"Um, number three, I think."

He pretended to read the documents he was holding when he looked over at the monitor, at the rows of file names, dozens of dates and times. Saminski glanced back over his shoulder and the implication was clear: he wanted some space. Chris stepped back, dropping his right hand—the one holding his phone—into his pocket.

"There are only two meetings on that date. One at 11 a.m. and the other at 6:12 p.m., nothing in the afternoon."

That "meeting" beginning at 6:12 p.m. had to be Anders and Kaitlyn. "Hey, I know you're in a hurry, so you can just send both of them to my email," Chris said.

Instead, Saminski clicked on the first file and a video player popped up. The camera had begun recording as a barrel of a man with a shock of silver hair entered the room just ahead of Chris.

"Okay," Dov sighed impatiently. "This it?"

"Yep, that's the one," Chris said, watching himself enter the room on the video.

"I can't email it. File's too big. Got a flash drive handy?"

Chris leaned over to open his desk drawer. He pulled out a fresh flash drive with the AndersLaw logo printed on the side and handed it to Saminski.

"Really appreciate this, man. You're saving my bacon!" Chris said, hoping he didn't sound as nervous as he felt.

Saminski copied the file, pulled the flash drive out, and handed it to Chris. "No problem. If you're done here, I'll lock up behind you," Saminski said as he stood and moved to the door. It was not a request.

"Oh sure, just let me grab my stuff and I am *outta* here!" Chris dropped the flash drive in his briefcase.

Saminski stepped aside to let him pass.

Chris felt triumphant. He was one step closer to getting his hands on that video, thanks to Mr. Badass Chief Security Officer.

As Chris walked past him, out the front door, Dov called out, "Enjoy your evening."

"What's left of it," Chris said, waving as he entered the elevator.

When the elevator door whooshed shut, Chris exhaled and hugged himself as he blew out short, quick breaths. He couldn't believe he'd gotten away with recording Saminski as he logged into the security server.

As he drove out of the parking garage, he slowed as he passed Anders' personal parking space. "Fuck you, and fuck Kitty, too," he said as he rolled past.

Now, Chris could replay the video he'd recorded, replicate Saminski's keystrokes, and he'd be able to access the server to download that incriminating video, and then . . . then, he would rain a little hell down on Kaitlyn and Anders for their betrayal.

But the tingle of victory was overshadowed by a tsunami of panic. He felt thoroughly exposed. Everything he said could, and would, be used against him in a Court of law. He didn't know how or when, but he feared it would all come crashing down around him.

He knew how to quiet those fears, though. He'd stop at Durant's on the way home. Have a drink. Drop a hint.

Chris Fischer was lining up the phases of his revenge like tin cans on a fence rail, and he couldn't wait to shoot them down. After spinning a little rumor for Frost and Weisman, he'd managed to get Dov Saminski to retrieve that video of his meeting with Sunnyside Solar. All while he snagged his own video of Dov's hands on the keyboard.

He pulled up to the valet at Durant's, the popular watering hole and gossip wallow for attorneys. He was hoping to run into Eileen Sanders, a partner at Sherman Wright and a Durant's regular. She was just the kind of aggressive, well-placed attorney to pounce on the rumor that AndersLaw was ripe for a buyout. And luck was on his side. As he walked through to the bar, there she was, sipping a glass of wine.

As he approached, one of his colleagues from his days clerking at the Arizona Supreme Court slipped onto the barstool next to Eileen, placing a palm on her thigh. They were dressed up, like they'd been out for the evening, which made Chris hesitant to approach. He didn't want to crash date night.

He needn't have worried though, because Eileen saw him and waved him over.

"Hey Chris! You're everywhere these days! Are you stalking me?" She laughed, her magenta lips parting to reveal even rows of nubby white teeth.

"I was going to stalk you, but you were already here, so I didn't have to," Chris shot back with a grin. He turned to the brunette at Eileen's side. "Hey, Monica! Haven't seen you in ages."

She grinned and leaned forward to give him a little sideways hug. "Yo bro! You're looking good. It's been a while, hasn't it?" She turned to Eileen. "Back in a minute. Wanna grab another couple of Cabernets?"

As Monica walked away, Eileen watched her for a second, then turned back to Chris.

"Where's wifey tonight?"

"She's at a baby shower," he said. "You two look pretty fancy. Where've you been?"

"Symphony. Very posh. Now we're starving for red meat. Wanna join us?" Eileen asked.

"Love to," Chris said. "But I don't want to be the third wheel."

"Don't be silly. You and Monica can catch up while I stuff my face with ribeye."

Chris smiled. "In that case, thank you. I could use the distraction."

"Yeah? What's up? Did you lose some big ass merger deal?"

"I wish that's all it was," he sighed.

"Jesus, Fischer, you look like someone stole your bike. What's going on?" Eileen waved down the bartender. "You want wine, Chris?"

He nodded as Eileen ordered three glasses of Cabernet.

"Oh nothing. Work stuff. Probably just the rumor mill on overdrive."

"About what? I mean, you're all a bunch of kitten kickers, so how much worse could it be?" Eileen rolled her eyes and took a long sip of wine as Monica returned.

"I shouldn't . . ." Chris looked around the bar to see who might be within earshot.

"Babe, our table's ready," Monica said, nodding toward the dining room as she picked up her glass of wine.

"I invited Chris to join us," Eileen said. "Hope that's okay?"

"Of course." Monica smiled at Chris. "I wanna hear what's going on with one of my favorite alums."

The maître d' led them to a crescent shaped booth near the back of the restaurant and a server brought menus, water, and bread.

Eileen paused until he left, then turned to Chris. "Okay, what's burning a hole in your mouth?"

"Something going on?" Monica asked.

"Oh, it's probably just a bunch of bitching and moaning." He took a sip of wine to soothe his suddenly dry throat.

"You're among friends, Chris. God knows I have no one to tell," Monica said. "Well, except my cat."

"I'm sure you've heard the Anders are divorcing? It's making things weird at the office these days. All the senior partners are flipping out."

"The old dudes always get nervous when there's a divorce in the ranks. Figure they're next to get served with papers," Monica said. "And with good reason."

"Doesn't really affect you though, does it?" Eileen asked.

"I don't know, probably not. But . . . things are a bit tense. The seniors are wigging out over Anders setting up a charitable trust, which is somehow related to his divorce." Chris shook his head. "Probably nothing but bluster."

"Who are we talking about, Chris? Which seniors?" Eileen's dark eyes bored into his.

"Does it matter which ones?"

"You're talking to the original honey badger, and she don't care." Monica let out a cackle. "She'll rake your skin off if you don't tell her."

"Okay, but this goes *nowhere*," Chris said. "Or I'll be screwed."

"We'll see. It might be that this goes somewhere very good for Chris Fischer," Eileen said, a slow smile settling on her face.

"Watch out, Chris, or you'll end up getting promoted," Monica said, arching an eyebrow.

"Okay, but seriously . . . I'll deny everything." Chris took a swig of water. "I overheard Jim Frost and David Weisman complaining about the trust because Anders is funding it with their deferred comp. And hooboy, are they pissed."

Eileen slowly put her glass of wine down and smoothed the table cloth. "Chris, I want every slimy little detail."

26

DUI

"Here's to you, Fi," Camelia lifted her glass. She hadn't seen Fiona Burke since her friend had located an obscure article for one of Byron's cases. "For coming up with that law review article. I was Byron's pet that day, thanks to your excellent research skills!" Camelia took a long sip of her martini.

The three friends were sharing appies and cocktails at Vito's, a hip neighborhood bistro. Their lively conversation was pierced with periodic shrieks and howls of laughter.

"It's nothing a third year law student couldn't have located for you," Fiona responded in her characteristically self-deprecating way. They'd known each other since Camelia's first job out of law school—a disastrous two years in BigLaw—where Fiona was the research librarian, back when there still was such a thing. "Got me out of my little bubble for a few minutes, though. But tell us, how are things at the office? Are you recovering from that awful mess?"

Camelia shrugged and scrunched her mouth to one side, focusing on her martini glass.

Mandy noted the gesture. "You've been through the wringer, Cam. And I know you're seeing Dr. Chavez, but . . . do you want to talk about it?"

Camelia gave her friend a weak smile. She'd met Amanda Moray, Psy.D., at a family law conference on vicarious trauma almost a decade ago. They'd ended up snickering inappropriately at all the wrong things and immediately became fast friends. She knew Mandy could see right through her, but she glossed over it anyway.

"No, I'm fine. But thank you both for your concern. I mean, *yes*, there's a ton to process, but I'm working on it with Dr. Chavez. It's just . . . my job is making me nuts. The horror stories and constant bickering start to blend together after a while, and I hate that I'm getting numbed to real life heartbreak. Plus, I have to say, I'm a little tired of the crazy."

Amanda grinned and shook her head, red hair shimmying around her shoulders. "*You're* tired of crazy? You should come hang out at my office!"

They all laughed and sipped their drinks, but Camelia could feel the weight of their expectation for something more.

"Really, I'm okay. I just need to think about what I want to do next, because I'm sure as hell not making partner, and that means it's time to move on," Camelia said.

Fiona's arched brows shot up. "What? And leave Byron? That gorgeous hunk of Scot?" She flicked a wave of ash blond hair away from her face.

Amanda looked from Fiona to Camelia and back again. "Our girl is about to fledge, Fi. So, forget about Byron! This is huge! Tell us everything!"

"Slow down, Mandy. There's nothing to tell at the moment," Camelia tipped her glass as their waiter passed, indicating another round. "I've been thinking about it ever since my Auntie Freda died. Then Leon brought it up again after the Josh Campbell ordeal. It freaked him out. Too close to home. He thinks I should go out on my own so I can control my schedule and the type of cases I take on. And I think he might be right."

A frosty martini appeared at Camelia's elbow as the waiter refilled water and whisked the empty glasses and plates away.

"Darling, you're brilliant. You know it's not a question of *if*, but *when*. I mean, Byron took you under his wing, but he can't keep you under his thumb," Fiona said. "Even if he is gorgeous."

Amanda laughed. "God, Fi. You really have a thing for Byron, don't you?"

"Why, Dr. Moray. I'll have you know it's purely physical. Nothing more," Fiona said, barely containing her laughter.

"Keep your panties on for a minute, Fi. Cam, we need details!"

"I'm still in the mulling stage, but if I leave, it won't be until one of my worst cases is final. And I'm planning to ask Cate to come along. I mean, *if* I decide to leave," Camelia said.

"Jesus, Belmont, I think you've made a decision, even if you won't admit it." Mandy counted off on her fingers. "One, it's been on your mind for months. Two, your husband is supportive. Three, you're not making partner. Four, you know your assistant will jump at the chance to accompany you. I'd say you're ready." She sipped her sangria and nodded at Fiona. "Do you agree?"

"Absolutely. Now, the most important part. Where will your offices be?" Fiona asked.

Their conversation wound down after talking through a few office options. Camelia glanced at her phone. It was after 9 p.m.

"I better get going." She reached for the bill before their server could even set it down so her friends wouldn't see how she'd outpaced them on cocktails.

"It's on me, Fi, I promised." Fiona and Amanda protested, but Camelia waved her corporate card and said, with more conviction than she felt, "No, no, no. This is my treat for finding that law review article. Besides, the firm is paying."

Neither of her friends would have allowed her to drive had they been paying closer attention, but thankfully they weren't. She would be extra careful. After all, Vito's was only a few miles from home.

Driving home, Camelia felt the warm release of alcohol coursing through her veins. Her legs were loose and rubbery. She felt alive and happy, and a little numb and sleepy.

Until a Phoenix Police Department patrol car pulled up behind her. Her palms began to sweat as she checked her speed. She set her cruise control at thirty-nine miles per hour. That cop wouldn't get a ticket out of her tonight.

But he stayed on her tail for way too long and she was beginning to think she'd made a critical error. There was no way she would pass a field sobriety test, and forget about a breathalyzer. Her pulse was pounding now, and she was trying to sort out some kind of excuse, a story, a way to wiggle out of it if he pulled her over.

The cop's lights came on.

Just as she figured she was done for, he pulled into the left lane and sped past her, sirens blaring.

Jesus, Mary, and Joseph. That was way too close.

She realized she'd been holding her breath, and exhaled. The fist holding her stomach in its grip was still twisting the air out of her. But she wasn't going to let that monster push its way into every nerve ending. Not tonight. She was okay. No need to panic.

Almost home.

All she had to do was make it a few more blocks without screwing up. Because the last thing she needed was a DUI. Next thing you know, she'd have an ignition lock with a breathalyzer, just like so many of her clients. What the hell was she thinking, drinking all those martinis? What if Byron got wind of it?

She knew she had to stop freaking out over every little thing, but anxiety had its own agenda. Drinking shut down the panic, but created a whole other set of problems. And Camelia had no idea how to rein it all in without everyone finding out what a train wreck she had become. She pulled into the garage and quickly glanced in the visor mirror to see how bad she looked.

Good enough.

She opened the back door to two wiggling dogs, their tails slapping her legs as she walked into the kitchen.

"Hey Leon, I'm home," she called out as she rubbed Caesar and Calvin's ears.

"In here," Leon called back.

"Bring you anything?"

"I've got a beer, thanks," Leon responded.

Camelia poured a glass of wine, gulped half of it, topped it up, and headed to the den. Leon was sprawled on the sofa watching the Suns basketball game on TV. Camelia paused to turn on the gas fireplace, then curled up beside him, wine in hand. Caesar and Calvin flopped down on their beds in front of the fire, groaning and stretching.

"They been walked?" she asked.

"Yeah, I took them out earlier." Leon glanced at the wine and then at Camelia. "How was happy hour?"

All these weeks of holding the booze at bay, and here she was, fuzzy headed and thick-tongued. She'd drank her progress—dirty, with extra olives—and now she had to start all over again. Camelia felt shame creep over her as she set her glass of wine down.

"It's always good to see Fi and Mandy. How about you? How was your day?"

"I think it was a damn good day," Leon said. "That Spanish client is shaping up to be a bigger account than I'd hoped for, so the business should be in the black in no time."

"Oh, babe, that's great," Camelia said. "And what is it that you do again?" She laughed at Leon's eye-roll.

"Tech support. That's all you need to know, little lady. I do tech support," he chuckled. "And how was your day?"

"Never easy, but nothing I can't manage." She let the lie slip down over her and it felt right.

"Wanna watch a movie?"

She laid her head back on the sofa as Leon read the newly released Netflix titles out loud. Camelia was warm and cozy from the fireplace, and drowsy from all those martinis.

"I think I better make it an early night, babe. I'm going to have a shower and hit the hay," she said.

Leon looked at his phone. "Okay. I'll finish watching the game, then."

Camelia rolled off the sofa and stumbled a bit as she leaned down to kiss Leon.

"Hey, easy there cowgirl." Leon looked at her intently. "How much did you have to drink tonight? I could have picked you up, you know."

"I'm just tired, and I've still got some vertigo," Camelia said, brushing off his concern. "I don't think Josh Campbell is out of my system yet, ya know?"

She saw the skepticism in his face.

"Seriously, how much did you have to drink tonight?"

The guilt that came with his question made her just a little angry.

"I don't know. A couple of martinis? We weren't exactly counting."

"But you *should* be counting. Because the last thing you need is to get busted on a DUI. Just . . ." Leon paused and took a deep breath. "Call me next time. You know I'll come get you, no questions asked. It's not safe."

She picked up her glass of wine, patted Leon's shoulder as she passed, and headed for the hall. "Don't stay up too late, okay?"

"I'm not kidding, Cam!" Leon shouted at her back.

Who is he to judge?

Leon. That's who. The guy who always did the right thing. Who always tried to protect her. But he didn't understand. Leon didn't get stressed over every single thing that came along. He was methodical and precise, but he wasn't a pathological overthinker.

Not like me.

Why should he suffer just because she couldn't handle her caseload, her clients were driving her nuts, she didn't really like her boss very much, and she was drinking away her misery? It wasn't his problem.

The little stab of resentment turned inward. Camelia felt the subtle numbness of vodka in her cheeks, her legs, her mind. She did a U-turn and headed back to the kitchen, where she grabbed the half-empty bottle of wine from the counter and padded silently to the bedroom.

I've already blown it, so what's a little more gonna hurt?

Camelia stood under the steaming hot shower gulping the last of the zinfandel. She hated herself for being such a weak, pathetic excuse of a human. As she toweled off, she wondered if it was time to come clean with Dr. Chavez. Otherwise, how was she ever going to get off this booze cruise? She stuffed the empty wine bottle in the bottom of the hamper and fell into bed, turning off her alarm. Tomorrow was Saturday, and she just wanted to sleep in.

Her old friend alcohol was neatly sweeping away all her waking worries, so by the time Camelia passed out, she was confident tonight was just a blip.

Tomorrow is a new day. A new Day One.

27

REDUCED SPEED AHEAD

FRIDAY, MARCH 4

It had been a boring, plodding week, a rare respite from the usual roller coaster of hearings, meetings, drafting countless letters and motions, and frantic trial prep. But, with just a few hours left on this Friday afternoon, Camelia found herself furiously tapping her pen on a legal pad, too twitchy and restless to take advantage of the down time to catch up on all the tasks she should have been focusing on.

It was the lull in activity that threw her.

Suzanne Anders was in Sedona with her kids. All of her other clients were in the process of settlement or between hearings. Camelia's report on Josh Campbell's suicide was finally complete and emailed to the coroner. And, as soon as the Anders case wrapped up in another few months, she would be able to jump ship. But there was a lot to do before that could happen.

Before she could ward it off, a flood of images rushed forward to ratchet up Camelia's heart rate. Every minute she wasn't hyper-focused on work seemed to instantly fill with vivid memories of Josh Campbell's brains splattered all over the glass wall of the lobby. Cate's white face and trembling hands as she steered Camelia into her office. Leon's fearful eyes as he picked godknowswhat out of her hair. Her hands began to shake.

Dr. Chavez had tried to prepare her for the PTSD and trauma reactions that threatened to derail her when she least expected it. But even Carlos with his big, sad eyes and big, sad vocabulary couldn't prepare her for being mentally slammed into a brick wall over and over. Camelia shook her head to dislodge the slide show of horrors running through her mind.

She needed to talk to someone who didn't know about Josh Campbell and wouldn't ask her forty-seven times if she was okay. Her mother was off on walkabout somewhere in Peru. Her Auntie Freda was dead. But there was someone. Rita Becker, her second cousin and lifelong friend. Camelia hesitated. Then, before she could change her mind, she picked up her phone.

Rita picked up on the third ring. "Hey Cam, what's up?"

Camelia could hear the radio and traffic noise in the background. "Is this a bad time?"

"Just driving to my next client, so I've got about ten minutes," Rita said.

"Haven't talked to you in a while. Thought I'd call and see how things are going."

"I'm hanging in there," Rita said. "You?"

"I'm okay. A bit of a slow day at the office and my mind got to wandering . . . any updates on Kenna and Mick?"

"Yeah, Mickey was sentenced last week and Kenna called, hysterical, as usual." Rita sighed. "She said Mickey's gonna appeal, so who knows how long that will take."

"It must be rough for Kenna," Camelia said.

"Yeah, well," Rita huffed, "she has her own sentencing to worry about. Her hearing's in April, when she's out of rehab. Sobriety seems to suit her, though. She sounded better than she has in years."

"Wait, what? I thought she was in *rehab* rehab, like physical therapy, for the burns," Camelia said.

"Oh, she is. But it only took about a minute for them to figure out she's an addict, so she's also getting treatment for that. Hopefully it will stick."

It should be a relief that Kenna was getting sober, so why did Rita sound less than optimistic? Maybe she was skeptical because Kenna had never been particularly dedicated to self improvement, especially if it meant sacrificing her precious rye and Coke and prescription painkillers. But Camelia didn't want to dwell on Kenna's issues. Not when they hit so close to home.

"Hmm, well, I hope she finds her way. How are you and Dave doing?"

"We're good. Dave's pretty happy with the regular hours now that I'm working in hospice, and I'm quite liking it since I've settled in. More than I expected, anyway. And you?"

"I'm okay. Just . . . you know, the usual. But you're probably already at your client's place, huh?" Camelia said.

"Yeah, I need to go. Call me on Sunday and let's catch up, okay?"

The two old friends said their goodbyes and Camelia turned back to her computer screen.

Since the *situation* with Josh Campbell, Camelia had not given much thought about the events of the holidays. But now, after talking to Rita, Auntie Freda's death and the Christmas fiasco was again at the top of her mind. After Auntie Freda died, Rita's younger sister, Kenna Shores, and Kenna's son, Mickey Shores, had been arrested for drug trafficking. No thanks to Camelia and Dave Becker discovering a cache of drugs in Auntie Freda's garage.

Curious about the details she didn't dare ask of Rita, Camelia wiggled her mouse and did a quick search. The first story to pop up was dated just a couple of weeks ago.

Regina Realtor Sentenced to 8 Years for Fentanyl Ring

Camelia skimmed the article. Mickey plead guilty. That's why it happened so fast. So why hadn't Rita called? Or, for that matter, anyone else in the family?

Just as a tiny stab of indignation began to rise, it was kicked back down the stairs by a flash of shame. Of course, Rita and the rest of them didn't contact her. Camelia's persistence was the only reason there was an arrest and a trial. No one in the family was particularly grateful that she'd figured out how Auntie Freda died, and they were sure as hell not happy when she'd turned Mickey's stash of fake fentanyl over to the RCMP. It was weird, because she'd always considered her relatives to be upright, law-abiding citizens. Somewhat morally superior. Above the fray. But the façade quickly fell apart when it was one of their own breaking the law. For some of them, at least, their virtue only applied to culprits outside the family.

She skimmed the next couple of articles, but they were older, and the information was no longer relevant.

Eight years. Eight measly fucking years.

As far as she was concerned, the punishment was a slap on the wrist considering Mickey's fake fentanyl had—accidentally or not—killed Auntie Freda. Or, if that wasn't *exactly* what killed her, it sure as hell contributed to her death. And almost killed Kenna in the process.

Camelia sighed. Maybe the length of the sentence didn't matter in the long run. Maybe what really mattered was that Mickey and his dealer buddy, Andy Yin, had been caught, their stash of deadly drugs confiscated, and they were going to prison. But based on what she knew of the two of them, they'd probably just learn to be better criminals while serving their time. Assuming, of course, Mickey kept his smart mouth shut, because that could get him into *real* trouble with his fellow inmates.

It was a stark reminder. These were the kind of people she'd be dealing with, day in, day out, if she left the firm to offer investigative services. Was she really up for hobnobbing with idiots and gangsters?

What the hell am I thinking?

She remembered something Leon said after Auntie Freda's memorial, when she'd first brought up leaving the firm. He asked how she would handle it when the bad guys got away with their crimes. Leon knew her only too well. Knew how Camelia bridled at the uneven hand of justice, how lots of criminals are never caught, or get off scot free on a technicality. And now, with just a few months to plan her transition, she realized it was her weak spot. Just like she'd underestimated Joshua Campbell's desperation, that naïve, ridiculous idealism would be what tripped her up every time. It was the thing that would rip her heart out and leave bitter cynicism in its place.

If I let it.

But wasn't she already cynical? And if she was in charge of her own client base, couldn't she pick and choose who she dealt with? Wouldn't she be able to devote her time to people she *wanted* to represent instead of a bunch of clients she was *told* to work with?

Leon had encouraged her to leave the firm, to find another way to practice law. When she balked, he said *everything is out of reach unless you plan for it*. He wasn't wrong. The only antidote to her fear of stepping out on her own was careful planning.

She opened a document on her computer and started typing. It was a brain dump, random notes about everything to be accomplished before she could actually leave McCaffrey Rhodes & Rodriguez. When she finished typing, she looked back over what she'd written. The sheer volume of details was overwhelming.

Dov Saminski had just dropped Aaron at the office after a meeting when Jim Frost's assistant called his mobile.

"Hey Dov. Any chance you can pick up Jim and Dave from Phoenix Country Club? They were out wooing a new client and neither of them are fit to drive," she said.

"Sure, I'll head over now. You can let them know I'll wait out front. Do I need to arrange to have their cars picked up?" Dov hoped not, but knowing them, he'd be ferrying vehicles for a couple of hours.

"They didn't ask, so I guess that's a no," she said. "Thanks, Dov!"

The Phoenix Country Club wasn't far from the office, but the Friday afternoon traffic snarl was already underway, and it took longer than it should have. When he finally pulled up in front of the Club, Jim Frost and David Weisman were laughing and shaking hands with three others. Most of their clients were corporate types, business owners, and CEOs, but that group couldn't have looked more like lawyers if they'd tried. And no one had asked Dov to run a background check, which he *always* did for new clients. It made him wonder if these were clients at all, or more likely just a group of lawyer buddies cozying up for a drunk afternoon on the firm's dime.

With a friendly wave, Jim and Dave bounced over to the town car, sliding in on fumes of wine and cigars.

"Good afternoon, gentlemen," Dov said. "Back to the office?"

"Nah, we're done for today. Can you drop us at my place?" Jim asked.

Dov pulled away from the curb. "Sure. And buckle up, please."

At first, the two men were silent, quietly checking their phones. But after a few minutes of grinding through rush hour traffic, Dave leaned over and spoke in a low voice to Jim.

"It all sounds great on paper, but how are we going to convince the missus to join us?" Dave said.

Dov heard the slur in his words and was relieved to be driving them home. Because if they got busted for DUI, he'd be driving them *everywhere*.

"I can handle her," Jim said. "I've known her a long time, and we have a good rapport. Besides, she's probably ready to stick a knife in him even more than we are."

"If you can play up the benefits, especially the instant payout for her shares, I can't imagine she'd say no. It would streamline the divorce, that's for sure," Dave said.

Even though his senses were on high alert, Dov always pretended to be part of the background. But at the mention of a divorce, he knew who the missus was: Suzanne. He strained to hear more.

"She's a smart woman, and rumor has it she's every bit as pissed off about that charity as we are," Jim said. "I don't think it will be as hard a sell as you might think. And I can always put Ginny on her. She's pretty persistent when she wants something, and god knows she wants this deal to go through."

Dave sighed. "Yeah, I guess. But this whole thing has me pretty puckered if I'm honest. Because if word gets out—"

"It won't. You heard what Eileen said. We're ninety percent there." Jim laughed. "Let's finish debriefing at my place."

"Gotcha," Dave said, and went back to scrolling on his phone.

Dov's eyes were on the road but his mind was darting around, gathering up the bits of intel the two senior partners had just dropped. He could tell something big was going on, but what were these two up to that was so hush hush? And who were those other attorneys at the Club?

More importantly, why would they involve Suzanne?

All Chris Fischer could think about was watching everyone leave the office so he could put the next step of his plan into play. He drank a soda and ate half a bag of chips, updated his profile on LinkedIn, surfed Instagram, and balanced his checking account. A few minutes after 8 p.m., he walked down the hall, checking to see who was still around. He hoped it was just him and Jeff Petronelli, his only true friend, remaining. Sure enough, Jeff was in his office.

He tapped on Jeff's door frame. "Yo, man. It's getting late. You ready to head out?"

Jeff's head popped up, obviously startled. "Dude. I'm starving and thirsty as hell," he said with a laugh.

"Same. Give me a minute to pack up," Chris said.

"Are we the last ones?" Jeff started tidying his desk.

"Yep. Balvinder left a few minutes ago."

Jeff called out as Chris walked away. "Two minutes!"

Chris walked swiftly back to his office, shut down his computer, placed his phone and key card out of sight, and grabbed his jacket and briefcase.

"Let's roll," Jeff said as he walked past Chris's office.

"I'll call the elevator, if you wanna get the alarm," Chris said as he caught up to Jeff.

"Deal."

Chris watched as Jeff paused to swipe his key card and set the alarm before joining Chris at the bank of elevators. When the elevator arrived, Chris fished in his pants pockets, then smacked his palm against his forehead.

"Aw shit, I forgot my phone. Hold the elevator, and I'll be right back." Chris wondered if he sounded natural, because to his own ears he sounded like a community theatre dropout. He tapped his jacket pockets. "Even worse, I don't have my key card."

"And here I thought you were ready. You're as bad as Rachel," Jeff said, shaking his head. "Here's my card. And hurry up. I'm starving."

Swapping key cards with Jeff might be overkill, but it would allow Chris to come and go without the Fischer name popping up when it shouldn't be.

"You got it," Chris said as he turned away. He disarmed the alarm, unlocked the door, ran back to his office, grabbed his phone and key card, tucked Jeff's key card in his pocket, and jogged back to the lobby.

"Thanks, man, just let me set the alarm," Chris called out to Jeff. As he entered the elevator, he handed Jeff his own key card. "Here you go."

It was so easy.

The two men rode the elevator down to the parking garage, chatting about the new pitcher for the Diamondbacks. When the elevator doors opened, Chris stepped out.

"I'll be right behind you. First one there orders the beer?"

"You got it," Jeff said over his shoulder as he walked to his car. "See you in a few."

Chris waited and, when Jeff rolled past, he tapped his horn and pulled slowly out behind him. He was so proud of thinking of every detail.

This was going to be a perfect crime.

28

ROLLING STOP

MONDAY, MARCH 7

After a weekend of tiptoeing around the liquor cabinet and pretending she wasn't feeling the full brunt of sobriety, Camelia was relieved to be back at work. At least at the office she could put her own life on the shelf while she dealt with other people's wrecked marriages and tit-for-tat custody battles. She was in the midst of hammering out a terse response to opposing counsel's stingy settlement offer in one of her cases when Cate tapped on her door.

"Sorry to interrupt, but Suzanne Anders is on line three, if you have time to talk to her," she said.

"Any idea what it's about?"

"She's just checking in to see if we got a ruling on her estate plan and where we are with the Motion on the charitable trust," Cate said.

"I told her we hadn't received a ruling on either one, but I think she wants to hear it from you."

"Let me pull up the case docket now to see if anything new has landed, and I'll be with her in a minute," Camelia said.

Cate walked out and Camelia could hear her relaying the message to Suzanne on the phone.

Camelia scrolled through the online docket, but there were no new rulings, either on the estate plan, life insurance beneficiaries, or on her Emergency Motion to Stay Transfer of Community Funds, intended to block Aaron Anders from robbing the firm's retirement savings in the name of his newfound cancer charity.

She picked up her handset and stabbed the blinking button.

"Suzanne, welcome back. How was Sedona?" Camelia asked.

"Oh, Cam, it was exactly what we needed as a family," Suzanne said. "And the weather was perfect, so we spent every day hiking up in the red rocks, taking a ton of photos. Even with the hard conversations, it was probably the best time we've ever had together. It's amazing how much I enjoy my kids when their father isn't around."

As Suzanne relayed the highlights of her Sedona weekend, Camelia searched her inbox for any new emails from the Court, even though she knew it was too soon to expect a ruling.

"And now that the kids know about my diagnosis and their father's ridiculous *charity*," Suzanne said. "They're feeling betrayed. And not a little pissed off, too."

"That's understandable. They love their mother and no doubt expected a bit more compassion from their father," Camelia said. "I've looked through the docket, and nothing new was posted today. I filed the Motion immediately after the hearing, but it was only two weeks ago. I'm not surprised Judge Bailey hasn't posted his decisions yet."

"I figured as much. It's just . . ." Suzanne sighed. "Is there any way to speed up the judge? I mean, he knows I don't have a lot of time, right?"

Camelia's breath caught in her throat at Suzanne's blunt concession. "I called Judge Bailey's judicial assistant on Friday, and she said it was on the judge's desk, but I don't know how deep that pile is. I'll let you know as soon as I hear, okay?"

"Of course, thank you. I'm just trying to get everything sorted before . . ." Suzanne heaved another sigh. "Before I have to rely on others to do things. And I have no way of knowing how soon that might be."

Camelia's eyes burned with tears. She cleared her throat.

"Oh, Suzanne . . . I'm so sorry. And I'm on it. I'll call you back," Camelia said, as she hung up.

She buzzed Cate. "Can you get Judge Bailey's JA on the line, please?"

"I can try! Their phones are always jammed, but I'll put her through if I can reach her," Cate said.

Camelia was tapping her nails on the desk when Cate transferred the call. After giving the judicial assistant the case number, she asked about the pending rulings.

"Sorry, Ms. Belmont, but Judge Bailey hasn't had a chance to rule on either Mr. Ashcroft's Emergency Motion or your Motion for a Stay. He did deny the respondent's Motion to Transfer the Case to Conciliation Court, though."

"Well, that's something, I guess. Any idea when he might have a chance to work on the other two?" Camelia asked.

"Sorry, but it might be a couple of weeks yet. We're swamped and there's a judicial conference all next week."

Camelia thanked the JA and hung up. Anders was going to get his way without even trying because even a simple divorce could easily take a year. But Suzanne didn't have a simple divorce and she didn't have a year, either. Hell, she might not even have six months. And there was *nothing* Camelia could do to deliver the *one thing* she wanted most before she died: a divorce.

Camelia stood up, slipped into her suit jacket, and walked down the hall. She pushed open the heavy bathroom door and did a quick sweep of the room.

Empty.

She entered the handicap stall at the far end and latched the door. She shoved her hand down to the bottom of her blazer pocket and pulled out her copper flask. Her emotional support flask. The one she'd almost thrown away.

Almost, but hadn't.

That happy hour with Fiona and Amanda had set her back. Way back. To the starting line.

Again.

She toyed with the flask before putting it back in her pocket. She exited the stall and stood at the long counter, washing her hands. But then, she paused at the door.

I'll stop tomorrow.

After all, what's one more day?

She turned on her heel and went back into the end stall, latching the door before she unscrewed the cap. Camelia tipped the flask back, letting the cool liquid flow down her throat. The burn at the end felt so good. It was like the essence of the vodka, the spirit of the spirits—she smirked at her own play on words—was burning away all her grief and shame and anxiety. All her worries evaporated on the fumes of vodka.

Camelia washed her hands, fluffed her hair, and walked back to her office. She had focus and purpose now. She would call the JA back, disclose what she had to, and beg for a ruling. Then, Suzanne would be able to breathe again.

And maybe, so will I.

29

REVELATIONS

WEDNESDAY, MARCH 16

Suzanne was just finishing her morning smoothie—a disgusting concoction prescribed by her new oncologist—when her phone rang. She was so shocked at the caller ID that she picked up immediately.

"Jim? Is everything okay?" She could count on one hand the number of times Jim Frost had called her. His wife, Ginny, was always the one to make the social arrangements.

"Good morning, Suzanne," Jim said. "Yes, everything's fine. Didn't mean to startle you. Is this a good time? I just need a few minutes."

"Of course. What's on your mind?"

"I wanted to talk to you about this charity thing Aaron's working on, along with some firm business."

Suzanne let loose the breath she'd been holding. "Oh that. I don't know much about it, but my lawyer's looking into it. And in case you're wondering, I had nothing to do with it and I think it's BS."

"That's a relief, because it was a surprise to us, too. But there are some other issues, as well . . ." Jim's voice trailed off.

"What kind of issues? Because you know I've never been involved in the day-to-day of the firm." Suzanne sipped her muddy green smoothie.

"Issues like . . . well, forgive me for being blunt. Because of your divorce, there's a business valuation in process."

"Yes? That comes with the territory," Suzanne said.

"Of course. But we think . . . we're concerned that the valuation may come in low, which devalues all our shares." Jim sighed. "And we're not getting any younger, are we Suze? I mean, I'd like to actually retire one of these days."

"What makes you think the valuation will come in low? I thought the financials were in pretty good shape," Suzanne said.

"They were, until Aaron set up that charitable trust. He intends to fund it using our deferred compensation. Anything Aaron does with those funds, like moving them out of the designated savings account, has a direct impact on the value of the firm."

"In other words, Aaron's funding the charity with your money, taking it off the books, which immediately makes your shares in the firm worth less."

"Yeah, that's the bottom line. Now, before you get the wrong idea, we *all* support you, Suzanne. And if you needed a dollar, we'd give you five. But to make a *public announcement*, and to pledge our *deferred comp* to the charity . . . it's not what we signed up for." Jim's laugh was bitter. "Ya gotta hand it to Aaron, though. He sure knows how to get us all puckered up and sweating bullets."

"It's his gift," Suzanne agreed, her own voice edged with sarcasm. "And I get it, Jim. But if you're asking me to have a word with Aaron—"

"Oh, no, no, no. That's not at *all* why I'm calling. The truth is, we're *done* talking to Aaron. We want to talk to *you*, Suzanne."

"Who's *we?*"

"The senior partners. Well, except Aaron. We're having a shareholder meeting this evening at my house, and we want you there. I know it's short notice, but we just got the call . . . we're going to vote on a proposal, but it's no good unless you're with us," Jim said. "Frankly, we need you for a majority."

"Okay, I'm sorry, but you're not making a damn bit of sense right now." Suzanne was thoroughly confused. "I'm not a *partner* so I can't vote."

There was a long pause before, finally, Jim spoke again. "Suzanne, you've been voting by proxy for a couple of years now."

"*What?* What the hell are you talking about?" Jim had to be mistaken. "I don't own any shares of the firm, so I couldn't have voted, even by proxy."

"But you *are* a shareholder. I can't believe Aaron didn't tell you. Jesus." Jim sighed. "A couple of years ago, the statutes changed, allowing non-attorneys to own shares in law firms. At that time, Aaron owned sixty percent. But right away, he put twenty percent of the firm's shares in your name. It was an outright grant, no vesting schedule. Very smart tax move, actually. And we all assumed you knew, because your signature was on the proxy form every quarter when Aaron exercised your vote."

Suzanne rifled through her memory. She vaguely recalled Aaron shoving a handful of blank forms in front of her, demanding her signature. It was before their big blowup, before he moved into the casita. Aaron said the forms were related to one of their investment stocks, and she'd just whipped out a pen and signed the whole stack without another thought. Like she'd done so many times in the past.

"But isn't Aaron still the *de facto* majority shareholder?" Suzanne asked.

"Not without your shares, Suze. He holds forty percent. The rest of us senior partners hold forty percent collectively. You hold the remaining twenty percent—"

"Jim, this is all news to me." Suzanne tried to make sense of what he was telling her. "That sonofabitch never mentioned anything about this." She slammed the gross smoothie on the counter.

"Well, I'm telling you now. Because," Jim inhaled. "We'd like to pitch a proposal to you tonight. If you're up for it."

She didn't respond. Her mind was whirling. She'd need her business attorney present for something like this, but could she convince him to show up on such short notice?

"And, in case I wasn't clear, Aaron doesn't know about this meeting, and we would like to keep it that way," he added.

That was just fine by her.

"I see. And exactly what are *we* voting on tonight?"

"It's the kind of thing you need to hear, and see, in person. I'm not trying to be dodgy, but Dave has a whole presentation for you. You know how he is. Mr. PowerPoint. And here's my pledge. If you agree to come, you can ask any questions you want, and we will answer them as truthfully and completely as we are able. You can withhold your vote if you don't like the proposal. And, of course, you can leave at any time," Jim said. "Just, please, come hear what we have to say. No obligation and completely confidential."

Suzanne could feel her pulse quickening. She was furious with Aaron for duping her yet again. And she'd love to know how she'd voted at all those meetings. But this clandestine invitation made her nervous as hell. The senior partners were no better than Aaron as far as she was concerned, and she had to assume she would be walking into a viper's nest if she attended. But it also sounded like an opportunity she shouldn't let slide, even if it was just to see what they were up to.

"What time should I be there, Jim?" Suzanne said. "And I'll warn you now, if he's free, I'll be bringing Barry Solomon, my business attorney."

Jim chuckled. "We wouldn't have it any other way."

After a tedious day of trying to focus on work, Chris left the office with one more task in mind before the annual firm gala. It was just days away, and tonight was his opportunity to inspect Kaitlyn's laptop, see what she and Aaron had planned for Saturday night. He knew they were up to something because she'd tried to get him to go in on a group limo with some other associates, which was definitely not her style. When he told her he couldn't commit to the limo because he'd volunteered to be the DD for the Petronellis, he'd watched relief wash over her face. But then, when she encouraged him to spend the night at Jeff's rather than drive all the way back to Tempe after dropping his friends off, he knew. Kaitlyn was definitely planning a hookup with Anders.

When he pulled into the garage, Kaitlyn's side was empty. She'd said she was going to some Arizona Women Lawyers thing which meant she'd roll in after eleven, tipsy on wine. If she wasn't lying about that, too. More likely she was straddling Anders right about now. A flicker of jealousy kindled a little flare of rage and he forcefully slammed the door as he entered the dark, silent townhouse.

After changing into sweats and a t-shirt, Chris poured himself a beer, pulled up a stool to the kitchen island, and popped Kaitlyn's laptop open. He typed in kittyhawk84, the password she used for everything. It didn't work. He tried again. It still didn't work.

He typed in 84kittyhawk and the display opened to her home screen. Jeez, she was dumb. She probably thought all her shit was safe because she 'changed' her password. As if no one would be able to crack her code. Then it occurred to Chris that, since he was the only person with access to her laptop, she'd changed the password to lock him out. Ha!

Nice try.

Her chat app was in the system tray, and it didn't take long to find a thread called *Lion's Den*. Unlike all the other group chats between her and her friends, there were only two members of that channel: Kaitlyn and someone called Ace. Close enough. At first glance, the messages looked pretty bland. Boring even. But then he noticed the pattern. They were talking in code.

Meetings.

Discussing reports.

Drafting motions.

Not that hard to figure out what it all meant.

Chris thought about packing a bag and walking out on his cheating wife right that minute. He took a deep breath. No. He wouldn't get all huffy and storm out. Not before he completed his mission. Plus, quarterly bonuses wouldn't be reconciled and paid until the first week of April. Based on the firm formula, between the two of them, Chris and Kaitlyn would be receiving a nice, fat check. And it was all community property. Money he was going to need for a fresh start without her.

He turned his attention back to an exchange yesterday.

KF: Meeting after the firm event?

A: If you want to discuss the reports, sure. Transportation sorted?

KF: C is DD for the JeffP and I'll have his car. I can meet any time after your motion.

A: You should prepare for the meeting ahead of time. I will arrive when you've had time to review.

KF: I'll wave on my way out.

A: I'll be right behind you. ☺

KF: You wish! xoxo

God, she was a shameless, lying whore. And so was Anders. Just by being so obvious, though, they were making this a lot easier on Chris's conscience.

He took a photo of the screen then shut the app. As he was about to close her laptop, he remembered the flash drive in that folder Kaitlyn brought home a few weeks ago.

Why the hell did she have that Sheridan exhibit file, anyway? That godawful case had been closed for years, which was why seeing it in their bedroom closet had fired up his curiosity. While Kaitlyn was in the shower washing off whatever sins she'd committed earlier, he'd grabbed the traffic device and flash drive in a fit of anger. Chris knew that if Anders—or even worse, Janice—realized Kaitlyn had lost those exhibits, she'd be in a world of hurt. But why had she been carrying it around in the first place?

He jogged down the hall to the garage and opened his gun safe. There, in the back, behind the hunting rifles he no longer used, was the device, safely wrapped in plastic and stuffed in a canvas ammo bag, along with the flash drive that had been in the folder.

Chris walked back to the kitchen and plugged the drive into Kaitlyn's computer. On the list of files there were a couple of Sheridan exhibit documents and one titled *Sheridan Gambit*. The date on the file was January 26 of this year.

What the hell was that about? No one had worked on the case in ages, and he would sure as hell remember if a word as unusual as 'gambit' had been thrown around during trial. He clicked opened the document and began to read, but the bullet points didn't make sense: a man's name, a phone number, a date, a gas station, a dollar amount, time, and intersection. He read it again.

The Sheridan Gambit

- ✓ Berto G
- ✓ 602-825-2332
- Sat 03/19
- Chevron @ Glendale/16th mens room in tank
- $10,000 half before / half after
- midnight approx. text @15 min
- Tatum / Lincoln

What did make sense is that Kaitlyn had made a list, because she was compulsive about it. She made lists for everything: planning her day, meals, vacations, and especially her cases. Said it gave her a sense of accomplishment to check everything off, but Chris figured she just wasn't smart enough to retain the information. So what, exactly, was she checking off this time? And who was Berto G?

Chris read through the list again and again.

A cold horror swept through his limbs as he realized what he was looking at. If it had to do with that device . . . it was a plan, a script, a blueprint for death. And who would Kaitlyn want dead more than her interfering husband? As for the timing? It was perfect. She wouldn't have to share her fat bonus with him if he was dead and gone. Hell, she'd get his bonus too!

Fucking heartless bitch.

He couldn't believe it, yet it was all right there, in writing. Was Kaitlyn really going to use the faulty traffic preemption decoder to cover up a fatal accident? Was that what her cryptic notes meant? As his eyes skimmed the list over and over, he began to fill in the blanks.

$10,000. Chris felt sick as the realization came to him. That's what it would cost to kill him. And all this Berto guy had to do was push a button to get a green light, then crash into his car. It would look like Chris was at fault.

Sat 03/19. The date of the AndersLaw annual gala. Of course. Everyone would just think it was an accident; he'd drank too much and ran a red light.

Lincoln and Tatum. If Kaitlyn had her way, Chris would die just blocks from the Paradise Valley Country Club.

Even Chris had to admit it was a pretty clever scheme. He glanced back at the date the document was created. At the time, Kaitlyn hadn't known Chris would be driving the Petronellis home. But she knew now. Would she have gone through with it anyway? He couldn't imagine she would do such a thing, but then he never would have imagined she'd plan to kill him, either.

Well, she wasn't going to get away with it, was she? He laughed, but it came out as a dry *huh-huh-huh.* He had the device. He had her list. She couldn't get rid of him that easily. And, now that he knew what she was up to, he'd make damn sure she got a dose of her own medicine. He was in control now.

Chris tried to shake off the revulsion, the rage, and the hot prickle of humiliation that his discovery brought. But the idea was already thrumming in his mind, the image of a plan quickly forming. He knew what he had to do, and he would not hesitate.

Not for a fucking second.

30

U-TURN AHEAD

SATURDAY, MARCH 19, 5:35 PM

As he made his way to the Paradise Valley Country Club for the AndersLaw Annual Firm Gala, Dov Saminski's thoughts turned to a cherished memory. It was a few years back, at another black tie event, much like the one he was headed to this evening.

Suzanne had twisted her ankle coming down the stairs in a pair of sky high Jimmy Choos. She'd laughed at herself when she asked Dov to drive her home early. *What was I thinking wearing these death traps?* He remembered her clinging to his arm as she limped to the car in her heels, her ankle already twice its usual size. When they arrived at the Anders' Paradise Valley house, she couldn't put weight on it. She threw one arm around his neck for stability. Without thinking, he bent down and scooped Suzanne into his arms. She threw her head back and let loose a deep, throaty, laugh. That deadly sexy laugh. When he set her down inside the back door, her arm lingered around his neck for a moment and their eyes met. Dov could feel the electrical charge between them, saw the look in her eyes and then . . . she pulled away and stepped back.

He sighed at the recollection.

That's when I should have left town.

Dov was 38 years old when he landed the contract with Aaron five years ago. He was a perfect fit for the demands of the firm and its very finicky owner: no ties, no commitments, no Mrs. Saminski, no daycare drop offs.

Then, a couple of months into the job, Dov met Suzanne Anders.

Her dark wavy hair, sea blue eyes, and teasing smile were a beam of warmth hitting him in the heart. She was Arizona sunshine on a winter day. Sure, she was more than a decade older than him, but Saminski didn't care. He worshipped her. He loved her laugh and her ankles and the way her hair swung on her neck. He loved the way she looked at him. *Really* looked at him. As if he were the most interesting man on earth. He loved her husky voice, murmuring in the dim hush of the car. And the way she smelled, the fragrance of her perfume lingering, wafting around him all the way home. She was way out of his league, and *completely* off limits, and he wished none of that mattered as much as it did.

Ever since Suzanne called him this morning, he realized he hadn't been honest with himself. Or her. And those feelings were creating the type of moral conflict he wasn't used to dealing with. So much of his life had been black or white, right or wrong. But this . . . this was right *and* wrong.

He powered his window down, letting the dry desert air wash over him.

This mild March evening was paradise compared to growing up under the howling Hawk, the brutal wind that barreled across Lake

Michigan, down the alleys of Chicago, and right through the second-hand clothes he'd worn as a kid. But Saminski didn't wear thrift store hand-me-downs any more. That fat AndersLaw paycheck made it easy for him to wear much nicer clothes. And it smoothed over some of the more questionable tasks requested of him. Like a good little soldier, Dov never batted an eye or asked questions.

Until now.

He'd known pretty much from the get go that Aaron was whoring around, but it went with the territory. He knew the type of guy he worked for and, at first, he just looked the other way, kept things discreet, tidied up after Aaron. It wasn't his job to judge.

But as he got to know Suzanne, and saw the flicker of pain in her eyes when Aaron sent her home while he stayed behind, it rankled. Now he was in a true double bind: he wanted to walk away from the job because Anders was such a jerk, but if he did, he would probably never see Suzanne again.

Would she even notice?

But whether Suzanne would notice his absence or not, the whole situation was already unbearable, even before Anders called him in for a chat the previous Monday. And that's when Dov knew he had to make a decision.

"Have a seat, Dov," Aaron said, his elbows on the desk, looking oddly relaxed. "I know you overhear things, so I thought I'd clear the air. I don't want any misunderstandings."

"You know me, boss," Dov said. "Hear no evil."

Anders smirked. "What you'll hear is that Suzanne has cancer and she's insisting on a divorce." Anders straightened in his chair. "It's a touchy situation at the moment, so I want you to steer clear of Mrs. Anders. She's not on the payroll, so she won't be getting the royal treatment from us anymore, understood? No driving her around to her doctor appointments or yoga or what have you, no running her errands or doing her bidding. Period. She's cut off."

Dov had never been one to display his emotions, but he'd had to work to keep the sneer of disgust from his face.

You fucking asshole.

He'd left the meeting as quickly as he could, seething at Anders' cold treatment of Suzanne. Dov wasn't sure what, if anything, he could do about it, but the edict stuck in his throat for days. All he knew for sure was that his next move had to be the right one. For Suzanne.

He hadn't even figured out what that *right move* might be when, just this morning, Suzanne called to ask if he could give her a ride to the firm gala.

Not ready to show his hand just yet, he made an excuse. "I'm sorry, Suzanne. I'm on duty for the firm event. But I'm happy to send someone from my team to pick you up."

"I appreciate it, but that's okay. I was just hoping . . ." Suzanne paused, sighed. "Totally understandable under the circumstances. I'll find my own way, Dov. Thanks." Her tone had cooled.

"Circumstances?" Dov asked.

"The situation between Aaron and me. I mean, we're in the middle of a divorce, and . . ." Suzanne paused. "Well, you're *his* man. Not mine. So, it's best if I keep to myself. Nothing personal, Dov. You know that."

Nothing personal.

Except it was *all* personal.

He knew he didn't have a snowball's chance in hell with a woman like her, but if not for Suzanne, Dov would have left long ago. He had enough savings, and was fed up with Anders' relentless need for approval, along with his demands for increasingly shady—if not illegal, then certainly unethical—*missions*, as he called them. Saminski snorted. As if a guy like Anders would have the first clue about a mission.

This job is worthless without her.

Of course, the job was worthless anyway, because Anders was off the rails. Even though Kaitlyn was on her way out, Dov could see how careless Anders had become around her. She already knew way more about his dealings than she should have, including firm matters that were none of her damn business and way above her pay grade. Dov had tried to warn Aaron that Kaitlyn was different from his other side pieces. She was a clever attorney with big ambitions—but lean on ethics—making her a dangerous adversary. But Anders ignored him.

It was like that idiotic land deal. Dov had warned him about that, too. Nothing good ever came out of investing with the Saudis. But no, Anders had it all figured out. Until it fell apart. His boss was long past listening to anyone about *anything* these days, including who he should—and, more importantly, should *not*—be getting into bed with, literally and figuratively. Lately, Anders had gone so far as to relegate Dov to duties more fitting a chauffeur and errand boy than Chief Security Officer. Not that Dov gave a shit about any of that, as long as he still got paid.

But what Suzanne had said? That bothered him. A lot. Her words still rang in his ears.

You're his man, not mine.

He rolled his shoulders. It stung, because she was right. He'd covered up countless trysts for Aaron, so what else would she think? Suzanne wasn't stupid. She knew he'd been Anders' right hand this whole time, doing his bidding, at his beck and call, day or night. Cleaning up his messes—and there were a *lot* of messes. That's what the security contract called for. That was the promise he'd made. And that's why he was pulling in $175k a year. She must think he was pandering for Aaron solely for the sake of that paycheck. What Suzanne didn't know was the only reason he was still on the job was to spend time with her a few times a month.

Being *Anders' man* was not at all who Dov wanted to be. He wanted to be the man who escorted Suzanne home *every* night. He shook his head. He needed to make a stand, once and for all.

The vague ideas that had been floating around in his mind since that meeting with Anders began to coalesce. If he could expose Anders' affair with Kaitlyn Fischer, give Suzanne something to use in the divorce proceedings, she would realize Dov was *her* man, not Aaron's. The bonus would be Anders getting a big dose of payback for the way he'd been treating Suzanne. If he avenged her, though, Dov Saminski would lose his contract and maybe even get sued.

And he didn't give a good goddamn either way.

As he pulled into the Paradise Valley Country Club, Dov did a quick scan of the parking lot. It was almost deserted, which is exactly what he was counting on. The afternoon golfers would be long gone, and the AndersLaw guests wouldn't be here for another hour. He liked the idea of a clean slate before the party started: no lingering drunk-ass golf bro getting obnoxious because the Club was closed for a private party. No loose ends.

Now, all Saminski had to do was check in with his temporary team, two guys and a woman he'd hired to supplement the Country Club security staff. He liked having his own people around him at these affairs, and this group was a tight one. Ex-military, easy to lead, fairly well disciplined.

They would be working the party undercover because, as Saminski had learned the hard way, there were always pickpocket waiters, bartenders selling roofied drinks, or a pro turning tricks in the locker room at this kind of private event. His job was to make sure no one from AndersLaw embarrassed themselves, or Suzanne, or—god forbid—Aaron.

After going over their assignments and testing their team phones, Saminski stepped outside, to the back of the Club. He paced the length of the loggia where clusters of tables were set up. Beyond the vast greenways of the golf course, pink mountains glowed in the sunset. From a security standpoint, it wasn't ideal. Anyone with bad intentions could come at them from anywhere on the course. But from an aesthetic point of view, it was sublime. He paused for a moment to appreciate the dense greens rolling away from the patio, pushing up close to the rocky slopes in the near distance. He rolled his shoulders inside his tailored grey suit jacket.

Show time.

Guests had begun to arrive, huddling together near the bars on the patio, excited laughter rising above the hum.

Saminski did what he always did: observe.

31

THE MICKEY ALIBI

SATURDAY, MARCH 19, 5:49 PM

Chris Fischer was distracted by his own ruminating thoughts as he slapped on some cologne. Tonight would be the first time he and Kaitlyn would be face to face with Aaron and Suzanne Anders since he'd caught his wife and boss pawing each other in the conference room. Chris wondered how Kaitlyn would react. Would she be cool, contrite, or brazen? Not that he cared. Not anymore.

Stepping into the walk-in closet, he slipped on a pair of boxers and scanned the selection of neatly rolled ties in his drawer. He must have thirty, all muted shades of grey, gold, and blue, except for one wildly patterned Mickey Mouse tie his nephew had proudly presented to him for law school graduation. Chris smiled to himself. No one at the party would forget that tie.

He wrapped himself in his robe before walking down the hall to the kitchen. Kaitlyn was already there in bra and Spanx, makeup done, her hair wrapped around giant rollers, pre-gaming for the AndersLaw annual firm gala this evening. She sipped a glass of wine as she tapped her perfect French manicure on her phone screen.

Chris slid onto the barstool next to hers and poured himself some wine.

"We need to leave in about a half hour."

Kaitlyn drained her wine glass. "I'm so excited. It's going to be a great party!"

He shrugged. "I guess." Chris nodded at her empty wine glass. "Are you sure you aren't going to need a ride home? Because we could just take an Uber."

He watched her face. He'd known his wife long enough to discern her little tells. Like now, when she wouldn't meet his eye, stabbing at Instagram with a glossy nail.

"I'll ease up later. Which I wouldn't have to do if you hadn't volunteered for the good deed of the day." Her eyes glittered with indignation. "You could always back out on Jeff and Rachel."

He poured another splash of wine in his glass. "No, I can't back out. Jeez, Kit. I said I'd be their DD, and they're counting on me for the favor."

"Pretty big favor, if you ask me. They could have left their car here and got a ride with us."

"It doesn't matter if their car is here or at the Club. If they're drinking, they're not gonna be driving," Chris said. "They have *children* to think about."

"Sounds like a Jeff problem," Kaitlyn said. "And since you're the DD, you're the one who better slow down on the wine."

"Just having a snort. Gotta gird my loins for the Aaron Anders Shit Show." Chris sipped the earthy Beaujolais.

"Oh, what*ever*. It's the Suzanne show tonight. She's the *guest of honor*," Kaitlyn said, making air quotes. "More like the poster child for this dumb charity everyone's been scrambling to put together."

He watched as she scrolled social media on her phone, noticing the things she tried so hard to cover with makeup and bravado. Her eyes were puffy and Chris suspected she'd been drinking last night. Again. She didn't get home until after midnight, then slept in the guest room. But this morning, she'd been up early making their smoothies, like she always did. Like nothing had happened. He hadn't confronted her, but Chris had known immediately what was going on. He knew she'd been with Anders by the way she talked too fast, the way her eyes slid away, the way she held her elbows close to her body, as if she would fly apart at any moment.

And now, here she was, chugging that damned expensive French wine, chattering about nonsense. Lying right to his face. A cold fury spread through his chest as the realization that she was stalling settled in. The only reason she hadn't already left him was because she was waiting for Anders to get divorced.

As he watched her uncoiling the last of the rollers from her hair, he was surprised at how quickly desire had turned to revulsion. It soothed him a bit to know he had everything he needed—or he would in a few hours—to take both Anders and Kaitlyn down. He would destroy both of those traitors. And, bonus points, do Suzanne Anders a huge favor at the same time. God only knows how many Kaitlyns she'd had to endure over the years.

Kaitlyn glanced down to the slim gold Cartier watch—his fifth anniversary gift to her—hanging loosely against her wrist. "Shit. We gotta get a move on."

Chris stood and put his wine glass in the sink. "Can you be ready in ten?"

He didn't wait for an answer as he walked down the hall. Was this really how marriages ended? He glanced at the wedding photos on the wall of their bedroom as he passed. Had he ever been as happy as he'd been that day? Kaitlyn's hair was pinned up with a daisy crown and ribbons. She was laughing, radiant. Hadn't she been in love, too? They'd had so many dreams for their life together. What happened to make it all evaporate like so much fairy dust?

Chris heaved a sigh and hung up his robe, then slipped into his best suit, a deep blue Armani that cost more than his first car. His father owned one suit, the dark grey one he wore to weddings and funerals. He would faint if he saw his son's closet.

He tucked a pale blue shirt into his trousers, and held the Mickey Mouse tie up, appraising its artistry. It was the opposite of boring. Yes, this would be perfect. He stood in front of the full length mirror in their bedroom, fiddling with his tie.

"Are you almost ready? We need to leave in about two minutes," Kaitlyn called from the bench at the end of the bed. She slipped her feet into a pair of designer heels with open toes.

"Yep, just perfecting my Windsor knot," Chris said as he turned to face her.

"Mickey Mouse? You're kidding, right? The dress code is black tie, Chris." She rolled her eyes and huffed an impatient sigh.

"No, it's black tie *optional*." He smirked. "So, I'm wearing my best suit."

"That tie is perfect if you're twelve years old and on the debate team. But for an actual *attorney* attending the annual *firm gala*? Uh-uh. Nope." Kaitlyn waved a curl of blond hair over her shoulder.

Chris turned back to the mirror as he smoothed Mickey's head with his palm. "Well, you always complain that I'm too predictable, so . . ."

"You aren't serious! Chris! For real!" Little splotches of color were rising on her cheeks. "You cannot wear that crappy tie to the most important party of the year!"

"I'll have you know this tie is one hundred percent silk." He tugged on his collar and turned back to her. "And I'm one hundred percent going to wear it. Also, the party isn't *that* important, Kit. It's just an excuse to get drunk on free booze and gossip with our co-workers. At least I'm giving them something fun to talk about."

Kaitlyn stood to face Chris, tilting her chin defiantly, her mouth pulled into a taut, disapproving line. He could tell she was desperately swallowing her words.

Chris stepped back and appraised Kaitlyn's outfit. She really was a gorgeous woman. Too bad she was also a lying bitch.

"You look amazing," Chris said. "New dress?"

"Thank you. It's a David Koma. And, unlike you, I'm careful how I dress because I'm interested in furthering my career, not getting demoted to the kids' table." She shook her head as she turned away.

Who is David Coma? And why would she care about dressing to impress if she was setting up Anders for a harassment suit? Liar.

"Hey, my career's just fine. A funny tie won't make or break me." Chris slipped his arms into his suit jacket.

"Fine. Wear whatever you want. It's your reputation on the line." Kaitlyn looked at her watch. "Just hurry up."

"We've got plenty of time. Don't worry so much," Chris said.

"Easy for you to say, *Mickey*. I have a career to manage," she retorted, her heels clicking down the tiled hall toward the garage.

As he accelerated up Highway 51 toward the Paradise Valley Country Club, Chris gripped the steering wheel with clammy hands. He had to focus. One thing at a time. But all he could think about was the risky trick he was going to pull off later. This clandestine stuff was making his stomach roil with nerves, and he felt almost dizzy with adrenaline. But it would all be worth it when the incriminating video footage of Kaitlyn and Anders was in his hot little hands in just a couple of hours. The whole firm would be at the stupid party kissing the ring, fawning over Aaron. And that meant he wouldn't have to worry about Saminski or anyone else walking in on him. His alibi would stick because *everyone* would remember seeing Chris at the party wearing a crazy Mickey Mouse tie.

It's all falling into place.

But Chris had already waited until the last minute and who knew when he would have another chance like this, with literally *everyone* from the firm at the party.

It has to be tonight.

7:05 PM

Dov Saminski turned as Kaitlyn shrieked into focus, leading a pack of already half-drunk associates. He was onto her game. That grasping little bitch thought she was in charge of the affair with Anders, that all those tasty tidbits of valuable information had promoted her, somehow. But Dov knew better. Anders was already getting tired of her. She didn't have much time before he moved on to the next pretty young thing. The only question was, would he be able to slip out of her grip as easily as he had all the others?

And what about Kaitlyn's husband, Chris Fischer? Dov studied the awkward, thin man parked at the bar. Did he have any idea what his wife was up to? He seemed blissfully oblivious, haw-haw-hawing too loudly about something as Jeff Petronelli clapped him on the back.

The firm bumpkins.

Office Bee arrived wearing a floor length dark blue gown with rhinestones framing a plunging neckline; the same one she'd worn every year he'd attended. Saminski smiled to himself. Janice was thrifty with a dollar, but not with the cleavage.

As a rush of guests poured in, Saminski made a loop, keeping his eye trained on Suzanne. Out of everyone here, she was the only one he cared about. By the end of the night, she would know Dov Saminski was his *own* man.

And the Almighty Aaron Anders would just have to get over it.

32

NIGHT MOVES

SATURDAY, MARCH 19, 10:00 PM

The AndersLaw annual firm party was everything Chris Fischer expected. Open bar, too much food, hideous centerpieces they were all expected to bid on, and Aaron Anders at the center of it all. As dinner wound down and the speeches commenced, Chris's heart rate ticked up. He'd seen enough. There was no way to know exactly the best time to slip away, so he excused himself to the relative quiet of the men's room to think it through one more time.

Locked in one of the massive water closets at the Club, he went over the evening in his mind. Even though he hadn't needed more evidence to support his suspicions, Kaitlyn's actions tonight erased any lingering regrets that might have crept in. He'd watched her from the edge of the room, appalled at her shameless behavior. Anyone looking would see how her eyes followed Anders. Occasionally, Kaitlyn and Anders' eyes met, and Chris could see the hunger around her mouth. She used to look at him like that. Chris knew the sizzling frenzy of passion that would follow.

Just not with him.

There was no other way to interpret it. He hadn't been foolish enough to buy into her flimsy story about entrapping Anders in a sexual harassment allegation in order to get a big payout, not for one second. But as for her plot to be free of her husband? Chris hadn't seen that one coming.

He shifted against the water closet wall and tapped his phone. 10:05 p.m. It was now or never.

His salvation was in the Bermuda grass surrounding the Club. Made him wheezy. Even though his lungs were fine right now, his stupid allergies were a handy excuse to get him out of the party the same way it got him out of playing golf with the ass-kissers at the office.

He opened his texts with Kaitlyn and thumb-typed.

> Forgot inhaler, gotta run home and grab it.
> Too much grass.

As soon as it sent, Chris washed his hands and strode purposefully to the front entrance, waving Jeff Petronelli's valet ticket. As soon as he settled in the SUV, he set his stopwatch.

A couple of minutes later, Kaitlyn texted back a thumbs up.

By that time, Chris was already speeding like a maniac to the office towers downtown.

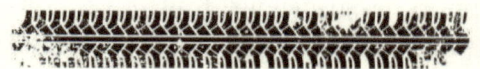

10:26 PM

Chris circled the block until he finally found a spot two streets over. Parking at the office was out of the question. He couldn't risk one of the many security cameras in the parking garage catching sight of him as he donned his flimsy bit of disguise.

He opened the console and pulled out Jeff's amber-tinted sunglasses before stepping out of the car. He walked to the liftgate of the SUV and popped it open, hoping to find Jeff's gym bag. Jeff had a gross habit of wearing the same sweaty gear to the gym all week, swapping it out every Monday for a fresh kit. And, as expected, there it was. Chris rifled through the bag, grabbing a ball cap and a moderately stinky hoodie, two sizes too big. He slipped off his suit coat, laying it neatly in the back cargo area, before pulling the ball cap low on his forehead and carefully zipping the hoodie over his Mickey Mouse tie.

Okay, let's do this!

He jogged down the street just like any guy out for a run. Turning the corner, he entered the parking garage, careful to keep his head down.

Chris pulled out the key card he'd swapped with Jeff a couple of weeks ago. Anyone checking the key log would think Jeff had been in the office. And even if they checked the security video footage, they wouldn't be able to tell who was on camera.

He took the elevator to the office and, swiping Jeff's card, slipped through the door. Pausing at the entrance, Chris held his breath, listening.

The humming silence around him was empty and pure.

He turned on his heel and quickly walked to his office. Unlocking the door, he slipped into his chair and pulled his keyboard close. Chris tapped in his password, then pulled out his phone and scrolled to a note, reading off the file path under his breath. When asked for an admin user name and password, he carefully entered the user name AndersSec1 and the password, which was a string of numerals and symbols followed by the initials DS. Then he held his breath, praying he'd accurately translated Saminski's keystrokes from that shaky bit of video he'd grabbed when he was looking over the Chief Security Officer's shoulder.

The system paused for what seemed like an unreasonably long time. And then . . . he was in.

Jeez. Is it really that easy?

Chris pulled open the top drawer of his desk and grabbed a fresh flash drive emblazoned with the AndersLaw logo, thankful that Office Bee handed out boxes of them like candy. He tapped on the video file from January 9 at 6:12 p.m. and watched as Kaitlyn and Anders entered the conference room. He didn't have the time—or the stomach—to watch, so he closed the file and copied it to the flash drive.

Then, to be doubly sure nothing screwed up, Chris removed that flash drive and inserted another. This time, after copying the video, he opened it on both drives to verify the files had copied and would play. Now that he was sure he had the footage he wanted, he clicked back to the main directory and looked for the lobby camera folder. After deleting the footage of himself entering the office a few minutes ago, Chris referred back to his notes for the step-by-step instructions for removing a file—permanently—from the server. He right clicked to empty the trash, and verified that he wanted to permanently erase the file.

There would be no record that he'd come into the office, and on Monday he could delete the bit of lobby footage of him leaving the office. It was important that no one know he'd been here, but what really mattered was getting rid of that video of Kaitlyn and Anders crawling all over each other. It meant he had total control of the narrative now, and there was nothing either of them could do about it.

He could feel sweat forming on his neck as he checked the time. He'd already been gone over a half an hour and still had one more task to manage. He inserted the flash drive he'd found in the folder Kaitlyn had brought home and clicked on the *Sheridan Gambit* file.

He still wasn't sure what the file name meant, but it damn sure didn't have anything to do with the case, and Chris would know, since he'd been second chair with Anders. When the document opened, he scrolled down to the phone number. Chris pulled a new phone from his pants pocket and dialed.

A man answered on the second ring. "Bueno." He sounded angry.

"Berto? Habla inglés? It's about tonight." Chris hoped the guy spoke English, because if he didn't, this was going to be a short conversation.

"Quién es éste? Who's calling?"

"New team, new phone," Chris said. "We still on for tonight?"

"Kinda late notice, bro. And why the fuck you calling me?"

"Sorry, I—"

"Just drop the gear and cash at the Chevron on Glendale, then text like we said. I need ten, fifteen minutes lead time." Berto hung up.

Chris stared at the phone, silent in his hand. His eyes stung with tears. Until this moment, he realized a little wisp of hope had clung to his heart. But now, everything he'd suspected Kaitlyn of planning had been confirmed.

He hastily texted Berto's number.

Just shake her up. Nothing serious.

Chris glanced at the time. He had to get the hell out of here and back to the party before people started to notice.

He closed Kaitlyn's *Sheridan Gambit* file, automatically hitting *Save* when prompted, then ejected the flash drive. He stood and pocketed the slim phone and the flash drives. Then, he unlocked his credenza and removed the envelope containing the device—he'd smuggled it into the office yesterday—and ten thousand dollars in cash. He locked his office door behind him, and sprinted to the front door. Chris swiped Jeff's card to lock up and, head down, raced for the stairs.

10:39 PM

When he rounded the corner toward Jeff's SUV, Chris froze. A Phoenix cop car was parked at the end of the block, lights flashing. His heart started hammering in time with the red-blue-red-blue-red-blue pulse of the lights. He was panting from the short run, and sweat was dampening his hairline. What if Saminski had some kind of app to access the security cameras remotely, and saw Chris in the lobby? It wasn't out of the question. Could he have called it in already? Would the cops show up this quickly?

Jesus. I gotta stop being paranoid.

Chris walked around to the back of the SUV and opened the liftgate. He pulled the hoodie off and used it to wipe the sweat from his neck and face. Then, he tucked the ball cap and hoodie back in the gym bag, and pressed the button to close the liftgate. Slipping into the driver's seat, he looked in the rearview mirror. His hair was slicked to his head with sweat. As soon as he started the car, Chris turned the AC on full blast. He ran his fingers through his hair and tousled it up a bit so it would dry faster.

Hell, I'm almost James Bond.

Except he was just a farm kid named Christopher.

10:52 PM

Chris raced to the Chevron station at 16th and Glendale, jumped out of the car, and speedwalked to the men's room. He desperately jiggled the door handle. Locked. He exhaled, slowed his breathing, and strolled into the station.

"Key to the men's?" he asked the cashier.

The woman glanced up from her phone and silently passed a key attached to a wooden spoon across the counter. Chris walked back around the corner of the building, unlocked the door and entered the small, brightly lit bathroom. He was supposed to hide the device and half the cash inside the toilet tank. He took the device out of the padded envelope, and wrapped it in a couple of rough, brown paper towels. Then, he dropped the device into a freezer size Ziploc bag, along with five thousand bucks in fifties. Sliding the lid off the tank, he dropped the plastic bag inside and prayed it didn't leak.

Chris grabbed another couple of paper towels to wipe the sweat from his face and exited. After dropping off the key, he jumped back in Jeff's SUV and roared out of the parking lot, heading east on Glendale toward Paradise Valley.

Arriving back at Paradise Valley Country Club, Chris tossed Jeff's car keys to the valet and stopped off at the men's room. He checked his stopwatch. He'd been gone fifty-four minutes and almost set a land-speed record getting to the office and back again. Catching his reflection, he did a double take. His color was high, and his normally neatly parted hair stood up in spiky waves. It didn't look half bad. As he washed his hands, he played with his wedding band.

Time to drop the charade.

Chris dried his hands and dropped the ring in his pocket. He tousled his hair a bit more and added some of the hair product set out on the counter. He undid his top collar button and loosened his tie. Pulling his collar away, he dabbed the sweat off the back of his neck with a paper towel and swished a paper cup of minty mouthwash.

He took one last glance in the mirror. For once, he liked what he saw. He stepped out of the men's room and collided at full speed with—of all people—Suzanne Anders.

"Oh my gosh, are you okay?" Chris said, bending toward her to grasp her shoulders. Suzanne smiled and stepped back as he dropped his hands to his side and his manners kicked in. "I'm so sorry for plowing into you like that, Mrs. Anders. We've met before, but not sure if you remember? Chris Fischer, senior associate." He held out his hand.

She was a beautiful woman, but even more attractive up close. It was her eyes. Their watery blue depth, tinged with humor and curiosity, drew him in. It was like looking into one of those deep, clear lakes back home.

"No harm done and please, call me Suzanne. Nice to meet you, Chris, and I apologize if we've met before. I'm so bad with . . . wait, did you say *Fischer*?" She looked at him more closely. "Yes, I remember now."

Chris was sure she was going to say something else, but she didn't have to. It was all there in her eyes. She knew.

"Anyway, Chris, are you having a good time?"

"It's a great party, Mrs. . . . Suzanne. This might be the best one yet!" Chris offered his right elbow. "May I escort you to the ball, madame?" He winked at her.

Suzanne laughed and affected a drawl. "Why, I'd be delighted, kind sir."

So, this is the woman Anders was cheating on. She was charming, pretty, and obviously intelligent. Anders was a damn fool because, in Chris's mind, trading Suzanne for Kaitlyn was a step down, not up.

As they approached the bar, he paused.

"May I buy you a drink?"

"Oh, no, I'm fine thanks, but you go ahead. I'll see you later," Suzanne said, and continued walking.

As he stepped to the bar, he smiled at the bartender.

"Pinot noir, please," he said, sliding his credit card across the bar.

"Aren't you with the party?" the bartender asked. "The bars outside are fully hosted. Unless you just need to burn some cash."

Chris looked up. The bartender had a wide-eyed, teasing expression, and a smile played around her full mouth. She had one pierced eyebrow and was holding a bottle of wine mid-air, waiting for him to decide.

"Well, I'm here now, so I'll take the wine. But thanks for the heads up."

"I like your tie, by the way."

"Oh, thanks. Thought I'd give the fellas something to live up to." He grinned.

The bartender turned away to pour the wine. Chris caught her looking at him in the mirror behind the bar. She lowered her eyes, smiling.

He self consciously rubbed his bare ring finger.

Kaitlyn wants me gone? So be it.

The bartender placed the glass of wine on the bar, swiped his card, and handed him the receipt.

"Have fun. And I'll be here if you want a refill. Or . . . whatever."

She smiled again. There was no mistaking the invitation.

"Thanks." He could feel his cheeks flush.

Chris headed for the loggia where most of his coworkers were milling about, chatting. A few were still seated, finishing their drinks, discussing work, no doubt. He was headed to the other side of the patio, looking for Kaitlyn, when Jeff intercepted him.

"Dude, where were you?" Jeff looked at him quizzically. "Did you skip out for a haircut? You look . . . different, man."

"Really?" Chris swallowed, hard. Was his whole plan about to go south? "Different how?"

"I don't know. What did you do to your hair?"

"Huh?" Chris reached up with one hand, reflexively ruffling his hair again. "I'm just overheating a bit with all this hot air in the room. Is it messed up?"

"Yeah, but it looks kinda hip." Jeff peered at him through narrowed eyes. "It's more than that, though. You look . . . like somebody hit you with a GQ bomb or something. Stylish, even. Very uncharacteristic," Jeff laughed. "You're making me look bad."

Chris smiled and tipped his glass to Jeff's. "Well, whatever it is, I'll take the compliment. No matter how backhanded."

"That tie though," Jeff said. "You've got balls, bro. I could never get away with it. Rachel would kill me."

"Pretty sure Kaitlyn feels the same, but I figure I can pick my own outfit at least once a year, right?" Chris said, relieved the conversation was back in safe territory. He glanced around the room. "Speaking of the wife, have you seen her around?"

"Nah, all the girls are over by the dance floor."

Which meant Kaitlyn likely hadn't even noticed how long he'd been gone. Chris couldn't believe how well his plan was working out. Turns out, he was a pretty damn good secret agent, after all.

Meanwhile, Jeff was getting wasted on free Scotch and his wallet—with Chris's key card tucked inside—was in his suit jacket, now hanging on the back of his chair.

As for Kaitlyn? She'd played right into his hands.

33

FAREWELL TOUR

SATURDAY, MARCH 19, 11:00 PM

Suzanne always enjoyed a party. Any party, really. Even if attending her scheming husband's annual firm gala meant she had to pretend everything between them was fine, at least she would have an opportunity to see some of the long-term employees—the few she actually liked—one last time. And, even if the silent auction was nothing more than a bunch of over-valued golf weekends and spa packages, at least everyone was having fun, enthusiastically donating money for the doomed charity created in Suzanne's name.

The extra sparkle came with knowing this was AndersLaw's last hurrah, although only Suzanne and the senior partners were in on that little secret. Which is why she had to go along with this ridiculous charade. For now.

She took her assigned seat at the head table, smiling graciously at the firm's four most senior partners and their wives. But if she was going to get through the night without blowing it, she had to push her anger down and do what she'd done so many times in the past. Have an ice cold martini and pretend nothing was wrong.

Finally, after what seemed like an eternity, Aaron finished his annual State of the Firm speech. Office Bee took the podium to moderate the White Elephant Auction, a hilariously competitive bidding war over worthless tchotchkes that kept everyone occupied while the Silent Auction bids were tallied. Desserts and liqueurs were being passed around, and the dance band was warming up. Suzanne noticed the senior partners were studiously avoiding him, but Aaron seemed oblivious to their snub as he put on the dog for a circle of adoring associates.

Suzanne excused herself from the table, but Ginny Frost and Sarah Weisman followed her into the ladies' room.

Ginny waded in first. "When we heard about the divorce, we were so worried about you, Suze," she said, her hard blue eyes sizing up her own image in the full-length mirror. "And then cancer, on top of it all? Jim and I will support you in any way we can, hon."

"Oh, absolutely. David and I are here for you. Anything you need." Sarah's freshly Botoxed face remained stoic as she tried to smile.

Suzanne knew better. They'd both known about the divorce for months, and who knows how long about her diagnosis, but neither of them had reached out. And now they cared? Pfft. They were vultures who'd hitched their wagons to men not much better than Aaron.

"Thank you so much for your belated concern," Suzanne said. "But I assure you, I'll be *just fine*."

Suzanne swept out of the ladies' room with a barely suppressed laugh. She sure as hell wouldn't miss the fake, grasping friendships and all those groveling lawyers sucking up to Aaron as if he were the anointed one. For years they'd all gone along with her husband's shady deals and infidelities. It was all fine, as long as they benefitted, too. Well, that was all in the past. At least for Suzanne.

She straightened her shoulders and headed back toward the party. The hallway was a cocoon of hushed quiet. It settled around her neck and the cool hum of the air handlers made her a little sleepy.

As Suzanne passed the men's room, a tall, reed-thin man hastily exited, bumping into her. He swung around and gripped her shoulders, as if she would topple over.

"Oh my gosh, are you okay?" he said, bending toward her. Suzanne smiled and stepped back as he dropped his hands to his sides. "I'm so sorry for plowing into you like that, Mrs. Anders. We've met before, but you may not remember me." He held out his hand. "Chris Fischer, senior associate."

Suzanne clasped his hand and looked up into his puppy dog eyes, which seemed to hold a bit of mischief. Or maybe he was tipsy.

"No harm done and please, call me Suzanne. Nice to meet you, Chris, and I apologize if we've met before. I'm so bad with . . . wait, did you say *Fischer*?" She looked at him more closely. "Yes, I remember now."

Yes, this was the man Kaitlyn arrived with. He was actually very good looking in a wholesome, fresh-scrubbed kind of way. She caught herself. She'd been staring. And he'd been looking right back at her with a knowing look in his eyes. Could it be that he was aware of the affair? Suzanne gave her head a tiny shake. This was neither the time nor the place, but perhaps she and Chris should have a heart to heart in the near future. For now, though, she needed to keep up appearances.

"Well, Chris, are you having a good time?"

"It's a great party, Mrs. . . . Suzanne. This might be the best one yet!" Chris offered his right elbow. "May I escort you to the ball, madame?" He winked and smiled.

Suzanne laughed and affected a Southern drawl. "Why, I'd be delighted, kind sir."

What a darling he was!

As they approached the bar, he paused.

"Buy you a drink?"

"Oh, no, I'm fine thanks, but you go ahead. I'll see you later," Suzanne said, and continued walking.

When she got to the doors to the loggia, Suzanne glanced over her shoulder to see Chris Fischer leaning in close to the bartender as she poured a glass of wine. Strange that he would pay for wine at the bar, when the firm's hosted bars were just steps away on the patio. Then again, the bartender was a striking young woman. It shouldn't surprise her to see him flirting. After all, his wife had been falling all over Aaron at the head table. Who knows. Maybe they had an *arrangement.* No, he wasn't the type. Too kind, too charming. More likely was just getting a bit of payback.

Maybe I deserve a little of that, too.

It had been impossible, earlier in the evening, to miss Kaitlyn's loud arrival. Suzanne immediately recognized her as the brash blond who'd made herself at home at the casita. She'd strutted into the party wearing a too-short red dress and a too-big smile, demanding the attention of the entire room. Even though she came in on her husband's arm, there was no arguing with the evidence. She was Aaron's tart *du jour.*

Not that Suzanne gave a damn who he slept with, not anymore. Aaron was just another cancer, as far as she was concerned, but at least he was one she could cut out of her life and be done with. Even so, Suzanne resented them both for their audacity and lack of decorum. In a perfect world, they would be the ones dying of cancer and she—the innocent bystander in all this—would be vibrant with health, enjoying a fling of her own. She shook her head to break the spell.

There was no point tossing a coin into that poisoned well.

There were hours yet to go, but Suzanne was bone tired. It wasn't just the chemo, although that certainly drained her batteries. This was more of a psychic exhaustion and she knew why. She was tired of living in Aaron's orbit. He was always the center of attention, while she was nothing more than his pale moon. There wasn't enough air in the room for Suzanne. Not when Aaron was around. Whatever interest she had left—for him, for this life, for anything he'd touched—fizzled into a puff of ash.

She wasn't going to waste one more second of her precious time on these stupid events. Suzanne grabbed her beaded clutch and swept the room with her eyes. Everyone had gravitated to their own little clique, drinking or dancing or circling Aaron like mindless groupies. No one would even notice she was gone. And that was perfectly fine. She preferred a quiet escape, an Irish Goodbye.

Suzanne was down the hall and halfway to the exit when she felt a warm palm on her elbow. She didn't have to turn around to know it was Dov Saminski. She could smell him: cedar and mountain air.

"If you're ready to go, I can walk you out," he said, tipping his elbow toward her.

"Oh, no need, but thank you." She couldn't look at him. No matter how much she wanted to, he was her husband's employee.

Aaron's man.

Dov didn't respond, but his arm was still extended.

She couldn't remember the last time Aaron had escorted her *anywhere*, but she clearly remembered the night Dov carried her into the house after she'd sprained her ankle in a pair of too-high heels. Maybe that frisson of electricity between them that night so long ago wasn't just her imagination.

Finally, Suzanne turned to look at him and saw something barely suppressed in his eyes. What was that look about? Or was she just reading her own wishes into it? Because to her, his eyes seemed full of longing for . . . something else. Suddenly, she saw Dov in a much different light.

She smiled. "If you insist, Dov. Thank you." Suzanne gripped a firm knot of bicep.

When they reached the doors, Suzanne paused to retrieve her valet ticket from her bag. When she looked up, maybe she moved her head too fast, or maybe it was the fatigue, but she staggered with a bit of vertigo. Saminski's arm was around her waist before she could right herself.

"Whoa, Suzanne, are you okay?" His forehead was creased with concern.

"I'm fine, just tired," she said.

Dov leaned closer, his scent and the look in his eyes sending a wave of heat through her body. Why did he have this effect on her? She was acting like a damn teenager. Ever since that night he'd carried her into the house, she'd managed to keep her distance. Tonight, though, it seemed all her defenses were down.

"Really. I'm okay," Suzanne turned away before Dov could see the flush of pink rising from her throat.

"No," Saminski said quietly. "You're not."

His grip around her waist tightened.

"Come on," he said as he began to lead her outside. "I'll drive you home."

She paused before speaking. "Dov, you know . . . I just—"

"Just this once." His eyes implored her. "You seem really tired and I would never forgive myself if something happened."

She wasn't going to put up a fight. Not tonight. And screw Aaron. If he didn't like it, he could take it up with her some other time.

"You're right. I am tired."

What could it hurt, after all? Yes, he might be Aaron's man, but it was a short ride home, and she would be sitting in the back where he couldn't read her face. Where he wouldn't guess how he made her feel.

She allowed Dov to steer her to the concrete bench near the entrance. "Dov, can you grab my car keys from the valet and give them to Aaron before we leave?" Suzanne held out the blue card she'd been clutching. "I don't want my car left out all night."

"I can take care of—"

"I know you can, but so can he," she said. "I wouldn't even be here tonight—and neither would my car—if he hadn't insisted. So let Aaron figure it out, for once."

Dov nodded. "I'll see to it. Just wait here, and I'll pull the town car around as soon as I take care of this. Won't be a minute."

Suzanne sank down onto the bench. After the valet handed him the keys, Dov turned back toward the Club, eyeing Suzanne as he walked past. She gave him a thin smile, not trusting her voice.

What was she getting herself into?

34

DQ DRIVE THRU

SATURDAY, MARCH 19, 11:07 PM

With Suzanne's car keys in his pocket, Dov began making his way to the back of the Club as he considered his options. If he handed over Suzanne's car keys to Anders, his boss would question him, and he had no good answer for why he was about to disregard a direct order by driving Suzanne home.

Steer clear of Mrs. Anders. She's cut off.

The last thing he wanted right now was a confrontation with Aaron while Suzanne waited on the curb. But if he could get her car home some other way, without either Suzanne or Anders knowing the details, he could put off the inevitable to another day.

The party was still going strong as Dov's eyes swept the loggia. Aaron was off to one side, clutching a fresh Cuban cigar, animated by the attention of a cluster of adoring newbies. Dov had witnessed this scene dozens of times, and he knew better than to interrupt. Not when Aaron had the floor. And it was a perfect excuse for Dov to find an alternative solution to the dilemma of those keys in his pocket.

He spotted Kaitlyn inside, swinging her hips to the music and laughing with Margo Nelson, head of bankruptcy, at the edge of the dance floor. He stepped inside and waved Kaitlyn over.

"What's up?" She asked as she approached.

"Can you do me a favor?" he asked.

She cocked one eyebrow. "What kind of favor?"

"Kind of a big ask, but I need Mrs. Anders' car delivered to her house." Dov looked Kaitlyn in the eye as he held out Suzanne's keys, dangling from a large sparkly blue *S*.

"You can't manage that yourself?" Kaitlyn sneered as she took a sip of wine.

Dov tilted his chin toward the patio. "You know how he is." He could see the satisfaction on her face at the acknowledgment, the two of them cozily sharing space in Aaron Anders' inner circle. "He wouldn't want me to trust Mrs. Anders' keys with just *anyone*, Kaitlyn."

Kaitlyn smirked.

"Mrs. Anders asked that Mr. Anders take her car home, but . . . he might have other plans? Of course, doesn't matter to me what happens *after* Mrs. Anders' car is delivered."

She grabbed the keys and stared at them for a beat, then looked up at Dov with a sly smile. "You're right. Aaron would absolutely want me to take care of this."

He was careful not to roll his eyes. She'd see just how special she was soon enough. He caught her looking around the room.

"The gate fob and garage door opener are in the glove box." Dov watched as her eyes slid away. "Your husband doesn't know I'm asking, in case that's what you're worried about."

"I . . . I'm not *worried* about anything." Kaitlyn looked at her watch.

"You know what, never mind. Just hand off the keys to Mr. Anders when he's done. I shouldn't have asked."

"No, I'm . . . it's not a problem."

Dov gave her a knowing smile. "I'm sure Mr. Anders will reward you appropriately for your *service*."

Two pink blotches appeared on Kaitlyn's cheeks and her eyes narrowed. "You better watch your mouth, Saminski. It's gonna get you in trouble one of these days," she hissed.

It felt good to have gotten under her skin a little, but he didn't have time to waste on one-upping Aaron's silly side piece. Suzanne was waiting.

As he walked past Aaron and his circle of admirers on the loggia, Dov caught his eye and gave a little salute. Aaron nodded in return.

11:10 PM

Dov pulled the town car up to the entrance of the Club and jumped out to open the door for Suzanne.

Then he saw her, deflated, slumped on the bench as if the wind had gone out of her. He wasn't ready to face the thought of Suzanne being sick, never mind dying. He could handle a guy blown up on a battlefield, but this was different. Saminski didn't have any experience with this. It unnerved him.

It didn't help knowing he was about to contradict a direct order from his employer, something he'd never done before. He assumed

Kaitlyn would rat him out, and he'd have to answer for his actions, but at least it wouldn't be tonight.

So much for the good little soldier.

He moved in close to Suzanne and extended his hand to help her up.

"All set," he said.

Once they were settled in the car, Dov pulled out of the Paradise Valley Country Club parking lot, stopped at Tatum Boulevard, and signaled to turn left, toward the Anders estate.

"Dov, can we take the long way?" Suzanne asked from the back seat. "I'm tired but totally wired, if that makes sense. I think a little drive might help me unwind before I go home. If you have time?"

"Sure thing. Do you want music?" he asked, flicking the turn signal to the right.

She said yes and Dov tuned in to a jazz station playing sultry cocktail tunes. He headed north on Tatum, then east on Shea, the long way around to the Anders estate in Paradise Valley. As they approached Scottsdale Road, Suzanne tapped his shoulder.

"Do you mind if we make a stop before we head home?"

"Sure. Where to?"

"No judgment?" she asked.

"No judgment."

"My new doc has me on a strict regimen, so it's been an age since I had anything naughty," Suzanne said. He could hear her little laugh. "I'm dying for an Oreo Fudge Blizzard, if you can believe it."

"You know what's crazy? I've been craving a Blizzard all day. And it just so happens there's a Dairy Queen right there on the corner." He laughed. "You planned this, didn't you?"

She giggled. "I'll never tell. But let's just do the drive through," Suzanne said, as Saminski pulled into the Dairy Queen parking lot. "I think I'd like to enjoy my Blizzard in my jimjams."

"No problem," Dov said. "You'll be in your civvies before you know it."

As they waited for their order, Dov checked his watch and turned off his phone. He'd already instructed Beau Harris, the team leader and tonight's valet at the Club, to debrief in the morning. As of now, Dov was off the clock. Whether Anders liked it or not.

Their ice cream treats tucked into the cup holders, he pulled out of the parking lot, turning toward the Anders' Paradise Valley enclave. He glanced in the rearview mirror to see Suzanne's head leaning against the window, her lips slightly parted, eyes closed. His heart swelled.

Dov cruised down quiet side streets, a hint of her perfume sweetening the air. By the time they arrived at the Anders estate, his thoughts had wandered off into forbidden territory, and he'd lost all sense of direction. His heart was racing, but—finally—he was ready to lay it all out on the table. For her.

11:33 PM

Dov waved the fob to open the gate at the Anders estate and drove the short distance to the house, pulling into the crescent shaped drive. He backed up to the garage and, as he turned off the engine, he heard a muffled moan from the backseat. Dov glanced over his shoulder to see Suzanne wince as she moved to unbuckle her seatbelt.

"Everything okay?"

"Mmmhmm. Just a bit stiff from those godawful banquet chairs," Suzanne said.

Dov exited the car and opened her door, but Suzanne just sat there, her hands limp in her lap.

She took a deep breath and gave her head a little shake. "Whew. I guess my party days really are over." She swiveled in her seat, started to stand, then hesitated.

Dov reached down. "Here, let me help," he said, holding out his hand.

Without looking up, Suzanne put her hand in his, and leaned into it. As she stood, Dov put his hand on the small of her back to steady her.

"Let's get you inside."

Dov helped Suzanne navigate the flagstone steps to the front door, where he punched in the numbers to the keyless lock. He pushed the door open with one hand, steadying Suzanne with the other. She kicked off her shoes in the entrance.

"Jesus, it feels good to get those off. Even these so-called sensible shoes are a pain!"

Dov looked at where the shoes had fallen, surprised to see a low square heel instead of the spikey stilettos she usually wore.

"Can you get the alarm?" Suzanne asked. "I'm going up to change."

"You go ahead," Dov said, punching in the alarm code. "I'll grab the ice cream."

He turned and headed back out into the chilly night air. The brightest stars pierced the dark, clear sky overhead, the golden glow of the city hovering on the horizon. Dov took a deep breath.

She seemed so frail just now.

How could he tell her . . . everything? Would she be offended? Outraged? Amused at his clumsy confession? It didn't matter. Tonight might be his only chance to finally confide his feelings. This was his moment.

Unless she's too tired.

Either way, he would tend to Suzanne, make sure she was okay and tucked in for the night. Then, it was time to bring this shit show to a head. He would avenge her in the only way he could, short of challenging Anders to a duel or a fist fight. Dov knew he could easily take Anders if it came to blows, but he had a better idea of how to bring Anders down, and it wouldn't take so much as one swing to do it.

From the outset, Dov had had his suspicions about Chris Fischer's story that he needed to review video from a client meeting. As Fischer crowded in behind him, it had made Dov uncomfortable and impatient. As soon as Dov entered his password, he got a whiff of what Fischer was up to. But he wasn't about to make a fuss without investigating first. After Fischer left, but before he locked up for the night, Dov opened the *other* video file from the same date, the one that started at 6:12 p.m. Dov had laughed out loud. So that's what Fischer had really been after—a cringe-worthy scene that turned awkward and embarrassing when Fischer walked in on them. Dov didn't know what Fischer was planning to do with that video and he didn't care.

Dov was going to use it for his own ends, to expose Anders—and Kaitlyn—for who they were. And he was the last person Anders would suspect of releasing it. All it would take was an anonymous email delivered to the president of the State Bar and the senior partners, with a fifteen minute segment of security video. Even if Anders wasn't disbarred over it, he would be deeply humiliated. Just like he'd humiliated Suzanne time and time again.

He leaned into the car and pocketed his security team flip phone, then grabbed the two melting Blizzards. Back inside, Dov draped his jacket over a barstool, and fiddled with his shirt cuffs as he waited for her in the expansive kitchen. Moments later, Suzanne joined him, pulling her hair up in a ponytail. She was wearing a loose sweatshirt and yoga pants in a pale shade of blue that made her eyes glow.

"I heard someone around here has a Blizzard with my name on it," she said, grinning.

"Special delivery, ma'am. Care for a bowl?"

"I'd love one. They're in that cupboard right behind you. I'll get the spoons," Suzanne said, opening a drawer on the kitchen island.

"Just one spoon," he said quietly. "I'll take off, now. I know you're tired."

Suzanne glanced up, meeting his eyes. "Of course, it's your choice. But as soon as I got those party clothes off, I got a second wind and I'm up for company if you are."

How's a guy supposed to say no to that?

35

Getaway Car

Kaitlyn flushed as she thought about Aaron openly staring at her all evening, secretly returning her smiles, flaunting their affair in front of the entire firm. He seemed to be daring Suzanne, or Chris—or anyone else, for that matter—to challenge him. It thrilled a shiver out of her that they were moving to the next stage.

It's about damn time.

Even Ginny Frost, wife to senior partner Jim Frost, gave her a friendly smile and laughed out loud at Kaitlyn's clever little quips when she'd visited the head table. Kaitlyn knew it was Ginny's way of signaling her acceptance of the situation. A new queen was ascending and Ginny, at least, realized where her allegiance should lie.

Then Saminski showed up asking favors, which just underscored Kaitlyn's rapidly rising position in Aaron Anders' world. Even the Chief Security Officer was acknowledging her emerging status.

The keys to Suzanne's car had sizzled in Kaitlyn's palm. She'd barely wrapped her fingers around the keys when the idea came to her, and it was a fucking brilliant one, too. Driving Suzanne's precious car was a particularly sweet triumph, as if everything that had once belonged to Aaron's wife was now being handed over to Kaitlyn. And those keys were the perfect excuse for surprising Aaron with a dangerous, sexy rendezvous. A fitting finale to a triumphant evening.

There was nothing stopping her tonight. Not Chris, who she'd encouraged to spend the night with Jeff and Rachel. Not Suzanne, the soon-to-be dead ex. Not even Aaron, not anymore.

Whether Aaron had meant to let it slip or not, he'd entrusted her with a dangerous revelation. Maybe it was just bragging, showing off how powerful and brilliant he was, or maybe he'd been a little drunk. Or maybe he thought it didn't matter what he told her, because *she* didn't matter. But since his confession one night in early January, she was now the only other person who knew about that traffic preemption device besides Aaron. And maybe Gerry Sheridan. It was every bit as faulty as the plaintiffs had said, and that was *very* valuable information. Even Chris, who'd worked on the case with Aaron, had no clue. It was the kind of thing that would have eaten at the Eagle Scout and, had he known, she knew he wouldn't have been able to keep it to himself.

The device—a traffic light preemption gadget sold by Sheridan Electronics—allowed emergency vehicles and first responders to control traffic lights so they could pass through intersections without delay. If they came to a stop light, an ambulance driver or cop or fire truck could hit a switch and change the lights to green in their direction, and red for crossing traffic. Or that was how it was *supposed* to work. But some of the early models—including the one they had in evidence—had a faulty circuit, and while it turned the first responders' light green, it delayed in turning the opposite light red.

Kaitlyn immediately saw the potential, leading to her cleverly orchestrated Sheridan Gambit.

Regardless of whether he ever used it, though, what Kaitlyn knew about the faulty device could—and would—blow up Aaron's whole career if he didn't follow through on all his sweet pillow talk promises. For now, she was content imagining his lusty delight when he found her waiting naked in his bed when he got home. Soon enough, though, Aaron would be either divorced or widowed and she'd have a big fat diamond ring on her finger. Kaitlyn would be the *new*—and much improved—Mrs. Anders.

Or else.

Just now, as she was leaving, she'd itched to crash the circle of adoring associates, slip her hand in his, and walk out of the party on Aaron's arm. But he was holding court with the new crop of Baby Lawyers, and she knew the drill. Aaron loved regaling the newbies with his war stories and courtroom anecdotes, spinning his own legend. And why not? He was one of the top defense attorneys in the country. He deserved their accolades.

So, instead of the scene she longed for, Kaitlyn sent him a silent message, waving the keys to Suzanne's prized car. The devilish grin Aaron shot across the room was all the confirmation she needed.

She glanced around. The last thing she wanted was another confrontation with her Boy Scout husband, especially now that she'd finally appeased him enough that he'd stopped scrutinizing her every move. But she needed to give him a heads up that she wasn't driving their car home.

The party had broken into camps: indoors dancing, outdoors smoking and drinking. Chris wasn't the dancing type, so she walked out to the loggia. No sign of Chris, but there was his idiot friend, Jeff

Petronelli. Even better. She skirted a group of tipsy legal assistants and sidled up to Jeff.

"Hey Jeff, can you let Chris know I'm running an errand for Mrs. Anders?" She turned toward the exit. It wasn't a lie. Not really. She *was* doing Suzanne Anders a favor, delivering her TR4 as requested, even if Suzanne didn't know about it. "I'll figure out a ride home."

Right after I finish delivering a little surprise of my own to Mr. Anders.

11:34 PM

Something was off. From the bar, Chris watched Kaitlyn wave a keychain and smile at Aaron before grabbing her wrap. She stopped to say something to Jeff, then headed for the exit. He'd followed a few paces behind to see for himself if she was actually leaving, heading out to meet Anders.

He stood in the shadows, flattened against a column as Kaitlyn dropped into an old Triumph. Saminski had been talking to her, dangling a set of keys in her face. When Kaitlyn snatched them away, Chris had no doubt it was connected to her rendezvous with Anders later. Keys to his legendary downtown condo, maybe? But why was Saminski giving her keys here, at the party, in front of everyone? Now it appeared they were car keys, instead.

Whose car is that?

It wasn't Anders' Porsche, that was for sure. Chris didn't recall seeing that car around the office, and he would have remembered the vanity tags: BBY BLU. As Kaitlyn pulled away from the curb, Chris hit send on a text message and dropped the cheap phone in his suit pocket.

10 min warning - Old blue Triumph convertible

Meanwhile, his mobile phone dinged. Kaitlyn.

Running errand for Mrs Anders. Will find my own way home.

Like hell you are.
But at least that explained whose car she was driving.

11:37 PM

"Would you like me to lower the top for you, miss?"

The valet who'd been watching Kaitlyn struggle with the manual release on the Triumph convertible finally took the hint and offered his help.

"Thanks." She dropped her chin and looked up through a fringe of Playboy Blond hair, the perfect shade of blond she'd selected at the salon last week. "I'm just clueless with mechanical things."

With the convertible top secured, Kaitlyn gave the valet a twenty and a smile. As she slid into the driver's seat of Suzanne's beloved blue TR4, she silently thanked her father for insisting all his kids learn how to drive a stick. A whiff of perfume mingled with old leather hit her nostrils. It smelled like something her mother would wear. If her mother had Suzanne's kind of money.

Her hips felt loose beneath the silky fabric of her dress as she settled in the car seat. A cold breeze made her nipples pucker and goosebumps rise on her legs, and then it was gone, warm spring air enveloping her once more. She smiled under the heat of the valet's gaze as she buckled up, but it was Aaron on her mind as she pulled her wrap over her shoulders. She was about to drive away when she thought better of it. Jeff was drunk. What if he bungled the message and Chris misunderstood, waiting for her to return? Things could get ugly. She needed to make sure Chris left her alone tonight. Taking out her phone, she thumb-typed a message.

> Running errand for Mrs Anders. Will find my
> own way home.

She hit send and gave a little wave to the valet as she shifted into first, pulling away from the curb. Would anyone notice she'd taken Suzanne's car? She glanced in the rearview mirror, but no one else was around and the valet was already busy texting on his phone.

Kaitlyn loosely gripped the steering wheel with one hand, shifting gears with the other, as she sped to Aaron's home in Paradise Valley. Her belly was taut with anticipation of the night ahead. The spring air, soft and cool on her bare arms, was saturated with the lush scent of orange blossoms. She had the top down, the wind tangling her honey-blond hair, whipping against her face as she drove through dim, deserted streets. She loved the fertile late-night hush, expectant with promise.

She glanced up to the clear, black sky above the glow of the city, where a tiny star winked at her from the bowl of a buttery crescent moon.

A good omen.

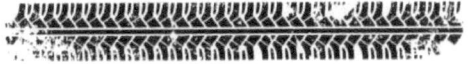

Chris slipped back into the Club, stopping at the bar on the patio to pick up another round for Jeff and a Perrier for himself. He took a long look around at his co-workers before turning back to the table he was sharing with Jeff.

How many of them know about Kaitlyn and Anders? All of them?

Chris washed down the bitter taste of shame with a slug of Perrier, and handed Jeff the Scotch on the rocks. He tossed his phone on the table.

"Dude. You are a gentleman and an enabler." Jeff grinned. "Thanks again for being the DD."

Chris's phone dinged.

"Somebody's pinging you, man."

Chris nodded at his phone. "Yeah, Kaitlyn's off to run—"

"Aw, shit, man. I was supposed to tell you. She was looking for you a few minutes ago," Jeff said. "She's running an errand for the boss's wife. Sorry, bro. I might be drunk."

"Ya think?" Chris laughed. "Good thing you've got a ride."

Jeff laughed and clapped Chris on the back. "I owe you a big one, you know that right?"

Chris smiled to himself. Jeff had already done him a big favor with the key card, even though he was completely unaware of the swap. Plus, the longer he stayed at the party waiting to drive Jeff and Rachel home, the less likely anyone would remember Chris had been gone for almost an hour.

"Yeah, seriously, no problem. Rather see you have some fun and get home safe."

"Rach looks like she's enjoying herself," Jeff said, craning his neck toward the dance floor. "I might even get lucky tonight if I take her a couple of tequila shots. Be right back."

As soon as Jeff stepped away from the table, Chris slipped into his empty chair and pushed his hand into the breast pocket of Jeff's jacket. It had been more than two weeks since he nabbed Jeff's key card and, now that his mission was complete, this was a perfect opportunity to return it. And it needed to be *now*, because shit was about to get crazy, and he could not have his friend implicated in any of it. His fingers closed around Jeff's slim metal wallet just as a hand clasped his shoulder. His head whipped around.

"How's it going, Christopher? Having fun?" Office Bee perched on the chair next to him, clutching a flute of champagne.

He exhaled. "Oh, hey Janice, great party, and you look *fantastic*," he said, smiling as he gestured at her dress. He had the wallet in hand, but he had to get rid of Office Bee before Jeff came back.

She looked up at him through a cluster of false eyelashes. "Aren't you just the sweetest thing? So, what's—" Office Bee began.

"Did Mrs. Anders find you? She was looking for you a few minutes ago," Chris said.

Office Bee's eyes darted to the dance floor, then swept the loggia. "Uh oh. Never good when the boss's wife is hunting you down. Do you know where she went?"

"Last time I saw her, she was headed to the ladies' room," Chris said. His palm was sweating around Jeff's high tech wallet.

"Sorry to bail on you, hon," she said, rolling her eyes, cleavage jiggling as she rose to leave. "I better go see what Miss Suzanne wants."

Chris exhaled and looked around to make sure no one was watching. He pushed the lever on the wallet and pulled his own key card out. He wiped Jeff's card on his pants—fingerprints!—then slipped it into Jeff's wallet. He was just dropping the wallet back into Jeff's suit jacket as his friend approached with another fresh Scotch in hand.

"You just missed Office Bee," Chris said, raising his eyebrows in a comical expression.

"Oh god. What did she want? Are your billing reports late?" Jeff snorted. "That woman takes her job way too fucking seriously, if you ask me."

Chris laughed. "And you don't take yours seriously at all, so it's a wash."

"I'll have you know I'm a very serious . . ." Jeff burst out laughing.

"Yeah, who am I kidding? At least I'm not out there doing the Electric Slide, like Rach. But hey, she's having a good time." He shrugged.

Chris looked at his watch. "So, whaddya think? Another hour?"

Jeff drained his glass. "If we can drag Rachel off the dance floor, sure. But if you wanna head out . . ."

"No, no. I'm good. Just trying to decide whether I have time for a glass of wine. Gotta pace myself, you know?"

"Go for it. The babysitter's spending the night." Jeff drained his glass with a loud sigh and licked his lips. "Fucking decent of the old man to have 'em put out the good stuff, hey? Rach never lets me buy Laaa … lapfrog … shit, I can't even say it."

"I think it's pronounced luh-froyg," Chris said.

This was one of the things he liked about Jeff: neither of them came from money and they were both from small farm towns. They had a country boy bond over their lack of worldly finesse, sharing an enthusiasm for the little luxuries that accompanied a law career. Like good quality booze.

Jeff giggled and held his glass against his cheek in mock adoration. "It's la-di-fucking-da is what it is! You oughtta have some while it's on the house," he said. "Instead of that Two Buck Chuck house wine they're pouring."

Chris nodded. "Why do you think I'm buying my wine?"

Jeff wiggled his eyebrows. "And here I thought it was because of that hot little number doing the pouring." He giggled to himself.

"Why Jeff, how impertinent. I'm a married man!" Chris said, in a fake southern drawl, laughing.

Jeff looked serious all of a sudden. "Yeah, but, Kait left you high and dry so . . ." Jeff raised his hands in a gesture of surrender.

The words hung between them.

Did Jeff know?

Did everyone know?

36

HOME STRETCH

SATURDAY, MARCH 19, 11:37 PM

Aaron Anders had kept the senior partners at bay all night, avoiding their grasping wives and furtive whispers. He'd held half a dozen tempting young women a little too close on the dance floor, vaguely aroused by the promises in their overly made-up eyes. He'd slapped the backs of several new associates, giving them something to brag about later. He'd even been generous with Suzanne, smiling at all the right times, spinning her around the dance floor to get the party started.

All while keeping Kaitlyn in her fiery red dress at a respectable distance, so the rumor mill wouldn't kick off again. He'd caught her eye a couple of times to warn her off.

He smiled as he recalled the whispered invitation of one of the new associates as they'd danced. Dierdre Riley had dark hair that fell in thick waves over her smooth shoulders, and hazel eyes that snapped with humor and cunning. She wasn't his usual type, and maybe that was for the best. Yes, the evening had been a resounding success as far as he could tell.

Aaron's phone buzzed mid-sentence as he retold another of his favorite war stories to a clutch of rapt associates, Dierdre included. He held up his hand, signaling a pause. He'd seen Saminski's little salute a while ago, and assumed it was him texting.

Aaron pulled his phone out of his pocket, held it up, and said, "Yet another client who can't live without me for even one evening. Remember this, people. If you want to make it to my level, there's no such thing as a night off."

He wheeled away from the group, taking long strides to the end of the loggia. Tapping the screen, he read the text:

Baby Blue departed 23:29

The message was from the valet, one of Saminski's team. Aaron had requested a heads up when the TR4 left the property, and Beau Harris had done as asked.

Aaron had seen Kaitlyn leave a few minutes ago, too, and that meant she was at least being discreet about their plan to meet up later at the condo. He'd hoped to break it off with Kaitlyn tonight. But when he'd confronted her about breaking into the casita, she'd handed him a threat wrapped inside her declarations of love. And that meant Aaron was stuck, for now, with a demanding girlfriend he couldn't afford to get rid of. But with both Suzanne and Kaitlyn gone home, Aaron wouldn't have to dodge any judgmental looks while he sampled an *amuse bouche* of Dierdre Riley.

His smile widened as he walked back to the clump of shiny-cheeked associates, awkwardly sparring in their new suits and cheap shoes, hungrily smacking their lips, watching his every move.

"I've put out the fire for now, but one of you will be getting an assignment Monday morning." Aaron winked at Dierdre. "Now, where was I?" he said as he picked up telling his story.

He held their attention for another hour, regaling them with courthouse gossip, funny anecdotes about a certain senator, and scathing jokes about opposing counsel. Aaron could do this all night. But he also knew to leave his audience hungry for more. Not that the gaggle of fawning associates wouldn't sit here all night lapping up any crumbs he offered, but the party was winding down and he'd done what he set out to do.

By shielding himself with adoring Baby Lawyers, he'd avoided any unpleasantness with the senior partners or Suzanne and kept Kaitlyn from falling all over him in front of the whole firm. But Aaron could feel fatigue tugging at his sleeve. By the time he drove downtown to the condo, it would be another forty five minutes before he could crawl in bed with Kaitlyn. It was time to go.

"Well, kids, it's been a delight, but this old man needs to go home. If you're drinking, make sure you're not driving, and I'll see you all on Monday," Aaron said with a jaunty wave.

A chorus of thank yous went up as he turned to leave.

With a satisfied smile, Aaron stepped away, heading toward the doors that would lead him through the Club to the parking lot, where Saminski would be waiting to drive him home. But, as he approached the doors, he inwardly groaned. Chris Fischer and Jeff Petronelli were seated in his direct path at the end of the loggia. Fischer's back was to him, but as he tried to slip past unnoticed, Petronelli hailed him.

"Aaron! Man of the hour! Great party, dude!" Petronelli raised his glass as he called out.

God, that guy is such a bonehead.

"Glad you're having fun. Be safe getting home, okay?" Aaron responded.

"Got it covered, boss! My man Chris is the DD tonight," Petronelli said, reaching over to slapping Fischer's shoulder.

Aaron corrected course and veered toward them. "Gentlemen, I hope you and your lovely wives enjoyed the evening." Aaron glanced around. "I guess the ladies have taken to the dance floor and sidelined you two left-foots, huh?" He laughed.

Petronelli tapped his nose with his forefinger. "Nailed it. Well, Rach is out there flinging herself around. Kaitlyn's long gone."

Because she's already waiting for me.

Aaron's senses tingled. He loved cat and mouse games.

"Oh? And where did Mrs. Fischer get off to this evening? I hope she's not under the weather?" Aaron smiled magnanimously at Fischer's tensed jaw.

I know exactly where she is, Fischer. Do you?

"You'd know better than me," Fischer said. "Kaitlyn said she was running an errand for Mrs. Anders, so you'll just have to ask your *wife*, I guess."

Aaron's smile did not falter, but his mind immediately raced to a dozen scenarios that were not on his agenda. What the hell would Kaitlyn be doing for Suzanne?

Jesus Christ.

"Women, huh? They're always up to something, and the less we know the better!" Aaron barked a laugh. "See you Monday!" He turned on his heel and walked briskly through the Club to the front entry.

Kaitlyn's lies were repeating on a loop in Chris's mind.

You coming home with me tonight?

Why wouldn't I?

Running errand for Mrs. Anders.

Not that it mattered. Not anymore. She was going to get what was coming to her for humiliating him like this in front of everyone. Chris thought about Anders' taunting words. He was just fucking with him, now. Because Aaron Anders knew *exactly* where Kaitlyn was. Or so Anders thought.

Chris glanced at his phone: 12:37. By now, his cheating wife would be calling a tow truck.

"You know what, you guys are gonna shut this place down, so I think I can afford one more glass of wine. Be right back," he said, as he stood. Come to think of it, that bartender *was* a hot little number, and she seemed pretty interested. What's good for the goose . . .

"Uh huh, you do you, buddy. Just be ready to roll by 1:30, okay? Cuz it's a long drive home and I have to take the monsters to soccer practice in the morning," Jeff said, waving his drink in the air as Chris walked away.

Chris strolled slowly toward the bar, not yet willing to fully admit why he was pulled in that direction. Even so, he was enjoying the sensation of being someone else. Someone besides Christopher Fischer, North Dakota farm boy, Eagle Scout, senior associate, Kaitlyn's cuckold, and all-around doormat.

Fuck all that. I'm a free agent now.

He walked to the end of the bar, and pulled up a stool in a dim corner beside a yellow puddle of lamplight. He could feel her dark eyes following him as he sat down. He pulled out his phone to read a text message. She stepped in front of Chris and placed a cocktail napkin on the bar.

"And what's your pleasure this time, cowboy?"

"Mr. Anders?" The valet stepped forward with his hand out.

Beau Harris. Saminski's guy. The one who'd texted him earlier.

"Yes, Beau, everything go smoothly tonight?" Anders asked as he handed over his valet ticket. He wanted to ask whether he'd seen Kaitlyn leave, but he wasn't about to tip his hand to some rent-a-cop he'd only just met.

"Smooth as glass, sir. I can drive you home, if you like. Just need to pull your car around," he said.

"Where's Saminski?" Aaron snapped. "He's supposed to be on duty tonight."

"He was called away, but wanted to make sure you were taken care of," Harris said. "In case you were ready to leave before he returned."

First Kaitlyn, now Saminski. Both AWOL. Aaron's temper was flaring, but there was no need to put it on display. He took a deep breath.

"Returned from *where*?"

"He didn't say, sir."

"Well, thanks Beau, but I don't need a ride." Aaron nodded at his car, parked just a few yards away. "Mine's the black Panamera."

Actually, it was just as well that he was on his own given how standoffish Saminski had been lately. He wouldn't have to make any awkward small talk.

"Sir, I'd be happy to drive you. Mr. Saminski said I'm supposed to—"

"And who do you think gives Saminski *his* orders?" Aaron smiled at the man until he nodded.

Harris sprinted away. It only took a couple of minutes before he pulled the Porsche up to the curb, but in that time, Aaron had grown even more impatient. Harris got out and held the door as Aaron handed him a $100 bill and slid into the driver's seat.

Aaron slammed the door and put the car in gear. As he squealed away from the curb, he saw the valet put his phone to his ear.

Who the hell is he calling?

Aaron had a moment of panic. Was this mess with Kaitlyn going to come back to haunt him, even after he'd been so meticulous?

37

BEDTIME STORIES

Suzanne wanted nothing more than to spend the rest of the night listening to Dov's voice, feeling the reassurance of his steady presence, but she hesitated to invite him to stay. What would that say about her, after her righteous railing at Aaron for his infidelity?

Then again, they'd been living separately for more than a year and their divorce was in process. It wasn't like she was ever going to reconcile with him. Plus, she felt like celebrating because—despite it being her scheming husband's annual firm event—tonight was also Suzanne's farewell party. Good riddance to all the showmanship and fake comradery. She would never again have to attend another event for, or with, Aaron. Just knowing she wouldn't have to see any of those people again made her feel lighter than she had in years. It was cause for celebration. But it also meant tonight might be the last time she would be alone with Dov, now that her duties to Aaron and the firm were solidly in the past.

Even though it wasn't fair to Dov, given all the circumstances, Suzanne wanted to prolong this evening, to savor it. She didn't want to get Dov in trouble, but maybe seeing the car out front would give Aaron pause. She knew how his mind worked. If he saw the town car outside, he would begin to question whether or not he could trust his Chief Security Officer. It would disrupt Aaron's smug little universe where everyone was there for one reason: to serve, support, and coddle him. Then again, given how Mrs. Fischer had been dangling her carrots in front of him at the party, Suzanne doubted Aaron would be back on the property tonight. He was probably already at his downtown condo with Kaitlyn.

She wondered how Dov would account for his whereabouts, since he wasn't at the Club to drive Aaron home. What would he say? Did it even matter what Dov told Aaron at this point? No doubt, Dov would end up kowtowing to Aaron. Like he'd always done. Or would he?

From the way he'd been looking at her tonight, Suzanne was beginning to think Aaron's hold on Dov wasn't as iron-clad as she'd once believed. It was almost as if Dov was . . . what? Interested? Curious? Feeling sorry for her? She used to be good at interpreting the signals, but she'd been married for so long and, besides, Dov wasn't like any other man she'd ever known. But one thing she wasn't mistaken about was the undercurrent of chemistry between them that, when she thought about it, had been there all along.

She replayed that night Dov had driven her home after one of a zillion society galas, when she'd twisted her ankle in those stupid Jimmy Choos. He'd shocked her by swooping her up and carrying her into the house. She couldn't forget the way his arms felt around her, lifting her out of the car as if she weighed nothing.

"As soon as I got those party clothes off, I got a second wind and I'm up for company if you are."

He hesitated, and his eyes slid away. She felt like a fool.

She should tell him to leave. Now.

All Dov heard was *I'm up for company if you are.*

The invitation was too tempting, even for Dov. It was what he'd hoped for, but never expected. Not after her cool dismissal earlier in the day, when she'd referred to him as *Aaron's man.* Had that only been this morning? He wondered what had changed.

Dov turned back to the cabinet and took down two bowls.

"Sorry, bad idea," Suzanne said. "You're probably exhausted."

He tapped both Blizzards into the bowls and looked over his shoulder with a smile. "To be honest, it's the best offer I've had in ages." Dov turned, holding the two bowls of ice cream, motioning for Suzanne to lead the way. "After you, madame."

"Right this way, sir."

Smiling, she stepped away from the island, into the family room, switching on the gas fireplace and a dim lamp before sinking into a corner of the deep sofa. Suzanne tucked her feet under her as she pulled a fluffy throw over her lap.

"Stupid, huh? Eating ice cream wrapped in a blanket with a fire going?" Suzanne huffed a little laugh.

Dov handed Suzanne her bowl and eased onto the other end of the sofa.

"It's kinda decadent, if you ask me," he said.

"Speaking of decadent, did you have any of that potato cheese custard thing tonight?"

Between spoonfuls of ice cream, Suzanne and Dov recapped the night: comparing notes on the rich food, laughing over the ridiculously fierce bidding for silly prizes, and grumbling about the petty factions of the firm's attorneys and staff, while carefully skirting the touchy subject of her divorce.

The gas fireplace had warmed the room—too warm for Dov—and he rolled up his sleeves. Suzanne was playing with the fringe of the throw, staring at the fire.

It's now or never.

He quickly checked the team phone for messages and saw that Anders had left the party at 12:37 a.m. He glanced at his watch: 12:52 a.m.

Shit.

It was so much later than he'd realized and Aaron could be banging on the door any minute now.

Unless he's somewhere else, banging Mrs. Fischer.

"I'm so sorry," he gulped. "I completely lost track of time. I'll just take these bowls—" He leaned forward to stand.

Suzanne pushed one bare foot against his thigh. "Dov."

He froze at the electric charge of her touch, then glanced at her as his hand gently rested on her foot.

"I didn't mean to—"

"Do you have to go? I know it's not fair of me to ask, and I will not be the least bit offended if you do, but I'm not sleeping much these days, anyway." She shuddered and pulled the throw over her arms. "Damn chemo gives me the chills. Sorry, don't mind me. I'm just—"

He swallowed the lump in his throat and interrupted her. "You're just a beautiful queen who needs someone to tell you a bedtime story as you drift off to sleep in front of the fire. And you're in luck. I know a lot of stories."

She pushed her other foot out from under the throw.

"Your hands are so warm."

He pulled her feet onto his lap, cradling them in his hands, gently rubbing her toes.

"I can't believe you're this cold with that fire going," he said.

Suzanne's hands popped out from under the blanket as she shifted her feet away and turned toward Dov. "My hands are like ice."

Dov scooted closer and took her hands in both of his. "You're not kidding. Lucky for you, I'm basically just a big heating pad."

Their eyes met. Dov's breath caught in his throat. Suzanne's cheeks flushed and she let out a soft laugh.

"Oh, you're a lot more than that, Dov." Her smile turned wistful. "At least to me."

His mouth was on hers before he could rein himself in. She returned the kiss, hungrily, clasping his face in her hands. His heart was pounding ninety miles an hour, terrified of what he was about to do. But fear wasn't going to stop him now. He pulled her onto his lap, wrapping his arms around her as she nestled her face into the hollow between his shoulder and neck.

"Thank you, Dov. For everything." Suzanne sighed. "But about that bedtime story. Shouldn't I be in bed first?"

He stood, lifting Suzanne with him. "I think that's the very best place for the story I'm about to tell you."

Dov didn't care what happened now, next, or ever. This was officially the best night of his life.

38

DANGEROUS CURVES

SATURDAY, MARCH 19, 12:35 PM

Aaron pulled up to the pump. He loved the Panamera, but she was a thirsty little gas hog. As the tank filled, Aaron pulled out his mobile phone and messaged Kaitlyn.

R U at the Den?

The Lion's Den. That's what Kaitlyn called his downtown condo which, over the past few months, had become their bolthole. It was close enough to the firm that Kaitlyn could walk over, leaving her car conspicuously parked at the office. When she'd wagged her keys at him earlier, he knew that's where she was headed.

The pump clicked off, Aaron locked the gas cap, and slid back into the car. She hadn't responded to the text. He felt a little stab of pain run across his left shoulder and fished in his pocket for a nitro tab. Nothing. He pulled out his wallet to see if he had one stashed there, but he'd taken it halfway through the firm party as a precaution. He opened the console, even though he never left anything like that in the car.

It didn't matter. He'd just swing by the casita, grab his meds, and he'd still be at the condo in less than an hour. As he pulled out of the gas station, he said, "Call Kaitlyn."

Her phone rang about a dozen times before voicemail picked up. Knowing her, she'd turned her phone off to avoid her clueless husband and was already propped up in Aaron's bed, halfway through a bottle of champagne.

When he arrived at the Paradise Valley home, Aaron slowed to tap his fob on the gate sensor. He smiled to himself in the dark.

His estate. *His* home. *His* property. Very soon all of it would be his, and he would answer to no one. Not even his interfering children or, god forbid, a high maintenance young wife.

I'm the king of this goddamn castle.

As the Porsche's headlights swept the driveway, he slammed on the brakes. The firm town car was backed up to the garage of the main house.

What the hell?

Saminski had no business being here, especially at this hour. He was supposed to be on duty, either at the party, or off doing whatever the hell it was guys like him did behind the scenes. But he *definitely* should not be *here.* Harris reported that Suzanne left the party over an hour ago. He could see the text message in his mind's eye.

Baby Blue departed 23:37

His wife's Triumph would be in the garage, as usual. But why was Saminski here?

Aaron took a deep breath. Was there a logical explanation?

Tentacles of doubt began to creep into his mind. When he thought about it, Saminski had been off his game the past couple of weeks. Distant, distracted, more formal than usual. And his security reports were terse, no banter or chitchat. Even when Aaron reported the Saudi's threats after Josh Campbell botched that land deal, Saminski had seemed pretty damn casual about it. He'd expected Saminski to at least act indignant. Instead, he'd just mumbled something about managing it.

Aaron eased his foot off the brake and the car coasted down to the guest house. He blew out a frustrated sigh. People were going off script. He needed to get ahold of Kaitlyn, beg off for tonight. Aaron couldn't head downtown now. He needed to be *here*, where he could manage Saminski swiftly, appropriately. And without having to manage a drunk Kaitlyn, too. And why did she make up that dumb story that she was running an errand for Suzanne?

Aaron was agitated now. He exited the car and pocketed the keys as he glanced back up to the house.

His breath caught in his throat and his heart galloped ahead.

Other than the landscape lighting, it was pitch dark except for a light in the family room in the main house. He took a deep breath. It was probably nothing. Suzanne probably just left the lights on when she went up to bed. He looked at his watch: 12:52 a.m. She was never up this late.

So why was the town car *still* here?

Fucking Saminski. Would he really have the nerve?

A bolt of pain, like lightning in the desert sky, flashed across Aaron's chest.

Jesus Christ. Not another fucking heart attack.

He had to get to his meds. Aaron blew out a long exhale and made for the casita, gasping at the stabbing pain in his chest.

He entered the key code and opened the door, leaning against the door jamb to catch his breath. He flipped a light switch and beelined for the kitchen, where his heart medication was tucked safely in the cabinet next to the fridge. It couldn't be another heart attack. That first one had been . . . a stupid mistake, snorting godknowswhat with that fucking prossie. He'd fully recovered, the doctor said. *Good thing you work out*, he'd said.

But his cardiologist had warned about angina, and he'd been right. It came on without warning, at the most inopportune times.

Aaron put two tablets under his tongue and grabbed a bottle of water as he made for the living room. He sank back into the sofa and kicked off his shoes, holding the prescription bottle close to his face, squinting at the label in the dim light.

If pain does not subside in 15 minutes, call 911.

He pulled his phone out of his pocket and set a timer.

Then, he texted Kaitlyn. That bitch better not be making a mess of things behind his back.

Where are you? Need to hear from you NOW.

First Kaitlyn, then Saminski! Why couldn't they just do as they were damn well told? That car parked at the main house was burning a pathway through Aaron's skull and his rage was growing, consuming all the other thoughts in its way.

He hit Saminski's number. It rang once and went to voice mail.

Aaron could barely speak, he was so furious. "Saminski. What the fuck is going on? Why is the town car in my driveway? Call me back NOW." He jabbed at the phone to hang up, then dialed again. Voice mail. He hung up and dialed again.

One more chance.

Voice mail. Aaron slammed his phone down and his hands clenched into fists as he screamed at the coffee table.

It felt good to let his rage off leash for a minute, but he collapsed back onto the sofa as another bolt of pain burned a path across his chest.

If Aaron hadn't been afraid of dying of a fucking heart attack on the way up the hill to the main house, he'd already be there, tearing a strip off Saminski. But whatever Saminski was up to would have to wait because these chest pains were making it damn hard to breathe. He stood up and walked to the bar, grabbing a bottle of Remy and a highball glass.

He sat back down, splashed some brandy in his glass, and drank a mouthful. He would just calm down, have a little nightcap, and wait for Kaitlyn and Saminski to respond. Because they would. If they knew what was good for them.

That repose lasted all of a minute before Aaron jumped up and started pacing the floor. But the pain was too much. He clenched his chest at another wave of searing, stabbing pain, then collapsed back onto the sofa. He popped another nitro and, instructions be damned, washed it down with a gulp of Remy.

Where the fuck are Kaitlyn and Saminski?

Aaron had a moment of wondering if they were together, the two of them, in *his* house. Good lord. Wouldn't that be just the best thing ever? He could send both of them packing, and good riddance. Start over. Fresh. No baggage.

He shook his head. He'd never be that lucky.

Aaron pulled up Kaitlyn's number. The phone rang and rang, a dozen times at least, before going to voicemail. He dialed again. And again.

There were still bolts of pain shooting across his chest. He should be at his condo rolling around in the sheets with Kaitlyn right now. But if she was gonna play games, *fine*. He could use it against her to good effect. Maybe the breakup wouldn't be as messy as he'd feared.

He glanced at his phone: 1:16 a.m. He poured another glass of brandy and dialed Kaitlyn's number one more time as he lumbered down the hall to his bedroom.

Answer me, you crazy bitch.

39

DEATH KNOCK

SUNDAY, MARCH 20, 2:15 AM

The sharp chime of the security app on Suzanne's phone snapped Dov out of his dreams.

It took mere seconds for him to realize where he was and what that warning bell meant. Someone was at the gate. He looked at his watch as he struggled with the sheets tangled around his legs. It was the middle of the damn night.

Who the hell would be here at this hour?

He was already flipping through scenarios as he rolled off the edge of the bed, grabbing his boxers as he stood. It was part of his job to know the estate's schedule. Anyone who had any business being here at this hour would have the gate code or a key fob. Whoever was out there wasn't family or staff. Even so, there was no way he'd be the one to answer the call. The last thing Suzanne needed right now was to be in the middle of a scandal, fueled by the kind of nasty rumors that would erupt if a man other than Aaron Anders picked up.

Dov scanned the dim bedroom, lit only by the reflection of the pool lights below. He quickly pulled his clothes out of the jumble on the floor. As he dressed, his mind was already formulating—and just as quickly discarding—plausible explanations for why he was in the home of his boss's soon-to-be-ex-wife. He could easily imagine the smug look on Aaron's face if he caught him here, in Suzanne's bedroom. That bastard would love nothing more than to use it against her.

He never should have fallen asleep.

But, right now, he didn't have time for regrets. Right now, he needed to get Suzanne up, quickly. Dov crossed to the windows and pulled the drapes closed before moving to her side of the bed. Settling on the edge of the mattress, he leaned over, gently rubbing her arm.

"Suzanne. Suze, wake up, love," he said. "Someone's at the gate."

Shit. Did he just call her love?

She curled against his thigh and sighed.

"Come on, wake up now," Dov said a little louder as he turned on the lamp.

She startled awake. "Wha-what time is it?" Suzanne pressed her fingertips to her eyes.

"It's just after two. Here, have some water."

He held out her water bottle as the gate chime rang again.

BINGBINGBINGBING.

Whoever it was, they were insistent.

"Is that the gate?" Suzanne mumbled before taking a long swallow of water.

"Yeah, somebody's here." Dov leaned down to kiss her exposed shoulder. "Come on now."

Suzanne tugged at his arm. "If this is a dream, don't wake me up," she sighed.

Dov smiled. "If this is a dream, maybe we can get rid of whoever's at the gate and go back to bed."

BINGBINGBINGBING.

"Crap, where's my phone?" Suzanne looked around the room. "I'm blind without my contacts."

"Here you go," Dov said, passing the phone to Suzanne.

She tapped the screen, holding the phone out in front of her. "This better be good."

"Sorry for the early hour, ma'am. Paradise Valley Police," he said. "May I ask who I'm speaking with?"

"Suzanne Anders, why? What's this about?"

There was a short pause before the man spoke again. "Ma'am, we need to have a word. It's urgent."

"Come on up." She swiped her phone closed before Dov could object.

"Suzanne!" Dov hadn't meant to shout, and she stopped, shocked by his tone. "I'm sorry," he said, his voice gentler now. "But why did you do that?"

"You heard the guy. It's the cops," she said.

"At two in the morning?" Dov shook his head, his mind already cataloging the possibilities, none of them good. "Unless someone died—"

"Someone died?" Suzanne sat up straighter, fully awake now.

"No, I'm sure no one's died." He regretted alarming her, but *goddammit!* She had to be more cautious. "Suze, the whole point of a security gate is to . . . you know. Provide security. It's not much protection if you just open the gate for anyone who shows up, without even verifying their identity."

"They said they were the police."

"Exactly. That's what they *said*. But you have to ask more questions before you push that button to let someone in."

Suzanne stared at him, her eyes wide. "Jesus, Dov . . . what kind of questions could I possibly ask to make sure they're actually cops?" She looked startled.

"When someone's at the gate in the middle of the night, you gotta ask *why*. And maybe even use that fancy security camera to take a photo. Just . . . to be cautious." Dov suppressed a sigh. There was no hiding the fact of his presence any longer. "Look, it's probably nothing, but just in case it is . . . well, this is where my job takes over."

She gave a little salute and a smile. "Yes, sir."

"I'm serious, Suze. Let me answer the door and verify their credentials, okay?" Dov didn't want to alarm her, but he wouldn't always be with her when someone came around in the middle of the night. Although, the idea of spending all his nights with her was pretty appealing, even if it meant never getting a full night's sleep again. *Especially* if he never got a full night's sleep.

Focus.

Pushing aside the idea of delicious nights like this one with Suzanne, Dov turned away so she wouldn't see him tucking a small Glock 42 pistol into his waistband. "They'll be at the door any second, Suze. Go to the closet and don't make a sound."

He held his finger to his lips and, after assuring himself she was following his instructions, he turned to leave the bedroom. Motion-sensor lights lit the path ahead as he sprinted down the stairs while Dov checked off a list of potential threats. A couple of unhappy clients, but they were white collar types more prone to breaking a reputation than kneecaps. That one former girlfriend—the one that had verbally accosted Suzanne at that legal conference—was always suspect, but she was living in Seattle now. The only other imminent threat was related to that land deal that had fallen through. But Josh

Campbell was the organizer and he was dead, so surely they wouldn't come after an investor. Or would they?

What if those fucking Saudis were serious after all?

He ran his hands through his hair and wondered how much trouble he was about to cause. Because when Anders found out . . .

Approaching the front door, Saminski glanced at the video monitor beside the door and saw two uniforms on the step. He pushed the intercom button.

"Can you identify yourselves, please?"

Trust no one.

The older of the two stepped up to the doorbell camera, holding his badge up. "Detective Luna, Paradise Valley PD. This is Officer Sherman." The younger man stepped forward with his badge.

"What's this about?" Saminski mentally recorded their badge numbers.

"There's been a car accident, and we believe . . . well, until a minute ago, we believed it involved Mrs. Anders."

Why would they think that? What the hell had Kaitlyn done?

"Officers, I'm sure you understand I need to verify. Give me a second," Saminski said. He pulled out his mobile phone. It only took a second to find the Paradise Valley non-emergency number in his contacts.

A duty sergeant picked up on the second ring. "Paradise Valley Police, how can I help you?"

"I'm calling to verify that Officers Luna and Sherman were dispatched to the Anders' residence," Saminski said, then recited their badge numbers.

"Hold on a second, and I'll check," the cop said.

Saminski could hear a dispatch radio in the background, along with the tapping of a keyboard.

"Yep, Luna and Sherman should be there now. Is there a problem?"

"No problem, just want to make sure they're legit before I open the door," Saminski said. "Thanks."

Saminski slipped on his shoes. He pulled his shirt out over the weapon at his back and jerked the door open, startling the younger one, who took a step back.

Paradise Valley Police Department. Not much better than rent-a-cops, in his opinion. Dov looked at Det. Luna. He was an older guy with a lot of hard miles on his face and a paunch that testified to more beer than cardio. The other one was just a kid, but already soft around the middle. He almost laughed out loud. Dov could take these two out with one hand tied behind his back. Maybe his feelings for Suzanne were making him a little *too* protective.

The older guy gave Saminski the once over, then flipped his notebook open.

"Sorry to wake you, Mr. Anders—"

"No problem." He held out his business card. "Dov Saminski, Chief Security Officer for AndersLaw—"

"*Uh huh,*" Det. Luna said as he took the card. The sarcasm wasn't lost on Dov. "Are Mr. and Mrs. Anders home?"

"Yes, Mrs. Anders is here." Saminski stiffened as he noticed the look that passed between the two cops. No doubt they'd be gossiping all the way back to the station.

"May we come in?" Det. Luna asked.

Saminski smiled. "I think we both know that's not going to happen. Now, if you'll excuse me, I'll get Mrs. Anders."

Suzanne was still groggy, but she took a deep breath, plastered a smile on her face, and stepped forward onto the portico, pulling her fluffy robe closer.

"Good morning, gentlemen. A little early for brunch, isn't it?"

Det. Luna stared at her for a beat before asking. "Are you Suzanne Anders?"

"Yes, I am. Why?"

"Do you own a 1967 Triumph TR4A, light blue, license Arizona BBYBLU?"

"Yes, Baby Blue. That's my car. Why? Oh, crap. Don't tell me it was stolen."

"Ma'am, I don't wanna be rude, but . . . do you have some ID handy?" He cleared his throat. "We just need to quickly verify your identity before we go any further."

"Sure, of course," she said. "Just a second." She turned and stepped back inside, as Saminski stood silently on the steps, hands jammed in his pockets.

Seconds later, Suzanne came out and handed her license to Det. Luna. "Here you go."

He held up his flashlight to inspect it, looking from the license to Suzanne and back again. He handed her the license as he glanced at the other officer.

"Mrs. And—"

"It's *miz,*" she interrupted. She wasn't Mrs. anyone. Not anymore. "But please, call me Suzanne."

"Is your car home this evening?" he asked.

"No, there was a party tonight . . . last night, I guess. At the Paradise Valley Country Club. I left my car at the Club. Why?"

"Officer, I gave the car keys to one of Mr. Anders' employees to pass along to him before I drove Ms. Anders home last night," Saminski said.

Det. Luna's expression was grim, but one eyebrow rose in silent judgment. Suzanne didn't care. Let them think what they wanted.

His eyes shifted back to Suzanne. "Why did you think your car was stolen?"

"I don't . . . I thought that's why you were asking. But obviously, I wouldn't know if it was stolen or not." Suzanne felt her irritation rise. It was too goddamn early in the morning for this guessing game. "What's this about?"

"Your Triumph was involved in a car accident earlier tonight, and we're trying to find out who was driving since," Det. Luna gestured at Suzanne, "clearly, you're alive and well."

"Wait, what do you mean *alive and well?*" Saminski asked.

"I'm sorry to be the one to break the news, but your car is totaled and the driver died at the scene." Det. Luna cleared his throat again. "Any idea who might have been driving?"

"Oh my god," Suzanne gasped and her hand flew to her mouth as tears filled her eyes. "Aaron."

"Jesus Christ," Saminski muttered.

"Are you telling me Aaron was killed in a car crash?" Her voice was becoming shrill. "Is that what you're saying? Just tell me!" She looked at Dov, then back at Det. Luna.

"No, no, sorry to alarm you. We're almost certain Mr. Anders was *not* in the vehicle," Det. Luna glanced at the other officer again. He seemed nervous. "Who else might be driving your car?"

"Well, the *only* person who would be driving my car is me or my ex-husband, unless it was stolen." Suzanne swiped the tears from her eyes. "That was my *mother's* car."

Det. Luna gave her a puzzled look.

"Shit. I'm sorry. That doesn't matter, obviously. And I have no idea who would be driving. I'm very sorry for the person who died, whoever it is, and I'm happy to cooperate, but the truth is, I left my car at the Club and that's all I know about it."

"And how did you get home, ma'am?"

Suzanne gestured at Dov. "Dov drove—"

"As I said, I drove Ms. Anders home," Saminski said. "It's one of my duties as Chief Security Officer to transport members of the family when necessary."

Det. Luna trained his gaze on Saminski. "Do *you* know who might have been driving the car?"

"As I said, I gave the keys to one of the firm attorneys to pass to Mr. Anders. I'm confident she would have delivered the keys as requested."

She. Who the hell did Dov give my car keys to?

"And what time was that?"

Saminski paused. "It was right around 2300 hours."

"Who was the employee you gave the keys to?" Det. Luna asked.

"One of the associates, Kaitlyn Fischer," Saminski responded. "Mr. Anders was in the middle of something, so I asked her to deliver the keys to Mr. Anders when he was free."

Aha. So that's why Dov didn't name the employee right off the bat.

"So, what was going on at Paradise Valley Country Club last night?"

"We . . . AndersLaw . . . my ex-husband's law firm had their annual party last night. It was a private party. The Club was closed to the public," Suzanne said.

"Who was there?"

Suzanne thought about it for a minute. "Club staff, obviously. And then everyone from the firm. Partners, attorneys, staff . . ."

"Besides Club staff and employees of the firm, who else was there?" Det. Luna asked.

"Nobody besides spouses, plus ones." Suzanne shrugged.

"My security team was also on site, and I can provide their contact information," Saminski said. "To the best of my knowledge, everyone on the property was either Club staff, an employee of the firm, or their guest. The party was supposed to end at zero two hundred hours, but I can call one of my team to verify, if that will help."

"It would. Can you do that now?" Det. Luna asked.

Saminski nodded as he pulled his phone out of his pocket. He tapped a number into his phone as they all watched him, waiting.

"Sorry, he's off duty and not answering. Can I have your number, so I can get in touch when I reach him?"

Det. Luna pulled a couple of business cards out of his pocket and extended one to Saminski and one to Suzanne.

"Now, if you're done with Ms. Anders . . ."

"For now, yes. You can email the info to the address on my card. And if you think of anything or hear from anyone with information about your car, give me a call," Det. Luna said. "We'll be in touch when we have anything further. Sorry again for waking you."

"Thank you, ma'am," the young officer mumbled.

As the two cops stepped away to leave, Det. Luna paused, and turned back toward Suzanne.

"You said *ex-husband?*" He glanced west, down toward the guest house. "So, Mr. Anders doesn't live on the premises?"

"Well, he lives in the casita." Suzanne pointed down to the guest house. "When he's not at his condo downtown."

"Do you know if he's there now?"

Suzanne glanced down the driveway.

"His car's there. Do you want me to call him?"

"No, that's okay. Do you mind if we check for ourselves?"

"Not at all, just follow the walkway." Suzanne was already turning to go back in the house when one of the officers spoke again.

"Hang on, I'll need the address of that condo and Mr. Anders' mobile phone number." Det. Luna stepped forward to offer her his notebook and pen. "Just in case he's not here."

Suzanne scribbled the information in the notebook and handed it back.

"I'll unlock the gate for you," Suzanne said. "So, when you're done you can just drive through. It will close behind you automatically."

"Thanks again, ma'am," Det. Luna said. "Sorry for the bother."

As she closed the door, Suzanne turned and raised an eyebrow at Dov.

"Why on earth would you give my car keys to Kaitlyn, Dov?"

40

CRASHED

MARCH 20, 2:29 AM

After the visit from the cops, Suzanne shuffled back to the kitchen ahead of Dov, and scooted onto a barstool at the island. She tapped her fingernails on her water bottle.

"I'm waiting for an answer, Dov. Why did you give Kaitlyn my car keys?"

He blushed. "I . . . because I'm a coward. I didn't want to start a row with Aaron right in the middle of the party."

Dov wasn't making sense. "Why would giving him my car keys start *anything*?"

His mouth tightened. "Because . . . because he's a jerk. A few days ago, he ordered me not to drive you *anywhere*," Dov said. "And if I gave him your car keys, well, he would wanna know how you were getting home."

Now she understood why, when she'd called yesterday morning to ask for a ride, Dov had sidestepped the question. "Aha! That explains why you tried to hand me off to one of your flunkies yesterday."

"I didn't want to raise any flags with Aaron," he said, sheepishly. "Not until I . . ." Dov's mumbled words trailed off.

She nodded. "Mmmhmm. I see. So my devoted husband was just trying to make my life a little bit more miserable? And he used you to do it?"

"Pretty much. When I went back inside with your keys, he was surrounded by a group of new associates, holding forth, as he likes to do. But Kaitlyn was available and—"

"And you know about their fling, so . . ."

Dov studied his hands. "I . . . yes. I know. And I also know that Mrs. Fischer likes to be *helpful* when it comes to Aaron. I figured she could be trusted to pass the keys along."

"You were wrong about her, though." Suzanne suddenly had a disturbing thought. "You don't think she was driving my car last night, do you?"

Dov shrugged and shook his head. "I don't know. I hope not, but I honestly don't know."

They sat in silence for a few moments.

"Okay, I don't want to make it weird, but—" she said.

"No worries. I get it. I'll make myself scarce," he said, and began to turn away toward the front door.

Was Dov already regretting last night? How could he not be? Suzanne leaned over and grabbed his arm.

"No, nothing like that. I mean," she sighed and took a sip of water. "I just . . . I don't want to give Aaron any more ammo than he already has."

"I understand, but," Dov took her hand in both of his. "I don't want to leave you to face him on your own."

"Oh please. I'll be fine. But if I know Aaron, as soon as those cops are done talking to him, he'll be marching in that front door spoiling for a fight." Suzanne sighed.

"Don't worry." Dov rolled his shoulders. "I can handle Aaron."

But she'd already made her decision. "So can I. Believe me. I've had years of practice," she said.

"I just think I should—"

"No, Dov, you shouldn't. Please." Suzanne gave a little shake of her head. "Don't give him the satisfaction of walking in and finding us together. He would love nothing more."

"He's already seen the Town Car outside, so . . .?" Dov turned his hands up in a questioning gesture.

"I'll manage that. All he needs to know is that I asked for a ride home, then demanded you stay to make sure the property was secure. Because of the rash of break-ins lately." Suzanne smirked. "Of course, the only break-in was by his girlfriend, but whatever."

"Well, if I have anything to say about it, you won't have to put up with his bullshit for very much longer," Dov said, rubbing his thumb over the back of her hand.

She looked over at his earnest expression and smiled. He was being very sweet, but Dov had no idea what was about to be unleashed. Suzanne did, though. She'd dealt with Aaron's furies more than once.

"With any luck, I'll be divorced in a few months."

He bent toward her, wrapped her in his arms, and gave her a lingering kiss. "Good. Because last night was the best night of my life, and I don't want it to be our last."

So, he wasn't regretting it after all. Suzanne sure as hell didn't regret one second of their passionate tumble into bed. But she had to be practical right now. Sort out this business with her car. And deal with Aaron.

"Dov, last night was wonderful, and you've not seen the last of me, I promise. But I think it's best if I handle this on my own, you know? I'll text you as soon as I know anything."

Dov had hesitated, but in the end, he agreed to leave Aaron to her. Good thing, too. Because she could well imagine the scene Aaron would make if Dov was here when he arrived. Not because he gave a damn about her, but just to prove he could.

2:29 AM

Aaron groaned as he rolled over. The chest pains that had plagued him last night finally resolved after the fourth nitro tablet, but he felt wrung out. Beaten up. Old. At least it wasn't another heart attack. Just the fucking angina that now crippled him at the worst possible times.

BINGBING

Who's ringing the goddamn doorbell at . . . what the hell time was it?

He looked at his phone: 2:29 a.m.

Still no message from Saminski or Kaitlyn.

Maybe it was Saminski at the door, and he better have one hell of a good story to explain himself. The doorbell rang again. Aaron pulled on a pair of joggers as he called out.

"Hang on, hang on."

He stumbled to the front door, shirtless. Aaron jerked open the door and was startled to see two Paradise Valley cops standing there, hands resting on their bulky belts.

"Aaron Anders?" the older one said.

"That's me. How did you . . . what's going on?" Aaron's brain was scrambling to figure out how they got through the security gate.

"Det. Luna, PV Police, and this is Officer Sherman. Sorry to bother you, but your wife . . . sorry, *ex*-wife, said it was okay to come down to ask you a couple of . . ." Det. Luna stopped. "Sir, are you alright?"

Aaron could feel his pulse galloping away, and the cop's voice was drowned out by the sound of his heart pounding in his ears.

Jesus Christ.

"Mr. Anders? Are you okay?" Det. Luna repeated.

"I'm . . . uh, sorry . . . I was asleep." He had to get hold of himself. "I need some water," he said, turning back into the house. "Come on in."

Slow breaths. I have nothing to hide.

"This won't take but a minute, Mr. Anders. We've already spoken to Ms. Anders and your Chief Security Officer," Det. Luna, glanced at his notebook. "Samin…"

"Saminski," Aaron offered. "How did you get hold of him?"

The officers exchanged a look. The younger one seemed embarrassed.

"Well, sir," Det. Luna spoke slowly, as if carefully choosing his words. "He's onsite."

"What do you mean *onsite*? He's here? On the property?"

Det. Luna nodded, then gestured toward the main house. "He's up at the house."

Still? At this hour? That fucking backstabbing snake.

Aaron could feel his face get hot. An uncomfortable fullness behind his eyes. His blood pressure was spiking.

"Mr. Anders, your ex-wife's car," he flipped back a couple of pages in his notes. "1967 Triumph TR4A, light blue, license Arizona BBYBLU, was in an accident tonight."

Aaron took a long sip of water. He knew that whatever he said right now was crucial.

Go slow.

"I have a black Porsche Panamera, and that's what I drove home last night, so I'm not aware of any car accident involving my wife's car."

"Mr. Saminski says he gave the keys to one of your employees, a . . ." Det. Luna thumbed through his notes. "Kaitlyn Fischer. According to him, she was instructed to give you the keys. Did she give you those keys?"

"No, she didn't. I left the party alone around 12:30, after Ms. Fischer had already left."

"So, you don't know who was driving the Triumph? You didn't give the keys to anyone?"

Aaron recalled Kaitlyn leaving the party. Flashing him a set of keys.

"I didn't . . . she didn't give me any keys."

"Okay, so Kaitlyn Fischer *didn't* pass the car keys along to you. Do you think she would have taken Ms. Anders' car for some reason?"

He now knew damn well why Suzanne wasn't driving her own car. But there's no way Kaitlyn would take the TR4 on a joy ride. But if she wasn't driving, who was? Who had the goddamn keys?

"No, I mean, Ms. Fischer wouldn't have any reason to take my wife's car. So, was it stolen?" Aaron took another sip of water.

"It's certainly possible, but we don't know as of now. The car was involved in an accident a couple of hours ago, just down the road at Lincoln and Tatum. Thankfully, it wasn't you or Ms. Anders, but someone died in that crash," Det. Luna cleared his throat. "And we're trying to find out who. Can you think of anyone—"

Aaron swallowed. "N-no. I saw Ms. Fischer leave the party around 11:30 p.m., and I . . . I assume she left with her husband."

He licked his lips. He knew damn well she hadn't left with Chris, but it seemed like the right thing to say. "I left about an hour later, gassed up my car, and came home. Suzanne's car *must* have been stolen."

Aaron's mind was a blur of potential scenarios. If the Triumph was stolen, that would explain why Saminski drove Suzanne home. Kaitlyn couldn't have been driving the TR4 because she was driving Chris's car, since Fischer was the DD for the Petronellis.

"The keys were in the ignition, sir, so it wasn't hot-wired. But we've taken enough of your time." Det. Luna pulled a business card from his pocket. "Call me if you think of anything or hear of anyone who might have driven the car last night, even if it's just a rumor."

Aaron stared at the card for a long beat.

The keys. Kaitlyn had waved a set of keys at him as she left the party. He saw it in his mind's eye like the replay of a movie. Now it made sense. Those were not keys to the Lion's Den after all.

"Sure, yeah. No idea who the driver was, huh?"

"Not yet," Det. Luna said, as they stepped onto the front sidewalk. "We're waiting on an ID. But we'll call you when we find out."

Aaron closed the door on the cops and leaned against the door. His breath was coming too fast.

Fuck fuck fuck.

Who was driving Suzanne's car?

It sure as hell wasn't his soon-to-be-ex, who was apparently alive and well and banging the help. And not just *any* random staff, either. Saminski was in *his* house with *his* wife.

But that left one person unaccounted for. A shimmer of cold sweat burst through Aaron's pores as a massive bolt of pain shot through his chest.

Kaitlyn still hadn't called him back.

41

CAUTION: SLIPPERY CONDITIONS

SUNDAY, MARCH 20, 3:47 AM

There were no other customers pumping gas at the Arco on Highway 587, south of Loop 202, when Chris idled up to the pump. It was about as far south as you could get and still be in Maricopa County, and not that far from Jeff's place.

He'd already dropped Jeff and Rachel off and would meet up with Jeff later to get his car back to him but, right now, he had one last detail to manage. Chris took his time gassing up Jeff's SUV, his eyes swiveling left to right, watching for someone.

A few minutes later, his eyes followed a gleaming red, late model Ford pickup bearing black and white Sonora license plates as it pulled up at the adjacent pump. A muscular Latino in faded Levis and a Def Leppard hoodie jumped out and stepped around the gas pump.

"Hey man, . . ."

"Berto?" Chris asked.

After a brief exchange, the guy jumped back in his pickup and roared off, headed south. He would be across the border in a couple of hours with a year's salary in his pocket.

As Chris pulled out of the gas station, a thrill pulsed through his body. Planned to fucking perfection.

SUNDAY, MARCH 20, 10:19 AM

Chris squeegeed the glass shower door before stepping onto a thick cotton rug to towel off. Even after an hour on the rowing machine and the coldest shower he could stand, his mind was still grinding.

All because of Kaitlyn.

Last night was just one more humiliation, but this time it was public. Kaitlyn hadn't taken her eyes off Anders for a minute, following him around like a lost puppy. Did she honestly think Chris wouldn't notice? That they could just get away with it? Then, as soon as his back was turned, Kaitlyn was off running an *errand* for Mrs. Anders. What a lame excuse. Lying bitch. Texting that she would find a ride home was just salt in the wound.

He'd been replaying every detail of the evening, of his humiliation, over and over. The fake smiles and dumb jokes. The drunken comradery. And Kaitlyn in her too short, too red, too revealing dress. Just another stupid chick who thought she'd bagged the prize buck. Chris almost felt bad for her, but why? She brought all this on herself. She was greedy. She was a liar.

But it all worked out just fine for Chris. Better than fine, if you considered the cloakroom canoodle with that sweet bartender. Volunteering to drive Jeff and Rachel home afforded Chris a perfect excuse to be among the last to leave the party. Then, even when Kaitlyn changed her plans, he was still able to seize the opportunity. Talk about Scouting up! Last night was a perfect example of pivoting and profiting from an unexpected opportunity.

As for Kaitlyn, Chris was clear when he told the guy, *just enough to shake her up.* That's what he'd paid for: a warning, something to rattle her cage a bit. *Nothing serious.*

And all night, Chris had kept his cool, despite the itch to throttle her and Anders both. He made sure everyone saw him at the party, including Office Bee and Mrs. Anders. He'd even been civil to Aaron when he left. And he made sure to say goodnight to at least half a dozen others as he escorted Jeff and Rachel to their car. He'd even tipped the valet a fifty-dollar bill—and looked him straight in the eye when he did it—to make sure the guy remembered him. Besides, he had an airtight alibi if anyone noticed he'd left the party: his inhaler.

But that alibi would fall apart if anyone discovered him on that few seconds of security footage in the firm lobby. He reassured himself that no one would be looking, and he would get rid of it tomorrow, first thing, when arrived at the office. Besides, there was no reason for Saminski to look at security footage. He'd seen Chris at the party, too.

He had to focus on one step at a time, one *baby* step at a time. He could not afford to get distracted or overwhelmed. And he would not allow himself to be pulled under by the riptide of fear rolling over him.

What if I get caught?

He shook his head. None of this was his fault.

Today, Chris would release that video to the senior partners and their wives. He'd initially thought it best to hold off, wait for his bonus. But then, Chris realized none of the partners, including

Anders, would dare withhold his bonus while he was sitting on this video bomb. And the minute their checks were deposited—didn't Kaitlyn say her bonus was going to be huge?—it would be time for the *big* reveal. Literally hundreds of clients would see what the Almighty Anders had been up to on their dime.

Let's see how Kaitlyn and Aaron like it when they're on the receiving end.

He couldn't even blame Anders. Not entirely. *Everyone* knew what kind of man he was, and Kaitlyn was a fool if she thought there was a future there. He'd seen the look on Anders' face when she crashed the head table, crushing her tits against his shoulder as she fake-laughed at some dumb joke. It wasn't love in Aaron's eyes. More like boredom, even a hint of disgust. Chris figured it was already over, or would be soon. And knowing Kaitlyn, she'd come crawling back, asking for forgiveness.

But it didn't matter if Anders was done with her. The bastard could have her, for all Chris cared. He wasn't interested in Anders' castoffs. Just the thought of it made him gag.

Both of those cheating assholes will get what they deserve.

It was perfect patio weather, so Chris stepped through an oversized glass door onto the concrete slab, already warm under his bare feet. He settled in a shady spot under the pergola with his laptop and an ice cold glass of lemon seltzer.

He needed to make a couple of calls, the first to Mrs. Anders. Chris felt like they'd had a moment of understanding between them, but he wanted to make sure she knew all about her husband's slimy ways.

Chris logged onto the firm's online platform and went to the firm directory. He clicked on Aaron's name. Suzanne's mobile was still listed as his emergency contact.

Chris turned his phone on and saw that Kaitlyn still hadn't called or texted. But he had three voice messages from an unknown number.

Damn spammers!

He swiped his phone open and tapped in Suzanne's phone number. She picked up on the second ring.

"Hello?"

"Mrs. Anders? Not sure if you remember me? Chris Fischer. We met last night . . ."

"Oh, hello, Chris. Of course, I remember you," Suzanne said. "How can I help you?"

She was gracious, but he could hear the confusion in her voice.

"Well, it's a bit embarrassing, to be honest. I, uh . . . my wife, Kaitlyn Fischer, said she was running an errand for you, so . . . I'm just wondering where she got off to, because she's still not home." He took a sip of seltzer.

There was a long pause. He heard Mrs. Anders blow out a breath.

"Chris, I'm sorry, but I didn't ask your wife to run an errand on my behalf. Nor would I *ever* ask an associate to do my bidding. I'm not that kind of partner's wife."

"Sorry, I didn't mean to imply . . . it's just that . . . I guess I misunderstood. Kaitlyn texted . . ." His heart was hammering against his ribs. Just as he'd suspected, it was all a lie.

"I think there's been a mistake. Maybe your wife was doing . . . *something else*. Something for Aaron," Suzanne said.

Chris took a deep breath.

He hated what he was about to do. She seemed like such a nice woman. But, from the way she'd looked at him last night when he introduced himself, and the way she said 'something else' just now, it sounded like she already knew. Maybe this wouldn't be such a shock to her after all.

"Yeah, about that," Chris said. "I hate to be the one to tell you, but I think—"

"You're not telling me anything I don't know, Chris. I'm not blind," Suzanne said. "Or stupid."

"Of course not, no. So I guess Kaitlyn's the reason you're getting a divorce?" Chris blurted out. It gave him a cold satisfaction to lay the blame.

Suzanne laughed. "Well, one of many. There's Kaitlyn. And Bobbi. And Tara. And a dozen others."

I knew it!

Of course Kitty had been played. How could she be so stupid, so naïve, thinking she was special, that she'd be the next Mrs. Anders? There she was, wagging her ass all over the Club last night, acting like it was only a matter of time before she traded up for something bigger, flashier. And fake. Because that's what those two were. Fakes.

And they're done for.

"I'm sorry—"

"No need to apologize for my own mistake. We both married interesting people, Chris. Exciting people. But we didn't marry *good* people. If you need a divorce attorney, I can recommend Camelia Belmont."

Chris shook his head. "Whaaat? Are you kidding? I've already had a consult with her."

Suzanne laughed again, gently. "Well, we're both in good hands, then. Let Camelia know we talked," Suzanne said. "And if you want to find Kaitlyn, I suggest you call Aaron."

"That's my next call," Chris said. He thanked her and hung up.

He pulled up Camelia Belmont's number on his phone and tapped. On a Sunday morning, he knew he would get voicemail, but it didn't matter. The important thing was for her to have his message first thing Monday. He couldn't wait to see Kaitlyn's face when she was served with divorce papers. At work.

". . . after the tone." The recording beeped.

"Camelia, Chris Fischer. Looks like I'm a go for the divorce, so please have your assistant schedule me for your first available. I'll email over our tax returns and some other details you're gonna need.

Oh, and let me know how much the retainer will be. Talk soon." He hung up.

The next call was going to be a lot more satisfying. It was time to let Anders know that Chris was all done pretending.

He got up. Walked around the patio. Stretched. Drank some water. Then dialed his boss.

The phone rang straight to voicemail. Chris hung up, frustrated and confused. Anders drilled it into all of them that *accessible attorneys were in-demand attorneys*, and if they were awake, they were expected to answer their phones. Anders himself *always* picked up, unless he was in Court or in a meeting. Chris tapped on the number. It rang again, then went to voicemail.

An unbidden image of the two of them, rolling around in the sheets, came barreling into his head. He could just see Kaitlyn, smug in her hold over Anders while he gobbled up her frantic, desperate attempts to please him. Kaitlyn, blithely believing she had Aaron wrapped up tight, even as Anders planned his exit. Because that's how this would end. Especially now that she'd gone and wrecked Mrs. Anders' car.

He hung up and dialed Kaitlyn's phone. It went straight to voicemail, too. Chris had no doubt they were together. She would have called Anders to come get her after the accident, and now they were probably running around like chickens trying to do damage control.

"Good morning you lying little bitch. Don't bother coming home. You're all his now."

He hung up and a bitter smile punctuated his face.

It was going to be a hell of a lot harder for Anders to scrape Kaitlyn off his boot now that she knew Chris wasn't waiting around to forgive and forget.

Now, before his next step, Chris needed a little bracer, something to take the edge off. He walked inside and poured two fingers of

Scotch, then retrieved one of the flash drives from his briefcase before going back outside.

He inserted the drive into his laptop and clicked on the folder, pulling up the video footage of Anders and Kaitlyn in the conference room. He watched the much older man pawing at his young, beautiful wife. His mouth filled with saliva as nausea overwhelmed him. Chris knew he was on the right side of this mess, but it still made him sick to watch. He took a gulp of Scotch to wash down the aftertaste of their cheap, vulgar groping.

When he'd finished watching the video, Chris clicked on his VPN and selected UAE as his country, then uploaded the video to Kaitlyn's Vimeo account. Next, he logged into a new Hotmail account, KittyHawk84, and opened the draft of an email he'd written days ago. Chris reread it, changing a word here and there. He clicked Schedule Send and set the time for 8:00 a.m. Monday morning, a nice slap in the face to start their week. As soon as it landed in the partners' inboxes, this video would create the kind of stink those two would never be able to wash off.

Fuck them both to hell and back.

42

CLEAN UP CREW

MONDAY, MARCH 21, 7:47 A.M.

After being caught at the Anders estate on Saturday night, Dov braced himself for the lambasting he expected as soon as Anders arrived at the office. Pulling into his reserved spot, Dov's mind turned back to the unsettling events of Saturday night.

They now knew it was Kaitlyn Fischer who died in Suzanne's car. An unfortunate accident, according to Det. Luna. Yes, Kaitlyn died in Suzanne's car, but it had *nothing* to do with Dov. She'd made the decision to take off in the Triumph, not him.

Keep telling yourself that.

He gave himself a mental shake. He needed to focus on the one thing he could control: the video footage of Anders and Kaitlyn. Because suddenly, that video footage was a lot more valuable. Some people might even think it was a motive for murder. But for Dov, the video was a way to bend Anders over, convince him to give Suzanne her fair share and walk away.

He headed to his office with a strategic plan of attack, all the tools at his disposal, and a clear goal in mind. Eager to get underway, Dov logged onto his computer, opened the security camera file server, and typed the date in the search bar: *January 9.*

When the search results came back, there was only one video file in the folder from Conference Room 3, the "war room" where Kaitlyn Fischer and Aaron were caught *in flagrante*. It was time stamped 11:00 a.m. And Dov knew exactly what was on that video, because it was Chris Fischer's meeting with his client. So where was the *other* file?

Dov knew it had been there the day after he'd downloaded that Sunnyside Solar video for Chris, because he'd viewed the footage in its entirety the next day. It was Fischer's suspicious behavior, his flimsy excuse—overacting, Dov thought—that prompted him to go back to view the files. Both videos had been there then. But now?

Nothing.

Where the hell was that file? Why wasn't it here?

Calm down.

All he had to do was slow down, focus, and he'd find it.

Dov rolled his shoulders as he recalled Fischer hovering behind him when he pulled up that meeting video. Fischer wasn't nearly as dumb as he looked, and one thing was certain: Dov needed to be a helluva lot more cautious around these lawyers. They were slippery as hell!

It made perfect sense, though. Of course Chris would be after the video of Kaitlyn and Anders. But to what end? Was it for a bit of revenge? Blackmail? Was it to cover up the affair so no one would discover he'd been cuckolded by the boss?

Dov had just verified that the trash folder was empty and was about to run a recovery app to restore the video when his office phone buzzed. He glanced at his watch. It was 8:03 a.m. Anders was right on time. He took a deep breath and picked up.

"Saminski," Anders growled. "We're gonna have a chat about your priorities. But right now, I need information. Did you see anyone drop a package in the interoffice mail?"

"Well . . . no. But I don't monitor internal mail."

"Don't you have cameras on the mail room?" Anders asked.

"No, just the lobby and conference rooms, as directed," Dov said. "Is something wrong, sir?"

"Just wondering where some of this shit comes from. Because *someone* sent me an old client exhibit through interoffice mail, and . . . never mind." Anders paused. "And to be clear, after Saturday's fiasco, Janice will be setting up a time for your review." Anders hung up.

Dov released a sigh and twisted his neck to get rid of the kink. That *review* was no doubt going to be Anders firing him. He'd known it was coming but was grateful for the unexpected reprieve. Yeah, he'd rather Anders just get it over with, rip the Band-Aid, and Dov could be on his way. But before he was locked out of the firm's computers, he needed to grab this video footage. Anders' delay was working in his favor.

Dov turned back to his bank of monitors. The lobby camera showed a slow stream of attorneys and staff arriving. The conference rooms were all dark. He went back to searching for the missing video when, a few seconds later, his peripheral vision caught the security camera in the third conference room click on.

Dov watched as Aaron, carrying a shipping envelope under his arm, crossed to the overflow files lining the wall of the room. He stuffed the envelope into a file box stacked among all the others. Then, he quickly turned and left the room.

What the hell is Anders doing?

Nothing Dov had just witnessed made sense. Why would Anders file anything for himself, when they had a whole crew of clerks to manage that task? Especially coming on the heels of his odd question about interoffice mail.

It definitely warranted an investigation.

Dov was already on his feet and moving quickly to the conference room. Once there, he scanned the stacks of boxes. Anders had gone to the right corner of the room, where literally dozens of boxes full of documents were stacked in neat rows. Only one with the lid askew. The file clerks wouldn't be so sloppy. Not with Janice clucking over their every move. He read the label: *Sheridan Electronics*. That was an old case, closed ages ago. Something was tapping on the door of his memory, trying to remind him of . . . what?

Popping off the lid of the file box, he immediately saw the padded envelope. The label on the front said "Sheridan Trial Exhibit". Dov didn't know what it was, but it had to be significant. Anders wouldn't be taking it upon himself to refile just any old exhibit.

Although he was dying to know what was so important to Anders, Dov wasn't about to open it in the conference room, with the cameras rolling. It would have to wait. He would take the file home to study, where he wouldn't risk getting caught. Dov walked back to his office with the envelope and a fresh set of questions. Something about this was off. The case was closed, but hadn't someone just mentioned Sheridan recently?

Who the hell was it?

He shook his head. Even more pressing right now, and the task he needed to concentrate on, was recovering that video of Kaitlyn and Anders.

Back in front of his computer, Dov set the file recovery software to run. While he waited, he pulled up the key card log. As he skimmed the report, he saw two entries on Saturday evening: Jeff

Petronelli, in at 10:26 p.m. and out at 10:38 p.m. When Dov last saw him at the party, Petronelli was three sheets to the wind. So what the hell was Jeff doing at the office on Saturday night?

He tried to recall a time during the party that Jeff was absent, but from what he remembered, he was around all night. Dov pulled up the security video footage from Saturday night and fast forwarded to 10:25 p.m. As a figure came into view, Dov stopped and whistled. Chris Fischer. Saturday night, while everyone else was getting hammered, Fischer was here, in the office. To get that file.

He opened his email and saw that Beau Harris, his team leader and valet at the party, had sent his report as requested. According to Beau's report, Fischer's grey Acura SUV never left the party at all. It was still parked at the Club when Harris went off duty at two a.m.

Dov scrolled through the report. Sure, Fischer's car never left the Club, but Petronelli's white Toyota Highlander left at 10:07 p.m., and returned at 11:01 p.m. Chris, that sneaky little shit, had used his buddy's key card *and* his car.

Dov picked up his phone and dialed Beau Harris.

"Hey Dov, did you get my report?"

"Yep. And that's why I'm calling," Dov said. "I'm just wondering if there were any cars left at the Club on Saturday other than the grey Acura SUV on your report?"

"Hang on a sec, and I'll check," Beau said. Dov could hear the clicking of a keyboard in the background. "No, that was the only car left behind. And is something going on? The cops called me yesterday about a 1967 blue Triumph TR4A."

"That's why I'm calling, too. Do you remember the driver?"

Beau paused. "Yep. Here it is. She departed at 11:33. Good looking woman. Am I in trouble for something?"

"No, nothing to do with you. She had the keys," Dov said. "But she was in an accident after she left the party. Fatal hit and run down at Lincoln and Tatum."

"Holy shit, man. Sorry to hear that," Beau said. "In case they're looking at liability, she seemed competent and sober when she left."

"Thanks for verifying, Beau."

Dov hung up. Kaitlyn died in Suzanne's car, but . . . was it really an *accident*? And was that video the reason? People had killed for less. And even if it wasn't a motive for murder, what was Fischer going to use the video for?

It would make sense he wouldn't want that incriminating video popping up as a potential motive. But, again, how would he have known Kaitlyn would be driving Suzanne's car, when Dov himself hadn't known until the last minute? It seemed almost impossible. No, if the accident *wasn't* accidental, it had to be Anders behind it. Dov didn't know how, but all his instincts led to that conclusion.

And if Dov had let Suzanne drive herself home . . . A shudder ran down his back. He didn't know how—yet—but he was *sure* that sonofabitch Anders had planned to kill her Saturday night. It was only a momentary fatigue that saved Suzanne's life.

How the hell did Anders do it?

Dov glanced at the folder and stuffed it into his backpack. Maybe the answer was in there.

His software dinged a notification. The file was recovered. He copied the video to a flash drive, shut down his computer and prepared to head home to inspect that package Anders had filed. In the elevator on the way to the parking garage, he thought again about Saturday night with Suzanne and everything that had happened since.

What a difference a day makes.

43

TSUNAMI HAZARD

MONDAY, MARCH 21, 8:12 A.M.

Before she even got to the office, Camelia was already dreading a long list of crappy tasks. The ride upstairs was still making her heart gallop, but thanks to Dr. Chavez, she was able to hold the panic at bay. Mostly. But she could feel it there, lurking, waiting for an opening, every time she stepped into the elevator.

As soon as she pulled the heavy glass door open, Cheri's head popped up and she picked up her phone.

"Cate? She's here," Cheri said, then looked back at Camelia. "Cate needs to see you immediately."

Oh no. What now?

"On my way," she replied.

As she hurried down the hall toward her office, Camelia saw Cate standing in her doorway hugging a case file.

"Sorry to jump on you first thing, but we've got an issue," Cate said.

"Come on in." Camelia brushed past Cate and tossed her briefcase on the floor, then hung her handbag and jacket on the hook on the back of her door. Her stomach was already tying itself in a knot, and Cate's worried expression just made it worse. "What's going on?"

Cate closed the door and sat in the chair opposite Camelia's. "We have some serious shit hitting the fan. Have you checked your voice messages and email?"

"No. You know I'm under doctor's orders to leave all that for office hours. What happened?"

"I don't even know where to start." Cate took a deep breath.

A rush of adrenaline hit Camelia's system as panic began to set in.

What have I screwed up now?

"Crisis one. We got an anonymous email a few minutes ago. The email address is KittyHawk84 at Hotmail, which apparently belongs to Kaitlyn Fischer. I thought it was spam at first but . . . you need to look at it."

"This sounds serious." Camelia tapped on her keyboard. She scrolled down and found the email. As she read the message, she felt lightheaded. "Holy shit," she whispered.

"Wait 'til you see the video," Cate said, shaking her head. "And before you ask, yes, I scanned it for malware."

Camelia tapped on the video link and enlarged it full screen. She watched as Anders and a blond woman sat at a conference table, appearing to review files. The camera was situated somewhere above and slightly behind them, likely mounted on the ceiling.

Without looking away, Camelia asked, "So this is Kaitlyn Fischer?"

"According to the email, yes," Cate said.

Anders swiveled the woman's chair to face him and placed his hand on the back of her neck, pulling her face to his. He roughly kissed her as he shoved his other hand up her skirt. Kaitlyn responded by undoing Anders' trousers. The scene quickly escalated to full on amateur porn. Camelia watched for a minute, shocked, but also a little bit fascinated. She clicked the video off, and laughed out loud.

"Jesus, Mary, and Joseph. Anders is in the shit now. I would *love* to know what he did to piss off his side piece, because this kind of thing tanks careers," Camelia said. "And it's all the leverage Suzanne ever needed. Can't wait to enter this as Exhibit A."

Cate stared back at her with wide eyes, her lips drawn in a tense line.

"What? It's funny as hell, if you ask me," Camelia laughed. "Well, probably not funny to Chris Fischer, but—"

"Definitely not funny to Chris Fischer. Which brings me to crisis number two. Kaitlyn Fischer died in a car accident Saturday night."

Camelia searched Cate's face for the punchline. She must have misunderstood.

"I'm sorry, *what* did you just say?" Camelia could feel her brain lurching, grabbing puzzle pieces, jamming them together. She blinked, hard. "Did you say she *died?*"

"Yeah. Kaitlyn was driving Suzanne Anders' car when she was in a fatal car accident just a couple of miles from Suzanne's house," Cate read from her notes. "Suzanne called this morning and gave me the short version, but she wants you to call her."

"You've gotta be fucking kidding me! Why was she driving Suzanne's car? What the hell happened?" Camelia stood up from her desk and held up her hand. "Wait, hold on. I need to call Suzanne right now. Can you do me a favor and bring me a coffee?"

"No problem. I need a refill, too. My brain is already scrambled and it's not even nine o'clock," Cate said as she stood and walked to the door. "We can address the rest of the shit show when you're done with Suzanne. Be right back with caffeine."

As Cate pulled the door shut, Camelia dialed Suzanne's number, anxiously tapping her pen on her legal pad as it rang.

"Camelia! Did Cate tell you—"

"Yes, and I'm speechless." Camelia said. "Are you okay?"

"Me? Oh, I'm great, actually," Suzanne said. "I mean, besides this awful mess."

"Well, that's a relief. Now, can you start at the top and tell me everything you know?"

Suzanne took a deep breath. "Okay, from the top. The AndersLaw annual firm party was Saturday night at Paradise Valley Country Club. Everyone who works at the firm was there, including Chris and Kaitlyn Fischer. I recognized Kaitlyn right off as the woman who dropped off that file at the casita a couple of weeks ago."

"Wait, why were you at the AndersLaw party?"

"Oh, didn't you know? I was the so-called guest of honor while Aaron rolled out his big cancer charity and shamed everyone into donating. He pressured me to show up since it was sort of *my* party," Suzanne said. "Anyway, I went, and I'm glad I did. It reminded me why I'm leaving him. It was actually a great farewell tour."

"Okay, we'll come back to that," Camelia said. "Please, go on."

"Well, it was the usual firm shindig. Open bar. Everyone got pretty loose. Mrs. Fischer included. She was panting after Aaron like a dog in heat." Suzanne paused. "And he made his rounds of the sweet young things, which is par for the course."

"*Uggh.*" Camelia grunted in commiseration. "I'm so sorry."

"Meh. I'm used to it. I left early, around eleven thirty, because I was tired—too tired to drive, thank god—so, I got a ride home. Around two in the morning, the cops showed up at the door wanting to know where my car was. At first, they thought I was the one in the accident, and I think it shocked them that I was at home." Suzanne huffed an exhale. "But since I was in bed asleep, they figured someone—they didn't know who at that point—must have stolen my car from the Club and got into an accident."

"That's so weird," Camelia said. "You drive some fancy vintage car, don't you? Is it totaled?"

"Well, not that fancy, but definitely vintage. It's an old Triumph TR4 my mother passed down to me. And yeah, it's totaled. I'd left my car at the Club, and expected Aaron to bring it home. Clearly, he didn't." Suzanne blew out a sigh. "The cops called last evening to tell me it was *Kaitlyn* driving my car. Hit and run with a dump truck, and she died at the scene."

"Holy crap." Camelia's mind was rushing from one theory to another. "Why on earth was Kaitlyn driving *your* car just a couple of blocks from *your* house?"

"Really good question, isn't it? I tried to call Aaron yesterday, but he's not answering, which is also very strange. Unless he's in Court or a meeting, he *always* picks up. Even for me."

"Is he at the casita?"

"He was there Saturday night, but he left before I got up Sunday morning and hasn't been back. I assume he's at his condo. And get this, Sunday morning around ten, Chris Fischer called—"

"How did Chris get your number?" Camelia paused from furiously scribbling notes.

"Had to be the firm directory. Anyway, Chris called looking for his wife. Apparently, Kaitlyn didn't come home Saturday night. And now we know why, but he didn't seem to know she'd been in an accident. Of course, neither did I, at that point."

"But why would he call you?"

"He seemed to think Kaitlyn was running some kind of errand for me, but I don't have any idea what he was talking about. I figured Kaitlyn didn't go home because she was shacked up with Aaron for the night, and I told Chris as much."

"Oh boy. That can't have gone over well," Camelia said.

"He didn't seem surprised. In fact, I'm sure he was about to tell me the same thing! Then, this morning, I received that email," Suzanne's voice grew quiet. "It went to all the senior partners, their wives, the president of the state bar, the head of the litigation group, along with you and Spencer."

"I saw," Camelia said. "That's gonna sting."

"No kidding. And I can't help but think Chris Fischer was behind it," Suzanne said. "I mean, the timing . . . Kaitlyn couldn't have sent that email, could she? Very odd, if you ask me."

"It's beyond odd, Suzanne. Did you tell the police about the video?"

Suzanne sighed. "Yeah, I forwarded it to Det. Luna, but Aaron had already reported it. And the cops want me to go to the station to make a statement, but I'm not talking to *anyone* unless you're with me," Suzanne said.

"Suzanne, I can tag along for moral support, if you want, but I'm not a criminal attorney," Camelia said. "Byron should go with you, since he's the criminal expert."

"That's fine," Suzanne said. "Feel free to schedule it any time that works for you guys. All I have on the calendar these days are doctor appointments, and I can always reschedule those."

"Does Cate have the contact info for the cop? Did you say Detective *Luna*?"

"Yes, I gave Cate his phone number," Suzanne said. Her voice dropped. "Camelia, I'm kinda freaked out. It was *my car* that crashed.

Everyone, including Aaron, thought I would be driving my car home. What if it wasn't an accident?"

Camelia caught her breath. "Do you honestly think the crash was meant for you?"

"I don't know. It's just . . . the cop was acting weird, and it almost seemed like he didn't think it was an accident, either."

"Well, in my experience, cops always act weird, but I'll see what I can find out. In the meantime, are you okay? Do you feel threatened by . . . I don't know, anyone? Aaron?"

"No, I'm perfectly safe," Suzanne paused. "Dov Saminski made sure of that."

And how, exactly, did he do that?

After finishing up the call with Suzanne, Camelia buzzed Cate to come back to her office.

"Okay, Suzanne's rattled, but she's okay. You said there's more?"

"Yeah, crisis three: Ashcroft has been blowing up my phone, but I'm letting it go straight to voicemail and Cheri is fending him off. For now. It hasn't even been a half hour and he's already emailed once and called three times about that video. His voice mails are getting crazier by the minute, but basically, he's accusing Suzanne of murder and doxing and I don't even know what else," Cate said.

"Yeah, I skimmed his email while I was talking to Suzanne. It sounds like he's on a rant about nothing, but are there specifics from his voice messages I should know?"

"No, he's just throwing spaghetti on the wall, repeating the same thing over and over. He's accusing Suzanne of rigging her own car to kill Kaitlyn because, according to him, she's viciously jealous." Cate sighed and shook her head. "And then he says Suzanne must have emailed the video to ruin Aaron's reputation and cover her own tracks."

"Oh *really?*" Camelia threw her pen on the desk. "So, he's going to commit slander and libel and set himself up for a bar complaint based on nothing but his stupid hunch?"

"Yeah, I figured you'd like that. But you know how slimy he is. Everything is *possibly* and *maybe* and all the right words to make sure he's just this side of breaking the law. He wants you to call him," Cate made air quotes. "The exact minute you arrive."

"Good thing I don't work for Ashcroft, huh?" Camelia sighed.

"Like that would ever happen." Cate laughed. "Oil and water."

"Oh my god, can you imagine how Anders lit Spencer up over that video? Ha! I almost feel sorry for him!" Camelia laughed. "But I don't think we need to worry about good ol' Spence. He's just covering his own ass. Or what's left of it after Anders is done kicking it. I'll let him stew for a bit, because I have to talk to Byron."

"Yeah, the sooner the better, because he's in trial this afternoon." Cate looked down at her note pad and flipped the page. "Now, crisis number four is actually pretty sad, and I'm not even sure it matters. Chris Fischer left a message on Sunday morning asking for an appointment at your earliest convenience to begin the divorce paperwork," Cate said, looking expectantly at Camelia. "What's the protocol?"

"Given the situation, there's no one to divorce. With Kaitlyn dead . . ." Camelia paused. "Call Chris back and let him know I'm happy to consult with him about next steps or we can set a time with Arturo to talk about probate."

"Will do," Cate said, writing notes.

"What time did he call?"

Cate looked at her notes. "The voice message was left at 10:29 a.m."

"Make sure you save the voice file. I don't know if it's significant, but," Camelia looked at her notes, then clicked on her email folder. "Suzanne brought up an interesting point. She suspects he's behind the email because it landed this morning, after Kaitlyn was already dead. I have to admit, the timing is pretty strange, isn't it?"

"This whole Monday is the weirdest I've ever seen, and that's saying a *lot*." Cate stood and headed for the door. "And just in case you thought your day was gonna be a cake walk, you have a call at one with the malpractice provider over that complaint Joan Hallman filed back in December."

Camelia put her head in in her hands. "Is it martini time yet?"

Cate gave her a sympathetic smile. "Not even close, boss."

Camelia grabbed her legal pad and a pen, and headed to Byron's office. Despite her explanation that she wasn't criminal counsel, Suzanne insisted the only way she was going to give a statement to the Paradise Valley Police Department was with Camelia in tow. What Suzanne didn't know is she'd inadvertently handed Camelia the opportunity she'd been waiting for. An excuse to convince Byron to let her start shadowing him. It wasn't much, but it could be the start of the criminal defense mentoring she had been hounding Byron for.

Byron's door was open and he was tapping furiously on his keyboard, his brow furrowed in concentration.

Camelia rapped her pen on the doorframe. "Hey Byron, I need fifteen or twenty minutes to talk about the Anders case. Is now good?"

Byron looked up, then at his watch. "I can spare ten minutes, and then I have to get back to this summary judgment response. So, stick to the facts," he said.

Camelia understood that Byron was busy. But they were *all* busy. And when he needed help, she was expected to drop everything and jump on it. Like she'd done for Jim Gerson, Byron's drunk pilot, and dozens of others. But when Camelia needed help, even for the high profile client he'd *insisted* she take on, Byron would only give her a begrudging ten minutes. A knot of resentment was taking root.

She quickly went down the list of facts she knew, and relayed that Suzanne needed criminal counsel, but insisted that Camelia be by her side when she gave her statement.

"That's not how this works, Belmont. Tell your client I will arrange a time and date that works with my calendar, but you won't be there. We'd have to double bill her."

By his tone of voice, it was impossible to tell if he was angry or just stressed by adding one more thing to his calendar.

"Byron, it's Suzanne Anders. She can afford the fees, and she specifically asked me to be there for moral support. Remember, you wanted me to coddle her. Plus, I'm really curious as to what happened to her car. I mean, someone could have tampered with it, thinking Suzanne would be driving, so—"

"Cam, stop. You've got a full caseload, but your billing is still *way* down. Not that I'm blaming you, but that Campbell mess ate up a lot of billable hours for everyone. You have a lot of catching up to do and Anders isn't your only case."

Camelia couldn't believe her boss would be so callous. But then again . . .

Classic Byron.

"There's no reason for you to attend a routine interview and, besides, you don't know the first thing about criminal law," Byron said.

"Which is why I want to go. You know I want to learn the mechanics of criminal defense. We talked about this a year ago."

Byron closed his eyes for a moment, his jaw clenching and unclenching, then looked directly at Camelia. "We talked about a *lot* of things a year ago. But right now, the firm needs an experienced, efficient divorce attorney, not a rookie criminal attorney. And if you can't manage your client's expectations, I'm happy to let her know who's in charge."

"Jesus, you don't have to be so snarly. I'm just trying to be helpful," Camelia could feel herself getting defensive, so she took a slow breath to quell the urge to tell Byron to go screw himself.

"But you're not being helpful, are you? Because if you were being *helpful*, you'd stay in your lane, work on a settlement in the divorce, and keep your nose out of the criminal investigation."

The look on Byron's face was enough to tell her there was no wiggle room.

"Now, as I said, you had ten minutes. If there's nothing else?" He turned back to his monitor, dismissing her with a tap on his keyboard.

Camelia spun on her heel and stomped back to her office, slamming the door.

Clearly, Byron was never going to give her a chance. It wasn't even ten o'clock and she'd already had her world rocked and received a good stripping from Byron. She hadn't even called Ashcroft yet. This day was just getting worse by the fucking minute.

Camelia opened her desk drawer and pulled out her little copper flask. As she unscrewed the cap, she thought about how Byron had spit the words at her. *You don't know the first thing about criminal law.*

She took a long swig of vodka and the burn in her throat immediately calmed her.

It's time to make an exit strategy.

44

JUST THE FACTS

MONDAY, MARCH 21

Cate stood in the doorway to Camelia's office. "Jim Duncan's on line four on the Hallman matter. And do you want me to order something for lunch so it will be here when you're done with your call?"

Camelia looked up from her computer and nodded. The little buzz from this morning's bolt of vodka had worn off and now she was hungry and tired.

"Thanks, I'll have that chicken salad from Duck & Decanter. And can you close my door?" Camelia picked up the handset and pushed the blinking light on her phone.

Cate gave a little wave and shut the door.

Jim Duncan, the malpractice attorney assigned to her case by the professional liability insurer, had worked with Camelia on prior complaints. He was smart, pragmatic, and she trusted him. He also understood that family law attorneys get more bar complaints than all the other specialties, and was good-natured about it.

"Jim, Camelia here. How bad is it?"

As he talked through the pros and cons of Joan Hallman's claims, Camelia's mind was busy thinking about Suzanne Anders' crashed car when she realized Jim had stopped talking.

"Sorry, what was that?" she asked.

"I said, does she have anything other than her *opinion* that you were drinking the day of the mediation?" Jim asked.

"I don't . . . no."

"You don't know?" Camelia heard the concern in Jim's voice.

"No, she doesn't. Joan's looking for a scapegoat because the trial didn't go her way. On the day of mediation, I was in the conference room with her all day until she stormed out. None of us left the building. So, no, I didn't go bar hopping."

"So, when she says she smelled alcohol on you at mediation, she's making it up, right?" Jim asked.

Well, no, Jim. The fact is, I tossed back a couple of ounces in the ladies' room because Joan Hallman is an insufferable bitch.

"I carry Listerine with me. I had a gargle after lunch, so maybe that's what she smelled." Camelia's palms were sweating. This is why she had to lay off during work hours. Covering her tracks all the time was exhausting. "I honestly don't get why she thinks I tanked the mediation. Joan was the one who walked out in a huff when the mediator schooled her about the unreasonableness of her demands."

"She insists it was your job to advise her on the likely outcome of trial, and I quote, *in a way she could understand*. And she says you didn't do that because you were under the influence," Jim said.

"Joan has an MBA, and is the comptroller for a tech company, so this claim that she didn't understand what we were *all* telling her is pretty lame."

"Look, I just want to be sure you and I are on the same page, because . . ." Jim sighed. "I've heard a rumor or two."

A flash of rage quickened Camelia's pulse.

Fucking Ashcroft.

"Jim, if you're referring to Spencer Ashcroft's little smear campaign, you should know he's full of shit," she said, a little louder than she'd intended.

"Okay, but he's been saying . . ."

Camelia was ready to recite the *mostly* true excuse she'd practiced in her head the night before. She couldn't exactly tell her professional liability attorney she was having panic attacks, but she had to tell him something.

"Oh, I know what he's been *saying.* And here's what *I'm* saying. I was on my period and hadn't had breakfast. Then his client had a heart attack and it was very . . . upsetting. Obviously. And that prick Ashcroft barged into the ladies' room like he owned the place. He saw me sitting on the floor with my head between my knees to keep from fainting, and made up his own version of the facts." Her cheeks burned with anger and shame at the memory. "It was just low blood sugar, but Ashcroft exploited the situation. And me. Which is what jerks like him do. And I really don't want to hear another word about it, understood?"

"Whoa, there, Nellie. I'm on your side, remember?" Jim laughed. "I like your fire, though. You must be fun in the courtroom."

Camelia took a deep breath and blew it out slowly. Jim *was* on her side, and he'd always been a good advocate for her.

"Sorry. You hit a nerve. Ashcroft managed to spread that lie all the way to my boss's office. I would have already made partner if it weren't for that asshole." Well, maybe.

"Ouch. That *sucks*. And if you say Hallman is wrong, then she's wrong. Even if she was right, I don't see how she could prove it. I'll send a letter over to her lawyer and see if we can wrap this up. In the meantime, quit doing shots in the bathroom, wouldya?" Jim laughed.

Camelia tried to laugh in response, but it came out as a little croak. The comment hit way too close to home. "Good advice, as always, Jim. Talk soon."

She'd no sooner hung up than her phone buzzed.

"What's up, Cheri?"

"There's a Det. Luna here, from Paradise Valley police. He says Suzanne Anders gave him your contact information, and he'd like a word," she said.

"He's in the lobby?" Camelia clicked on her calendar. No appointments, except with that chicken salad. Until now.

"Yeah, said he was in the area." Cheri lowered her voice. "Do you want me to get rid of him?"

Camelia thought about it for a few seconds.

Might as well get it over with.

"No, I'll meet him in the main conference room in a few minutes, thanks," Camelia said, and hung up.

She buzzed Byron's extension, but it went straight to voicemail, so she rang Sonia.

"Hey, is Byron available? There's a cop in the lobby who wants to talk to me about the Anders case, and I need backup."

"Sorry, he's on a telephonic with Federal Court and he's going to be a while. Check with one of the associates. The new guy, Ken Stafford, maybe?" Sonia's voice was flat.

"Got it. Everything okay?" Camelia asked.

"Of course. Why wouldn't it be?" Sonia snapped.

Camelia couldn't help but wonder if there was trouble between Byron and Sonia, and frankly, she hoped there was. Byron had no business screwing around with his assistant. Or anyone else, for that matter. He was no better than Anders! Not to mention that an office scandal would tarnish the dazzle Byron—and the whole firm—was currently enjoying thanks to Josh Campbell's suicide. The publicity had sent a drove of people to the firm with their hands full of life's misfortunes. Camelia shuddered. They were all profiting nicely on Campbell's death. No matter how posh it looked from the outside, it was all blood money.

"No reason. I'll buzz Ken, thanks." Camelia hung up and rang Ken Stafford's extension. He was a fairly new associate, so she barely knew him, but any attorney in the room with her was better than none.

He answered on the first ring.

"Ken, Camelia Belmont. I'm about to have an informal chat with a cop in the main conference room, but Byron's tied up, and you know the rules. No one talks to law enforcement without an attorney present. So, can you please come to my office right away?"

"Yes ma'am. On my way," he replied.

Baby attorneys were always so cooperative. It was a nice change from the roadblocks and snark she was getting from Byron lately.

Camelia had barely gathered up her notepad and the Anders client file before there was a light tap on her door. A young man with a tousled mop of black curls stepped into her office and pulled the door closed behind him.

Damn! These days, all the new associates looked like they should still be in college.

"Any idea what the police want to talk to you about, ma'am?" His pen was poised over a legal pad.

"First, call me Camelia. Second, yes. My client is Suzanne Anders. Her husband is Aaron Anders of AndersLaw. One of the senior associates from his law firm, who also happened to be having an affair with Mr. Anders, was driving Suzanne's car on Saturday night when she was in a fatal car accident a few miles from the party.

Opposing counsel is making noises that Suzanne Anders is somehow involved." Camelia moved toward the door. "Oh, and we got an email early this morning with a video of Anders and the associate having sex in a conference room. And that's about all I know. Ready?"

He whistled as he looked at her with eyes that matched his sage green suit.

"Yes, ma'am . . . Camelia. Lead the way," he said, holding the door open for her.

I could get used to being treated like I matter.

"Cate, we'll be in the main conference room with the PV police," Camelia said as she walked past Cate's desk.

"Got it," Cate replied. "And your lunch is in the fridge, when you're done."

"Thank god. I'm starving," Camelia said over her shoulder as she briskly walked down the hall.

A few steps later, Ken rushed ahead of her and held open the conference room door. Camelia stepped inside and plastered a smile on her face as she held out her hand.

"Camelia Belmont, divorce counsel for Suzanne Anders. This is Ken Stafford, criminal defense associate with the firm," she said, nodding at Ken. "How can we help you?"

"Thanks for seeing me without an appointment. I'm Detective Sergeant Luna, Paradise Valley Police, and this is Officer Sherman. We're part of the team investigating the fatality of Kaitlyn Fischer on Saturday night," the older man said as he shook Camelia's hand.

"Please, have a seat," Camelia offered as she sat down. "I'll do what I can, but I have to observe attorney client privilege, so I may not be much help."

"Yep, I know the drill. Suzanne Anders says you're representing her in her divorce case, and I'm interested in some basic facts."

"Okay, but I thought this was about a car accident," Camelia said.

"Correct. But we investigate every fatality. So, did Suzanne Anders suspect that Aaron Anders was having an affair with Kaitlyn Fischer?" Det. Luna asked.

Camelia glanced at Ken. He blinked and gave an almost imperceptible shake of his head.

"I can't really give an opinion on what Ms. Anders knew or didn't know about Kaitlyn Fischer. I can tell you, because it's public record, that Mr. Anders is a known philanderer." Camelia paused for a sip of water as her stomach loudly growled. "Sorry for the whale song. I haven't managed to eat lunch yet."

Det. Luna laughed, revealing a row of very white teeth against his sun-weathered skin. "We won't be long. Do you know *anything* about Aaron Anders and Kaitlyn Fischer?"

"I know way more than I ever wanted to," Camelia said, raising her eyebrows. "I was greeted this morning with a very naughty video attached to an email from an anonymous source. Have you seen it?" Camelia asked.

"Yes, Mr. Anders reported it. We have a digital forensics expert looking at it now to figure out who sent it. Any theories?"

"Who knows? I'm sure Aaron Anders has made plenty of enemies along the way." Camelia glanced at Ken, who was furiously writing notes. He gave her another small shake of his head. "For all I know, he sent that video himself. But your guys will figure it out soon enough."

"Do you know Christopher Fischer, Kaitlyn Fischer's husband?" Det. Luna asked.

"That's attorney client privileged information," Camelia responded.

"Well, it's not all that privileged, because Ms. Anders reported that you're representing him, too. Kinda odd, isn't it? I mean, representing the two spouses of the cheating couple?" His eyes were trained on her face and Camelia knew he was watching for a twitch, a tell. "I don't care about who gets the sofa or whatever. We're just trying to get a picture of what was going on in Kaitlyn Fischer's life that might lead her to be driving her boss's wife's car."

"I was not officially retained as Mr. Fischer's attorney," Camelia said.

Det. Luna heaved a sigh. "Look, if she was distracted by marital problems, that might be one explanation for her accident. If she was having a fling with her boss, that might explain the car. Either way, I've got a 32 year old woman at the morgue who had to be ID'd by her dental records, and I'd like to know why."

"I have no idea why she was driving Ms. Anders' car, and I don't know why she had an accident. *And* I have rules to follow," Camelia said.

"Well, I can get a subpoena," Det. Luna said.

"Do what you have to do, but to be clear, I'm not trying to be obstinate. We're always happy to help law enforcement, aren't we Ken?"

Ken's eyes widened a bit as he nodded. "Absolutely. I mean, to the extent that our cooperation doesn't run up against the attorney client privilege, which remains intact despite a warrant, other than the exceptions stated in the rules."

"Okay, Einstein. No need for all that," Det. Luna said to Ken. He turned back to Camelia. "Let's start with Suzanne Anders. Why is she getting a divorce?"

"Public record, you can answer," Ken said.

Det. Luna shot Ken a look, and the younger officer smirked.

"It's all laid out in our Petition for Dissolution, sergeant. Nothing unusual about it. Ms. Anders is seeking a divorce and equitable division of marital assets. And there is a claim for marital waste based on Mr. Anders' infidelity," Camelia said.

Her stomach grumbled.

"And was Kaitlyn Fischer the reason for the divorce?"

"Not really. As I said before, Mr. Anders has quite a reputation. Mrs. Fischer was just one more in a long line," Camelia said.

"So, you don't think Ms. Anders would have had any special reason, I mean besides the obvious, for wanting Mrs. Fischer dead?" Det. Luna asked.

Camelia barked a laugh. "Not at all. I think . . . in fact I *know* that all Ms. Anders wants is a divorce. She couldn't care less about Kaitlyn Fischer or any of the others."

"Maybe that video tipped her over the edge, though," Det. Luna said.

"Ms. Anders received that video along with the rest of us, more than thirty six hours after the accident," Camelia said.

Det. Luna smiled and nodded. "Good catch, Counselor. But Mr. Anders' attorney," he shuffled a couple of pages in his little notebook. "Spencer Ashcroft. He thinks Ms. Anders is behind the video, and that she tampered with the car."

Camelia shook her head. "And you believe that windbag? He'll say whatever it takes to take the heat off his client. If anything, I'd be looking at Aaron Anders. You know. Side piece suddenly becomes inconvenient, etcetera."

Det. Luna laughed again. "Well, that's another interesting theory. And no, I don't think Mr. Ashcroft has much evidence for his claims." He flipped through his notes. "So, about Christopher Fischer . . ."

"As I said, I met with Mr. Fischer, but I was not formally engaged to represent him," Camelia said. "And, now that Mrs. Fischer is deceased, he won't be needing a divorce."

"Isn't that a pretty strong motive?" Det. Luna asked.

"No more so than any other divorce. It's not like Chris Fischer was going to get filthy rich overnight because his wife died. Unlike Aaron Anders." Camelia took a sip of water and gave Det. Luna a hard stare to drive home her own theory. "If my client had been driving her own car, as everyone *expected* . . . well, Mr. Anders would get the whole pie. And it's a pretty damn big pie. North of ten million. I hope you're looking at that possibility."

"Thanks for the tip. But back to Fischer. You met with him about his divorce?"

"I met with him once, and our meeting is covered by the attorney client privilege. I can't tell you what we talked about."

"Do you think Mr. Fischer killed his wife?"

Camelia knew the shock of that question registered on her face. She thought about Chris Fischer: gangly, awkward, but who knows? The email they'd all received could have come from him. But stealing a video and blasting revenge porn wasn't the same as murder.

"I thought you said Kaitlyn was in a *car accident* in Ms. Anders' car? How would Mr. Fischer have anything to do with that?" Camelia asked.

This cop was starting to annoy her. He kept knocking on the same door, hoping she would drop her guard and break the privilege.

No way. Not going to happen.

"All good questions. While we assume this was just an unfortunate accident, when there's a fatality involving our Paradise Valley community members, even tangentially, we have to look at all angles," Det. Luna said.

"Sounds like white privilege to me," Camelia smirked.

Det. Luna just raised his eyebrows and continued. "It's still nagging me that a dump truck full of gravel was hauling ass through PV on a Saturday night." He shrugged. "But the truck was reported stolen, and whoever was driving it is in the wind. So, it's likely just the usual hit and run. Driver got spooked and took off, and we'll probably never find him. Now, all I need to do is verify all that, so I can go home and have a long nap. Is there *anything* you can tell me about *anything?*"

Camelia thought about it for a moment, and decided the information was fair game. It had nothing to do with the Anders divorce, and would be a nice bone for this cop to chew on.

"There is one thing . . . this disclosure in no way compromises or waives Suzanne Anders' attorney client privilege. And I have a witness," Camelia nodded at Ken. "A couple of weeks ago, Kaitlyn Fischer showed up at the Anders' estate in the early evening. She apparently had the gate code, because she drove onto the property without ringing the security intercom. Mr. Anders has been living in the casita for about a year, but he was not home at the time. Ms. Anders was home, and happened to observe Mrs. Fischer's movements from the main house. Mrs. Fischer went into the casita carrying a file folder. When she left, she no longer had the file."

Det. Luna nodded. "Is that so? And what was in this file folder?"

"Um . . ." Camelia looked at Ken, but she could tell by his expression that he didn't know whether this information was fair game or not. "Client trial exhibits."

As the senior officer looked at his partner and then back at Camelia, she couldn't tell if he was doing it for effect, or he really meant it when he said, "Now, why wouldn't either of the Anders have mentioned that, I wonder?"

A flutter of panic caught in Camelia's throat. Had she just put Suzanne in Luna's crosshairs?

45

LOVERS AND OTHER LOSERS

MONDAY, MARCH 21

If Det. Luna was confused as to why Suzanne hadn't reported Kaitlyn Fischer visiting the casita a couple of weeks ago, Camelia was doubly so. There's no way it could have slipped Suzanne's mind. Luna seemed like the permanently suspicious type, and Camelia figured being on the police force of one of the wealthiest communities in the country afforded him the luxury of being hyper-meticulous. And now, if Det. Luna hadn't already considered Suzanne a person of interest, finding out she hadn't mentioned Kaitlyn's visit to the casita would definitely put Camelia's client on the cop's radar.

As she rushed down the hall, Ken Stafford in her wake, Camelia's mind was humming. When they reached Cate's desk, Camelia paused to place the Anders file back on the active case shelf before turning to Ken.

"You were great in there, thanks," she said.

"My pleasure. Do you want a debrief or should I just email my notes?" Ken pushed a curl out of his eyes.

"Email's fine. Right now, I need to talk to my client." Camelia turned to Cate. "Can you get Suzanne Anders on the phone, please? It's about her statement to the police."

"Got it," Cate said. "And Ken, copy me on the notes, please."

"Will do." The young associate gave a quick nod and turned away, walking swiftly down the hall.

Cate grinned at Camelia. "Whew. Is it warm in here?" She fanned herself and laughed. "And is it just me, or is he too young to have a full time job?"

"All the newbies look like they're too young to drive, even," Camelia shrugged. "But you know what? Boy Genius was totally on point in that meeting. I think he's a keeper, actually."

"I hope he sticks around. Because it's high time the partners started taking diversity a little more seriously," Cate said. "I mean, there's Arturo, but he's a partner and doesn't really count."

"Yeah, it's overdue, isn't it? Maybe someday they'll even hire another woman! Anyway, I gotta talk to Suzanne right away. Just ring her through when you have her on the line." Camelia crossed the hall into her office.

She shut the door and slid behind her desk. A couple of minutes later her phone buzzed.

"Suzanne, hey, thanks for taking my call," Camelia said. "I wanted to talk to you as soon as possible, because I just finished meeting with the PV cops and . . . I was caught off guard. They didn't seem to know Kaitlyn Fischer had been at the casita."

"They didn't?" Suzanne sounded momentarily confused.

"No, and it raised a red flag because neither you nor Aaron mentioned that Kaitlyn had been on the property a few weeks ago." Camelia took a deep breath and a sip of water. "So, now they think there's something there."

"Well, shit. How the hell was I supposed to know Kaitlyn was driving my car? I mean, why would I even mention her at all? It was the middle of the damn night, and I was asleep when Dov . . ." Suzanne drew in a sharp breath. "When they arrived at my door. I was pretty out of it. I guess I just wasn't thinking straight."

Camelia was pretty sure she knew what Suzanne was about to say when she caught herself. *When Dov woke me up.* Jesus. Were those two having an affair? In the middle of Suzanne's divorce?

"Well, okay. That makes sense, but be sure to clarify when you make your statement." Camelia could understand why Suzanne wouldn't have brought Kaitlyn up, but there was another issue. "Now, is there something you need to tell me about Dov Saminski? Starting with why he drove you home from the party?" Camelia paused. She didn't want to pry, but then again, if Suzanne was going to have a fling, why the hell couldn't she pick someone other than her husband's strongman?

"Just between us?" Suzanne asked.

"Just between us. I'd like to make sure you're not putting yourself in a situation that might bite you in the ass later."

"Well, it's not like I'm going to need a prenup," Suzanne laughed. "But, between you and me—and I mean *strictly* between you and me—Dov and I sort of . . . connected."

Holy shit, girl.

"Ooookay. Are you . . . I mean, did you . . ." Camelia wasn't sure how to put it without being rude. "Are you sure he's a person you can trust?"

Did Suzanne just giggle?

"Oh, I'm pretty sure I can trust Dov with my life. You don't have to worry about him, Camelia. He's . . . he's on my side."

"And how can you know that, Suzanne? Look, your private business is your private business, but I don't want Aaron manipulating his employee just to trip you up. So, fair warning, I think spending time with anyone affiliated with Aaron is a bad idea," Camelia said.

"I get where you're coming from and thank you. But it's really okay," Suzanne said. "Anyway, I'll tell the police all about Kaitlyn when I go to make my statement. Have you scheduled it?"

"Well, that's another thing." Camelia took a deep breath. "I can't attend that meeting with you, Suzanne. I'm a family law attorney, not a criminal attorney, and my boss doesn't want us to make any missteps in protecting your rights. He's going to appear with you for the statement, and you'll be in good hands. Byron's the best—"

"Oh, really? What if I want you there anyway? Don't I get a choice?" Suzanne asked, and her voice pitched up an octave.

"I get it. You're used to working with me. But Byron was firm on this point. I'm not a partner and I'm certainly no criminal attorney, so I'm in no position to argue with him. Byron will make sure you're fully protected."

"Fine. I'll handle Byron, then," Suzanne said. "Because at this stage of my life, I will not be told how my representation is going to be managed, and by whom. And if Byron doesn't like it, well, I'll just find another criminal attorney. They're a dime a dozen."

Camelia sighed. Suzanne didn't know what she was up against with Byron. Or maybe she did. Being married to a man like Aaron Anders had surely taught her a few things about handling overbearing men.

"Do you want Byron's direct number? Because this needs to be managed quickly. I do not want you even remotely in the frame for what happened to Kaitlyn Fischer, so let's get that statement scheduled, okay?" Camelia said.

"Absolutely. I'll call Byron as soon as we hang up, and get on his calendar," Suzanne said. "And Camelia, thanks for worrying about me. But when it comes to Dov, I'm perfectly safe. I trust him completely."

"I hope so. It's the least you deserve. And I'll wait to hear from Byron. Knowing him, I'll hear him all the way down the hall. Good luck!"

Camelia had no sooner hung up than Cate was in her doorway holding a take-out container and a glass of iced tea.

"Before you do one more thing, please eat. Otherwise, someone is going to steal your lunch and you're going to pass out!" Cate set the container on Camelia's desk.

"Thank you. Jesus, what a day," Camelia said as she popped the top off her salad and began eating.

"Yeah, and there's not going to be a good time for it, but you probably need to call Chris Fischer when you're done." Cate shook her head. "Poor guy. It's all over the news. Do you want me to send flowers over to his house?"

"No, not flowers," Camelia said around a mouthful of chicken salad. "He's a string bean and needs food. And this salad is a good place to start. Pick out five good meals from Duck and have them delivered. Stuff that will keep."

"Yeah, that's a better idea." Cate turned and walked to the door. "I'll leave you to it," she said as she pulled the door closed behind her.

With the first bite of chicken, Camelia realized how hungry she was. Ravenous, in fact. She was just shoveling another forkful into her mouth when her door flew open and Byron stormed in. Behind him, Cate scurried to pull the door shut.

Great. There goes my peaceful lunch.

"Sorry," Camelia mumbled through a mouthful of food. "I wasn't expecting company." She waved at the chair opposite hers.

"I just got off the phone with Suzanne Anders. I thought I was very clear about my position on this, and yet she seems to think your presence at the Paradise Valley Police Department is negotiable," Byron said. "So, who gave her that idea?" He sat down and crossed his arms across his chest.

He's itching for a fight.

Camelia swallowed. "I told Suzanne I wasn't coming along for her statement to the cops, and that you were going to manage it. She disagreed. I told her it wasn't a suggestion and, since I'm not a partner, I have no sway over such things." Camelia took a sip of tea. "You wanted a Scottsdale socialite on the client docket. Well, here she is, demands and all."

"You think this is funny, don't you?" Byron glowered at Camelia over his glasses. "The interview is Wednesday at 3:45 p.m. at the station. You are *not* to bill her for your time and you are *not* to say one word during the interview. Am I clear?"

Camelia almost laughed out loud. So *that's* why he was so pissed off. Suzanne had gotten her way.

"Got it, boss. I'm just there for moral support. And to take notes."

"Not one word, Belmont." Byron got up and turned to leave. He paused at the doorway. "Email me a summary of the timeline of events before you leave today."

Byron slammed the door behind him and Camelia let out the breath she'd been holding. And then she burst out laughing.

But right behind the laugh was a pang of regret. Where was the Byron she'd loved and admired all these years? When did he stop being her cherished mentor and friend? And why was he antagonizing her every chance he got? The realization came quickly, and with a sting. Byron was hoping she would get tired of all the cold snubs and harsh words, and leave of her own accord. He was done with her.

"Chris? Camelia Belmont," she said. "I know it's probably not a good time, but—"

"Yeah, not even sure why you're calling. No need for a divorce now, is there?" Chris Fischer said. His voice was flat, almost angry.

"Chris, I'm so, so sorry. It's just a terrible thing to happen, so I wanted to reach out to see if I can do anything for you."

"Like what? I've been spared the divorce circus, so there's nothing left for you to do."

"I know, I know. But if you want or need any other kind of assistance . . ." Camelia barely knew him, but she'd become kind of fond of the gawky puppy of a man jilted by his grasping wife. "I know a lot of people. Therapists, grief counselors, probate attorneys, you name it. Seriously, I want to help," Camelia said.

She could hear Chris let out a ragged sigh, and wondered if he was crying.

"I know. I'm sorry. Just a really rough couple of days," Chris said, his voice a low murmur. "But there's nothing anyone can do. Not now."

"Do you have any idea what happened? Why Kaitlyn was driving Suzanne Anders' car?" Camelia thought maybe, if he talked about it, it would be a relief. She wasn't prepared for his angry response.

"No. Why the fuck would I?" His voice came out in a snarl. "Suzanne Anders asked Kaitlyn to do her a favor, so she left the party early—"

She couldn't tell if he was grieving or guilty. "What kind of favor?"

"I have no idea. That's what Kaitlyn said right before she left me high and dry at the party. Said she'd find a ride home. And that's all I know."

But Suzanne said she never asked Kaitlyn to do anything on her behalf. So, who was Kaitlyn *actually* doing favors for these days? Aaron Anders, that's who.

"Okay, I'm sorry. I didn't mean to cause you any more pain," Camelia said. "When someone from Duck & Decanter rings your bell this evening, answer the door. Cate and I are sending some food over for you, okay? And call me if you need anything, Chris. Anything at all."

"Thanks for the gesture. And yeah, I have your number. Anything else?" Chris said.

"Take care of yourself," she said and hung up.

It was not the conversation Camelia had expected and it left her unsettled, concerned, and more than a little bit suspicious. She glanced at the clock on her monitor. It was already after five and she still hadn't sent Byron the summary he'd asked for. She opened a blank document on her computer and began the list of events as she knew them, but there were so many things that just didn't make sense.

Was there something other than fatigue that convinced Suzanne Anders to leave the party with Aaron's Chief Security Officer?

Why didn't Suzanne have Saminski drive her home in her own car, then get a cab back to the Club, instead of leaving her car there for Aaron?

How did Kaitlyn Fischer get her hands on Suzanne's car keys?

Was there something wrong with the car that caused the crash, or was Kaitlyn drunk?

Det. Luna said a dump truck hit Suzanne's car in the intersection at Tatum and Lincoln. What the hell was a dump truck doing out at midnight on a Saturday night in a posh neighborhood like Paradise Valley?

And how was it that Kaitlyn Fischer was conveniently killed in the car owned by her lover's wife? It was just too . . .

What if Det. Luna's hackles were up for a good reason? Wouldn't Aaron Anders have expected Suzanne to be driving home that night, in her own car, alone?

The first inkling she'd had of anything going on between Kaitlyn and Anders was her consult with Chris Fischer. Then, the next thing she knew, Suzanne reported Kaitlyn showing up at the casita to drop off a package. It was an anomaly, according to Suzanne, that anyone—especially a girlfriend—would show up at their Paradise Valley estate just to deliver a file. What was so special about that particular file?

Camelia swiped open her phone and went to the photos folder. She selected the shots from that evening and forwarded them to her email. When it arrived in her inbox, she downloaded the photos and opened them, scaling them full screen.

Why the hell was this so damned important that Kaitlyn Fischer broke protocol and delivered it to Aaron's very off-limits home?

Was this file somehow related to the accident?

46

FOR THE RECORD

WEDNESDAY, MARCH 23

Camelia was dreading this afternoon. Byron was on the warpath, and she was going to have to spend god knows how long sitting in a stuffy police interview room with him and Det. Luna.

Despite having looked forward to this opportunity for a long time, Camelia didn't want to learn criminal procedure with Byron like this. Suzanne had given him an ultimatum, and Byron was convinced Camelia had put her up to it. He was pissed off, and nothing she said was going to change that.

She stuffed a legal pad and a fresh pen in her briefcase as Cate came to the door.

"Do you have everything you need for the meeting?"

"Yeah, I'm just there as an observer. Byron made that crystal clear." Camelia pulled on her suit jacket. "But if you've got a spare pot of honey for Byron, I could sure use it, because man, he is being a bear about this."

"Byron will be fine," Cate said. "I mean, you know how he is. Mantrum today, gone tomorrow."

"I hope so, but honestly, Cate, things have shifted. He seems . . . different," Camelia said. "Anyway, can you please call Suzanne and let her know I'm on my way to pick her up?"

"Will do. You have the directions to the station, right?"

"Yes, and I'll be back right after," Camelia said as she brushed past Cate. "Hold down the fort!"

She sounded more cheerful and confident than she felt. This afternoon was going to be tense.

Camelia had discussed Byron's outburst with Leon, looking for a reality check. But instead of agreeing that she was over-reacting, Leon reiterated his belief that it was time to start planning to go out on her own. Just the idea of it made Camelia's heart race. She'd always worked in private practice firms, surrounded by other attorneys, with a safety net of experience around her. And a paycheck. But if she went out on her own . . . there would be no net. She couldn't think about it now, or she'd be in full panic mode by the time they got to the police department.

Pulling up to the Anders estate, Camelia pushed the intercom button and waited for Suzanne to answer.

"Come on in," Suzanne said as the gate swung open. "I'll be right out."

Camelia pulled into the circular drive and waited, turning up the fan on the A/C. It wasn't even April and already too damn hot. As she muttered to herself about climate change, the passenger door opened and she looked up into intense grey eyes.

"Camelia Belmont?" A solid man with a cautious smile stood at the open passenger door.

"Yes. And you are?"

"Dov Saminski, Chief Security Officer for AndersLaw." He gave a slight bow of his head. "Suzanne will be—"

"I'm here, Dov. Be back in a bit." Suzanne tipped her face up and gave Saminski a little peck. "And stop worrying."

Suzanne slid into the passenger seat and buckled up as Camelia watched Saminski walk back into the house. He had the posture of a man at the ready and she admired the tight coil of muscles under his t-shirt.

Camelia glanced at Suzanne, who was also watching Dov walk away. When Suzanne turned back to Camelia her smile erupted into a laugh.

"My *body guard*," Suzanne said.

"So *that's* Dov Saminski?" Camelia smirked.

"The one and only," Suzanne said.

"He's not what I'd pictured."

"Oh?"

"He's a bit younger than I expected." Camelia pulled away from the house and down the winding driveway. "And he's . . . well, he seems very *fit*."

"You could say that," Suzanne chuckled. "Definitely no issues with *cardio*." She burst out laughing.

"We're going straight to hell." Camelia laughed along with her. "But until then, we need to focus. Byron is meeting us at the police station, and he's in a mood. I think you ruffled his feathers."

"Good. He had it coming. Since when does he get to dictate who I have on my legal team?" Suzanne flicked her highlighted bangs to one side. "These men. Always bossing us around. Even when I'm the one paying the damn bill."

Camelia wanted to add her own thoughts about Byron's tirade, but it was bad form. She had to keep up appearances.

"Byron's just trying to protect clients from over-spending. I'm sure you, of all people, can appreciate how quickly legal fees add up when you're not looking."

"Of course! How do you think Aaron paid for that outrageous house? But it should be *my* choice. If I want to double my fees to get the result I want, that's *my* decision, not Byron's." Suzanne huffed a sigh. "I've had enough of over-protective, condescending mansplainers. Hell, I've been married to one my whole adult life. And if Byron McCaffrey thinks I'm gonna roll over just because he says so, he's in for a surprise."

Camelia smiled. She liked this side of Suzanne.

But she didn't like this side of Byron and it brought her back, again, to the comparison of Aaron Anders and her boss. Maybe it was just the M.O. of successful litigators to be arrogant jerks. Or maybe they were two peas in a pod.

A broad shouldered woman with a copper-penny ponytail and a constellation of freckles across her face ushered them into an interview room. Camelia and Byron flanked Suzanne, who seemed to shrink under the fluorescent lights and muddy tan walls.

"Det. Luna will be right in," the woman said as she pulled the door shut behind her.

"Please remember, Mrs. Anders—"

"Byron, call me Suzanne, please."

"In here, you are Mrs. Anders. And I want to remind you that everything, including this conversation, should be assumed to be on the record." Byron pointed to the corners of the room. "This place is packed with cameras and microphones, so I never trust that those recording devices are off. *Ever.* If you want to discuss *anything*, we will step out to the parking lot, understood?"

Suzanne nodded her head.

"Also, remember to answer only the question asked. Don't give any information that isn't fully and completely true, or that wasn't requested, are we clear?"

"Yes, crystal clear," Suzanne said.

"So, if you are asked to verify something that is only partially true, you have to deny it," Byron said. "We can do explanations later, but this initial interview is to establish a timeline and the facts surrounding your whereabouts on the night of the party. Nothing more."

"Got it." Suzanne took a deep breath and placed her hand on Byron's arm. "And thank you, Byron. You have no idea how much it means to me that you've taken the time to be here. I know you're a very busy attorney, and with good reason, so I'm flattered to call you *my attorney* today."

Camelia looked down at her pad of paper and pressed her lips together to keep from grinning. Suzanne knew exactly how to play him.

"Of course," he said, and his expression softened. "It's part of your representation, and I'm happy to help. Camelia wanted to be here too, since she knows your case so well. It just makes sense that we show up together, a unified front to help you navigate this mess."

A light rap on the door announced Det. Luna and Officer Sherman, the same two who had shown up at Camelia's office. After introductions and cautions, Det. Luna turned on the recorder on his mobile phone and began asking questions. It was all foundational stuff, until he got to the part about Suzanne's car keys.

"As you know, the victim had your car keys," Det. Luna said. "So, your car may have been stolen, but it wasn't a random theft, was it?"

"How would Mrs. Anders know whether or not it was random?" Byron asked.

"Let me put it another way," Det. Luna's eyes narrowed. "Why did your husband's girlfriend have your car keys?"

"Again, Det. Luna, you're asking for speculation. Mrs. Anders has no way of knowing how Mrs. Fischer came across her car keys." Byron gave Det. Luna a raised eyebrow. "How about asking things she might actually be able to help with?"

"Actually, I do know—" Suzanne began.

Byron placed his left hand on Suzanne's wrist and held his right hand in the air. "May I consult with my client privately, please?"

Det. Luna and Officer Sherman exchanged a look. "Sure, by all means, we can leave," Det. Luna said.

"No, we'll step outside and be back in just a minute." Byron stood up and walked to the door.

Camelia followed Byron and Suzanne outside, where they gathered under the dappled shade of a palo verde tree covered in golden blooms.

"Okay, Suzanne. What you do you know?" Byron squinted against the harsh afternoon sun.

"I know that when I asked Dov Saminski to give my keys to Aaron, he didn't." Suzanne looked at the ground for a moment, and pursed her lips before continuing. "Dov went back into the party to deliver my car keys to him while I waited outside. But Aaron was in the middle of telling tall tales to a group of associates. He does *not* tolerate interruptions when he's buffing his image. So, Dov gave the keys to Kaitlyn Fischer, and asked her to pass them to Aaron."

Oh no.

"Why did he give the keys to Kaitlyn?" Byron asked.

"Because . . . Dov knew about their fling. And he figured she was the most reliable messenger." Suzanne's face fell into a grimace. "He assumed she would be happy to deliver the keys, along with whatever else she was providing Aaron."

"And why don't the cops already know this?"

"Dov told them he gave her the keys when they came to the house that night, but it sounds like they've forgotten. At the time, none of us knew Kaitlyn was the person in the accident, so it didn't seem all that important." Suzanne huffed a sigh. "We didn't find out who was driving my car until Sunday night. And look, no matter how it sounds, Dov wasn't responsible."

"Why are you so sure?" Byron asked.

"Because I . . . it was impromptu that I didn't drive home. Dov wasn't responsible, but some people, the cops in particular, might see him as a logical fall guy." Suzanne took a deep breath. "Based on his background, and the fact that he works for Aaron. Which is why I didn't bring it up again."

"Dov would have no reason to harm Kaitlyn Fischer," Camelia said. "But Aaron might have put him up to—"

Suzanne turned to Camelia. "Dov had *nothing* to do with what happened to Kaitlyn. I'd stake my life on it."

"Okay, let's get back in there and set the record straight, okay?" Byron shook his head. "And from now on, you tell me *everything*, understood?"

Suzanne nodded and followed Byron as he headed back to the police station. But now, Camelia's mind was spinning. What if it wasn't Chris Fischer or Aaron Anders at all?

What if Saminski was behind the whole thing?

She vowed to call Saminski in for a chat as soon as she got back to the office. He needed to stop straddling the AndersLaw fence. Because even if the investigation went nowhere, Kaitlyn Fischer's parents could still sue for wrongful death, and they would no doubt name everyone who'd come into contact with their daughter that night. Camelia knew damn well Anders would throw Saminski under the bus and never bat an eye. Saminski knew things, and it was time for him to start spilling his guts, or risk being eyed for something he didn't do. Camelia just hoped he was smart enough to know when to come clean.

When they stepped back into the interview room, Det. Luna was alone.

"Ready to finish up?" he asked.

"Yes, I think we've told you everything we can," Byron said. "Except for one detail you were already given. It clears up the issue of how Mrs. Fischer came to have Mrs. Anders' car keys. Suzanne, please tell Det. Luna what you told me in the parking lot."

Suzanne nodded and looked at Det. Luna. "When you showed up at my house in the middle of the night, I had no idea who had been driving my car, so it didn't seem important. But I want to clarify . . ."

"Clarify what?" Det. Luna leaned forward.

"Clarify is the wrong word. I want to *remind* you that Dov Saminski, the firm's Chief Security Officer, passed my keys to Kaitlyn Fischer at the party. He asked her to give them to my husband."

Det. Luna flipped through his notes. "Okay . . . I see here he did say that, but I still don't know why. Do you?"

"Yes, because Aaron was occupied. Dov was aware of the affair between them and knew Kaitlyn could be trusted to give the keys to Aaron later." Suzanne said. She took a sip of water. "But he was wrong. She didn't give the keys to him. Instead, it seems like she took my car for a joy ride."

"And you knew nothing of this?" Det. Luna's face was suddenly taut and menacing.

"Not at the time. I thought my keys went to Aaron. It was only when you guys showed up at my house that I learned Dov had actually given my keys to Kaitlyn." Suzanne swallowed another mouthful of water.

"So, just to be clear, you have no idea why Kaitlyn Fischer would have disregarded a request from the Chief Security Officer, acting on your behalf, and taken it upon herself to drive your car?" Det. Luna seemed to be losing his patience.

"No, I do not know why she would do such a thing," Suzanne said. "But I do know it was impromptu, because five minutes before she had my keys, I was intending to drive myself home in my own car."

"And what changed? Why did you decide you were not able to drive yourself home?" Det. Luna asked. "Were you drunk?"

"No, I wasn't *drunk*. If you must know, I have cancer. I'm in the middle of chemo treatments," Suzanne's eyes were hot with indignation. "I was leaving the party early because I was exhausted, but then realized I was too weak to drive. I asked Dov Saminski to drive me home. Which he has done many times before."

"Oh, he has, has he?" Det. Luna smirked. "Is that part of his job?"

Suzanne's cheeks flushed.

"My client isn't here for your snarky and inappropriate insinuations. I think we'll be on our way if you're all done with your questions, Det. Luna." Byron stood up and dropped his legal pad into his briefcase.

"Sure, that's fine," Det. Luna stood up. "This was just a formality, anyway. We're gonna end up closing the case, because there's nothing to indicate it was anything other than an accident."

Byron gave him a quizzical look. "Really? You already knew this, and wasted our whole afternoon?"

"Like I said, I have to make sure all the Ts are crossed. But yeah, we got word a couple of hours ago that the prosecutor doesn't consider it a criminal matter," Det. Luna said.

"So, what? Wrong time, wrong place?" Byron said.

"We've looked at the CCTV a hundred times." Det. Luna shrugged. "Maybe the traffic light malfunctioned, maybe not, but no matter how you look at it, it seems like it was just an accident. Wrong time, wrong place, as you said."

As they walked out into the heat of the afternoon, Camelia felt a shiver roll up her spine. Knowing the little bit she did about that traffic light preemption device . . .

What if the traffic light was working just fine?

After dropping Suzanne off at her house, Camelia debated with herself all the way back to the office. Det. Luna said the County Attorney was closing the case as accidental. That was good news for Suzanne. The last thing she needed was more stress. On the other hand, there was something lurking beneath the surface and Camelia had a feeling Kaitlyn Fischer's death was not an accident at all. She was also sure Dov Saminski knew *something* he wasn't telling. Hell, given his position, he probably knew where *all* the bodies were buried.

Camelia pulled into her parking spot and shut off the engine. What was she supposed to do, just ignore her instincts? She pulled her phone out of her handbag and scrolled through her contacts until she found Dov Saminski's number.

He picked up on the first ring.

"Hi Dov, Camelia Belmont. Do you have a minute?"

"Sure, what can I do for you?" he asked.

"I'd like to talk to you, privately, when you have a chance." Camelia paused, but Dov didn't reply. "If that's okay with you."

"What do you want to talk about, exactly?" Dov sounded a little more guarded than he had a second ago.

"I want to talk about why you gave Suzanne's car keys to Kaitlyn Fischer. I want to know what's going on down at AndersLaw that got an associate attorney killed. And I want to hear your side of things," Camelia said. "Because, I'll be honest, Dov. This whole *accident* theory just stinks to high heaven."

She heard him sigh. "You're right. It's time to compare notes." He paused and she could hear a keyboard clicking in the background. "I'm in the middle of something right now, but I can be there any time next week."

"Perfect, just call Cate to set a time," Camelia said. "And Dov, thank you."

She hung up and considered what Dov had just said. *Time to compare notes.* That didn't sound like a guy who was guilty of felony murder or manslaughter or whatever this was. In fact, it sounded like he was almost anxious to talk to her. She needed to be prepared.

Camelia pulled Det. Luna's business card out of her purse. As his phone rang, she took slow deep breaths to steady her nerves.

"Luna here."

"Det. Luna, Camelia Belmont. Do you have a minute?"

"Sure," he said. "What's up?"

"You said the County Attorney is closing the Fischer inquiry." How could she put it? "And I was wondering . . . can you tell me more about the possible traffic light malfunction you mentioned?"

"Not much to tell. Traffic lights are computer driven, so could be a bad circuit. But they operate in real time, so—"

"What does that mean, *in real time?*" Camelia asked.

"There's no data log that we can go back and check. But that intersection does have a red light cam. When the light turns red, it photographs any vehicle passing over the sensor in the road. There was no photo recorded in either direction," Det. Luna said.

"I see," Camelia tried to calm her voice, despite how that revelation made her throat tighten. "So that means there was no red light either direction?"

What if Aaron planted that preemption device somewhere?

"The city traffic investigators looked at the CCTV, and they say the light changed from yellow to green instead of yellow to red, so that's a technology issue. Just to be safe, they replaced the whole works," Det. Luna said.

She definitely had to dig deeper into that Sheridan traffic device.

"Okay, one more question. What about the video? Did you guys figure out who sent it? Because Mrs. Anders is getting sick of the accusation that it was her."

"The data says the video was sent from the United Arab Emirates through a VPN, so it's a dead end." He sighed. "Since the video was sent *after* Mrs. Fischer's fatal accident, it seems to me that whoever sent it didn't know she was deceased."

"Do you have a theory?" Camelia took a swig of water. "About who sent it, I mean?"

"Damn right. Jealous partners do that kind of thing every day."

"True. But which one?" Camelia asked.

Det. Luna chuckled. "Ya got me there. Pretty sure it wasn't Mrs. Anders, but that leaves Mr. Fischer and Mr. Anders as the likely suspects."

"Suspects for releasing the video, or for plotting a hit and run?" Camelia probed.

"Look, I don't know anything for sure, but my gut does. Sometimes you just get a hunch. But hey, the prosecutor wants cases he can *win*. And this ain't one of 'em." He heaved a sigh. "And this time, I agree with him. The dump truck was stolen, abandoned at the scene, and the driver is in the wind. If I'm right, whoever was driving was over the border before we even identified Mrs. Fischer. The CCTV doesn't tell us anything new, and we don't have any evidence or witnesses to prove it wasn't an accident. So that means *case closed.*" Det. Luna's voice was heavy with resignation.

"I'm sorry to have bothered you. It was just nagging at me a bit, but you've cleared it up." Camelia said. "Thanks for your time."

Camelia knew, in her bones, that Kaitlyn's death was *not* an accident. She might not have been the intended victim, but the "accident" itself was not the least bit accidental.

But how do I prove it?

She couldn't wait to talk to Dov Saminski.

47

TICK TOCK

FRIDAY, MARCH 25

Camelia could hear Suzanne's desperation, but she felt helpless to fix the source: Aaron Anders.

"I know it sounds like I'm being a drama queen, but the truth is, Cam, I'm exhausted," Suzanne said, her voice breaking. "And . . . with all the other stuff I'm dealing with right now, I don't have the energy to deal with Aaron, too. This divorce just has to be over with."

Camelia could hear Suzanne sniffling on the other end of the phone and it tore her heart out. She knew better than to get emotionally attached to her clients, but Suzanne's case was different. Even so, right now, Camelia had to focus on a solution to Suzanne's legal problems, not her health problems.

"How about mediation? If we can lock ourselves in a room with a good mediator, we could walk out at the end of the day with an agreement," Camelia said.

"Just tell me when to show up and I'll be there. Because," Suzanne sighed into the phone. "Otherwise, Aaron's going to wait me out, and my only revenge will be haunting him to the end of his days. And I'd rather start the haunting now." She laughed a little.

Camelia could feel her throat tighten with tears. Tears she had no right to. This was Suzanne's battle, not hers; and yet, she empathized. Maybe too much.

"Okay, I'll call Spencer right now, and let you know," Camelia said.

She hung up and dropped her head in her hands, unable to choke back the sob in her throat.

Okay, buck up. You've got a war to win.

Dabbing her eyes with a tissue, Camelia took a few deep breaths while staring out at Camelback Mountain.

Center yourself.

She wasn't doing Suzanne any favors by dissolving into a sobbing heap. She had to toughen up, kick back, fight tooth and nail for the one thing—the only thing—she could give Suzanne that would actually make a difference in her life. A divorce.

She took another deep breath and dialed Ashcroft's direct line.

"Spencer Ashcroft."

"Good morning, Spencer, Camelia Belmont on the Anders matter," she said, as if he wouldn't know why she was calling. "Do you have a minute?"

"I always have time for the ladies," he said. "What's up?"

Camelia rolled her eyes. "Just trying to get my client divorced. As usual. So, I was calling to find out if Aaron will agree to mediation," Camelia said. She held her breath, waiting for Spencer's usual sarcastic blast.

"Isn't that premature? We don't have the business valuation yet," Spencer said.

He almost sounded reasonable.

"True, but we can agree in principle, can't we?" She took a sip of coffee. "Assuming we agree on everything else, we could drop in terms about resolving the business buyout."

"Yeah, but that's just kicking the can down the road. We should just hold off. Unless you're worried you'll lose your client before you get another full day of billing out of her?"

The comment hit Camelia like a lightning bolt, igniting her anger. She tapped her pen on her legal pad in time to her pulse and swallowed all the words she wanted to hurl at this smug asshole. Almost all the words.

"Sounds like projection, to me. I mean, I get it. If I were you, I'd be looking at the clock, too. Just hoping nothing gets in the way of that bonus?" Camelia said. She shook her head at her own weakness. There was no reason to tip her hand about that premium she'd heard Anders promise Ashcroft in the hallway after their hearing, but it was out now. "Anyway, enough about you. Let me know if Aaron will agree to mediation. Sooner the better."

Camelia hung up and gripped her pen, digging deep grooves in the legal pad, before flinging her pen at the window.

"*Assholes!*"

There was a light tap on the door as Cate's head popped around the door frame. "Everything okay in here?"

"*Uggh*. Yes. Everything's fine. I'm just so sick of Ashcroft's bullshit," Camelia said.

"So, just another Friday, then?" Cate laughed.

"Pretty much. I just called to find out if Anders will agree to mediation, so let me know when he calls back," Camelia said. "Although I doubt it will be today."

"Got it," Cate said, backing out of the door. "Now, I have to get back to sorting the latest round of disclosures."

Camelia stood up and stretched, trying to loosen the tension in her shoulders. Ashcroft was a vile lapdog, but that's all he was. He wasn't the one directing this drama, Anders was. Even so, they both seemed to enjoy making Suzanne's life miserable.

How on earth did other lawyers manage this kind of stress day after day, year after year? It was no wonder she was popping Klonopin and tossing back the booze. How else was she supposed to hold onto her sanity and not just run screaming down the hall? How else was she supposed to sleep at night? And then drag her ass out of bed every morning to, once again, try to slay a dragon with a pen? It was fucking impossible.

No one was more surprised than Camelia when Ashcroft called her back an hour later.

"We're a go," Ashcroft said. "With one condition. We get to name the mediator."

Camelia couldn't believe it. "Who does Aaron want to use?"

"Judge Truman is our pick. Take it or leave it."

She'd had at least half a dozen mediations before retired Judge Steven Truman. He was old school, but he was also experienced, and she knew he could bring these two junkyard dogs to heel.

"I'll run it by Suzanne, but I don't see a problem," Camelia said. "And thank you, Spencer, for the prompt response. It was unexpected."

"We're just trying to be reasonable, Cam," he cooed. "Aaron really wants all this behind him."

They had to be up to something, but what? The only advantage Camelia could see was that it would give Anders a clear view of what Suzanne was willing to give up in order to be divorced. A common litigation tactic but, at this point, it didn't matter.

"Then we should have a very good day in mediation," Camelia said. "I'll arrange a date with Truman's office and email the details."

As soon as she hung up, Camelia called Suzanne.

"Suzanne, they agreed to mediation, *if* we use their choice of mediator," she said.

"Who do they want to use?" Suzanne asked.

"Retired Judge Steve Truman. Do you know him?"

"No, not really. I've met him at some bar functions, but we're not friendly," Suzanne said. "I think Aaron's been on a couple of committees with him, though."

"Well, their easy agreement to mediation smells like a trap, but then I don't trust Ashcroft as far as I can throw him. Who knows? Maybe Steve Truman will shame Aaron into settling."

"We have that video of Aaron and Kaitlyn Fischer," Suzanne responded. "Isn't that worth something?"

"If Kaitlyn were still alive, I think it would have been valuable. But now," Camelia paused. Was there anything left to gain out of that tragic ending? "I'm not so sure. Let's just go to mediation and try to get as many concessions as we can."

Suzanne sighed. "I guess that's all I can hope for at this stage. Just tell me where and when, and I'll be there."

Camelia hung up and buzzed Cate.

"I need you to call Steve Truman's assistant to schedule the mediation date. Do anything, and I mean *anything* to get on his calendar as soon as possible. Next week, if we can. And yes, you can disclose Suzanne's diagnosis," Camelia said.

"Got it, boss," Cate said. "I'm on it."

Camelia hung up and closed the file on her desk. How the hell was she going to be ready for a full mediation in just a few days? This kind of prep usually took at least a week. She had just begun drafting a list of the Anders' assets and debts to take to mediation when Cate buzzed her.

"Mr. Truman says you can have Tuesday, all day, beginning at 9:30 a.m., with attorneys in his office at 9:00 a.m. to brief him on the case," she said. "And you know how he is, so you should be there by 8:45."

"Absolutely, and good job," Camelia said. "I owe you for this."

"Damn right you do. I'd love a venti vanilla latte!" Cate laughed.

"You drive a hard bargain, but I'm good for it. In the meantime, we have a lot of work to do." Camelia sighed. "And Cate, clear my calendar. I'm going to need every minute."

48

OUT OF ORDER

TUESDAY, MARCH 29

The mediator's offices were a monochromatic space in a downtown high rise, decorated in dusty tones of beige and brown, with large pieces of what passed for abstract art on the walls. The receptionist—a doughy-faced 30-something man with sparse, stiffly gelled hair—greeted Camelia with an invoice.

When the bill was settled, the man led Camelia to a conference room with dingy carpet and a scuffed rosewood table straight out of the 80s. She placed her briefcase on the floor beside her chair and sat down just as the man returned, escorting Suzanne. Once alone, she turned to her client.

"How are you? Are you ready for today?" Camelia asked, scanning Suzanne's face. She looked tired, but her eyes were clear.

"I have to be, don't I?" she said. "I just want it over with, but . . . shit, they're here."

The door to the conference room opened and the mediator, a retired judge who was too old for the courtroom but too driven to retire, entered. Ashcroft was right behind him, strutting like an old rooster.

Steve Truman glanced around, his hands casually resting in his pant pockets. He lent a country club air to the drab room in his tan pants and Glen plaid sport coat over a starched white shirt.

"Seems like we're missing one," he said. "But I'm sure he'll be along. First off, counsel, we'll meet in my office so you can brief me on the case. Miss Anders, if you need anything, just ask Cory. We won't be long." Truman stepped back into the hall. "This way, counsel."

Ashcroft followed closely on Truman's heels while Camelia grabbed her pad of paper and pen.

She leaned over and whispered to Suzanne. "If Aaron shows up and you don't want to be cornered in here, just go sit in the lobby."

Camelia rose and walked swiftly down the hall to catch up to the two men, who were already being seated. Truman's office was a shrine to his years on the bench. One wall was covered with plaques and photographs of him beaming alongside politicians, judges, and even Supreme Court Justices Sandra Day O'Connor and William Rehnquist. The opposite wall was lined with law tomes and bound journals. Behind him was a wall of windows facing north with a view of the Central Corridor. Camelia slid into the remaining chair in front of his desk and leaned away from Ashcroft and his cloud of cologne.

"You know the drill, counsel. Give me the five dollar version," Truman said, his owlish eyebrows twitching in Camelia's direction. "You're the Petitioner, so let's hear it."

Camelia ran down the history of the case as succinctly as possible, giving only the barest of details. Until she got to March 19, the night of the AndersLaw party.

"And then, Steve, there was an unfortunate accident. AndersLaw had their annual firm party at Paradise Valley Country Club. My client attended, but only because Mr. Anders put on a farce of raising money—"

"A farce? I'd hardly call fourteen thousand dollars a farce," Ashcroft sputtered.

Camelia calmly stared at him. "I wasn't finished." She turned back to Truman. "Now, as I said, the only reason Ms. Anders attended was to save Mr. Anders the embarrassment of funding a charity, to which he insisted on attaching her name, without her present. Even though, like most everything else in their marriage, it was done without her consent. At the end of the evening, she wasn't feeling well, and got a ride home, leaving her car at the Club. Sometime after that, one of the senior associates, Kaitlyn Fischer stole her car," Camelia said.

"If she had the keys she didn't steal it, did she?" Ashcroft interjected.

"I still have the floor, Spence, so try not to interrupt," she said.

"Is that the woman I've been hearing about on the news?" Truman asked.

"Yes, sir. Anyway, she was driving Ms. Anders' car, and maybe she was a little drunk, because she ran a red and promptly hit a dump truck at Tatum and Lincoln. Unfortunately, Mrs. Fischer died at the scene," Camelia said.

"And what does this have to do with the divorce?" Truman asked.

"I was about to ask the exact same thing, Judge," Ashcroft said.

Truman hadn't been a judge for years, but he puffed up a bit at the sound of it.

Brown noser.

"Mrs. Fischer was having an affair with Mr. Anders, so there's an issue of marital waste," Camelia said.

Truman nodded. "Go on."

"The Monday after the accident, someone claiming to be Kaitlyn Fischer sent out a video to the partners of the firm, the Anders, and to bar counsel—"

"Actually," Ashcroft huffed. "I think we'll find that Suzanne Anders was behind that little stunt."

Camelia turned in her seat and glared at Ashcroft. "Unless you are prepared to defend a defamation case, I advise you to keep that conspiracy theory to yourself." She turned back to Truman.

"The video showed Mr. Anders and Mrs. Fischer having an embarrassingly *quick* bit of sex in the firm conference room." Camelia gave Ashcroft a smirk. "So, in addition to marital waste, because of the video, there is also an issue of marital tort. Either intentional or negligent infliction of emotional distress."

"Well, now, it sounds like emotions are running high. What do you have to say about all this, Spencer?"

Ashcroft leaned forward and began countering every point Camelia had made with flowery denials and sugar-coated admissions that he twisted to make Aaron Anders sound like an innocent victim.

"I think you'll find, your honor, that Mr. Anders is devastated by all of this. First, *out of the blue*, his wife of more than thirty years files for divorce. Then, he finds out quite by accident that she's dying of cancer. Then, as if those blows weren't enough, one of Mr. Anders' top associates was tragically killed in an accident. Any one of those, by itself, would knock an ordinary man down. Mr. Anders is no ordinary man, but even he's having a very hard time."

Camelia snorted.

"It's hardly out of the blue, Spence. Aaron's famous for dragging his dick through the payroll, if you'll pardon the expression," Camelia said.

"Now, Counsel, let Spencer finish," Truman said.

She sat back and listened to Ashcroft weave his tale of woe about Aaron Anders.

"And at the end of the day, Judge, Mrs. Anders is dying. It's patently unfair to allow her to reach out from her inevitable grave to claw back assets Mr. Anders earned by the sweat of his brow, when she'll be," he glanced at Camelia, "*long gone*. Suzanne has no possible use for these worldly things. It's pure spite, and Mr. Anders is heartbroken by Suzanne's callous vindictiveness. He's the father of her children, for Chrissake. And then there's her own infidelity . . ." Ashcroft shook his head. "Shameful."

This final flourish made Camelia flush with rage. "Once again, just brazen defamation of a dying woman. So, Steve, you can see why we haven't been able to settle on our own." A pent-up torrent of angry words crowded in her throat, but she had to hold it together for Suzanne's sake. She swallowed and stood up. "For now, though, let's get on with it, shall we?" Camelia turned on her heel and marched to the door where she paused, and glanced back. "Coming, gentlemen?"

She smiled to herself as Ashcroft, his face flushed with anger, muttered something about impatient women, and rose to follow her.

Suzanne was sitting in the lobby and Aaron was in the conference room, scrolling on his phone when they returned. Suzanne fell in behind Camelia and the four of them took their seats around the table, with Truman at the head.

He cleared his throat. "Now, I've heard from counsel and I am confident cooler heads will prevail so that we can settle this today. Remember, I'm here to help you put all this behind you, once and for all, so you can all live happily ever after."

Suzanne choked on a sob. Camelia glared at Truman.

Talk about tone deaf.

She had to get Suzanne out of that room before she fell apart. "We'd like to exercise our option to sit separately, Steve. If you'll excuse us, we're going across the hall."

Ashcroft offered a reptilian grimace.

"No need for all that, now is there?" Anders said, smiling like a choir boy.

"Oh, yes, of course, I should have offered," Truman stammered.

When Suzanne and Camelia stood up, Anders leapt to his feet. As Suzanne approached, he pressed up against her, pushing his palm into the small of her back.

"Here, love, let me get the door for you," he said.

Suzanne pushed his hand away. "Do not touch me ever again," she hissed and stomped across the hall.

As Camelia approached the door, Anders pivoted in front of her, purposefully brushing his arm against her breasts. Camelia's entire body went rigid as she twisted away from him. Her glare was met with a subtle, knowing grin. Anders knew *exactly* what he was doing. As usual.

But then, Aaron Anders *always* knew what he was doing. He wasn't the kind to leave things to chance. So, how did his girlfriend end up dead in his wife's car? What really happened to Kaitlyn Fischer that night? Was her accident really a botched attempt on Suzanne's life? Camelia couldn't help but feel he was somehow behind the whole thing, but she tamped down her suspicions. Maybe it was just wishful thinking, because she would love nothing more than to see Anders in a jailhouse jumpsuit.

Truman followed Camelia and Suzanne as they crossed the lobby. "Cory, please see that the conference room has fresh water for our guests."

Truman pulled the door to the conference room closed behind him.

"Now, you girls get settled and if you need anything at all, just ask Cory. In the meantime, I'll start with those two old bulls and see what I can get out of them, okay?" he smiled, pressed his lips together, and nodded as he left the room.

Camelia bristled. *You girls*. Of course, Ashcroft and Anders had readily agreed to Truman. He was one of them.

The mediation started off painfully slow. Truman went back and forth between the conference rooms—volleying offers and counter offers, rejections and rationales—all while pushing, trying to find a path to the middle. But Anders kept moving the bar. If Suzanne agreed to a concession on one point, he raised the stakes on another. Camelia soon realized today was a show of force, not a settlement negotiation. Anders was demonstrating to Suzanne that he would not back down. Ever.

They finally broke for lunch around 2 p.m., and Truman pulled Camelia and Ashcroft into his office. He motioned for the two lawyers to sit down.

"Camelia, if we're going to settle this thing, you have to lean on your client. Convince Suzanne to give up some ground. She's asking for a lot and I don't think Aaron is going to budge." Truman's voice sounded weary, resigned.

Ashcroft piped up. "I agree, Judge. I mean, we don't even know Suzanne's life expectancy." Ashcroft turned to Camelia. "Sorry, Cam. We're all upset about Suzanne's illness, but come on. How can Aaron make an offer of spousal maintenance when he doesn't know if it will be for a month, a year, or . . . who knows? It's not the least bit fair." He turned back to Truman. "I think everything should go to Aaron, and Suzanne should just go enjoy what's left of her life. I might be out of order here, but I know I can get Aaron to cough up twenty thousand a month, terminating upon her death, if Suzanne will agree."

"I'm not one for taking sides, but what Spencer says makes a lot of sense. Suzanne has no need for all those assets in the afterlife. Can't she just let it go?" Truman said.

Camelia could not believe her ears. She could feel her temper rising like lava from her belly. She bowed her head, closed her eyes, and took a deep breath. She blew it out in a long whoosh.

She lifted her head and looked at Truman and Ashcroft, so sure of themselves in their Rich White Man world. So smug, knowing their futures were tightly tucked in, warm and secure. What she was about to say could mean getting fired. Maybe even a bar complaint. She didn't care.

Let the fucking truth be told.

"Yes, Spencer, you *are* out of order. I think you're both forgetting that Suzanne has a *right* to divorce Aaron, even if she only has ten minutes left to live. She has a *right* to half the community assets and the *right* to bequeath her share to whomever she wants. Today, in order to settle, Suzanne was willing to accept a lot less than half. Turns out, that's still more than Aaron will agree to," Camelia said as she stood up. "So, we're done. I'm terminating mediation."

"No need to get emotional now, Cam," Truman said. "I think it's a mistake to end like this. Especially since your client doesn't have time on her side."

"Jeez, you women are so sensitive. We're just getting warmed up and you're already throwing in the towel? I thought you wanted a settlement. You're the one who asked for mediation, so what's your *problem?*" Ashcroft smirked.

That was all it took. Camelia shot out of her chair and the words came pouring out of her in a torrent.

"My problem? My *problem?* How about reading the goddamn statute? How about *equitable division?* Should I cite *Sharp v. Sharp* to you two, as well? You're both despicable. Steve Truman, your job today was to be a neutral facilitator, not Aaron Anders' agent. You say you're not one for picking sides, but you *have* picked a side. And now you have the *gall* to suggest Suzanne should give up her share of the marital estate because she's dying? Because it's no good to her anyway? But what about Aaron? He had a heart attack *in Court*, for Chrissake. Who's to say he won't die before Suzanne? I mean, life is fickle. Just ask *Kaitlyn Fischer.*"

She paused in her pacing to let her words sink in and clasped the back of the chair to steady her trembling hands. "As a former member of the Bench, Steve, you should be ashamed of yourself for even *suggesting* that a person be denied their rights based on their health. If *anything*, Suzanne's situation should cause you to be even more careful about preserving those rights because *it's all she has left.*" Camelia turned to Ashcroft.

"As for you Spencer, have you not one ounce of humanity left? You've spent all day doing your best to deprive a dying woman of her one desire: to be divorced from that narcissist in the other room. Oh, please," Camelia sneered. "Don't give me that look. You know damn well Aaron Anders is a whore who spends half his time banging the employees and the other half glad handing the likes of you. He's successful, yes, I'll give him that. But he's also a horrible, abusive lawyer and *everyone* knows it." Camelia took a deep breath.

Ashcroft's face was red and his eyes were narrowed to slits. "*How dare you—*"

"I'm not done, Spence, so save your questions for the end. The fact is, I'm ashamed of you both. And guess what. Suzanne is going to get a divorce, whether Aaron likes it or not. It's the fucking law, no matter what Aaron Anders wants! So maybe *you* should be the ones *letting it go.*"

Not waiting around to find out if she would be escorted from the building or just laughed out of the office, Camelia turned and walked out, slamming the door behind her. She speed-walked down the hall and into the conference room where Aaron Anders was scrolling on his phone.

"Mediation is over," Camelia said, and finished the last part silently. *And you can go fuck yourself.*

She slammed the door and walked to the glass walled conference room across the hall where Suzanne was sitting wide-eyed.

"Get your stuff," Camelia said as she stuffed files in her briefcase. "We're leaving."

Suzanne's forehead wrinkled in confusion, but she stood and followed Camelia to the elevators.

"Is everything okay? What happened in there?"

"Those old men started something and we are going to finish it for them."

Her words were far stronger than she felt. Her insides were shaking and she thought she might faint, but her outrage and sense of justice were bigger than her fear. Her internal moral compass was pointed toward truth and fairness, not the sham Ashcroft and Anders were trying to pull. Camelia wasn't going down without a fight.

If it was the last thing she did, she would protect Suzanne from those two wolves at the door.

49

HER FATHER'S DAUGHTER

TUESDAY, MARCH 29

Suzanne listened quietly as Camelia recounted the argument that precipitated her blow up, ending the mediation.

"You were right to stop the mediation, Camelia," she said when Camelia finally finished. "If they had their way, I'd probably end up with twenty-five grand and a gift card to Nordstrom's."

Camelia wasn't so sure. Even though Suzanne endorsed Camelia's decision, she wasn't convinced she'd done right by her client.

"So where do we go from here?" Suzanne asked.

"We'll make an offer" Camelia said, grateful for the focus on next steps. "And I'll file a Motion to Set Trial," Camelia said.

"We're not actually ready for trial, though, are we?" Suzanne squeaked.

"Not even close. But there's case law that says the Court can enter a decree, and tease out the details of the business buyout with a Special Master after the fact. That's the argument I want to make," Camelia touched Suzanne's arm. "In a worst case scenario, you'll be divorced even if we don't have the business valuation, and when the Special Master is done, you'll still get your half of the assets."

"Perfect. Let's do it," Suzanne said. "In the meantime, I'm heading up to Sedona for a couple of days to breathe some of that magical air and clear the cobwebs."

"God knows you need it. It was a rough day, all the way around," Camelia said.

They'd parted ways in the parking garage and, even with Suzanne's assurance that she'd done the right thing, Camelia replayed the whole scene in her head all the way back to the office.

Had she said anything that could get her sanctioned?

What if Ashcroft called Byron and reported on her tirade?

Truman might even make a bar complaint. Hadn't she called him biased and despicable?

Jesus Christ I'm an idiot.

Camelia had taken her one shot at getting a deal for Suzanne, and blown it on principle. Not that Anders had any intention of making a *fair* deal, but she still had a responsibility to Suzanne to eke out anything she could. And to consult with her before walking out and slamming Steve Truman's door off the hinges.

But the more she thought about it, the more she knew she was right.

It was clear to Camelia that even the fearsome Aaron Anders was getting old, his glory days firmly behind him. And a dying wife brought his own mortality into question. How long did he have left, especially after that heart attack? They still hadn't received his medical records, but his own health seemed to be a topic he was deeply uncomfortable with.

Still, Anders' health wasn't the issue here. It was Suzanne who was under the daily threat of a deadly disease. And it was obvious to her that even Truman would be relieved if Suzanne would just shut up and die. But would Anders be satisfied to sit back and wait for that to happen? Or would he take matters into his own hands? Just how far would Anders go? She couldn't shake the sense that Anders had a hand in Kaitlyn Fischer's death, but how? And had he really been aiming for Suzanne?

She opened her desk drawer and pulled out the little copper flask and shook it. There was barely anything left. She unscrewed the lid and tipped it back, pressing the threaded rim to her lips, sucking out the last drops.

Not nearly enough.

It was almost three o'clock. Not late enough in the day to leave, but certainly early enough to run an errand. Just down the street to the grocery store, where she could pick up a bottle, fill her flask, and be back in less than half an hour. She grabbed her handbag and headed for the door.

As she passed Cate's desk, she smiled and kept walking. "Be right back. Forgot to pick up my script."

After all, wasn't that what this was? A prescription to be filled? An antidote to the non-stop heart-thudding stress? Or was she just a lush, a drunk, a sloppy alcoholic lawyer like so many of her colleagues? Did it even matter what she called it?

Suzanne pulled through the gate in the rental car the insurance company had provided. Even though her own car was totaled, it didn't make sense to buy another car at this stage of what was left of her life. One less thing for the kids to deal with.

As she pulled up to the garage, she couldn't help but smile. Sedona would be a perfect remedy to all this mess with Aaron. She could set all the bitterness aside for a couple of days, order room service, and enjoy the red rocks and electric air shimmering under a turquoise sky. All she had to do was throw a few things in a bag, call her housekeeper to cancel the next three days, and text Dov.

As she unlocked the front door, her phone began ringing. It was Allison, her middle child. The one carrying her first grandchild. The one who'd told her philandering father she was pregnant before she told her mother.

Her father's daughter, through and through.

"Hey Alli. Hang on, just got home," Suzanne said as she dropped her handbag and kicked off her shoes. "What's up, kiddo?"

"Have you got a few minutes, Mom? I'd like to talk about the divorce, and all this shit with Dad." Her voice sounded contrite and a little hoarse, like she'd been crying.

"Sure. Do you want to come over?" Suzanne asked. She rarely got time with Allison alone, and would usually jump at the chance, but today she hoped Allison didn't want to meet in person. It would just delay getting on the road for the two-hour drive to Sedona.

"I wish I could, but I'm just taking a break until my next client's jacked up hamstring arrives," she said. "This won't take long. I just want your permission for something."

"And what's that?" Allison hadn't asked her permission for anything since high school, so this was definitely out of character.

"Well, we all know about the video—" she sighed.

"*What?*" Suzanne squeaked. "You haven't watched it have you, Alli?"

"Oh god no. I can't afford that much therapy." Allison paused.

"So, how did you find out about it?"

"I'm so sorry, Mom. Someone posted it to YouTube, and Avery got wind of it. But none of us have watched it, because . . . *ew*."

"What a nightmare," Suzanne grunted. "I wish you weren't finding out these things about your father this way."

"Yeah, well, maybe it will work in our favor. You know how Dad always jokes I'm his favorite? It's only because thinks he's got me wrapped around his little finger."

"That's how your father is, Allison. Always playing both sides against the middle," Suzanne said, but she was surprised at her daughter's insight. She hadn't considered Allison to be that thoughtful about the family dynamic.

"Well, he might have thought he had me eating out of his hand for a while, but that's in the past. I'm just disgusted . . . and Mom, it never meant I loved you less. I've just been such a selfish, greedy little bitch . . ." Allison's voice broke on a sob. "I'm so fucking sorry."

"Hey, Alli, stop it. It's not a crime to breathe easier by staying in your father's good graces. We've all done things we aren't proud of, just to keep the peace with Dad. Don't beat yourself up over it, honey. Really," Suzanne walked through to the family room and sank onto the sofa. "But what do you need permission for?"

"Okay, don't be mad, but . . . I talked it over with Alex and Avery. I want to negotiate with Dad for your settlement. He thinks I'm in his pocket, so he won't see me coming." Allison took a deep breath and blew it out. "Anyway, with a grandbaby in the oven, I think I can push him into something reasonable. And before you say anything, yes, I know I'm not the lawyer in the family. But I don't need to be. Avery drafted all the talking points, Alex threw in his two cents, and I'm the hostage negotiator."

Suzanne laughed. "So. My little brood have been plotting? Again?"

"Well, you know how we are. We band together when the shit hits the fan. And this time, the shit is all over the damn room, no thanks to Dad. So, we think it's his job to make it right," Allison said.

"Funny you should call now, because I just got home from mediation." Suzanne's hand ran absently over the arm of the sofa. A sudden memory of Dov made her sit up and clear her throat. "It didn't go well."

"Big surprise. I know you have a lawyer but, Mom, seriously. I know I can get a deal out of him. Because I'm his fave. Or so he thinks."

Suzanne paused. It didn't feel right to have her daughter negotiating on her behalf. After all, Aaron would soon be her children's only parent. They would need that relationship, going forward.

"I really appreciate the offer, but it doesn't sit right with me," Suzanne said. "I know I can't stop you, but as rotten as your father can be sometimes, we never wanted you kids in the middle of our arguments."

"Mom, this is not just an *argument!* Dad was screwing an associate *on camera*, in the firm conference room. And now she's *dead!* And Dad is just going to sail through all of it with that shit eating grin plastered on his face. He's doing whatever he can to put off the divorce, because he knows the law. Last man standing, and all that crap. I just want to make sure you get your fair share. And the last word," Allison's voice had become strident, agitated.

"Thank you, and you're right to be concerned. The three of you need to protect your inheritance . . ."

"What the hell, Mom! It's not about that *at all*. Give your share to the Humane Society. We don't care. We just don't think any of this is fair, and we're so pissed off at Dad. He needs to *pay*," Allison said. Suzanne heard her gulping something. "You said, when we were in Sedona, all you wanted was to die as a single mother. Which would be hilarious if it weren't so goddamn sad. Please, just let me do this for you."

Suzanne could hear Allison's sniffles through the phone. Her heart filled with compassion for her middle child. Squeezed between the first-born and the baby, Allison had somehow managed to carve out her own space. Now, Suzanne could see how much it had cost her. But she was an adult, and it was time to give her the reins, allow her to take the lead, to be front and center. Hot tears filled Suzanne's eyes.

"Oh, sweet girl, of course. Keep your values intact, but use your leverage to make a deal, if you can. All I want is my half, and a signed Decree," Suzanne said.

"Mom, if it's the last thing he does, Dad will be signing those papers," Allison said. She gave a little laugh. "Besides, I'm way more fit than Dad, so if I have to, I'll wrestle him! Thanks, I gotta go. Mr. Hamstring is here. Love you!"

Suzanne stared at the phone in her hand long after Allison had hung up.

Miracles do happen, apparently.

Her phone buzzed again and a smile burst through Suzanne's reverie. Dov was yet another unexpected miracle.

> I'm out front. If we hurry, we can catch a Sedona sunset. XO

50

DRUNK AT DURANT'S

TUESDAY, MARCH 29

Hours after the disastrous mediation, Dr. Chavez had just ushered Camelia into his office when she got a text message from Suzanne.

Call me tomorrow re settlement

Fear clamped down on her stomach like a vise. Could the terseness of the message mean Suzanne had been stewing over the aborted negotiations? Was she upset over not reaching a settlement? What else could it be?

Camelia sat down and quickly responded with a thumbs up. She rolled her shoulders and took a deep breath.

This, too, shall pass.

Dr. Chavez's therapy dog, a chubby corgi named Marcia Brady, immediately jumped on the sofa beside Camelia and stared at her with those big brown eyes.

"How's Little Miss today?" Camelia said, scratching the dog's ears. "And how are you, Carlos?"

He smiled, his own sad eyes crinkling at the corners.

"Well, I would say pretty good. My husband and I just closed on a cottage up in the pines, just outside Flagstaff. It will make the Phoenix summers a lot more bearable if we can escape on the weekends!"

Camelia grinned. "So that's where all my hard-earned cash is going? Will you at least name a room after me?"

"Absolutely!" Carlos laughed and flipped the page in his notebook. "Now, how about you?"

Camelia started to tell him about the blowup at Suzanne Anders' mediation, when she was blindsided by a burst of hiccupping sobs.

"And . . . and . . . and I just . . . I blew up. I lost my shit right there in Truman's office. I couldn't stop myself. I unloaded on him and Ashcroft." She paused to blow her nose as Marcia harumphed. "My patience for bullshit is just down to nothing, and it's gonna get me fired."

"What was it about this particular situation that set you off?" Carlos asked as he pushed the box of tissues closer to Camelia.

"My client deserves so much better," Camelia managed to say as she stifled another sob. "And she doesn't have much time to make a deal. Meanwhile, those bastards are just so smug and sure of themselves . . . and I'm . . . not."

"Compassion for your client is understandable and appropriate, so don't ever feel badly about being a human with feelings. Remember how we discussed compassionate detachment? As for those other lawyers, do you really believe they're better than you in some way?"

Camelia reached for a tissue, swiped at her runny nose, and sighed. "Well, aren't they? I mean, these men really do rule the kingdom, even if it's just the Phoenix legal world. They're all so clubby and chummy, so back-slappy and good old boy. It makes me fucking sick," she said, twisting the tissue.

"There's no argument that sexism exists, especially in your field. But I wonder if they really have all the power you think they do. I mean, you put the brakes on the mediation, and potentially saved your client from caving in to their demands from a position of weakness. So, didn't you slice off a chunk of their authority for yourself?" Carlos eyes were sparkling with interest.

Camelia could see that he loved this type of probing. The truth was, she did too. The unravelling of her own mystery was satisfying, even when it felt like a cheese grater against her skin. And when he put it that way, she could see that yes, she had wrested some power from those two old bags of wind. But what would it cost her?

"I suppose so. I just wonder what the blowback will be. My anxiety is through the roof. And I'm worried about the effect all this is having on my health. I'm a wreck pretty much all the time. And," Camelia paused. Should she go on? Tears welled in her eyes. She could feel the sobs lodged in her throat.

"And?" Carlos prompted.

"And I'm drinking too much. Way too much. Like . . . even like today," she whispered. There, she'd said it. Almost.

"Did you drink before you came here?" Carlos' voice was gentle, not accusing.

Camelia nodded. "Earlier. This afternoon."

"Before we talk about what *too much* means, tell me how the drinking helps," Carlos leaned forward, elbows on knees, and set his notebook aside. "How does it make you feel when you have a drink?"

"It calms me down. Gives me a little dose of confidence when I'm staring down the barrel of the stress cannon," she said. "Helps me forget . . ."

"Forget what?"

Camelia thought about it. What was she trying to forget? And was that even it? Was *forgetting* the reason for tipping that flask back every chance she got? The realization landed lightly at first, just a hint. Then it hit her.

"Wait a minute. That's all wrong. It doesn't help me forget." She looked up at Carlos and shook her head. "I think it's more like I'm drinking to remember. To remember what it's like to have confidence. To remember what it feels like when I don't have a knot in my stomach all day. To remember how to laugh about things and enjoy a meal and sleep all night." Camelia grabbed a fistful of tissues from the box beside her, dabbing at her tears.

Carlos slowly nodded. "So, you're drinking to remember *yourself*, is that it?"

"Yes, I think that's exactly it," Camelia said. She pressed a fresh tissue to her nose. "The problem is, I'm not sure *I'm* still in there, you know? It feels like the *actual* me is long gone, and even the memory of the real me is fading away. I'm becoming this . . . this hollowed out ghost of who Camelia used to be."

"That's pretty profound, isn't it? I mean, realization of these deep truths are the very foundation of our work here. And I don't want you to drop this thread. It's way too important to lose sight of." Carlos grabbed a remote control and soft guitar music came into the room. "Let's take five while you journal everything you just said, and how it's making you feel. We'll talk about it more, but I don't want you to lose the impact of this."

It seemed as if the clouds had parted for a moment, illuminating an aspect of herself she hadn't realized was hiding right there, in plain sight, all along. Carlos thumbed through a psychology journal while

Camelia dumped her thoughts on the page, trying to capture the important parts of her revelation.

She blew out a long exhale. Maybe she was finally getting somewhere. But then . . .

A memory of her father's flushed face came rushing forward. Not quite drunk, but he would be soon enough. That excited look in his eyes. He had a new idea that was going to propel them all to *Easy Street*. He was gonna be making the *big bucks*. It was as easy as *falling off a log*. All he had to do was get to Palm Springs, the Poconos, Tampa . . . wherever the next big timeshare resort was going up. *Just think how fun it will be, living in a resort town.*

Even as a young teen, Camelia could see it was a pretty flimsy dream. But it was the final straw for her mother. With no desire to leave her family and friends in Regina, she'd threatened divorce.

They held it together. For a while. But when Camelia left to attend university in the U.S., her father wasn't far behind. And he never made it big. Every job was a step down from the last. And now she was acting just like him. Drinking herself into believing she could just leave the firm and start her own investigation practice. Her stupid pipe dream was almost as futile as her father selling a week at a time in those slapped-together apartments. And a lot more dangerous.

Was she doomed to repeat his mistakes? It seemed like every time she thought she was moving forward, her history grabbed her by the hair and dragged her back down to the darkest places. All she'd ever wanted was to shine a light on those dark corners, help clean up life's injustices, to be someone brave who did important work. Instead, she was just a divorce attorney with an anxiety problem and a vodka habit.

Maybe that was all the "deep truth" she would ever uncover.

She recalled one of Carlos' instructions, years ago, to counter negative thoughts with gratitude, so she began jotting down her list:

she had a comfortable home, a loving husband, and an education that could be parlayed into . . . something.

She'd stopped writing, but was still lost in thought when Carlos turned the music down. It startled her, not realizing how much time had passed. She glanced up to see Carlos look at the clock over her shoulder.

"Time's up, huh?" Camelia asked.

"Yes, for today. But I want you to continue to journal on how alcohol brings a piece of your life back to you. Even if it feels like that's what vodka gives you, you know you're still in charge, right? You're still *you*, even if that's hard to remember on days like today. And alcohol doesn't have to dictate who you become."

On the short walk to her car, Camelia turned on her phone and saw two missed voice messages: Leon and Nina Garry. She listened as Leon explained he was meeting his former coworker, Jon, for nine holes of sunset golf and a burger. Nina Garry had called to see if Camelia wanted to meet up for a cocktail.

Nina was always full of interesting stories that buoyed her spirits but Camelia was bone tired. All she could think about was getting home, shedding her heels and bra, and curling up on the sofa with some takeout.

Camelia texted Nina.

Sorry, other plans. Rain check?

Camelia handed her keys to the valet at Durant's and walked into the steaming, bustling kitchen. She used to think it was gross that people could just walk through the kitchen like this, but she'd come to respect the transparency. No dirty secrets in Durant's kitchen!

Her eyes needed a moment to adjust as she stepped from the bright kitchen into the dim, moody atmosphere of the restaurant. The place was already packed, so Camelia placed her takeout order with the maître d'. With a twenty minute wait, she rounded the corner to the vast length of bar.

Camelia's breath caught in her throat. Chris Fischer was hunched over at the far end, but had glanced up as she approached. It was too late to pretend she hadn't seen him.

Shit. Just what I need.

Camelia took a breath and straightened her shoulders as she walked to the end of the bar.

"Hey, Chris," she said as she waved at the bartender. "I'll have a soda with lime and buy my friend here another."

"Thanksh, but he already cut me off," Chris slurred, not bothering to straighten up as Camelia took the bar stool next to his. She peered over at him. "Becush Ricky here thinksh I've had enough." He gave Camelia a rueful smile, then flipped the bird at the bartender.

Jesus Christ. Chris is hammered.

When Rick returned with her soda, he leaned over the bar and gestured to Camelia to come closer.

"If you're his friend, you better take him home," the bartender said. "He's been spouting a lot of stuff that's probably nonsense, but people are listening. I've already closed out his tab, but if he doesn't leave, I have to get security involved."

Camelia nodded at the bartender and turned back to Chris.

"Well, Chris, it looks like you got a head start on me," she said. "So, how about if I drive you home?"

"Don't need a ride," he said, swinging his head in Camelia's direction. "My car'sh out back with the valet."

"Let's not argue about that, okay?" Camelia leaned in and firmly gripped Chris's shoulder, lowering her voice. "Listen to me. The valet has your keys, and you know damn well they're not going to let you drive off the lot. If you don't let me walk you out of here and take you home, Rick's gonna call security. And then the cops. Believe me, you do *not* want to spend the night in the drunk tank, Chris."

Chris stared at her, not seeming to understand what she was saying. Then, he abruptly stood up, staggering against the padded bar. "Well? What are we waiting for? I'm ready to go!" he shouted.

Camelia waved her credit card at the bartender. As he stepped in front of Camelia and Chris, Rick held up his hand. "He's paid up and yours is on the house," he said.

"Thanks. Can you cancel my takeout order? For Camelia Belmont. I need to get this guy home."

"I'll take care of it," the bartender said. "And thanks for taking Mr. Fischer home." He turned to Chris. "You've got a true friend here, man. Take it easy!"

Camelia steered Chris back out through the main dining room, then through the kitchen. When they got to the valet stand, she gave the guy a twenty with her ticket and told Chris to hand over his ticket.

"We're not taking his car, but I need his keys," she said to the valet.

He gave Chris the once over and gave Camelia an understanding nod. "I think that's for the best," he said as he handed over Chris's keyring.

"I'm fine," Chris slurred. "But she'sh my lawyer and won't let me drive." He saluted Camelia.

Once they were in Camelia's car, and buckled in, she turned to Chris.

"How are you feeling?"

"How's it feel that my cheating wife died . . . driving Mish Andersh car? Well, no more curfew." He shook his head and pinched the bridge of his nose to stop the tears. "I'm fine."

"Chris, I'm so sorry . . ." Camelia put her hand on his shoulder. "But what I really meant was, are you gonna throw up in my car?"

He laughed and draped his arm over Camelia's shoulder. "I'm a lover, not a puker!"

Camelia sighed. This was not what she had in mind for her evening. She pulled up Chris's contact information from his consultation intake and tapped on the address. The nav on her dash lit up.

Starting route . . .

Chris had gone quiet, his head lolling against the glass as Camelia headed out of downtown and onto the freeway.

After minutes of silence, he startled her by speaking. "How'd it ever . . . come to thish? I've known Kitty since high school . . . never saw this coming."

"Of course not," Camelia said. "The accident was a big shock to everyone."

"Yeah, shocking . . . video," he said.

"I'm sorry. It must have been very embarrassing for you."

Unless it came from you.

"Privileged communications, Counselor," Chris mumbled. "I fucked up. I just wanted . . . scare 'em . . . screw Andersh . . ."

Camelia could feel her pulse quicken. She wasn't prepared—or the least bit equipped, no thanks to Byron—for a criminal confession.

"Chris, we can't talk about this right now, not while you're under the influence."

"I did what I did," Chris said, ignoring her. "Poor Kittyhawk . . . no walking it back, not now." He passed his hand over his face and smashed his fist on the dash. "There's gonna be . . . consequences."

Was this just about the video, or was there more he was trying to say?

"Chris, what the hell have you done?" Camelia asked.

"Nothin' good," he said as his head clunked against the passenger window. "Just payback . . ." His voice drifted off and Chris went silent.

A few minutes later, Camelia pulled into Chris's driveway and turned off the car. She looked over at him and realized he was passed out.

Memories of her own drunken bouts flashed across her mind. Chris's inebriation made him way too chatty, a little belligerent, and far too loud. She cringed, recalling how many times she'd been in his shoes. A hot rush of shame burned her cheeks.

Camelia tugged on Chris's arm until he woke up, then helped him stumble out of the car, stagger up the walk and through the front door.

"Wanna beer?" he asked as she placed his keys on the kitchen island.

"No thanks, Chris. And you sure as hell don't need a beer, either. You need to eat something, take some ibuprofen, drink some water, and go to bed. Then, if you want to talk—"

"You wanna talk about Sheridan and Kitty, dontcha?"

"Not tonight I don't. You're shitfaced drunk and you need to sleep it off. Call me tomorrow when you wake up."

"Sorry . . ." He turned away and Camelia could see his shoulders hitching with sobs. "I didn't want to come home . . ."

"Is there someone I should call, Chris? To come stay with you?" she asked.

"Like who?" he mumbled. "My Kitty's dead."

51

MALICE AFORETHOUGHT

TUESDAY, MARCH 29

Camelia didn't even bother trying to put the conversation with Chris out of her mind that night. After dropping him off at his townhouse, a raging wildfire of suspicions whipped through her brain as she obsessively went back over everything he'd said. But maybe she was reading too much into his mumblings. Chris had been falling down drunk, after all.

He could have been simply drowning his sorrows over the tragic death of his cheating wife. Or not. After all, how much grief would he actually feel for a woman who'd so blatantly screwed around on him? Maybe Kaitlyn's death was a relief. He'd seemed so heartbroken and forlorn, but was it remorse for what might have been—or for what he did? Not that alcohol was some sort of magical truth serum, but it *did* lower inhibitions. What was it about those slurred words that made her spidey senses tingle?

This is getting me nowhere!

Camelia started again at the beginning.

Chris said Kaitlyn left the party early, on her own, to run an errand for Suzanne. But Suzanne didn't know anything about the so-called errand. And why on earth would Kaitlyn do *any* favors for her lover's wife? It made no sense.

What did make sense—and was a reaction Camelia completely understood—was Chris's rage at Kaitlyn for ditching him in such a public way. Kaitlyn had crossed a line when she left the firm party alone, humiliating him in front of his friends and colleagues, and it was clear to Camelia that Chris wanted retribution.

So, did Chris get back at both Anders and Kaitlyn by sending that video out to the senior partners and the State Bar? Based on the timing, it sure looked that way and, if so, he'd crossed a line of his own. But what if that wasn't all he did? No matter how naive Chris might seem, it didn't mean he was incapable of doing something awful. But he had an alibi. He was still at the party when Kaitlyn died.

Assuming for a moment it was Chris, how could he have pulled off what appeared to be a simple car accident? How would he have known Kaitlyn would be driving Suzanne's car? Could Chris have somehow found a way to ensure Kaitlyn would end up with Suzanne's car keys? That seemed like a stretch.

Even though she hated to even think about it, Camelia had to consider Suzanne's possible involvement. Ashcroft had proclaimed pretty loudly that, as the spurned wife, she was the perfect suspect. But Camelia couldn't see how Suzanne could have had anything to do with Kaitlyn's death. After all, she was at home at the time of the accident. And, based on what Suzanne had let slip, she was rolling around in the sheets with Saminski at the time, so he had an alibi, too. Even so, a woman in Suzanne's social position had the means and the contacts to orchestrate something, especially with the help of a guy like Saminski. But what was Suzanne's motive? She wasn't jealous—those days were long gone—and she sure as hell wasn't trying to reconcile with Aaron. No, if anything, Aaron having a mistress was beneficial to Suzanne's divorce case.

According to Suzanne, she left her car at the Club. At the end of the night, in the general confusion of people leaving, demanding their vehicles, and designated drivers claiming cars for inebriated friends, who would even notice someone taking the wrong car?

Camelia turned her focus to Aaron. He was also at the party when Kaitlyn died. But a guy like Aaron Anders no doubt had people to take care of things so he wouldn't get his hands dirty. Which would point directly to Saminski, if he hadn't been with Suzanne. That fact didn't let Anders off the hook, though. Or Saminski, for that matter. After all, spending the night with Suzanne was the perfect alibi. And a guy like Saminski would have contacts—the kind who wouldn't hesitate to pull off a dangerous job for the right amount of cash. But Camelia just couldn't see it. No, it was Aaron she kept coming back to. She was sure he was involved somehow, she just didn't know how. Yet.

The critical question on Camelia's mind was whether Kaitlyn was the intended target or an accidental victim. The cops were about to close the case, chalking Kaitlyn's death up to an unfortunate accident. According to them, the car hadn't malfunctioned. Kaitlyn just happened to enter the intersection at the same time as the dump truck. *Wrong place, wrong time*, Det. Luna had said. Or was it?

Maybe, if Camelia could get her hands on the police evidence, she could make sense of all this. But, as Byron had so adamantly pointed out, she wasn't a criminal attorney and had no business getting involved.

By the time sleep finally arrived, the stars were beginning to fade in the eastern sky.

WEDNESDAY, MARCH 30

Dragging herself to the office after a fitful night, Camelia steeled herself for a conversation with Byron. No matter how much she dreaded it, she had to let him know about her conversation with Chris Fischer.

But first, she had to keep her word to call Suzanne and Chris.

After a brief chat with Cate about her calendar for the day, Camelia sequestered herself in her office and dialed Suzanne.

"Good morning! How's Sedona?" she asked when Suzanne picked up.

"Oh my god, it's perfect." Suzanne yawned. "Just what I needed."

"I got your message about settlement. What's on your mind?"

"Hang on. I just want to go to the other room," Suzanne said. Camelia heard her mumble to someone, "It's my lawyer."

Camelia wondered where Dov Saminski was at the moment and smiled to herself. She hadn't thought Suzanne had it in her, but liked the idea of her client grabbing some joy out of life at the eleventh hour.

"Okay, about the settlement. I got a call from my daughter, Allison, yesterday. She offered . . . well, sort of *demanded* to negotiate a deal with Aaron on my behalf, and I want to let her try," Suzanne said. "She has some leverage with him right now with the baby on the way, and she knows what I want, so I don't see the harm in it. Do you?"

"Does she really want to get in the middle of this?" Camelia asked.

"All three of them are smack dab in the middle of it all now, thanks to that video. Someone—and it sure as hell wasn't me—posted it on YouTube. My kids are *mortified*. And outraged." Suzanne sighed.

"Oh god, they haven't watched it, have they?" Camelia asked.

"I don't think so, but they've heard all about it."

"Well, I've met your kids. They're intelligent adults, and I don't see any reason why Allison can't give it a try. I hate that she'll be negotiating with her own father, but then again, it might be good for her. Let him know she's a grownup." Camelia scribbled some notes on her legal pad.

"I think Allison wants to atone for being Aaron's pet. And Aaron is all over her about the new grandbaby, so she's convinced he'll listen to her." Suzanne paused. "I think she'll be spitting in the wind, but I have to let her try. Even if she's doomed to fail."

"Does Allison have our list of terms?"

"She said Avery drafted the talking points and Alex gave some input," Suzanne said. "The three of them cooked this up on their own, which is very sweet in its own way. But no, they don't have the list you drafted for mediation."

"Okay, I'll email a copy and you can forward it on to Allison. But nobody signs anything until I look at it, okay?"

"Of course. And I know how Alli is. If she has a list, she'll stick to it," Suzanne said. "I hope you're not offended."

"Not at all. Whatever works! My goal is to get you divorced with the best settlement possible, no matter who comes up with the deal. I'll email the list as soon as I hang up," Camelia paused. "And . . . how's Dov?"

Suzanne burst out laughing. "You can't tell a soul, but I'm happier than I've been in *years*. He's the best medicine."

Camelia smiled. "Attorney client privilege. You deserve this."

"Damn right I do! And Dov wants you to know he'll be in to see you as soon as we're back in town." Suzanne paused. "Oh, one more thing. Detective Luna emailed and I'll forward it to you later, for the file. He says Kaitlyn Fischer's toxicology report shows she was just barely over the limit for alcohol but nothing else in her system. The driver of the stolen dump truck still hasn't been tracked down, and Luna figures they'll never find him."

"That's unfortunate, because he's the only person who really knows what happened, for sure." Camelia wondered what he'd seen that night. "Anyway, enjoy Sedona, and let me know how it goes with Allison." She hung up, opened Suzanne's file on her computer, and forwarded the list of terms to Suzanne.

Camelia had another sip of coffee and braced herself before dialing Chris's mobile. He might have more information about what the police had found out, assuming he wasn't still drunk. She listened to the ringtone a dozen times before she hung up. She dialed Chris's mobile again. And again. She could only imagine his hangover today, and hoped that was the only reason he wasn't answering. The last thing she wanted was for Chris to fall into the kind of desperate depression that had driven Josh Campbell to kill himself. She left a voice message and hung up.

She flipped over to a blank page on her legal pad. She didn't have much to go on, and the few facts she had were rolling around in Camelia's head like fog through a forest. Just when one thing seemed to make sense, it dissolved into a solid rebuttal of the theory.

Even though she knew she should be working on half a dozen other cases that needed attention—not to mention a hearing next week—and even though Byron would no doubt rip into her if he caught her poking around like this again, it was eating at her. Especially after seeing Chris last night. Because no matter what Det. Luna said, there's no way Kaitlyn Fischer's death was just a simple accident. Not in a deserted intersection where, according to him, *neither* vehicle ran a red light.

First question: How were Aaron Anders, Kaitlyn Fischer, and Chris Fischer connected, other than a workplace tryst? Because, in Anders' past, his flings seemed to end amicably. Not in murder.

Camelia stopped.

Murder.

That's what this was, she could feel it in her bones. All she needed was . . . a reason. Why Kaitlyn and why the night of the firm party? But that was the wrong question. Kaitlyn wasn't the intended victim at all. It had *always* been Suzanne. She was supposed to be driving the car when it was crushed in the intersection. And that brought Camelia right back to where she'd started. To the one person with the most to gain from Suzanne's death. Her husband.

It's always the damned husband.

But Anders wasn't the only husband with a big fat axe to grind.

Last night's conversation with Drunk Chris ran back through her mind. Was he merely grieving his wife, or was there more to it than that? After all, he'd been humiliated and scorned by his wife in a very public way. But how could Chris have had anything to do with Kaitlyn's death?

Focus! Find the connections!

The only logical cause of the accident was Det. Luna's theory of a traffic light malfunction and how could that be— Camelia gasped out loud.

Holy shit.

The device at Anders' casita. She opened the photo library on her phone and swiped until she found the six images she'd taken the night she met Suzanne at the guest house. The receipt for the device read Sheridan Electronic Imports.

The thread of an idea began to weave a path in her mind. That night at the casita, Suzanne said Aaron often used props to illustrate a point in the courtroom. If what the plaintiffs in the lawsuit said was true, the device at the Anders casita was more than just a harmless trial exhibit. Kaitlyn had delivered it to the casita, removing it from the firm's case file. But what use would Anders have for a faulty preemption device from a case that concluded years ago?

Unless he was going to use it against someone.

Kaitlyn Fischer's death *was* accidental. Because that deadly crash was intended for Suzanne. And the only reason Suzanne's life was spared was because she was too tired to drive herself home.

She picked up her phone and found Det. Luna's number.

"Det. Luna, Paradise Valley Police."

"Camelia Belmont here. I'm calling about the Kaitlyn Fischer matter," Camelia said. "Just a quick question for you. Do you think a traffic preemption device could have caused the traffic lights to malfunction?"

He paused. "I guess it's possible. If there was a first responder coming through the intersection," he said. "But there wasn't a fire truck or ambulance or police car anywhere near Tatum and Lincoln when the accident happened."

"So you think it was just some bug in the system that caused the traffic lights to all turn green at the same time?"

"It sure looks that way," Det. Luna said.

"Which means," Camelia pointed out, "it could happen again. Maybe even during rush hour. Has the city been out to check those lights?"

"The engineers were out bright and early the very next day," Det. Luna replied. "The traffic signals seemed okay, but they replaced the circuit boards, just in case."

"So, doesn't that mean something else happened? Something to make it so neither driver had a red light?"

"What are you getting at?"

"What if I had a preemption device? Could I make the lights change whenever I wanted?"

"Theoretically, yes. And then you'd be under arrest, because those things are closely controlled. Only available to first responders and law enforcement," Det. Luna said. "And, besides, one of those devices would have turned the southbound lights *red*, not green. I don't think your theory holds up."

"You're right. I was just a little surprised that Kaitlyn's death was deemed accidental, given the surrounding circumstances," Camelia said. "But when you put it like this, I can see there's really no other explanation."

"Not one we've found," he said. "And believe me, I looked."

Camelia hung up and tried to catch her breath. She needed to talk to Byron right fucking now, because this could be the smoking gun that pointed straight at Aaron Anders. She gathered her notes and gulped the last of her coffee. As she speed-walked to Byron's office, she tried to slow her racing thoughts.

Okay, calm down. Present the facts. Don't come off like a maniac.

Byron was standing outside his office door talking to Sonia when Camelia approached.

"Good morning, Byron, Sonia," Camelia said, trying to sound nonchalant.

"Hey Belmont, how's it going?" Byron asked, as Sonia turned away and slid into her chair.

"Can I have a few minutes on the Anders case?"

"Yep, I've got a half hour until my client meeting, so come on in," Byron said, turning into his office. He stepped behind his desk as Camelia shut the door behind them. "Everything moving along on the divorce?"

"Yes, well, sort of. Mediation didn't go well, but we're negotiating a settlement," she said. "And I wanted to talk to you because . . . let me start at the top. I saw Chris Fischer at Durant's last night. I stopped to give him my condolences, but he was hammered, and began talking about . . ."

"Oh Jesus, don't tell me you're wading into that again?" Byron shook his head and rolled his eyes.

"Wait, just hear me out. I couldn't leave him there, babbling into his bourbon at the bar. Not at Durant's, with every shark in town circling. He was saying a lot of things that could be . . . misconstrued. Used against him." Camelia's palms were sweating, now. "I wasn't about to let him make some stupid, drunken confession in public, so I drove him home."

"You *what?* Do you not have even *one* boundary? That guy is radioactive right now!" Byron's voice thundered across the desk. "Couldn't you have just called him a cab?"

"Maybe, but he's still a human being! And I consulted with him, so we do have an attorney client relationship." Camelia took a deep breath, trying to quiet her racing heart. "Anyway, I called him this morning, to get him to come in and talk to you, but he didn't answer."

"Good. Because he's not my client, Cam. Besides, it looks like they're going to rule his wife's death accidental. There's really no evidence otherwise," Byron said.

"But what if there is?" Camelia asked.

"What of it? It's not our case. And you're not a criminal investigator. So, you need to stand down." Byron picked up his Montblanc pen, twisting it between his fingers.

"There's a link, Byron. Between Fischer, Anders, and Sheridan Electronics, the people who make the traffic light preemption devices. I don't think it was an accident. And I think Suzanne Anders was the real target that night. Only she got a ride home, instead of driving her car." Her face felt hot, and her throat was dry, but she'd come this far.

"You see, that's the problem. You're full of *thinks*. Thinking something happened isn't *evidence*. Where's your proof? Your hunches might be good enough for the family bench, but it won't cut it in a criminal trial." His jaw was clenching and he'd started tapping his pen on the desk.

"Those traffic light devices were faulty, according to a lawsuit brought against Sheridan Electronic Imports. Aaron defended the case and he won. But not on the product liability issue. He won on technicalities and procedure," she said.

"Okay, so he's a damn good litigator. I don't think that's really up for debate. I win on technicalities all the time. What's your point?" His prominent temple vein was throbbing.

"Yeah, but Anders had one of those devices at his home," Camelia said.

Byron's eyes narrowed, and he leaned forward. "Really? And how do you know that?"

"I . . . uh, Suzanne saw a woman, who turned out to be Kaitlyn Fischer, enter the casita at their estate and," Camelia flushed. "She asked me to come to her house to see what Kaitlyn had dropped off, so I—"

"You *WHAT?*" Byron slammed his fist on his desk. "When was this?"

This wasn't going as planned.

"A couple of months ago. This woman just showed up at the house, went into the casita with a package, and then she left. Suzanne didn't know who she was and was worried about . . . you know, a stranger on the property." Camelia gulped.

"A stranger? Who has the keys to the house and delivers a package? Really? Is that the best you've got? Because I can tell you right now, even if it was solid evidence, it's tainted now." Byron glared at her over his glasses. "Jesus, Mary, and Joseph. Why can't you just leave this alone? It is *not* our problem."

"Well, it *is* my problem, because it's *my client's* problem. It could explain why Kaitlyn met that dump truck in the intersection." As she spoke, Camelia swallowed, trying to slow her heart, which felt like it was beating a hole in her head. "Don't you think I should at least tell the cops about this?"

"No, I don't think you should do anything of the sort. I think you should quit playing Nancy Drew, and I think you should leave Gerry Sheridan out of it. Please, Cam. Just march your ass back down the hall and focus on your own cases. Got it?" Byron pulled a file from the stack on the edge of his desk. "Now, if you're done, I have work to do."

How does Byron know the first name of the owner of Sheridan Electronics?

"Got it, boss. But for the record—" she began.

"For the record, I don't want to hear another word about it. Now go, before you really piss me off."

Camelia stood, turning toward the door. "Okay, message received."

"I'm going to have Sonia schedule a meeting for us in the next couple of weeks. It's time we had a heart to heart, Cam."

Camelia nodded and pulled the door to Byron's office closed behind her.

A heart to heart.

She knew what that meant.

The file in her arms suddenly felt like it weighed a ton. A ton of disappointments. A ton of being dismissed. A ton of never being taken seriously. It would never change. Byron would always see her as a bottom-of-the-pecking-order divorce attorney with no potential for anything more.

It's time to leave.

52

DADDY'S GIRL

THURSDAY, MARCH 31

Aaron Anders wasn't getting much sleep, and it was making him testy. He paced the casita's sheltered courtyard, relentlessly reviewing the night of Kaitlyn's death while sipping iced tea and puffing on a fat cigar. Would it all blow back on him, somehow? But that wasn't possible. When he last spoke to the cops, they said it was looking more and more like an accident. But they hadn't stopped sniffing around, despite his demands to the police chief that they wind it up quickly, before Kaitlyn's parents filed a civil suit. Which he would beat in a minute. After all, it was Saminski who handed Kaitlyn the keys to Suzanne's car. But he didn't need the bad publicity that kind of lawsuit would bring.

Aaron had often wondered if he'd miscalculated by getting involved with Kaitlyn, but it was all over now. Even if it had come to a tragic ending, he could finally exhale.

And, at this stage of his life, he could afford to be pragmatic about such things. Kaitlyn was nothing more than another fling—a spicy one, a dangerous one, but still just a passing fancy—regardless of how she saw herself. He hadn't appreciated the relentless rumors around the office, especially since he had a sneaking suspicion Kaitlyn herself had started some of them. It was her way of elbowing her way to the front of the line as Suzanne's successor.

Yes, he'd definitely dodged a bullet. Her craving to be the next Mrs. Anders was too strident, too insistent. And blatantly obvious to anyone paying attention. He could kick himself for letting her in on some of his more questionable tactics, because she'd already started dropping hints about how she could use that information against him. You never knew what a woman scorned was capable of, and Kaitlyn was the vengeful type. Well, now he could relax. He would be a lot more careful who he fell in bed with from now on, but at least this time, he was in the clear.

Well, not completely in the clear. He stubbed out his cigar and took a long swig of cold tea. Things were out of balance, and he hated this feeling of not being in total control of everything—and everyone—in his world. Not only were Kaitlyn's parents threatening a wrongful death suit, now Saminski had gone rogue, Suzanne's divorce lawyer was still screeching like a banshee, and Chris Fischer was unraveling.

Why couldn't these people just fucking manage themselves like grownups? Instead, Aaron was left juggling all their crap, cleaning up after everyone's mess. Not that he had a choice. He had to step up. He had a firm to manage, including some very upset attorneys and skittish staff who were having a meltdown over Kaitlyn's death. And then there was the video. Even though it had only been emailed to a handful of people, they were all people who could make his life hell: the senior partners, Suzanne, Ashcroft, Belmont, the president of the Arizona bar, and the head of the litigation division. But it didn't stop there. He'd gotten wind that the very embarrassing video was now out in the wild, creating havoc.

Even with Kaitlyn out of the picture, someone else—someone who would pay dearly as soon as he caught them—was out to get him. Who would have the nerve to release that footage? The cops still had no fucking clue who sent it, which meant his usual strategies—overwhelm, outmaneuver, threaten, or whatever other dirty tricks he could come up with—would not resolve the problem.

Whoever sent the video had access to the security camera files. There were only two people who had that access: Saminski and Office Bee. Janice would *never* cross him that way. Saminski, though. How the hell did he let this slip? His whole fucking job was to make sure this kind of shit didn't happen. Unless he was behind it.

No matter who sent that video out, Aaron was embarrassed to admit it had badly singed his reputation. The repercussions were echoing through every hall in the firm, and even through the corridors of the Courts. Although, in the eyes of some, his stock just went up. Aaron allowed himself a bitter smile.

But this wasn't just about the ding on his professional reputation or the sudden rise in his social capital. That damned video had changed the way his own children looked at him, and they were furious. Hell, Alex had shown up at the casita unannounced and gone off on a judgmental rant for over an hour. Avery wasn't even speaking to him. She just hit ignore every time he called. And now Allison—his eager to please middle child who had been curiously silent on the subject—suddenly wanted to talk about settlement in the divorce. No, things were definitely out of balance.

Aaron took Allison's sudden desire to get involved as a good sign, though. At least *she* was talking to him. He knew he could get her to see his side of things and, once she was back on board, she would convince her siblings to forgive him. Even better, she would become his weapon. He'd let Allison believe she'd beaten him down, because that would make her a better advocate for the deal with Suzanne. Which is why Aaron didn't mind negotiating with her. All he had to do was convince Alli she'd managed to get some big concessions, then she'd do the rest, persuading Suzanne to go along with whatever terms he was willing to permit. It was all about perception.

Aaron glanced at his watch, then stepped back inside the casita. A quick shower, then off to meet his daughter.

As he toweled off, Aaron considered the genius idea of using Allison as their go-between, and he wished he'd thought of it. He didn't know why she'd agreed to step in to negotiate a deal, but Suzanne was obviously behind it. She probably thought Allison could work him over emotionally. He chuckled to himself. If Suzanne only knew how easy it was for him to run all over Allison. She should have sent Avery, their youngest. That one had his killer instinct and wouldn't be so easy to convince. He smiled. That was Suzanne's mistake, and one she would regret when Allison started putting the screws to her.

As he slid behind the wheel of his Porsche, Aaron glanced up at the main house, his jaw clenching. He'd agreed to move into the casita to maintain appearances, give Suzanne a longer leash, while keeping his own hours. Their agreement was that she would step up for society and firm functions while, in exchange, she had free range of the credit cards. Until now, he'd thought it was an ideal arrangement for both of them.

He was still pissed off that she'd had the nerve to file for divorce after learning her diagnosis. If she'd just kept her wits about her, Aaron would have dutifully played the doting, grieving husband. But no, Suzanne just couldn't leave it alone. After all he'd given her. His time. His name. His money. *His children.* Now the bitch was getting exactly what she deserved.

He eased the car out of the security gate, picking up speed as he turned onto Tatum. As he pulled up to the historic resort, the valet recognized him and gave a little salute as he took Aaron's keys. He pointed to where Allison was already waiting on the patio near one of the fireplaces. Lon's at The Hermosa Inn is understated, discreet, not a see-and-be-seen kind of place, which suited Aaron. He didn't need nosy colleagues eavesdropping while he was negotiating his divorce. He was about to wave when he noticed Allison's stiff posture.

So that's how it's going to be, huh?

Hiding his resentment behind a wide smile, Aaron walked up to the table, leaning down to kiss Allison's cheek.

"How's my favorite MamaBear this evening?"

"Great, Dad. Just a little hungry, as usual," Allison said, pointing to a plate of crudités and hummus. "Help yourself."

"Thanks, but I think I'll skip the rabbit food," Aaron said, gesturing at a waiter. He ordered an Old Fashioned and the charcuterie board.

"It's great to see you both." Aaron nodded at Allison's belly. "Everything going well with my grandcub?"

"Yeah, we're both doing fine. Looks like we're gonna have a healthy bambino in just a few more weeks. Hard to believe," she said, rubbing her belly as she scooped up hummus with a carrot.

"That's great news. I can't wait to be a Grandpapa." As the words left his mouth, Aaron realized he meant it. It was a fresh start. A new beginning. A brand new human who wouldn't judge or resent him. He'd make sure of it. "Still no hint as to whether I'm buying blue or pink onesies?"

"Like we told you, Dad," Allison cupped her belly. "We're not getting hung up on that kind of thing. If you want to buy blue onesies, go for it."

"Good strategy, Alli," Aaron said. "And either way, I can't wait to spoil him and/or her."

"Well, about that," Allison said. She reached into her handbag and pulled out a folded piece of paper and a small notebook. "We need to get Mom settled before the baby comes. I don't want your divorce hanging over me while we're celebrating my little track star."

"Of course. Completely understandable." Aaron shifted in his seat as the waiter approached with his cocktail and appetizer. He took a long draw of his drink. "So, where would you like to start?"

"It doesn't . . . we can start wherever you like." Allison unfolded and smoothed the piece of paper. "But Dad, please don't be a dick about it, okay?" She raised an eyebrow.

"Oh, come on, Alli-Cat. I'm not gonna be a dick about any of it. Your mother wants certain things that aren't reasonable, but everything else . . . it's all up for grabs. Do you want to begin with real estate?" Aaron smiled at his daughter. "Fire away."

"Okay, fine. Real estate. We all know you don't want to sell the PV house, so you'll have to buy Mom out. Zillow says it's worth about five mil, so I'll put two point five on mom's side of the ledger. Where's the cash gonna come from?" She drew a couple of lines down the length of her notebook and labeled them Dad, Mom, then wrote 2,500,000 under Mom, before looking up.

"Well, there's a mortgage on the house, so the net is more like three point five. Put one point seven five in Mom's column," Aaron said, leaning over to watch Allison scribble over the numbers. "As for the cash, we'll have to do some horse trading, but she'll get plenty of money. Certainly enough for the rest of her life."

He heard Allison's gasp and looked up. She was glaring at him with tear filled eyes.

"What? Don't look at me like that. I'm just stating a fact."

"Jesus, Dad. Can you at least pretend to care a little? This is hard enough . . ." Allison dabbed at her eyes with her napkin and put her pen down. She drew a deep breath. "Okay, so what about the summer place?"

"Montana? That isn't on the table, is it?"

"Of course, it is. Why wouldn't it be?" she snapped.

"That's our family place. For all of us. Not something to be divvied up between your mother and I. Does she really want it sold?" Aaron watched Allison's face carefully. He knew how much she loved that property.

"Nobody said you have to sell it, but it belongs to you and Mom. Us kids don't have any ownership rights to that property. So yeah, we've always considered it to be a *family* getaway, but it's not ours. Not legally."

"But what if it was? Why couldn't Mom and I just deed it over to you kids and be done with it? My little grandbaby should be spending all her, or his, summers there." He shook his head as he took a bite of cheese. "I mean, we could sell it, but it was always meant to be a place for you kids, for the future. Even after your mom and I are long gone."

Allison swallowed a mouthful of pita and hummus, then washed it down with iced tea. He could see she was thinking, formulating a response.

"Okay, so sign the Montana compound over to the three of us, along with everything in it. I think Mom will agree to that," Allison said. "And what about the downtown condo?"

"You're ruthless!" he laughed. "The condo belongs to the firm, Alli. It's just a place to sleep when I'm in trial, so it's not really a personal residence, you know? It's a firm asset, and not on the table." Aaron took another sip of his drink. His patience was already wearing thin.

"Okay, but there's no line item for the condo on the list of business assets, so that will have to be fixed. What's it worth? A million?" Her pen hovered above her notebook, ready to record a value.

"I doubt if it's worth eight hundred, but I'll remind the accountants to add it into the business value. What's next?" Aaron asked.

"There's a long list, but the big line item is the business. It looks like your share is worth about eight million," Allison said, pointing to the folded piece of paper. "Not counting the condo."

"Well, it's not worth much of anything if I walk away." Aaron popped a date in his mouth and slowly chewed, waiting for Allison's response.

"Oh really, Dad? And where the hell would you walk to? You're not leaving your own firm and we both know it. So, from what I understand, you owe Mom four point four million for her half of the business, including half the condo." She began writing in her notebook.

"And what makes you think I can come up with that kind of cash? That's the *value of the business*, not the balance of the bank account. And there's a lot of blue sky in that number. I know you're new at this but, seriously, even you have to know it doesn't work that way. I would have to make payments, on a long schedule. And your mother doesn't have that kind of time." Aaron ran his hand across his chin. "So, instead of tit for tat, can we skip to the part where we talk about a reasonable overall settlement amount?"

"Sure. How about five million, plus Mom keeps her life insurance and her retirement funds?" Allison dropped her pen on her notebook. "Because that's totally reasonable given all these other numbers."

"Jesus, Alli. Now you sound like her. How about I pay Mom $25k a month until she dies, and she keeps her retirement funds, but I get the proceeds of her life insurance?"

Allison's cheeks flushed with red splotches. God. She looked just like her mother when she was pissed off. Aaron knew she was getting frustrated, but so was he. She wasn't equipped for this kind of deal making. She was a fucking physical therapist, for crying out loud. Allison understood pulled muscles, not the complicated financials of a high net worth divorce. She was being so typically simplistic. He wished Avery were sitting here. Even though she hadn't passed the bar yet, at least she understood the basics of negotiating.

"How about you give Mom what she wants for once in your fucking life?" Allison hissed. "Or you can say goodbye to me and your grandchild right now." She threw her napkin on the table.

"Oh, come on, MamaBear. Don't be that way. This isn't how negotiations work. You don't just literally throw in your towel," Aaron gestured at her napkin, wadded up on the table. "And start making threats just because I would like to preserve *something* of the estate I've worked my fucking ass off for my whole life. Fair doesn't always mean equal, you know. So, just calm down and let's talk about spousal support. How much does your mother need?" Aaron waved his glass at the waiter for another.

"*Calm down?* Boy, you sure know how to smooth talk the ladies, dontcha?" She rolled her eyes. "So, tell me, dear father, what good is $25k in spousal support if mom is . . . dead in, I don't know, a year? That would only come to $300,000. And that's sure as hell not half the estate, is it? I mean sure, it's a good deal for you—"

"How is three hundred thou a good deal? It's a damned expensive deal, but I want your mother to be comfortable for this last bit of her life. And then, when she's gone, who's left to take care of the family? Me. Grandpapa." He tapped his chest with his index finger. "That's who. And how will I take care of all of you if my money is pissed away in a divorce settlement? How can I make sure this new grandbaby has a paid ride to Stanford or Oxford or wherever, if you've bled me dry on asset division? Is *anyone* thinking about the future besides me?" Aaron pinched the bridge of his nose. His head was pounding.

Allison heaved a sigh and took another gulp of iced tea. "Okay, here's the thing, Dad. If Mom has her share of the estate, and she bequeaths it to us as she intends, then we won't need your help. Each of us will have our own nest egg. And that means you're free to spend all your money on whatever, *or whoever*, you want. Can't you see that?"

"Sorry, kiddo, but it just seems like no one is really considering how this is going to play out over the next twenty years. And I get it, emotions are running high. Your Mom's playing the cancer card, and—"

"Are you kidding me right now? Mom hasn't played *any* fucking card, Dad. She has Stage IV ovarian cancer. That is not a goddamn card. It's her life. I can't believe you." Allison snapped her notebook shut and began stuffing it in her handbag. "I'm outta here."

Aaron reached out and grabbed her hand. "Hey, Alli, hold on now. I know we can come up with something that works for everyone. Just hear me out." Aaron ran his thumb over the back of Allison's hand. "You and I have always been closer than the rest of them. Remember when you were on the track team, Alli-Cat? Our secret ice cream missions? There's always going to be an extra scoop for you at the end. You know that right? Fair doesn't mean equal, does it?"

Allison's eyes bored into him, but when she set her purse back on the chair, Aaron knew he had her.

"Okay, I'm listening." She pulled her notebook back out of her bag, and clicked her pen.

"Well, don't hold me to this, because I'm just spitballing, thinking out loud for a minute." Aaron loved this game. He would offer just a hint of what might be possible, then pull it back ever so slightly until Allison agreed. Then pull back a bit more, and a bit more, until he'd whittled the terms into a great deal. For Aaron. "What about the Montana place? I mean, you're the mother of my first grandchild, so maybe you should receive the legacy of our vacation home."

Allison rolled her eyes. "Really? And make me fight Alex for the rest of my life? No thanks, Dad."

"Yeah, he can be a bit of a prick about stuff like that," Aaron smiled. "So, what about the condo? You work downtown anyway, so instead of being out in the wilds of Ahwatukee, it might be nice to be closer to work—"

"Dad, we already own a house and the last thing I want is to raise my kid in a downtown condo, in the middle of the heat island." Allison scribbled in her notebook. "What about cash?"

"What about it? You know I'm always in a feast or famine cash flow battle with the firm. But how much are we talking about?" Aaron could almost smell her mind heating up as she fidgeted for a number.

"I don't know. What seems reasonable to you?" Allison sipped her tea and her blue eyes, so much like his own, narrowed.

Aaron weighed his options. If Allison went to bat for him with Suzanne, it could save him millions of dollars. Not to mention the priceless satisfaction of having won the battle on two fronts: his daughter, and his soon to be ex.

"I can probably come up with $500k right now, then another five hundred after Mom . . . after Suzanne passes." He leaned forward, elbows on the table, and grasped Allison's hand in both of his. "I would love nothing more than to make life more comfortable for my first grandchild."

Allison stared at her notebook for a minute. "Can you go to one point five?"

Aaron laughed and tapped his finger on his temple as he leaned back in his chair. "Now you're thinking like your dad. And for you? Of course, I can pull another half a mil outta my ass." He shook his head. "But seriously, if I do this, then I've got terms, too. And the first one is, this stays between us."

"I expected that. So, how about this. I get one point five, and Mom gets her retirement funds and $30k a month with a three year minimum?" She pulled her blond ponytail out of its scrunchie and ran her fingers through her loose hair.

Aaron thought about it for a minute, sipping his Old Fashioned, as he watched the waiter stoke the fireplace.

"Deal," he said, trying to tamp down the grin on his face. "As long as Mom keeps me as her beneficiary on the life insurance."

Allison slammed her notebook closed and stuffed it in her bag. "Well, at least now I know who you are." Her eyes narrowed into fierce slits. "If you think I can be bought off with an *extra scoop of ice cream* as you call it, which is actually *Mom's scoop*, you're stupider than I thought. Here you are, wheeling and dealing away Mom's money—not to mention her rights—while I sit here, pregnant with your grandchild. Do you even see the irony? Are you gonna pull this shit with my kid, too? You gonna promise them an *extra scoop* to turn them against me?"

"For the love of god, Allison, what the hell is your problem?" Aaron took a deep breath and glanced around to make sure no one was listening. He was trying to keep his temper in check, but not entirely succeeding. "I'm offering you a life-changing amount of money to lead our family out of this crisis. Because you're the one who can do that. You're the only one who can help your mother overcome her deathbed greed long enough to see what's really important. So, stop with the self righteous bullshit."

"Got it. Thanks for doubling down. Don't call me, I'll call you." Allison stood up and waved at their waiter. "Give him the bill."

As she walked briskly toward the exit, Aaron had to stifle a scream rising in his throat.

That vicious little bitch.

She was just like her goddamn mother after all.

Then he had to stifle a groan as a searing flash of pain ripped across his chest.

Jesus. Not again.

53

UNLIKELY ALLIES

THURSDAY, APRIL 7

When Camelia entered the conference room, Dov Saminski was standing with his back to her, looking out the floor-to-ceiling windows over 24th and Camelback, hands stuffed in his trouser pockets. Hearing the door, he turned and crossed to shake her hand.

"Nice to see you again, Dov," she said. "Thanks for coming in."

"Overdue, I think," he answered, firmly gripping her hand.

Camelia placed her legal pad on the table and slid into a chair while he hovered. He looked tense, out of his element.

"Please, have a seat." Camelia gave him a smile. "Just to reassure you, we have attorney client privilege, so you can speak your mind. In case that was a concern."

Dov pushed a hand through close-cropped, dark hair shot through with silver. Camelia could see why Suzanne was attracted to him: lean and muscular, well tailored clothes, and a quiet demeanor. He had to be late 40s, Camelia thought, based on those lines around his eyes. Or maybe he just wasn't the type to moisturize. He sat down and dropped his backpack into the chair next to him.

"Thanks. I'm here because I want to protect Suzanne," he pressed his palms to the table, "and I think we can help each other do that. That's it."

"What makes you think she needs protection, Dov?"

He took a swig of water. "I think Suzanne was the intended target of the so-called accident that killed Kaitlyn Fischer. Or at least the trail I've picked up seems to lead in that direction."

"Okay, lay it out for me from the beginning," Camelia said, her heart rate ticking up at Dov's words. "I'll stop you when I have questions."

"It all started . . . hang on." Dov pulled a tablet from his backpack and swiped it open. After a couple of taps, he said, "I think you know this, but back in January, Kaitlyn Fischer delivered a package to Anders at home. The reason I'm aware of it is because Mr. Anders called that night asking what I knew about Kaitlyn being on the property. Which was nothing. The next day, Mr. Anders asked me to change the gate code and key code for the casita. Because, and I quote, *I don't need someone like her taking advantage of the situation.*"

"And did you change the key codes?" Camelia asked.

"Yep. As ordered." He took a breath.

"And you don't know anything about the package she took to Anders' home?"

"No . . . well, I do now, but I'll get to that in a minute." Dov looked down at his tablet. "Then, a few days—"

"Do you keep a log of everything?" Camelia was itching to look at his screen.

Dov gave her a tight grin. "Of course. I'm in the security business. And sometimes *security* means having a reliable, contemporaneous record of—"

"An alibi?" Camelia smirked.

"Yep. An alibi. And it's a record kept in the ordinary course of business which makes it admissible as evidence. It's my safety net," Dov said.

"You've learned a few things hanging out with lawyers, haven't you?"

"I've learned to watch my back." Dov swiped his screen a couple of times. "Where was I? Oh yeah. On February 24th, Mr. Anders announced his new charity. It raised a lot of hackles, and the senior partners were raging mad about it. So mad they held a secret meeting at Frost's house."

"If it was such a secret, how do you know about it?" Camelia shook the cramp out of her hand.

"Jim Frost and David Weisman—two of the senior partners— had an offsite meeting at Phoenix Country Club, very hush hush. Except not so top secret that they didn't get me to drive them home. They'd been drinking, and since they think of me as just one of the hired help, they let a couple of things slip in the car. Those guys," Saminski shook his head. "They're almost as bad as Anders. Suzanne said they invited her to a meeting at Frost's house mid-March to hear a proposal on selling their shares to another firm."

Holy shit.

Would the senior partners really be mad enough to bail?

"Why didn't she tell me about this?"

"There's been a lot going on, and the deal's not final yet. A lot of things can happen between now and then, but Suzanne's business attorney, Barry Solomon, expects it to go through in a few days," Dov said.

"That explains why I had a message from Barry last week. Guess I better call him back." Camelia made a note to herself. "But wait a second. Can they sell without Aaron's vote?"

"According to Suzanne, the five of them make a majority of sixty percent," Dov said.

"That's *very* interesting news as it relates to the divorce and division of assets. Okay, what's next?" Camelia was dying to rip the punch line out of Saminski, but she could see he was a methodical, linear thinking guy. He had to work through each step.

"A few days before the firm party, Anders called me in and gave me very specific orders that I was no longer authorized to drive Suzanne *anywhere*. That was a big change because I *always* drove her to and from the events she attended with Mr. Anders. Parties, fundraisers, conferences, all of it." As if a cloud had passed overhead, Dov's grey eyes shifted to slate blue. "And recently, if none of the partners needed me, I'd been driving Suzanne to medical appointments a couple of times a week. But Mr. Anders made it very clear that was over. The timing seemed a bit odd to me."

"Well, they are in the middle of a divorce, so it makes sense," Camelia said. "Was there something else to it?"

"I'm just getting started." Dov took a sip of water. "March 19 was the annual firm gala. That morning, Suzanne called to arrange a ride, as she usually does. But I had to decline because of Aaron's orders." Dov tapped his fingers on the edge of the table. "I said I would have one of the team drive her, but she refused the offer."

"Okay . . ."

Dov's expression darkened. "The *only* reason Suzanne didn't drive herself home the night of the party was because I insisted. Against the boss's *direct* orders, but I didn't care at that point, you know? I mean, she was exhausted, could barely stand up." Dov heaved a sigh. "But *he* didn't know she wasn't driving her car home, did he?"

"No. I suppose not. But what about her car?" Camelia prompted.

"That's Suzanne's baby, inherited from her mother, and it's a garage queen. Mr. Anders always considered it a kidnapping risk for her to drive on her own, and Suzanne won't drive if she's having cocktails. Which is why Suzanne *never* drove herself to events, at least not as long as I've been around."

"But the night of the party was different," Camelia prompted. "Because you didn't drive her."

"Right. Suzanne drove her car to the Club. Which Anders had to have known. Hell, he might have even watched her drive off that evening before he left for the party. Anyway, later that night, when I saw her, it was obvious she was in no shape to drive herself home. I offered to have her car delivered to the house by me or one of my team. But she asked me to give Aaron her car keys." Dov glanced out the window, then at his watch.

"Why would Suzanne want Aaron, specifically, to drive her car home?"

Dov gave a little smile. "Honestly? I think she was just winding him up. I mean, Aaron *demanded* she attend the firm party, then wouldn't even extend the courtesy of a ride. And even though he wouldn't have to personally drive her car home, she knows how much he hates any kind of plebeian task. Suzanne knew he'd end up having to manage her car, and that was enough of a dig for her. But when I went to give Mr. Anders the keys, he was surrounded by a bunch of young lawyers, and I didn't dare interrupt. And . . ." Dov looked down at the table, as if steeling himself. "He would have asked how Suzanne was getting home. I didn't feel like arguing about it. Kaitlyn was handy, though, and I knew she'd jump at the chance to be Aaron's special girl, so I handed the keys off to her."

"I see. Did you ask her to drive the car back to the Anders estate?"

"I, uh . . . left that open." Dov heaved a sigh. "But I also made it clear that she should just pass the keys to Aaron. I don't know why she decided to drive Suzanne's car. Knowing her, she probably thought of it as a big fuck you to Suzanne."

"But Aaron didn't know anything about it, did he?" Camelia wrote a note.

Dov snorted. "If Aaron had known she was going to drive Suzanne's car, he would have been furious. He doesn't like *anyone* taking liberties like that."

"So, Aaron thought Suzanne would be driving herself home?"

Dov nodded. "Yep. Which is why I think he's behind the crash. I think it was intended for Suzanne, but then Kaitlyn changed the equation when she left the Club in Suzanne's car."

"So you didn't know *for sure* Kaitlyn would drive Suzanne's car?"

Dov shook his head. "No, we left before her, just after eleven."

"And can you prove that?" Camelia asked.

Dov pushed a stapled sheaf of papers across the conference table and pointed at a line item. "This is the valet log. See here? BBY BLU, that's Suzanne's license plate, left about twenty minutes after we did. From my valet's description and the Paradise Valley Country Club security cameras, we know it was Kaitlyn leaving in the Triumph. By that time, Suzanne and I were already at the Anders estate."

Camelia studied the spreadsheet. "So, you have an alibi."

"Not that I need one, but yeah. And Suzanne has one too, because . . . I was with her."

"Okay, so then what happened?"

"The Monday after the accident, I went over this log to see if there were any other anomalies. The valet recorded one car making two arrivals. Jeff Petronelli's. After arriving around seven, he left the party at 10:07 and returned at 11:01." Saminski took a deep breath and another sip of water.

Camelia raised her eyebrows and shrugged. "Why would Jeff whatshisname be of interest?"

"During those fifty-four minutes, he went to the office and accessed the firm security camera files—"

"What does that have to do with anything?" Camelia dropped her pen and leaned back. This seemed off topic.

"It wasn't Petronelli at all. It was Chris Fischer. I caught him on security video."

"What? That doesn't make sense either. Why was he in this other guy's car and how did Fischer access those files if he doesn't have permission?" Camelia tried to picture the man she'd met being some kind of hacker, but it didn't jibe.

"Fischer was the designated driver for Jeff and Rachel Petronelli, so he had the keys to their SUV. And he had access to the security server because, a couple of weeks ago, good ol' Farmboy Fischer hoodwinked me into revealing my login and password." Saminski slapped his forehead. "I know how he did it and, Jesus Christ, I'm embarrassed that I let him get away with it. Anyway, he did a swipe and wipe. Downloaded the video of Kaitlyn and Anders, then wiped the files. Or so he thought."

"Files? Plural?" Camelia asked.

"Two. There was also the security footage of him coming *into* the lobby on the night of the party. He deleted both files, but the underlying data is still there if you know what you're doing. And he didn't think about the footage of him *leaving* the lobby, or the building security cameras. He's on the elevator camera. Toothpick in a ball cap and a hoodie, getting off at AndersLaw. It was absolutely him."

"*Damn.* The police said the video of Kaitlyn and Anders came from an anonymous computer behind a VPN. They can't prove he was the one who released the video, so they can't press charges under the revenge porn statute," Camelia said. "But here's their proof!"

"Oh, believe me. The cops are the least of Fischer's worries. Anders wants a pound of flesh." Saminski played with the cap of his water bottle. "I haven't turned this information over to Anders yet, and I'm not going to. He'll have Fischer disbarred. Or worse."

"What Anders wants is beside the point, but what Chris did was illegal and needs to be reported. And even as shitty as releasing the video was, it didn't kill his wife." Camelia studied Dov's face for clues. "Although it sounds to me you don't think Kaitlyn's death was an accident."

"I guess the crash *could* be an accident, but Anders is *really* pissed off at Suzanne for having the nerve to actually divorce him and take half his fortune in the process. But," Dov paused. "I admit I'm not one hundred percent certain. Fischer comes across all meek and mild, but Anders was screwing his wife. That's gotta bring out the dark side, even in a good-natured Eagle Scout like Fischer. And then there's . . ." Again, Dov stopped.

"There's what?" Camelia prompted when the silence stretched thin.

Dov sighed. "Look, Camelia, there's always the chance—granted, it's a long shot—that this has nothing to do with Anders or Fischer. Or, at least, not the way we think."

"What's that supposed to mean?"

"Anders was involved with some . . . uh, less than aboveboard *situations*. There was this land deal, involving the Saudis—"

"This is too much of a coincidence," Camelia's mind snapped to the day Josh Campbell killed himself. He'd been terrified of some Saudi investors. "How many shady land deals involving Saudis can there possibly be in Phoenix?"

"Just one that I know of, at least recently. Josh Campbell wasn't—"

She started at hearing her former client's name coming out of Dov's mouth. "What do you know about that?"

"About what?" Dov looked puzzled.

"Josh Campbell. The land deal gone bad. All of that. How do you know?"

Camelia could tell Saminski thought it was common knowledge by the way he looked at her.

"Well . . . that's Campbell's gig. Or it was. He finds—I mean, *found* property that might be a little undervalued, lined up the development permits, put a package together, and recruited the investors."

"I didn't realize that was his whole business. I thought he was a commercial realtor," Camelia said.

"Well, he was more like a bookie, if you ask me, because those deals are always a gamble. The big money usually comes from offshore. Russia, China, India. In this case, a group of Saudi ranchers. But locals were throwing money at the project, too. Anders, Frost, Sheridan and a few others invested. It wasn't the first time this group's been in bed together. Hell, I think your boss, McCaffrey, was even in on a couple of their deals." Dov paused to take a sip of water.

Camelia almost choked. "I'm sorry, but did you say *Byron McCaffrey* was involved with these people?" she sputtered.

Why on earth would Byron be investing with that group of bandits? Was that why he warned her off Gerry Sheridan?

"Yeah, but not on this deal specifically. Pretty sure he made his money and bowed out early. Which was the smart thing to do." Dov nodded. "You probably read about the County clamping down on new grants for agricultural water rights. You need a ton of water for alfalfa, so the deal died, and the earnest money was lost. And it was a *lot* of money. The Saudis went into a rage, throwing threats at everyone, including Anders. Honestly, they're all a bunch of spoiled brats, if you ask me. But it sure spooked the other investors."

"Were their threats serious? Because Josh Campbell certainly thought so."

Dov tilted his head and squinted as if seeing the question from a distance. "I think it was just a bully bluff to recoup some of their loss, but you never know with the Saudis. They can be a ruthless buncha dudes. Very Old Testament." He shrugged. "Sorry about Josh, though. I hate to say it, but I think he overreacted. Not that you shouldn't take a threat seriously, but he should have waited it out."

"I wish he would have." If only Camelia had known . . . but would it have made any difference? Could she have talked sense into Josh if she'd had this information then? She gave herself a mental shake. Now wasn't the time for ruminating on that tragedy. She had more pressing problems to deal with. "I interrupted you. Was there more?"

"You know most of the rest of this already. I took Suzanne home, then later . . . around two a.m., the cops showed up. Monday morning, I headed to the office, as usual." He paused and looked uncomfortable. "I was expecting to get fired, so I went to clean up a few loose ends."

"No need to sugar coat it, Dov."

"Yeah, well, the truth is, I wanted to get to the office so I could give Anders a taste of his own medicine. I was going to distribute that video to a couple of choice people to humiliate him. Publicly."

"Sorry, you *what*?" Camelia knew she was staring, but she couldn't blink.

"Oh, believe me. I had every intention of using that video myself when I went into the office that Monday morning." Dov looked down at his tablet before meeting her eyes again. "But Fischer beat me to it. And I kinda want him to get away with it."

"I get it, he's kind of a big puppy. But I'm confused about something. He sent out the video with that vague email about the Anders house of cards and all that. I don't understand his end game. I get why he would send it to Aaron, but why copy anyone else?"

Camelia asked. "There's no blackmail value if you've already released the incriminating information."

"You're right. No one gets compensated for dirt people already know. But I don't think Fischer did it for money. I think it was just to screw with Anders' reputation and his cone of privilege. Fischer's way of letting Aaron know he hadn't gotten away with making a cuck of him." Dov's grey eyes were unrepentant. "And that's fine with me. Because it gave Suzanne—and you too, I guess—enough leverage to push the divorce through. That's all she wants."

"Okay. Maybe Fischer's motive wasn't entirely horrible, but the result was not only against the law, it created a helluva mess. Especially since Kaitlyn had just died." Camelia took a deep breath.

"The timing was awful. And yeah, Fischer might be petty and vindictive. But he really doesn't strike me as the kind of guy to release the video if he knew Kaitlyn was dead."

"I agree. I've only met him a couple of times, but he doesn't seem that callous." Camelia capped her pen and flipped the pages of notes over, thinking they were finished, when Dov held up his hand.

"There's one more thing. That Monday morning, while I was at the office recovering the video, Anders asked if I knew who sent him a package through inter-office mail. It was such a weird question. I mean, we don't monitor our own people like that." Dov shook his head. "Then I see Anders on the security video. He's in the conference room rummaging around in old closed case files. And that made my hackles go up."

"Why would that make you suspicious?" Camelia asked.

Dov took another swig of water and blew out a long exhale. "Because Anders doesn't file. Ever. But there he was, on camera, stashing a package in a closed case file."

"Okay, I'll grant you that sounds strange," Camelia said. "But not exactly criminal."

"I thought it was out of character enough that I should check it out. I mean, why would he be doing his own filing when we have half a dozen file clerks?" Dov leaned over and pulled a large envelope out of his backpack. "This is what he was putting away." He pushed it toward Camelia.

She peered inside and saw a flash drive. And a metal device that looked just like the one she'd seen at Anders' casita.

"Do you know what this device is?" she asked.

"Of course. I looked it up. It's a preemption device used by law enforcement and first responders to change traffic lights in an emergency. Imported by Sheridan Electronics. Gerry Sheridan is not only Anders' golf buddy and real estate investor, he's a client of the firm. They had a big case over this a while back." Dov blew out a sigh.

"I know. Anders won on a technicality," Camelia said. "The devices are faulty, apparently. Or at least some of them were. But Anders won the appeal and the case was dismissed." She could barely breathe. This was a lot of serendipity. "So tell me, Dov, can you think of a reason why Aaron Anders would show up at the office on a Monday morning, the day after his mistress is killed in a car accident, returning this particular exhibit? Which, from what I hear, should never have been removed from the office in the first place, per AndersLaw policy. The same exhibit Kaitlyn Fischer delivered to Aaron Anders a few weeks ago? The same exhibit that just happens to be a faulty traffic preemption device that would make someone think they had a green light, not knowing everyone else had a green light, too?"

Dov nodded. "It's too much coincidence to be a coincidence, isn't it? And being the Chief Security Officer, I couldn't just sit on this. I doubt if Anders or Fischer know these things have a memory card. This device," he pointed at the packet, "was operational on March 19 for thirteen minutes between 11:39 and 11:52 p.m. Which was when Kaitlyn Fischer was in her fatal accident. Prior to that, the only time it was operational was on October 10th and 11th, 2019, during the Sheridan trial." Dov sat back and crossed his hands behind his head. "You're the lawyer. What were Kaitlyn Fischer and Aaron Anders doing with this device?"

"I have no idea. Based on the discovery we got from Anders, Kaitlyn didn't work on that case. But Anders and Fischer did, so they'd have plausible reasons for having this thing," Camelia said.

"Do they though? That case was closed years ago. And I don't know why Kaitlyn would be taking the exhibit out of a closed case file to deliver to the casita, unless Anders asked her to."

"Okay," Camelia said. "So what do you want *me* to do with it? And with all this information you've shared? It's pretty damning stuff, *if* it's as you say."

"I know it's all kinda hard to follow, but I have no reason to lie. That's why I came to you. The one thing I'm sure of is that we have a common interest." Dov paused and looked down at his hands. "I will not let *anything* happen to Suzanne, if I'm able."

"Jesus, Dov. Do you really think—"

"Do I really think Aaron Anders would kill his wife? Yeah, I do. Do I really think Chris Fischer would kill his wife? Nah. Send out an embarrassing video, absolutely. But he just doesn't have the edge of a killer. My money is on Aaron. He has a *lot* more to lose, and I've seen him in action. I think he would weigh the risks and benefits, pull the trigger, and never flinch." Dov pushed the folder toward Camelia. "Take this to the prosecutor or whoever, but give it to someone who will listen."

"That's not how it works, Dov. You're going to have to be the one to turn it all over. Firsthand knowledge, and all that."

Camelia watched as he nodded in resignation.

"If you say so, but I don't exactly trust cops," he said.

"I know someone at the County Attorney's office I can rely on. Someone who can advise me on the best way to turn this over, since the case is already closed. But what happens when Anders finds out you delivered firm property to the cops?"

"The only reason I'm still working for Anders was to have an excuse to be around Suzanne. But now? I'm just waiting to be fired, which I expect will be any day now." Dov glanced at his phone and pulled out his wallet. "Anyway, that's what I came to unload on you. I've taken enough of your time. What's the fee for today? Do I pay up front?"

"Fee?" Camelia laughed. "I should be paying you! I may need to call you though, if I have questions. I'll need your number," she said.

Dov wrote a phone number on her legal pad. "That's my private mobile. Since I may not have the AndersLaw number much longer."

Camelia escorted Dov to the elevators and assured him she would be in touch. As she walked back to her office, an icy finger traced her spine, bringing on a shiver.

Dov Saminski had just dumped a treasure trove of information in her lap and she had no idea what she was going to do with it all. And if Byron found out she was still poking her nose in the criminal case, it would probably get her fired. But one thing was certain. Aaron Anders and Chris Fischer had a lot of explaining to do.

54

FRIENDS IN LOW PLACES

THURSDAY, APRIL 7

Back in her office, Camelia reviewed the notes she'd hastily jotted down as Dov Saminski talked. To capture the scribbles and arrows and abbreviations before her memory got fuzzy, she opened a new document and started typing.

The whole time she transcribed her notes, Camelia couldn't help but think about Skye Samson. They'd worked together years ago, and had grown close. Now, Skye was a rising star in the Maricopa County Attorney's Office and Camelia's only contact with the prosecutor. She pulled up Skye's info and dialed her number.

"Samson." Skye's voice startled Camelia, whose mind had wandered, trying to make sense of everything she'd just learned. "How can I help you?"

"Skye? Camelia Belmont. How are you?"

"Camelia? Oh my god, it's been ages. I'm good, but you," Skye tsked. "Mmm mmm. I heard about that client of yours. You okay?"

"Yeah, that was a bad day, for sure. But I'm fine. And I can tell you all about it sometime, if you want." Camelia took a breath. "I don't want to waste your time, and I was wondering if I could buy you lunch to pick your brain about a case. Off the record."

"You cut right to it, don't you?" Skye laughed. "I'm all in. Just name the date and time, but I'll name the place because you know I don't have the kind of expense account you do!"

"Deal. How's tomorrow?"

"You ain't foolin' around! And I can do tomorrow, but it will have to be breakfast. I have a trial all afternoon. Does eight work?"

"You're on," Camelia said. "Name your place."

They made their arrangements and Camelia hung up, suddenly feeling more optimistic than she had in weeks. Skye Samson was exactly the right person to consult. She was a friend, they had history, and she was smart as a whip.

Friday, April 8

When Camelia arrived at The Henry, Skye was already seated on the patio with a cup of coffee. After they hugged and complimented each other's successes, they settled in. Camelia pulled out her notes.

"I really appreciate you taking time to meet me. And I hope you don't have a conflict of interest." Camelia leaned forward and whispered. "It's regarding Aaron Anders and AndersLaw."

Skye's perfectly arched eyebrows flew up. "Oh, this has to be juicy. What dirty deed has Mr. A been up to now?"

Camelia laughed. "Oh, so you've met him?"

"His reputation precedes him." Skye rolled her eyes. "Is this about that associate that wrecked herself and died?"

"Yes, and please, *please*, this has to stay between us. At least for now. I just need your professional opinion."

A wiry guy with a blue crewcut approached and poured coffee before whipping out a notepad.

"Breakfast, ladies?"

They ordered, then doctored their coffees as Skye began to speak.

"Professional opinion, as in what would the County Attorney say? Or professional as in you need another set of eyes?" Skye flicked a box braid over her shoulder. "Because remember, my boss won't *officially* direct a law enforcement investigation. She'll only make a charging decision *after* law enforcement submits their evidence. But I'm happy to spout off about whether it sounds like there's enough to charge the case."

"I'll take it! At least you have a good idea of how things work. I'm just a lowly family law attorney, so I don't know the rules of criminal evidence, what kind of things are important or not." Camelia took a long, glorious sip of strong coffee and cream.

"Okay, lay it on me, but," Skye glanced around the patio. "Just use first initials. And I'll give you my best impression of a criminal attorney by poking holes in what you tell me."

"Good. That's what I need! Because I don't have time to get up to speed on criminal law."

"Why aren't you asking your hunka hunka burnin' boss? He's one of the best in town," Skye said.

"I *wish* he'd talk to me about it. These days, he just wants me to shut up, sit down, and focus on divorce cases. But this goes beyond just divvying up assets." Camelia looked down at her notes. "The information came to me from a very reliable source, and it's serious shit, Skye."

After their waiter delivered breakfast, Camelia began going through her notes, stopping now and then when Skye had questions, jotting down notes and questions she couldn't answer.

"So, what do you think? Is this something worth pursuing? Or is Mr. A going to get away—"

Skye interrupted her. "No conclusions. I want to keep an open mind."

"Good point."

"The land deal is nothing more than rich boys losing their lunch money, so strike that tidbit. Irrelevant." Skye tapped her pale pink fingernails on the table. "And there are some problems with the physical evidence. Chain of custody issues. Sounds like a lot of people have handled that device, including you, so fingerprints are pretty much useless. Besides, Mr. A and Mr. F both worked that case, so they had every right and reason to be handling it, carrying it around, or whatever."

"Yeah, but that case was closed years ago, so why would Mr. A have it delivered to his house, then return it to the office the day after K died?"

Skye's brow furrowed. "I agree it's strange, but it doesn't mean he actually *used* it. Plus, it sounds like K was the one carting this thing around."

"Then why would Mr. A suddenly order his security guy to stop driving S around? If he assumed S would be driving herself home from the party, it's opportunity." Camelia moved her notes aside as their breakfast dishes were cleared. "And he has about ten million dollars' worth of motive. As far as I can tell, Mr. A had motive, means, and opportunity. But then his wife went and blew it when she got a ride home."

"Someone's been watching too many Netflix mysteries," Skye laughed. "But you're right. It lines up. Even though it may not be *proof*, it sure sounds like it's worth a follow up interview. Is your source willing to make a statement?"

"Yeah, he seems like a stand up guy," Camelia said.

"Here's the thing. Right now, there is no case. Paradise Valley PD has no basis to call Mr. A or anyone else in for an interview." Skye dabbed at her lips with a napkin. "But if your source were to come forward, well, that's a different game, right? And girl, I would love nothing better than to sink my teeth into a case like this. It's what promotions are made of."

"I thought you might be interested," Camelia said with a smile.

"Nah, I'm *beyond* interested. Just try to get me to stop." She laughed and pulled her braids to one side as she leaned forward, whispering. "Have your source call the lead detective as soon as possible to make a statement and turn over the evidence. And he can tell the detective to call me *directly*, even if the cop isn't sure it's enough to pursue. Gotta lay my bricks carefully, you know. Because if this goes all the way, I want a solid gold road from Mr. A to hard time. No bumps. No potholes."

Camelia felt a nervous thrill run through her belly. On the one hand, she was grateful to Skye for mapping out how to present the evidence, and *hopefully* get a chance to prosecute Anders. On the other hand, she knew that as soon as Byron found out she'd been messing around in the criminal matter—and he would definitely find out sooner or later—she would get the full brunt of his anger. She had to be ready for whatever came next.

It was time to talk to Cate.

55

RULES OF EVIDENCE

TUESDAY, APRIL 12

Dov Saminski had only been in the waiting area of the Maricopa County Attorney's Office for a few minutes when a petite woman in chunky braids and even chunkier heels called his name. He stood up and followed her down a wide corridor to a small stuffy room with no windows. Det. Luna was already there, slurping on a huge tumbler of coffee.

Skye Samson placed a file, laptop, and her coffee mug on the table. "Thank you for coming in. I realize this might be awkward given your position, but in order to pursue charges based on the evidence you provided to Det. Luna, I have some follow up questions about your formal statement."

Dov nodded. "Yep. That's why I'm here."

"Good. I'll be recording our meeting. When we're finished, the tape will be transcribed. You will be offered an opportunity to review the transcript and make any corrections or additions you would like to make. Do you understand?"

"Got it."

Skye pressed typed something into her laptop. "First off, please state your name and address."

He recited his name and the address of his rental condo on North Tatum.

"Birth date?"

As she went through her preliminary questions, Dov shifted in his seat. This kind of tedious shit drove him nuts. And, it made him question whether he was really being a concerned citizen, or if it was just wishful thinking because of his feelings for Suzanne. Finally, Samson got to the point.

"You're here to provide further information about evidence regarding the car accident that occurred on March 19 at the intersection of Tatum and Lincoln in Paradise Valley. Is that correct?"

"Yes," he said.

"Well, go on then," Skye said. "Start at the beginning, and I'll stop you if I have questions."

Dov repeated his story. First Belmont, then Luna, now her. He was getting tired of saying the same thing over and over.

"And the physical evidence you provided supports all of these allegations?" Skye prompted.

"Well," Dov said. "It's not exactly a straight line."

Skye tapped on her laptop keyboard.

"Please describe these items for the recording, Mr. Saminski," she said, swiveling her computer toward Saminski. "And tell me how they relate to the information you just provided."

He squinted at the screen. "The first item is the valet log from March 19," Dov said. "The highlighted portion indicates that Chris Fischer left the firm party then returned in just under an hour in a vehicle owned by Jeff Petronelli. Fischer was Petronelli's designated driver the night of the party. A short time later, Mrs. Anders left with me in the company town car. About twenty minutes after that, Kaitlyn Fischer left in Mrs. Anders' Triumph. That's also highlighted."

She tapped her keyboard and another image appeared on the screen.

"This is a printout of the GPS unit from the traffic preemption device showing when and where it was activated. This device was active on October 10th and 11th, 2019, which is when Sheridan Electronics was on trial for product liability. It was also active on March 19th just minutes prior to Kaitlyn Fischer's car accident, then deactivated a thirteen minutes later, after the accident."

Skye nodded and clicked her keyboard again, switching to a new image.

Dov leaned in, examining the screen. "This is the traffic preemption device returned to the AndersLaw offices on the morning of March 21. I know that because I was in the office at the time, and watched Mr. Anders on the firm security cameras. The feed is live on my desktop, and I've provided a copy of the footage. I believe it is the same device Mr. Anders had in his possession a few weeks earlier."

Skye turned her laptop back toward her.

"Is there anything else you want to tell me about these items?"

"No, I think that's it."

"There's one big question in my mind, and maybe in Det. Luna's, too," Skye said, turning over a page of her notes. "All this thing does is change the traffic light. So why go to all that trouble when you can just hire a dump truck to plow into someone, do the hit and run, and call it good? Why bother making it look like some kind of traffic light problem, when car accidents happen all the time?" Skye looked at Det. Luna, then back to Dov.

"March is our number one vehicular fatality month," Det. Luna interjected. "And we have six or seven hundred traffic fatalities in Maricopa County every year. So, I'm with Ms. Samson. Why would anyone go to all this trouble?"

"Well, if you want my theory . . ." Dov looked from one to the other expectantly.

"Go on," Skye said.

"I know how Anders thinks. He's a skilled litigator, and he knows how to win a case on confusion alone. Baffle them with bullshit, as he likes to say. It's all about creating enough doubt that a jury can't commit to a verdict. And he's applying that strategy here, in my opinion. If he stirs up enough confusion about the cause of the crash, it will be too much trouble to prosecute, and impossible to win," Dov said. "Anders is raging mad about the divorce, and I believe he cooked up a plan to get rid of his wife using the preemption device. He didn't have to be anywhere near that intersection and he only had to hire one guy. One guy to steal a truck, crash into his wife in the intersection, take the cash, and disappear. But Anders' plan didn't account for contingencies, like Suzanne being too ill to drive." Dov looked from Samson to Luna, hoping for validation, confirmation that his instincts were on point.

Det. Luna's thoughtful frown and the way he tapped his coffee cup made Dov think that he, at least, was following. Skye Samson, however, was not so transparent.

"Interesting theory, I have to admit. For now, though, I have to verify the evidence, then Det. Luna and I will talk to my boss about whether it's enough to get Mr. Anders in for a chat. If everything pans out, we may have enough to file a direct complaint. If not, it goes to a grand jury. But either way, you'll be hearing from me. If the case goes forward, you'll be a key witness. If it doesn't, you'll have the right to receive your property back." Skye stood up. "Here's my card. Call me if you have any questions."

"Thanks, I'll wait for your call." Dov stood up and tucked her card in his back pocket as he headed to the door.

On the walk back to his car, all Dov could think about were the bridges he was burning. Whether he was on the right side of this fiasco or not, he would never get a positive recommendation out of Anders, and International Umbrella might even terminate him.

And sure, things were cozy with Suzanne at the moment, but what about when . . . if she needed more intense medical care? How would her kids react to having him in the picture? He could guess: they'd hate him. An interloper. Their father's hired gun, now sharing their mother's bed. He had to admit, it didn't look great when you zoomed out.

But Suzanne, with those clear blue eyes, had injected him with the most dangerous drug: hope.

What if, for once, everything worked out? What if Skye Samson—smart and hungry for this kind of case—put it all together and convicted Anders? What if Det. Luna found the guy who'd driven the dump truck and he testified? What if Dov could build a happily ever after with Suzanne?

What if dreams sometimes come true?

56

COLLISION COURSE

THURSDAY, APRIL 14

Camelia was reviewing Suzanne Anders' case docket online when Cate came into her office.

"Your file's ready, and the recording of Anders and Ashcroft is on this," Cate held a flash drive between her thumb and forefinger before dropping it in the file. "And the driver will be here in about 15 minutes. What else do you need?"

"I think I've got everything. It's just a status conference, so the most important thing is my current trial calendar so we can set a date in Court today," Camelia said.

Cate pulled a slim folder out of the file. "It's right here and I double checked all the dates this morning, so no matter when Judge Bailey sets the trial, you'll know if you have a conflict."

"Thanks," Camelia said. She still hadn't talked to Cate about coming along with her if . . . *when* she jumped ship. Now was not the time, but it had to be soon. "I owe you a long lunch. Do you want to schedule it? Anywhere you want."

"Yes, please! How about The Mission in Old Scottsdale?"

"Perfect," Camelia said. "And now, I better get going. Don't want to keep the Royal Pains waiting." She rolled her eyes.

Cate laughed. "I just hope Bailey doesn't sanction you for this. It's not exactly *by the book*, Cam."

"It depends on the interpretation. They were in a public place, with no expectation of privacy, and they were talking loud enough that my phone picked up their conversation from across the hallway. I was legitimately dictating notes on my phone. How was I supposed to know Siri would keep listening?" Camelia made a face of dread. "That's my story and I'm sticking to it."

"Good luck with that! I'll light a candle for your butt, just in case Bailey chews it off for eavesdropping." Cate placed the file in Camelia's rolling brief. "Time to go."

As soon as Camelia entered the Courtroom, she could feel the tension rolling off Anders and Ashcroft. Suzanne, following close behind her, sat down at the Petitioner's table just as Aaron approached.

"Good afternoon, ladies." Anders smiled beatifically. "Camelia, may I have a word with my wife? Privately."

Camelia looked at Suzanne for a response. She was dressed in a pale, buttery linen dress, accessorized with a placid, regal expression. Obviously, Dov Saminski was good for her, because Camelia had never seen Suzanne so composed.

"Oh, Aaron. Why on earth would I want to hear anything you have to say? And now? Just minutes before our status conference?" Suzanne blinked slowly and let out a little sigh. "Whatever's troubling your busy little mind will just have to wait."

Camelia stifled the laugh threatening to burst from her lips. Suzanne was definitely coming into her own, and the effect on Anders was clear in the flush of his cheeks.

"You don't have to be such a bit—" Aaron began.

Camelia put up her hand. "Stop right there. You do not have permission to call my client names. Not in Court, not at home, not anywhere, Aaron." She beckoned Ashcroft. "Control your client, Spencer. He seems a little snarly today."

"How dare you?" Anders hissed. "Do you have—"

"Spence, do we need to take a recess before the status conference even begins?" Camelia smirked and shook her head. "Calm down, Mr. Anders. You can't risk *another* heart attack."

Spencer crossed the aisle and touched Aaron's elbow. Aaron acted like he'd been electrocuted. He jerked his arm away, whirled on Ashcroft, and glared at him through narrow slits.

"I just want to talk to my fucking wife."

"Aaron, now is not the time—"

"It's time when I say—"

The bailiff pushed open the courtroom door. "All rise."

That shut him up.

Camelia sat down next to Suzanne and watched with more than a little satisfaction as Spencer tried to soothe Anders. She didn't know what was so urgent, but if she had to guess, she'd say it was related to his botched attempt to put one over on Allison in their settlement negotiations. Poor Aaron. Women were just being so damned mean to him these days! She smiled to herself. He had no idea how mean they could be. But he was about to find out.

After making their appearances, the judge went over their discovery schedule and then asked everyone to pull out their calendars.

Camelia leaned over and muted the courtroom mic. "Are you still okay with me bringing this up with the judge?" she whispered.

Suzanne nodded.

Camelia stood. "Your honor, before we get to calendaring the trial date, I have a small issue to clear up. May I approach?"

Judge Bailey looked grumpy about it, but waved her forward. She took the flash drive out of the file and walked to the bench. She leaned in and placed the drive on the edge of the bench – the elevated desk area separating the judge from the floor of the courtroom – and stepped back.

"What's this?"

"Your honor, it's an accidental recording of Mr. Ashcroft—"

"Hold on," Judge Bailey said. "Mr. Ashcroft, sidebar."

When Ashcroft drew up beside Camelia, he gave her a sharp glance before smiling at the judge.

"Go on, Ms. Belmont."

"As I was saying, I have an accidental recording of Mr. Ashcroft and Mr. Anders engaged in a conversation regarding an unethical agreement. Now, I understand the recording rules, but how was I to know Siri was listening?" Camelia could feel Ashcroft's eyes on the side of her head, but she refused to look at him, instead focusing on Judge Bailey.

"What relevance does this have to the case?" Judge Bailey asked.

"It sounds like collusion between Mr. Ashcroft and his client to stall this case," Camelia said. "And there's a cash bonus offered by Mr. Anders."

"That's an extremely serious accusation." Judge Bailey paused, his owlish eyebrows furrowing as he stared at Ashcroft.

Ashcroft was silent for a beat before he exploded. "I object to all of this . . . this . . . slander, your honor. Not only is Ms. Belmont casting aspersions, she's doing so with an illegal recording of an attorney client privileged conversation. I want this whole thing stricken from the record *now*." Spencer's face was turning red and beads of sweat had formed on his forehead. "This is *outrageous*, even for you, Camelia."

"Counsel, in my chambers." Judge Bailey said as he stood up. He grabbed the flash drive and headed for the door behind the bench. The bailiff rushed to open the door as Judge Bailey paused and turned to address the room. "We are in recess for fifteen minutes while I meet with counsel. I don't want any chitchat in my courtroom while we're gone, so Mr. Anders will wait in the hall until we resume, am I clear?" After they both agreed, he turned to Camelia and Ashcroft. "Follow me."

When they got to chambers, Judge Bailey shut the door and motioned to the two chairs in front of his massive desk.

"Ms. Belmont, start at the top. What is this about?" Judge Bailey sat down heavily in his chair.

"Your honor," Ashcroft said, his voice too loud in the silent room. "I obj—"

"I know you do," Judge Bailey said. "But I wasn't addressing you. Ms. Belmont?"

"Yes, your honor. After our last hearing, I was exiting the courtroom, dictating notes. Apparently, Mr. Anders and Mr. Ashcroft were having a conversation in the hall. I had paused in the vestibule to finish my thought. I have Siri enabled and it picked up their conversation. It was entirely by mistake." She paused to catch her breath. Jesus, she hoped Bailey wasn't going to rip her a new one. "I think it's best if you just listen for yourself, your honor."

"Mr. Ashcroft, what is your objection to me listening to this recording?"

Ashcroft sputtered. "I . . . well, it's patently against the rules, and the recording statute, and I certainly don't have my client's permission. So, your honor, I object *on all grounds.*"

"You were in a public place with no expectation of privacy. Do you know the substance of this recording, Mr. Ashcroft?" Judge Bailey asked.

Ashcroft had the good manners to blush. "Well, no. Not really. I mean, I talk to my clients about a lot of things. And all of them are *privileged.*"

Camelia could feel her palms sweating and her ears getting hot. Because it was exactly the objection she would make if their roles were reversed.

"I'm not convinced you have an expectation of privacy sufficient to protect attorney client communications in the hallway outside my courtroom. But even if you did, don't you agree that a violation of the ethical rules, or any other rule or statute, can overcome privilege?"

Ashcroft's voice was vaguely penitent. "It depends on the circumstances, I guess."

Judge Bailey plugged the flash drive into his computer and hit play. There was a rustling noise, and then men's voices. The sound was muffled.

"I'm can't make out what they're saying," he said.

"As I said, this was an accidental recording. If you turn up the volume—" Camelia said.

"Jesus Christ. Are you really going to indulge this? How is this even allowable? What happened to the rules of evidence?" Ashcroft said, his voice rising.

"Spence, when it comes to the rules of evidence, you haven't filed a Rule 2(b) Motion, have you? So, we're not under any obligation to observe strict compliance with the rules. Remember?" Camelia took some satisfaction in shoving that right back in his face after their last hearing.

"It's just between us until I rule otherwise." Judge Bailey was fiddling with his computer. "Either way, one of you won't like the outcome."

Ashcroft glared at Camelia before turning back to Judge Bailey. "Your honor, please."

"Here we go," Judge Bailey said. He hit play again. This time, the voices were amplified and their conversation—the bit that she'd captured—was loud enough to understand.

"What do you want me to do? It's not like I can just shut the case down," Ashcroft said.

"You don't have to do a fucking thing except stall. Just hold them off. Because you're not getting your fat bonus until I get Suzanne's life insurance," Anders replied.

"I'll do what I can, Aaron, but . . ."

Judge Bailey sat back in his chair and heaved a sigh. He ran his finger over the edge of his desk before looking at Ashcroft.

"Well, this is not very flattering." He took a deep breath. "Mr. Ashcroft, I don't need to tell you how bad this looks, do I?"

Ashcroft was hunched over in his chair, his face a dangerous shade of red, his hands balled into fists.

"Your honor, I . . . this is *outrageous.*" Ashcroft bellowed.

"Damn right it is," Judge Bailey shifted his gaze to Camelia. "And you know good and well this is a breach of ethics. So why didn't you just take it to the State Bar?"

"Your honor, I wasn't sure what to do. On one hand, Mr. Ashcroft is making an unethical deal and shady promises. That's on him. But we all know it's Mr. Anders calling the shots, demanding delays just so he can take advantage of Ms. Anders' health situation. *He's* the one who should be sanctioned. As for Mr. Ashcroft, that's up to you." She wiped her palms on her skirt, pretending to smooth it. "I really don't care if Spencer gets a bonus, but I do care that Mr. Anders is willing to bend all the rules to profit off his wife's death and screw her out of her share of the marital estate."

"Mr. Ashcroft, I'm putting you on notice that I will be turning this over to the State Bar for review. As for your client, I'll address him myself. On the record. In open court. Because if he thinks for one minute that I'll put up with even one wrong move from here on out, he's in for a surprise." Judge Bailey stood up. "Get back to the courtroom and do not say one word, either of you, to your clients. Leave that to me."

Camelia and Ashcroft gave their yessirs and followed Judge Bailey out of chambers, down the hall, and back into the courtroom. The whole way, Camelia's heart was pounding. She'd done it. She'd revealed their sinister motives, even though she was tiptoeing right up to the ethical line. Aaron was about to get his ass handed to him, and she felt almost giddy with relief. Because it could have just as easily gone the other way.

After Judge Bailey announced they were back on the record, he launched into a diatribe.

"Before we schedule trial in this matter, I would like to address the parties. I have consulted with your counsel in chambers regarding a recording made just outside these very doors a couple of weeks ago. That recording, Mr. Anders, paints you in a *very* unflattering light."

Aaron stood up. "Your honor, I . . ."

"Mr. Anders, sit down. You were not invited to speak. In this courtroom, you are not AndersLaw. You are Aaron Anders, a man in the middle of a divorce, who has taken some very unsavory actions. From this day forward, your case is fast tracked. I am designating it a priority, urgent matter. Ms. Anders, you will have a trial at the soonest date your counsel can be ready. Mr. Ashcroft, if you have a calendaring conflict with the date Ms. Belmont selects, I will personally get continuances in your other matters if you don't. As for the issue of a bonus or bribe, or whatever you want to call it, you, Mr. Ashcroft will answer to the State Bar. But you, Mr. Anders, will answer to me. I am taking the matter under advisement and will rule on your sanctions within the week. Ms. Belmont, what date will you and your client be ready for trial?"

Anders was beet red and jabbing the respondent's table with his finger as he furiously whispered at Ashcroft, who was almost the same shade of red. Anders stood up again.

"Judge Bailey, I do not believe you have the—" he began.

"Mr. Anders, I will not tell you again. Sit down. You have counsel and he will speak on your behalf unless I have a direct question for you. Is that understood?"

"But your honor, I have not had—"

"Mr. Anders!" Judge Bailey thundered. He grabbed his gavel and pounded it on the bench, harder than Camelia thought he needed to. "I am ordering you to sit down, *now*, and do not say one more word. If you can't control yourself, the bailiff will escort you from the courtroom. Am I perfectly clear?"

Anders mouth was set in a grimace and his face was flushed red, but he sat down, glaring at the judge.

Camelia flipped through her calendar and pointed to a date, as she hit the mute button on the courtroom microphone. Suzanne leaned over and whispered, "Can we be ready that soon?"

Camelia nodded. "If we use the preliminary business valuation numbers, without waiting for the full appraisal, we can. Are you okay with that?" she whispered.

Suzanne nodded. Camelia unmuted the mic.

"Your honor, we'll be ready for trial on May second and third," Camelia circled the dates on the calendar printout. "I am requesting a two day trial due to the complexity of the assets."

The clerk stepped up beside the judge and showed him something on the monitor. He nodded and made a note.

Ashcroft stood up. "Your honor, please, that's not nearly enough time to be ready for this kind of trial, and counsel knows it. We have expert reports to analyze, and—"

"Mr. Ashcroft, if Ms. Belmont can be ready, I trust you can, too. I expect *everyone* to show up prepared. I will not be granting any continuances. If you have pretrial motions, get them filed in the next couple of days. We are adjourned and off the record." Judge Bailey clicked the recording device on the bench and stood up. "I'll see you folks here in a couple of weeks," he said, as he exited the courtroom.

The second the door shut, Anders exploded at Ashcroft as Camelia and Suzanne strode out of the courtroom on a wave of triumph.

57

MAJORITY RULES

FRIDAY, APRIL 15

Even for Aaron Anders, a career litigator accustomed to the nonstop grind of litigation, it had been an exhausting week. It seemed like he was under scrutiny from everyone these days, including the Paradise Valley Police Department, who'd had him in for some less-than-friendly questioning about Kaitlyn's accident and the Sheridan Electronics traffic preemption device. As if he knew a goddamn thing about it. They were way out of line and he hadn't hesitated to let them know. But just to be sure, he'd called the Maricopa County Attorney. Aaron had helped that bitch get elected. The least she could do is shut down this bullshit inquiry into a fucking traffic accident.

And now this. Aaron wasn't a goddamn rookie. It had been three weeks since that humiliating video was emailed out and he'd hoped it would just blow over, die down, be forgotten. But when Jim Frost called, inviting him over for an impromptu get together, he knew damn well it was going to be an ambush. Screw them. He *was* AndersLaw, and all of them were expendable. Hell, he'd fire every damn one of them tonight, if he had to.

Aaron threw on a white linen shirt, untucked, and a pair of dark jeans. He debated whether to wear trousers instead, but decided not to give them the satisfaction of looking like he was walking into a business meeting. No, he would treat it as it was offered—just a friendly end-of-week gathering between colleagues at one of their homes. But he was sure he'd heard an icy threat under Frost's invitation.

Or am I just being paranoid?

The Frosts lived in a sterile, contemporary cube a couple of miles south of Anders in the Royal Palms neighborhood, just a few minutes away. Jim said they would start at 6:30, but Aaron had a hunch, so he opted for an early start. It was just after six p.m. when he slid into the back seat of the town car. He gave Saminski a curt greeting, then they headed for Jim and Ginny Frost's house.

He still hadn't dealt with Saminski, but they'd been sharing a cool detente ever since the night of the firm party. His Chief Security Officer had offered no explanation for why he was at the house that night with Suzanne, which Aaron actually admired. He had to hand it to Saminski. The guy had balls. But even though Aaron was furious, he couldn't fire him. Not until the investigation into Kaitlyn's death was officially closed. He couldn't afford to have Saminski on the outside. Not with the amount of dirt he had on Aaron. But that didn't mean he had to like having Saminski around. Or that he had to talk to him. Still, it made for a long, tense ride.

The tension spiked as soon as they entered the cul-de-sac. Aaron recognized David Weisman's Mercedes, Eric Bass's Tesla, and Chuck Preston's BMW lined up along the curb in front of Jim Frost's house. All the senior partners were here, but the fact that none of the junior partners had been invited confirmed Aaron's suspicions. This was an ambush.

"Saminski, do you know anything about this little gathering?" Anders hated having to rely on his Chief Security Officer, but he was the one person who might have the inside scoop.

"Can't say that I do," Dov responded. "I did overhear Jim saying something to Eric a couple of days ago, confirming getting together tonight."

"Fair enough," Anders said. "I'm gonna crash their party a little early. And don't go anywhere. Something tells me this won't take long."

"Understood." Saminski pulled into Frost's driveway, put the car in park, and stepped out to open Aaron's door. "It's a beautiful evening for drinks on the patio."

Aaron huffed a bitter laugh. "Something tells me my drink might be spiked with a little poison pill."

He walked up to the house and stepped through the open front door, not bothering to knock. He'd been here dozens of times over the years, so he knew his way around. Walking past the vaulted living room, Aaron passed into the open kitchen area, where Ginny Frost was stirring a pitcher of sangria.

"Good evening, Gin," Aaron said.

She startled at his voice, and quickly glanced to the patio. Aaron's eyes followed hers, where he saw the other partners already seated on a large sectional by the pool.

"Aaron, gosh, you scared the daylights out of me," Ginny said, coming around from behind the kitchen island. She held her arms open and approached Aaron for a hug. She smacked her lips near his cheek. "You look like trouble and you smell amazing!" She winked and giggled. "I love Dior."

"Sorry for sneaking up on you," Aaron said as he stepped back from her embrace. "Didn't want to be late for the party!" He gave her a smile.

"Can I offer you a drink?" Ginny asked.

"What's in the pitcher? Is that your famous sangria?"

"Sure is. Can I pour you a glass?"

Aaron took the glass and the pitcher. "I'll pour my own, but let me deliver this to the fellas. I don't want to keep them waiting."

"Oh, I don't think you're . . . I mean, you're not late. Everyone just got here," Ginny said. She seemed uncharacteristically flustered.

Aaron walked through the stark dining room and stepped through wide patio doors. As soon as his foot hit the patio, Jim Frost looked up. He raised his hand to wave and the conversation stopped.

"Aaron! You made it! We were just wondering where you were," he called out. "Come on over."

Aaron bared his teeth at the other men in an imitation of smiling. He could smell the tension.

"And here I thought I was early! Thought you said 6:30, but I must have misheard." Aaron set the pitcher on the coffee table after pouring himself half a glass of sangria. "Eric, Chuck, Dave, Jim." He raised his glass and took a sip. "Cheers!"

A mumbled *cheers* went up from the others as they eyed each other over their cocktails.

"What's the occasion? Tax day? Or are we just celebrating Friday?" Aaron glanced around the group.

"Isn't Friday a good enough excuse?" Jim said with a too bright smile. "As you can see, I had a great morning on the golf course." He touched his glowing, sunburnt forehead with a wince.

"Well, I'm up for celebrating," Eric drawled. He'd kicked his loafers off and his manicured bare feet were planted on the edge of the coffee table. "Won my wrongful termination suit and got a fat award from the jury. Two mil. And the defendants are appealing, so let the billing begin." Eric laughed, pushing his shirt sleeves up. "God, I do love a good appeal."

"Well, my week sucked, thanks for asking. My assistant gave notice this morning, so I'm once again looking for someone who knows how to draft a goddamn letter," Chuck complained. He pushed his hand through thick, wavy brown hair. "Of course, with my reputation and good looks, shouldn't take too long, huh?"

The others groaned.

"How about you, Aaron?" Jim swiveled his sunburned forehead toward him. "How'd *your* week go?"

Was it Aaron's imagination, or was there a sharp edge to his question?

"Guys, all my weeks are rough these days, with Suzanne . . ." he trailed off. "But I don't want to talk about her cancer treatment and all that. I'm just happy to have work to take my mind off all the sadness at home right now."

Jim glanced at Eric, then set his drink on the table and leaned forward, elbows on his knees. "I'm sure it wasn't easy to lose Kaitlyn, either. You two were pretty close."

Here it comes.

"Closer than I'm comfortable with, if you want the truth," Eric said, his Southern Kentucky drawl slipping out. "Aaron, you know I'm not the morality police, but good god a'mighty. Y'all been pretty loosey goosey lately."

"Yeah, Carol is livid about that video. Especially given the way Kaitlyn died, in Suzanne's car," Chuck said. "And if you must know, it's the reason my assistant quit. She said it was no longer the kind of firm she wanted to be associated with."

"And how does your assistant know *anything* about it?" Aaron asked.

"Jesus, Aaron. Do you really not know? Somebody leaked that video the day after we got the email. It's on YouTube," Chuck said.

Aaron felt his ears get hot.

Why isn't Saminski keeping me informed?

He looked at the three men before turning his gaze to Dave Weisman. He was the youngest of the senior partners, hand picked by Aaron twenty years ago. Dave was tan, fit, and one of those guys who looked good bald.

"Et tu, David?" Aaron said.

"Hey, it's not like that," Dave said. "We're just concerned friends, that's all. And we want to make things better for you. For all of us." He spread his hands in a gesture of peace.

But Aaron knew there were knives at the ready.

"And how do you propose to make things better? Do you have a cure for cancer up your sleeve?" Aaron smirked and took a sip of sangria.

Jim cleared his throat. "Aaron, this isn't an easy conversation to have, but we might as well get the business over with. We've all agreed," he glanced around to the others. "It's time to sell our shares and move on. Give you a chance to regroup after all the . . . trouble you've had."

Aaron felt the room tilt a bit. His head was swimming. A bolt of pain ran down his arm.

"Trouble?" He almost choked on a sip of sangria. "You call ovarian cancer *trouble*?"

Jim glared at him. "No, I do not. And you know damn well that's not what we're talking about here. It's been a long time coming, Aaron. Kaitlyn was one too many."

"Oh, really? Like none of you've ever had your hand in the cookie jar?" Aaron glared at each of them in turn. "Fucking hypocrites."

The click of heels on the patio heralded Ginny's approach and the men went silent.

"How about some chips and salsa? And I've made guacamole from the Barrio Queen's recipe book." She set a tray on the coffee table between the men, then looked up.

"It looks perfect, Gin," Jim said. "But we're in the middle of something right now."

She glanced around. "Don't mind me! I'm not even here! If you need anything, just whistle." Ginny waved as she walked back into the house.

Chuck started digging in the guacamole with a chip, cramming it into his mouth as if he hadn't eaten in a week.

Still stress eating, Charlie?

"It sounds like you haven't talked to Ginny about any of this, Jim." Aaron took another sip of sangria, trying to get his heart to slow down. "Maybe she'd like to weigh in on some of *your* side pieces."

"Never mind Ginny. She's ready to rip your face off over the charitable trust bullshit." Jim licked his lips. "But look, this isn't personal, Aaron. This is a business decision. Nothing more. We wanted to talk to you outside the office before we . . . the truth is, I've lost half a dozen clients already and I'm sure more are going to drop us. The staff have put all of us in the same box, assuming we condone your . . . shagging the help. And the female associates are about to declare mutiny if we don't come up with a one-strike rule for inter-office relationships."

"So far, four of our lady lawyers have tendered their notice in response to the video, citing a hostile work environment," Eric said. "And while I agree they're totally replaceable associates, the optics are unfavorable, Aaron."

The pain in his chest was making it hard to catch his breath. Aaron fumbled in his pocket for a nitro pill. He'd put one in his pocket, hadn't he? He couldn't remember, now. He wasn't finding anything other than lint.

"Gentlemen, I'm well aware of the challenges we're facing, no thanks to a greedy little slut who seduced me, duped me into an affair—"

"Oh, Aaron, please. Save that tall tale for your family. We know you better than that," Eric drawled. "You've been banging the help from day one. Not that I give a good goddamn. But when it hits the bottom line . . . You've been lucky up to now. But believe me, this mess with Kaitlyn is goin' to cost all of us. There's lost client revenue, then there's staff and associate turnover, and never mind the muddied reputation."

"Eric's right," Chuck said around a mouthful of tortilla chips. "This is going to cost us all, and not just in dollars. You know damn well I've been planning to apply to the bench this fall. Well, I can kiss that goodbye. I'll never get appointed now, not with your baggage on my back."

"How is *any* of this my fault?" Aaron said, louder than he intended. "I'm the goddamn victim here! My wife decided to divorce me after more than thirty years and *then* I find out she's dying of cancer. A rogue associate set me up, entrapped me in an affair I had *no* interest in, then exploited the whole situation by releasing that video which, again, *she set up*. And then she stole my wife's car and wrapped it around a light pole. How the fuck is *any* of that my fault?"

Jim cleared his throat. "You might feel like the rug is being pulled out from under you, but come on, Aaron. You aren't the *victim* of anything. Suzanne isn't divorcing you because she has cancer. Everyone in town knows about your affairs. We all know who you are." He looked to the others for reassurance. As they nodded, Jim continued. "But it's not just a bit of reckless fun anymore. Prostitutes at conferences, at least a dozen secretaries and paralegals, and now attorneys. But not just *any* attorneys. *Our own attorneys!* All told, the firm has paid out almost a million dollars over the years to hush up your girlfriends. The going rate's $50k. Did you know that?"

Aaron felt the weight of their judgment pressing down, tightening around his ribs. These two-faced bastards were actually accusing him of some kind of moral failure? He'd show them.

"I think it's called severance pay," Aaron said, rolling his eyes.

"Yeah? Well, whatever you call it, I think we got off cheap," Chuck said. "One lawsuit could have cost that much."

"No, Chuck, we'd be getting off cheap if we didn't have to pay off *any* humiliated girlfriends when Aaron cut them loose," Dave said. He turned to Aaron. "At this point, I think you need to admit you have a serious problem. Call it sex addiction if it makes you feel better, but I'd say it's more in the realm of unchecked narcissism."

"Oh, now you're a fucking psychiatrist, David?" Anders was working hard to modulate his breath around the pain radiating through his chest.

"No, Aaron. I'm not a psychiatrist, but my wife is. Unlike you, I still have a happy marriage, and don't think we haven't discussed your habits a *hundred* times." Dave poured himself some sangria and took a quick gulp. "She's the one who diagnosed you, not me."

Aaron looked around at the four men. He could see the daggers in their eyes, the disgust on their faces.

"Guys, this is an easy fix." Aaron steadied himself on the couch before standing up. "You're all released from your contracts. Your personal items will be delivered to your homes on Monday. As of now, your access to the office is terminated. And you can all go fuck yourselves." He turned to leave, but had only taken a step when Jim called out.

"Aaron, we're not done. You forgot something."

Aaron turned back to face him. He felt nauseous, woozy, and sweat was seeping through his shirt.

"Yeah? What's that, Jim?"

Frost had a satisfied smile on his face. "Based on our shares, we," he gestured at the other men. "Are the majority. Well, one of the voting members isn't here, but we *all* voted to sell. Eric, can you give Aaron his copy of the signed agreement, please?"

Eric stood up and handed Aaron an envelope.

"What the hell is this?" Aaron asked, tearing open the manila envelope.

"I warned you back in February we were all done playin' along with your charity scheme and your extracurricular shenanigans. This is a buy-sell agreement. By releasing us," Eric made air quotes around *releasing*. "You've bumped up our departure date by a month, but we could all use a couple of weeks off before we move into our new offices over at Sherman Wright."

Sherman Wright? What the hell were they playing at?

"Ha! Nice try. I'm still the *majority* shareholder," Aaron said.

His mind was spinning. He owned forty percent of the firm's shares and another twenty percent in Suzanne's name, which she didn't even know about. Each of these assholes owned ten percent. To get to a majority, they would all—including Suzanne—have had to approve the sale.

"Surely you haven't forgotten about the revised shareholder agreement you had us sign when the firm ownership statutes changed?" Jim said. "When you granted those shares to Suzanne?"

"Do the math. All four of us, *plus Suzanne's twenty percent*, equals sixty percent. Sherman Wright is now the majority shareholder of AndersLaw." Dave took a sip of sangria.

Aaron's vision was blurring. Suzanne agreed to sell?

"Suzanne would not have—" he stammered.

"Oh, wouldn't she?" Eric flipped to the back page. "Miss Suzanne's signature is right here."

"You can't do this!" Aaron said. "I'll sue every single one of you into the ground."

"No, Aaron, you won't. You don't have a case. We operated strictly within the terms of the partner contract *you* drafted. And, besides, it sounds like you're going to be busy with your criminal defense," Chuck said.

"What are you talking about? There is no criminal matter!" Aaron sputtered. "Kaitlyn's death was an accident."

"Save it for the jury. A little bird at the County Attorney's Office says a reliable witness turned up with evidence implicating you in Kaitlyn's death," Dave said. "Good thing we sold when we did. We'll get our cash out while the firm still has value."

Aaron couldn't think. His heart was thudding against his ribs and sweat was rolling into his eyes. He had to get out of here. Now.

"I'll read this over and get back to you, but everything I said stands. Don't even darken the door of AndersLaw unless you want to be arrested for trespassing."

He turned and walked as quickly as he could through Jim's fucking boring white on white house, out the front door, and down the driveway. Saminski was leaning on the car hood, scrolling on his phone.

"Take me to the condo," Aaron said as he planted his hands against the car. God, he felt so woozy.

"Whoa, Mr. Anders, are you okay?" Dov asked.

"Just get me downtown," Aaron said, faintly.

Dov opened the back door and Aaron collapsed into the back seat.

"I can have you at ER in just about five minutes," Dov said. "Or the casita. Either one's closer."

"No! Just take me to the fucking Lion's Den." Aaron gasped as he clutched his chest. "I don't need to go to ER and I don't want to be anywhere near my fucking traitor of a wife. Because if I see her right now, I'm gonna fucking kill that bitch with my bare hands. It should have been *her in that wreck*! F U C K!"

He saw the glare Dov gave him before he slammed the door, hard enough to rock the car. It was all the confirmation Aaron needed.

Screw him, too.

Dov pulled out of the driveway and headed downtown. Twenty minutes later, they entered the underground garage at Portland Place. Dov jumped out of the car and opened the back passenger door. Aaron was panting, soaked in sweat, and his vision was blurred.

"I really think you need to be at ER." Dov stood back as Aaron swung his feet out the car door. Dov extended his hand to help Aaron out of the car.

"I don't need your opinion, I just need my meds," Aaron snapped.

"Okay," Dov said. "Let's get you inside."

"Just open the fucking door," Aaron snarled. "I'll be fine."

Dov entered the code, pushing the door open as he stood aside for Aaron to enter. Dov walked to the elevator and pushed the button.

"I'll just ride up with you," Dov said.

Aaron didn't answer. He was actually grateful, because he wasn't sure he would make it under his own steam. When they arrived at the top floor, Dov walked ahead and entered the key code. He swung the door open for Aaron, who brushed past him into the condo. For a moment, Aaron sagged against the wall.

"What can I get you?" Dov asked.

"Just get the nitro pills and a bottle of water from the fridge. And then get the hell out," Aaron said.

Aaron staggered to the sofa and fell heavily into the plush velvet cushions. Dov placed the pills and water bottle on the coffee table, standing by expectantly.

"Are you sure—"

"I said *leave*, you fucking traitor. You were in on that scheme tonight, weren't you, Saminski? You knew all about Frost's plan, didn't you? And the way you've been cozying up to Suzanne, way above and beyond the call of duty. *You think I don't see who you are?*"

Aaron shouted. "Fuck off, Saminski. Get outta my face. You're fucking fired."

His legs were going numb.

As he chewed a couple of nitroglycerin tablets, he watched Dov silently turn and walk away, gently pulling the door closed on his way out.

Aaron screamed at the closed door, but his anger turned to agony as his heart convulsed in his chest.

He thought about calling Suzanne, but what was there left to say? She was a backstabbing, money grubbing bitch. Just like all the rest of them.

There was only one good, pure, beautiful thing left in Aaron's life, now. His thoughts turned to his new grandchild. He remembered the warm, milky smell of his own children, those squalling bundles of silky skin and little clenched fists. He smiled. His grandbaby was going to be the most perfect, beautiful, genius little girl ever. Even if Allison wouldn't tell him, Aaron *knew* it was a girl. She would love her Grandpapa so much she would *never* turn on him. Not like the rest of those traitors.

Another bolt of pain shot through his chest and down his arm, pulling a loud groan out of Aaron's throat.

Suzanne.

He should call her right now, let her know what she was doing to him. His phone slid out of his tingling fingers onto the floor.

How would she ever manage without him at the helm? How would any of them? They wouldn't. They'd all—every last one of them: his wife, his kids, his law partners, the lot—see how much he'd done for them. Every damn day of his life. They'd be fucking sorry.

He moaned as Death clutched his heart, wringing out his life force in agonizing spasms.

God, he was so tired. Too tired to fight anymore.

The evening light settled into a pink haze over the Japanese Gardens below as Aaron sighed out his final breath.

58

EXIT RAMP AHEAD

MONDAY, APRIL 18

Suzanne hit redial for the third time. "Dammit, Aaron, pick up!" she said to the empty kitchen.

Soon after their last hearing, Judge Bailey issued a favorable ruling on her estate plan and life insurance policies—they were all hers, now—so the beneficiary clauses were going to be changed with or without her spouse's signature on the little black line. She'd already met with her estate planning attorney to update her will, and as soon as the divorce trial was over in a couple of weeks, she was leaving on an extended vacation with Dov. But she had to manage this bit of unfinished business.

Based on the stern warning Judge Bailey had given him, she figured Aaron would sign off on the policies without Camelia having to take the forms to the judge. Except he wouldn't answer his damn phone. Aaron of all people. The man who demanded that everyone answer his calls at all hours. It went to voicemail again.

"Aaron, I'm not kidding. Call me as soon as you get this." She hung up and called Dov.

"Good morning, sunshine," Dov answered.

She could hear the smile in his voice. "Good morning yourself. Hey, have you heard from Aaron this morning?"

Dov hesitated. "No, but I can check his calendar," he said.

"Are you at the office? I thought you were fired?" Suzanne said.

"Yeah, I'm cleaning out my desk, archiving my computer files, that kind of thing. I'll have the formal chat when he gets in, but I want to be ready to leave when it's over," Dov said. "Clean exit."

"But Dov, you said he threw you out of the condo and fired you at the top of his lungs on Friday," Suzanne said. "What else does he need to say?"

"He was just having a mood," Dov said. "That's gotta be like the fifth time he's fired me. And I'm under contract, remember? I can't walk off the job until it's in writing, signed off by HR. Anyway, there's a meeting on his calendar, but let me check with his assistant."

Soft jazz music played as Suzanne sat on hold. A few seconds later, Dov was back.

"Darla says she hasn't talked to him, but he had a settlement meeting first thing this morning, and she doesn't expect him in the office until later this afternoon." Dov said. "Anything I can do?"

"No, I just need his signature on my life insurance forms but he hasn't answered my calls all weekend," Suzanne said.

"That's not like him," Dov said. "And I'm a little surprised he didn't have me drive him to the meeting."

"If you're fired, why would he?" Suzanne laughed. "And I'm sorry it had to come to that, Dov. But not the least bit sorry you won't be working for him anymore."

"He has his moments! I'll text you as soon as I see him." Dov paused. "And, I'd like to swing by later, if that's okay?"

"Absolutely! Come on over whenever you're done. Alma made a big pan of chicken enchiladas, so dinner's sorted. Text me when you're on your way, Love."

Dov hung up and felt the heat of a blush on his cheeks. She'd been calling him that lately, and he was both mortified and delighted. He shook his head. Silly courtship games. The type he'd always dreamed of.

Right now, though, a niggle of doubt about Anders was darkening the glow he'd felt at hearing Suzanne's voice on the phone. He glanced at his watch. Aaron was supposed to be in a meeting. He pulled up the firm calendar and read off the case name before opening the firm contacts. He entered the last name of opposing counsel, Bartlett, and clicked on the phone number as he picked up his handset.

After three or four rings, a man answered.

"Jason Bartlett."

"Mr. Bartlett, I work for Aaron Anders, and I'm just confirming that he arrived for your meeting this morning. His phone seems to be off, and his assistant has been trying to reach him," Dov said.

"Huh. That would explain why he's not picking up my calls. Because no, Aaron didn't show up this morning and I've been lighting up his phone." Bartlett said. "My client waited around for over an hour, but when Aaron didn't show, we adjourned."

"Please accept my apologies. Looks like we had a calendar conflict this morning that somehow got missed. We're looking into it," Dov said.

"Shit happens, but the timing wasn't great," Bartlett said. "Let Aaron know my client is out for blood. He's not accustomed to being stood up when we're supposed to be talking settlement. Have Aaron call as soon as you track him down, yeah?"

"You got it."

Dov hung up as a fat coil of dread unwound in his belly.

Aaron would die before he'd miss a meeting.

He'd looked pretty rough when Dov left him at the condo Friday night and, even if he'd hooked up with a new fling over the weekend, it wasn't like him to go silent like this. Dov grabbed his keys and phone, and sprinted for the elevator.

The condo was only a few blocks from the office. Going on foot would likely be quicker, but if he had to transport Anders, he'd need the car. As soon as the elevator doors opened into the parking garage, he ran to the town car and jumped in. The tires squealed all the way out of the parking garage. Dov dodged in and out of downtown traffic before turning onto Portland. He roared up to the curb, grabbed the car keys, and ran inside, jamming the elevator button repeatedly. The urgency of his errand took over. He couldn't wait. He entered the stairwell, taking the stairs two at a time.

He'd known when he left the condo Friday night that his boss was in a bad way and needed medical attention. Even though Anders had fired him and shouted at him to get the hell out, it was irresponsible to just leave. He'd been so furious about the way Anders was talking about Suzanne that it was a relief to close that door behind him. But Dov was Anders' Chief Security Officer. The least he could have done was call the fire department paramedics. Shame and regret pulled at him. His feelings for Suzanne had clouded his judgment, something he'd never experienced before now. It was an unforgivable breach of his duties. And it was completely foreign territory for Dov.

He burst through the fire door on the top floor and stepped into the hallway. He silently reviewed emergency medical protocol, and prayed it wasn't too late to administer first aid. As he approached Anders' door, he stopped short.

What the hell am I thinking?

He couldn't go back into the condo. If anything had happened to Anders—and the list of people wanting to smash his head in was growing by the hour—Dov would look like suspect number one. He took a deep breath and stepped forward to ring the doorbell so he would be on the doorbell camera. Proof he hadn't entered. He rang it twice before retracing his steps back to the car.

Once there, he called 911.

"I need an adult welfare check, as soon as possible," Dov said.

"What's the emergency, sir?" the dispatch operator asked.

"My boss was having a cardiac incident on Friday around seven p.m. He refused medical treatment, and asked that I take him home, which I did." Dov took a breath. "Since Friday night, no one has heard from him, and he's not answering his phone or his door."

"Is he violent? A threat to himself or others?"

"No, and he doesn't own a firearm," Dov said.

"Address?"

Dov rattled off the address for the dispatcher.

"We can send someone around in an hour or so," he said. "And what's your name?"

"Better be sooner than that," Dov said. "This guy is a big shot lawyer, and if he's alive, and finds out you took that long to show up? Oh man, there'll be hell to pay."

"Sheesh, okay, hang on," the dispatcher said. He put Dov on hold. A few seconds later, he was back. "Okay, a patrol car will be there in a few minutes. Sit tight."

Dov hung up and waited. He debated calling Suzanne, but there was no need to upset her. Not yet.

About fifteen minutes later, a Phoenix PD patrol car pulled up in front of Portland Place and two cops stepped out: a muscled up white guy and a wiry Latino. Dov got out of the town car as they approached.

"You the guy that called for a welfare check?" the white cop asked, hitching a thumb in his belt.

"Yes, Dov Saminski," he said. "Chief Security Officer for Mr. Anders. When I drove him home Friday evening, I suspected he was having a cardiac event, but he refused medical care. It's very unusual for him to go dark, and he missed a client meeting this morning."

"Do you have a key to the condo?" the Latino cop asked.

"I have the key code, so I can let you in," Dov said.

"If you've got the key code, why didn't you just go in and check for yourself?" Big White seemed annoyed.

Dov looked at him and shook his head. "That's not in my contract. No way am I gonna walk in by myself on either a crime scene or a sex party."

Wiry Latino laughed in short titters. "Let's hope it's door number two."

Dov led the cops inside, over to the elevators, and up to Anders' condo. He punched in the key code, entered the condo, disarmed the alarm, then stood aside.

"The last time I saw him, he was on the couch in the living room." Dov waved his arm in that direction. "I'll wait here."

But he already knew. He could smell Death all around him.

As the cops took his statement, an ambulance arrived to remove Anders' body, while whispering clots of nosy neighbors gathered in the courtyard. But now, with all the uniforms gone, Dov knew he should be doing a sweep of the condo to tidy up any loose ends—burner phones, ladies' underwear, porn, drugs, and god knows what else—but he just didn't have it in him. However Anders left things, that's how they'd be found.

That's what happens when you fire your Chief Security Officer.

Dov's concern now was how to break it to Suzanne. Even though Aaron had treated her badly—very badly, in his estimation—they'd shared a life. It was bound to be a shock, at the very least. He knew Suzanne well enough to know she would grieve. Maybe not for *this* Aaron, but for the Aaron she'd married all those years ago.

Dov took a deep breath and looked at his watch. It was already after one p.m. He started up the town car and pulled onto Central, heading north.

He had to talk to Suzanne before someone else did.

Suzanne's phone chimed BINGBING, alerting her to someone at the gate. She was surprised that it was Dov.

"Suze, I'm ahead of schedule," he said. "I didn't want to startle you by showing up unannounced."

"Come on up," Suzanne said.

When she heard the crunch of gravel on the crescent drive, she walked to the front door to greet him.

The second Dov stepped out of the car, Suzanne knew something was wrong. It was in the slope of his shoulders, the set of his jaw, the way his eyes telegraphed pain. She watched him approach, his footsteps heavier than usual. He seemed to almost run the last couple of steps, wrapping his arms around her, crushing her to his chest.

"Dov, sweetheart, what's wrong? What's going on?" Suzanne whispered.

He held on for another long beat before releasing her.

"Let's go inside," Dov said, taking her hand, leading her back into the house.

"Come sit down for a minute, okay?" Dov said, once they were inside.

He stepped into the family room and sank into the couch. Suzanne grabbed her water bottle and sat down facing him, cross legged.

"You're freaking me out, Dov. What's going on?"

He looked at her briefly, then his head dropped. "Not sure how to tell you, so I'm just going to say it." Dov took a deep breath and heaved out a sigh. "Aaron died sometime Friday night or early Saturday at the condo. They're pretty sure it was a heart attack."

Dead? Aaron?

She couldn't talk. She couldn't move. Hell, she could barely breathe. Was this real? She felt numb.

"I . . . what did you say?" Suzanne grabbed Dov's hand. "Look at me, Dov. What did you just say?"

His eyes, blue grey in the afternoon light, met hers. "I'm so sorry, Suze. They think Aaron died sometime after I dropped him off Friday night."

"He died on *Friday*?" Suzanne said. This couldn't be happening. "At the condo? Was he alone?"

Dov blew out a long breath. "Yes. He had a meeting at Jim Frost's house with the other senior partners. It didn't go well."

"I knew they were going to meet to tell him about the sale, but I didn't know it was Friday," Suzanne said. "He would have been in a rage."

"Yeah . . . he didn't want to come back here, and refused to go to ER. You know how he can be. Aaron demanded that I take him to the condo."

Suzanne began to laugh. And then continued to laugh. Then she couldn't stop laughing. Tears rolled down her face.

"Are . . . you . . . kidding?" She said as her laughter turned somber. "Is this even real?"

"Come here." Dov opened his arms and she fell against his chest. "It's real, Suzanne. Fucking bizarre and totally real," Dov rubbed her back. "And Suze, you need to call your kids before the news breaks."

"Oh god, Allison!" Suzanne sat up. "She'll be heartbroken."

"Yeah, this is going to be rough," Dov said.

"I have to tell them in person, but I only want to say it once. Please, Dov, can you hand me my phone? It's on the counter." Suzanne blew her nose. "I'll just text them to come over right away."

Dov retrieved Suzanne's phone and returned to the family room couch. He pushed the box of tissues toward Suzanne.

"What can I do?"

She shook her head. "I have no idea. But this is going to blow everything sky high. It will be an absolute shit storm as soon as word gets out."

"Give yourself a minute. Breathe. But then . . . you have to get in front of this. The deal with Sherman Wright . . . is there someone there you can warn? Or will it queer the deal?" Dov asked.

She had to think strategically, for once.

"So, no one at the firm knows about Aaron yet?" she asked.

"Not yet. But somebody is going to figure out pretty soon that he didn't show up for the settlement meeting this morning." Dov paused. "Suzanne, why not just talk to Darla and let her manage it? Or Janice?"

"Because of the buy-sell agreement, Dov. The ink is barely dry and now one of the shareholders is dead. Even though Aaron wasn't part of the deal, Sherman Wright could pull out because this is bound to bring the value of the firm down. Which means I don't get my money, and those senior partners don't get theirs either. They'll be on the warpath." Suzanne took a shuddering breath then looked around the room.

"But does it even matter? All of it . . ." He swept his arm around. "All of *this* is yours now, including majority shares in AndersLaw. I

502

think you should do whatever you want, never mind what anyone else wants. And I hate to say it, but that includes me. Don't listen to anyone except your gut and your lawyer."

She stared at him for a moment. "You're right. I didn't even . . . Jesus."

Suzanne got up and walked to the French doors, pulling them open to the veranda. She stepped outside and leaned on the railing overlooking the pool. Her mind was suddenly crowded with possibilities she'd never considered. Things she'd thought were out of reach—like the small, bright adobe bungalow she'd been dreaming of for years—were materializing in her mind's eye.

Dov came up behind her, wrapping her in his arms.

"I want to support you, but I'm going to head out while you talk to your kids," he said.

Suzanne pulled his arms closer and leaned her head back against his shoulder. "Yes, that's best. They'll need time to process. But do you mind coming back later? I'm gonna need the moral support."

"Any time. Just text me and I'll be here."

Suzanne turned to face him. Dov took her face in his hands and kissed her forehead. "I'll even bring you a Blizzard."

She laughed and stepped away, walking back into the house as Dov followed.

"You're too good to me!"

"Not nearly." Dov caught her hand and looked into her eyes. "And, Suze, I'm really sorry. I should have seen it coming . . ."

"Hey, none of that. Aaron already had one heart attack, and he didn't change even *one* bad habit, did he? I mean, he was still eating slabs of steak, washing it down with Scotch, and chewing on those disgusting cigars *all* the time. The man wouldn't eat a salad to save his . . . life." Suzanne paused, shook her head. "I can't believe I outlived him."

59

'Til Death Do Us Part

Monday, April 18

"Cam, Dov Saminski is in the lobby. He says it's urgent that he talk to you immediately," Cheri said.

What on earth would Dov want at 4:30 in the afternoon? He'd already turned over his evidence to Det. Luna, had met with Skye Samson to nail down his testimony, and Suzanne's divorce case was fast tracked with Judge Bailey. Camelia felt the grip of anxiety in her belly. What if something had happened to Suzanne . . .

"I'll be right there." She hung up her handset and rushed to the lobby, where Dov was seated.

"Good afternoon, Dov. Let's go somewhere more private, okay?" Camelia turned to Cheri. "Is the north conference room open?"

"It's all yours," Cheri replied. "And the fridge is freshly stocked, so help yourselves."

"This way, Dov," Camelia said as she stepped through to the hallway.

Entering the small conference room, Camelia took two bottles of water out of the beverage fridge and gestured for Dov to take a seat.

"So, what's going on, Dov?" Camelia placed the water bottles on the table between them as she sat down.

"Suzanne asked me to call you right away," Dov sighed. "But I was driving right past your office, so I stopped by, instead. I don't know how to break the news, but—"

"Jesus Christ, Dov, is Suzanne okay?" Camelia squealed.

"Oh, yes, sorry. She's fine." Dov's brow gathered in worried folds. "But . . . Mr. Anders is definitely not okay. He . . . god, what a mess. We . . . the cops found him dead in his condo this morning."

"*Holy shit,*" Camelia whispered, involuntarily. Then she caught herself. "Sorry, but that's . . . that's really shocking news. You caught me completely off guard."

"I get it. I've had a few outbursts of my own today." Dov gave a dry laugh.

"What the hell happened?" Camelia could not imagine Aaron Anders dead.

"Mr. Anders attended a partner meeting on Friday night. When it was over, he seemed to be in a bad way, and I tried to get him to go to ER, but he wasn't having it. I drove him back to his condo, downtown. Apparently, he had a heart attack later on Friday night." Dov released a long sigh. "When he didn't show up for a meeting this morning, I called in a welfare check. That's when the cops found him."

"I can't believe it." Camelia shook her head. "How is Suzanne taking it?"

"She was shocked, but given his lifestyle, I think she more or less expected another heart attack. Anyway, she's talking to the kids now, but wanted you to know so you didn't hear it on the news."

"I appreciate the consideration. Does Ashcroft know?" Camelia asked.

"Not yet, but he's my next call. He's not going to be very happy." Dov shrugged. "Not that I care, but it's my professional responsibility to let him know."

"And it's my responsibility . . . well, either mine or Ashcroft's, to notify the Court. Because now, there's no more divorce," Camelia said "But as soon as I call the Court, it's public record. I won't do anything until I hear from Ashcroft."

"I'll let Suzanne know," Dov said. "I guess this means the criminal investigation is dead in the water, too?"

"I'm sure that will be the end result. Even though there was clearly a second person involved, they haven't found the dump truck driver. And I'm sure Det. Luna's right. Whoever it was, he's long gone by now. Maybe even over the border."

Dov rolled his eyes. "So that's it?"

"No one has IDed him from the intersection cameras, and I doubt the cops will ever track him down, so yeah, that's probably the end of it." Camelia took a sip of water.

"What about Rocky Valley Landscape, the company that owns the dump truck. Can they shed any light on who was driving?"

"They reported the truck stolen from a job site, so no." Camelia shook her head. "Really, the best lead we had on what happened was Aaron, but with him dead and the driver in the wind, the case will have to be closed. But everyone knows it had to be Aaron. He wanted Suzanne out of the picture and wasn't going to wait around for her to . . . sorry, Dov."

He cleared his throat. "Actually, it was Kaitlyn's idea." Dov blew out an exhale. "Karma's a bitch, huh?"

"What are you talking about?"

"Kaitlyn. This was all her idea."

Camelia's heart rate jumped. "Jesus, Mary, and Joseph. Are you telling me you knew *all along* about his plan?"

Oh god. Did I misread this guy?

"I never said that," Dov said. "I just know who started the conversation. Aaron went along with it, but it was Kaitlyn's plan. She just got the timing wrong."

Oh my god. He knew. And he let it go forward.

"So this whole time . . . *you knew he was going to try to kill Suzanne?*" Camelia's voice had risen in volume and tone. She realized she was almost yelling when Dov drew back.

"No, god no. I didn't know *anything* about an *actual plan*. I put it together after the fact."

"Do I have to drag it out of you?" Camelia was losing her patience with his methodical style. "Just tell me what happened."

Dov had the grace to look sheepish. "A couple of months ago I was driving Anders and Kaitlyn back to the condo after a late dinner. I overheard her babbling about a surefire way to keep his estate in one piece and be free of Suzanne. She was kinda drunk, and Aaron shut her down, so I figured it was just hot air. But my ears perked up. She kept calling it the *Sheridan Gambit*, as if she'd ever played chess in her life."

Camelia recalled the note Kaitlyn had left at Anders' casita with that folder. *Sheridan Gambit research.*

Dov took a swig of water. "It's ironic now, though, since a gambit is the sacrifice of a pawn for a later advantage in the match."

"Chess player, are you?"

"I'm a Russian Jew. It's our national pastime," Dov said with a little smile.

"And when she died in Suzanne's car? What did you think then, Dov?"

Camelia wasn't sure about this guy after all. He was walking a pretty fine line between discreet and dishonest.

"I thought, first, I should light a candle, because although I have no idea how, Suzanne had been spared, protected. A miracle, really." Dov gave a slight shake of his head. "And then I thought it had to be an accident—a *real* accident, just like the cops said—because Anders wouldn't have killed Kaitlyn. Sure, she annoyed the hell out of him sometimes, and the affair was winding down. But he would have just broken it off with some fancy jewelry and a fat check. Like all the others."

"Then you saw him with that device from the Sheridan case, and thought differently?"

"That's when I figured it out. The *Sheridan Gambit*, as she called it, was referencing the traffic preemption device from Sheridan Electronics. Aaron *had* followed through with her idea, but he obviously didn't tell Kaitlyn what was going on. Which was smart, actually, because she's . . . she had a big mouth. When I saw him stashing that device on the Monday after the party, it all made sense. He implemented Kaitlyn's plan to kill Suzanne. Only it backfired spectacularly, because Kaitlyn *didn't know*. Otherwise, she never would've got behind the wheel of Suzanne's car." Dov crossed his arms and shook his head. "It's all such a tangled web of lies and . . . just a bag of crap. I was actually looking forward to going to trial and testifying against Aaron. He deserved to see the look on everyone's face when they found out what kind of scum he was. And now they never will. He'll be a tragic hero."

Camelia sat back and stared at him. She had misjudged him too quickly. Now that she thought about it, there *was* something special about him. It wasn't just his looks. Although his close cropped hair with a touch of silver, those steely grey blue eyes that could look right through you, and his lean, muscled physique nicely accentuated by the quality clothes he always wore didn't hurt. But there was much more to Dov; it was the way he observed people, listened to things, kept his mouth shut. He was a good mix of tough and presentable. She was going to need a guy like this if . . . *when* she went out on her own.

"You're probably right. But there's not much we can do about it now." Camelia took a sip of water. "So, you're at loose ends, huh?"

"Sort of. I'm out of a job, but I have a new hobby." He smiled and his eyes lit up. "I'm Suzanne's new chauffeur, bodyguard, and procurer of ice cream."

"You're a lot more than that, I think. I've seen the way she looks at you, Dov."

He blushed. "That's good enough for me."

Back at her desk, Camelia couldn't concentrate. She'd briefly filled Cate in, and now she was waiting for Ashcroft's call. She knew it wouldn't take him long after Saminski broke the news, so she just fidgeted, shredded mail, and watched the clock. An hour or so later, Cate transferred the call.

"Well, Belmont, you did it. You drove my client to his death," Ashcroft snarled as soon as she picked up.

"Spencer, I'm sorry about Aaron. But it had nothing to do with me," she said.

"Oh, how about that stunt you pulled in Court? You don't think that raised his blood pressure? Not to mention all your other antics?" Ashcroft was sputtering with rage. "You're such a high and fucking mighty—"

"I can tell you're upset, Spence. So, I'll save you some heartache and notify the Court that Mr. Anders is deceased and the divorce can be dismissed," Camelia said.

"You'll do no such fucking thing," Spencer replied. "Aaron was *my client*, and I'll be making that announcement to the court. In my own good time."

"We have a duty to promptly notify—"

"Don't tell me what my duties are," Ashcroft said. "Hold on."

The line went to a staticky rendition of Dolly Parton's "Nine to Five". Several minutes later, Ashcroft was back.

"Belmont? We're on speaker phone with Judge Bailey."

Ashcroft hadn't wasted any time.

"Good afternoon counsel, we are on the record in . . ." The judge read off the case name and number. "Mr. Ashcroft has advised that the matter should be dismissed on oral motion due to the untimely death of the respondent, Aaron Anders. Do you concur, Ms. Belmont?"

"Yes, your honor," Camelia said.

"Very well. The matter will be dismissed with prejudice and a minute entry will go out this afternoon. Is there anything else?" Judge Bailey asked.

"Your honor, just one thing. I know you were referring Mr. Ashcroft to the State Bar over his imprudent actions with Mr. Anders—"

"I object your honor," Ashcroft bellowed. "This is certainly not the time!"

"Just let her finish before you object, Mr. Ashcroft. You're getting ahead of yourself," Judge Bailey said.

"As I was trying to say before Mr. Ashcroft interrupted, I hope you'll show some mercy, your honor. Mr. Ashcroft was under the influence of a very manipulative and powerful client. He may not have acted honorably, but he was acting on his client's wishes. That's all I was going to say."

There was a long pause.

"Thank you for your input, Ms. Belmont," Judge Bailey said. "But I see the situation in a much different light. Mr. Ashcroft has *decades* of experience and is responsible for his own actions. It will be up to the State Bar to determine the appropriate sanction, but I have no sympathy for attorneys who think the rules—especially those designed to protect the public from chicanery and dirty dealing— don't apply to them because of their age and status in the legal community. We're adjourned."

The judge hung up and Camelia was left staring at her phone.

Well, she'd tried to soften the blow for Ashcroft. Not that he deserved it, but she couldn't help but have a little compassion. He was having a supremely bad day, after all. And she hoped that if she ever needed grace extended her way, someone else might do the same.

What had Dov said?

Karma's a bitch.

60

THE DEATH CARD

TUESDAY, APRIL 19

Camelia sat at her kitchen island, exhausted, hoping the coffee she was brewing would give her a much needed jump start. She hadn't slept well, tossing and turning, going over and over the events of the past month in her mind. She couldn't feel happy about Anders' death, but she didn't feel the least bit sad either. It was just so unsettling, but also, something about the way it ended felt rather . . . unfinished.

She poured a cup of coffee and took a long, scalding sip. Would Dov have passed the word to Det. Luna or Skye Samson? She kind of doubted it, so she left a message on Skye's mobile on her way out the door, warning her she would be stopping by.

She'd barely sat down in the waiting area at the Maricopa County Attorney's Office before her friend appeared in a striking kente dress and mustard yellow pumps. Skye led the way to her office and plopped into the chair behind her desk. Camelia pulled the door shut.

"I bet you want an update, don't you?" Skye laughed. "You gotta give us a minute to schedule the grand jury, Cam. Because the boss doesn't think—"

"Skye, that's why I'm here. Aaron Anders died Friday night."

Skye gasped. "Are you fucking kidding me right now?" Her voice went up an octave. "What the hell happened?" Skye leaned forward on her elbows.

"Heart attack, apparently. Saminski drove him home Friday night after a partner meeting, said he looked like hell, but—typical man—refused to go to ER. When Anders missed a meeting Monday morning, Saminski called the cops over to his condo for a welfare check. They found him already deceased."

"Wow. That's crazy. And here I was, just about to get promoted when I won that trial. Anders is . . . would have ninety nine percent been going to prison. And now you're gonna play the death card? Snatch me from the jaws of victory?" Skye shook her head.

Camelia laughed. "Counting chickens, much? But I get it. It's kind of disappointing that we won't get to see justice play out."

"Wait. You said he had a partner meeting on Friday night?" Skye asked.

"Yeah, not that it matters. Since the divorce wasn't final, Suzanne inherited his shares in the firm," Camelia said. "She's the majority shareholder now."

This time it was Skye who laughed. "You know Eileen Sanders, right? She was a class ahead of us in law school."

"Sure, I remember Eileen. She's at Sherman Wright now, isn't she?" Camelia said.

"Yep. We hung out over the weekend and . . . this is just between you and me for now, okay?"

"Of course! Give me the dirt!" Camelia said.

"Sherman Wright made a deal to buy out the senior partners at AndersLaw," Skye said. "And get this. Eileen said Chris Fischer was the little birdy who dropped the intel about the senior partners wanting out."

"What? How does she know Fischer?" Camelia asked.

"He used to clerk with Eileen's girlfriend at the Supreme Court. Anyway, Eileen said the senior partners couldn't sign fast enough. So ain't that somethin'?"

"Holy shit. Dov said Suzanne was part of a deal to sell, but I had no idea it was to AndersLaw's biggest competitor. Do you think that's what the partner meeting was about? They were breaking the news?" Camelia couldn't help but feel a moment of schadenfreude on Suzanne's behalf. "No wonder he had a heart attack."

"That's what I'm saying. Mr. A would have blown a gasket over that revelation, wouldn't he?" Skye paused. "Not that I wish ill of the dead, but damn. He kinda had it coming. Karma and all."

"Not the first time the K word's come up. But on the other hand, he'd already had one heart attack back in December, so this one could have just been bad habits catching up to him," Camelia said. "I can see, though, how losing his own firm in a shareholder coup would have been a catastrophic blow for Aaron Anders. As bad as dying, maybe."

"Yeah, he was definitely the alpha dog in his own house. So now what? You gonna come work over here now that you're a junior detective?" Skye teased.

"Thanks, but I'm not sure I'm cut out for the prosecution side," Camelia laughed. "There is change in the air, though. Anyway, I need to get to the office—"

"Hey, before you leave, since you're more or less Saminski's counsel and apparently we no longer have a case, can you take this property off my hands?" Skye swiveled her chair to grab a folder off her credenza.

Camelia stared at the folder on the desk between them. "Am I allowed to just take it?"

"I'll submit the forms, but yeah, there's no weapon or contraband here, and the last thing I need is *another* file to deal with." Skye gestured at the files piled on every surface of her office. "I'm sure someone at AndersLaw will want this back."

"No doubt. I'll take care of this if you call Det. Luna and let him know?"

"You got a deal."

Camelia stood and moved to the door. "Don't be a stranger!"

On her way to her car, Camelia considered the news about the Sherman Wright acquisition. Chris Fischer had made himself very useful. He was probably even part of the transition team, since he was in mergers and acquisitions. She wondered what he got out of the deal.

With the Anders case effectively over, Camelia didn't have any urgent issues demanding her attention. But when she pulled up her case calendar, she could see she didn't actually have any free time, either. Two of her cases were set for trial in the next couple of weeks. It was a never-ending cycle for which she should be grateful. At least her billables would be healthy this month.

She had just begun drafting the pretrial statement on one of the cases when her intercom buzzed.

"Cam, come to my office, please." Byron hung up before she could respond.

She sighed as she rose from her desk. Byron had no doubt heard about Anders and was upset she hadn't notified him. And he probably wouldn't care that she'd only found out late yesterday and had just now arrived at the office. She walked down the hall, gripping her legal pad in one hand and pen in the other. As she approached his office, she felt her body tense up. It never used to be this way.

"You wanted to see me?"

Byron didn't look up. "Come in and shut the door."

Camelia closed the door behind her and sat down while Byron finished typing. He pushed a file aside and leaned back in his chair.

"Remember when I said we were going to have a heart to heart? Well, this is it. Let's start with the Anders criminal case. You and I talked about it more than once. And more than once I specifically, directly ordered you to stay the hell out of it, didn't I?" Byron was nodding to himself as he talked. "But now I hear—"

"Byron, I didn't tell you about Aaron—"

He slapped his hand on the desk. "Do not interrupt me. As I was saying, I hear you've been talking to Det. Luna and one of the County attorneys. Poking around, asking questions, even setting up meetings. Is that true?"

"Well . . . I did call Det. Luna to ask him a couple of follow up questions," Camelia said.

"And didn't I specifically tell you the criminal inquiry was not our case, not your problem, and off the table?" Byron's prominent vein was pushing out of his forehead.

"Yes, but I—"

"But *nothing*! Stop making excuses! I told you to stay out of it and you didn't. I told you to leave Gerry Sheridan's name out of it, but you didn't do that either." Byron was punching the desk with his index finger. "And now it sounds like some law school chum of yours at the County Attorney's office is asking questions about a traffic device Sheridan's company sells. You know he's a friend of mine, right?"

"Byron, Aaron Anders died on Friday. None of it matters now." Camelia could feel her heart pounding and her temper flaring.

Byron smirked. "I know he's dead. But why didn't I hear it from you instead of from Det. Luna? Maybe you think Anders' death lets you off the hook, that it doesn't matter. But you'd be wrong about that. And I haven't even got around to that email you sent to Josh Campbell about not paying spousal maintenance. What the hell were you thinking?"

He had her there. "That was a professional opinion based on the case law and the facts presenting in the Campbell matter. I overstated my confidence, obviously. I had no idea Sorensen was going to award interim support, because it was never pled."

"Honestly, it's the least of your worries. And mine. My biggest concern right now is that I seem to have a rogue associate who can't stay in her own goddamn lane." He heaved a sigh. "And do you know what ethics counsel says to do with a rogue associate?"

"No, but I bet I'm about to find out."

She was tired of maneuvering Byron's outbursts, dodging his temper. What happened to the Byron who brought her into the firm? The mentor who taught her how to shine in the courtroom?

That Byron was long gone.

"Jesus. The sarcasm doesn't look good on you right now, Cam." Byron picked up his Montblanc pen and twirled it between his fingers. "Ethics counsel says rogue associates are to be terminated at once. Walked to the door. Do not pass go. Because they are a liability."

Camelia didn't respond. There was nothing to say. If she was being fired, well, so be it.

"Are you even listening?" Byron's steely gaze burned into Camelia's face.

She might as well let it all out. He was going to fire her anyway.

"Yes. I heard every word. But there was no question posed. In rebuttal, I don't consider myself a *liability*. In fact, I thought I was on partner track until recently. But I can see now that you have a much lower opinion of my value to the firm than I do." She took a breath. "If you want me gone, just email the severance letter and I'll sign it. But if you want me to stay on, you've got to quit treating me like a fucking red-headed stepchild. Because honestly, Byron, I'm exhausted. Not just because of the caseload, which is ridiculous, by the way. But because of you."

"Oh, *do tell*. How have I *exhausted* you, Cam?" Byron's brogue was breaking through as the sarcasm dripped off his lips. "Is it by demanding that you do your damn job?"

"This. This is what's exhausting. Dealing with your tirades. Having you tell me over and over that I'm not qualified to do criminal work, but that's only because you've pulled back your offer to mentor me. Dangling the promise of partner in front of me, meanwhile Brett hasn't even been here three years, spends half his time playing pickleball, and he's already been voted up. Breathing down my neck over billables, all while you're calling me into meetings with *your* clients, *on the house*. But you're billing them for that time, aren't you?" Camelia swallowed. Might as well go all in. "And watching you and Sonia bat your eyes at each other in the case meetings is frankly tiresome, too. I thought you were better than that. Hell, I thought Sonia was *so* much better. Turns out, you're not much different than Aaron Anders. Who, I just recently learned, was one of your investment buddies. Along with Josh Campbell and Gerry Sheridan, to name a few."

Byron's face turned a dangerous shade of mottled red. "Goddammit, you've got a nerve. Who the hell do you think you are?" Byron threw his pen on the desk. "That does it—"

"Does what? Gives you grounds to fire me? Because all I'm saying is the truth. If it pacifies your conscience to tell everyone I'm an uppity, backtalking bitch who didn't show the right level of respect for your position, go ahead. But for what it's worth, I don't appreciate the lack of respect you've shown me lately, either. I'm a grown ass woman and a pretty damn good lawyer, but you act like I'm not worth your time." Camelia stood up. "I loved this job, and I admired you, respected you. I don't know what happened, but I'll await your severance letter."

As she turned for the door, Byron spoke. His voice was a low growl. "Walk out that door, Cam, and we're done. No turning back. I'm warning you."

Camelia stopped in her tracks, but didn't turn around. What the hell did that mean? Was he firing her, or was this just another test of her willingness to kiss the ring? It hit her, then, like cold water. She was never going to make partner, and why the hell would she even want to? Why would she continue striving to impress a boss who didn't value her skills? Why would she tolerate being diminished at every turn? Was she really that desperate? That low on confidence?

She had to make a split second decision. Sometimes you can just feel your fortunes hanging on a word, and Camelia knew this was one of those moments. This was it. Her Death card. And only she could decide whether or not to play it.

She could kowtow to Byron *again*, or she could gather up all the strength she had and just walk out the door, carrying the consequences on her shoulders.

The timing was awful, but it probably always would be. She hadn't even talked to Cate yet. And Leon would likely be pissed off about the impulsiveness of her decision, even though it had been his idea.

She turned to face Byron. The anger had drained out of his face, leaving a sneer of contempt. It was all the validation she needed.

Without a word, she turned and walked out, gently closing the door behind her.

The end of a goddamn era.

61

ROAD TO FREEDOM

THURSDAY, APRIL 28

"I can't believe how hot it is. And it's not even May!" Cate threw her purse on a chair as Camelia stood up to hug her assistant.

Former assistant.

"Thanks for meeting me for lunch," Camelia said as Cate sat down across from her.

"Hey, it was already on the calendar! Besides, the halls are on *fire* with gossip and I couldn't wait to see you. Get this. Yesterday, Sonia quit. Loudly." Cate took a long sip of water. "There were fucks given. Actually, they were thrown with great force at Byron's head. So, it's been a big week over at the office. But what about you? How are you doing?"

After Josh Campbell's violent end, all the competing thoughts—should she stay and fight for her seat at McCaffrey's table, or leave and make her own way—had kept Camelia awake at night for weeks. Then, it all coalesced into one scary, yet unavoidable, conclusion. If she was going to move up, she had to move out. When she'd seen the contempt on Byron's face, it had been like clouds parting, lighting the way. Their season was over.

"I'm actually way better than I thought I'd be. Kinda weirdly calm, actually." Camelia leaned aside as a server brought iced tea and their waitress approached.

"You ladies need a minute?" the waitress asked.

"Give us five," Camelia responded.

The waitress nodded and walked away as Cate sugared her tea.

"Okay, Sonia was juicy tidbit one. Juicy tidbit two? I guess you're indispensable, because Byron says he's shutting down the family law department. Which, now that you're gone, is basically me and the file clerk. So, yeah." She blew out a sigh. "I need a vacation."

"Jesus. That's a lot to go down in just over a week," Camelia said. "Are you okay?"

"Oh, I'm fine. It's not the end of the world. I found this job. I'll find another one." Cate looked at Camelia. "I mean, I've already had quite an interesting offer."

Shit.

Had she already missed her window with Cate?

"Yeah, I've been meaning to tell you . . . remember when Ashcroft and Anders came to the office for that meeting? Well, Spencer made his move. Offered me a job. Then things got hectic and I forgot about it."

"He *what?*" Camelia recalled how rattled Cate had been after that meeting. "You're not actually considering it?"

Please say no.

"Well, what do you think? I mean, *come on*. How could I turn down a rare opportunity to be a shark wrangler in Arizona?" Cate laughed, rolling her eyes. "I mean, it's so *tempting*, because who wouldn't jump at the chance to mop up after blowhards like Ashcroft? Ha! No thanks. I'd rather work in a daycare, because at least there the shit is real."

Camelia laughed. "Thank god. Because I didn't get a chance to talk to you after . . ."

Cate grinned. "After you ripped Byron a new asshole and marched out of the office like a warrior queen?"

"It wasn't like that. I lost my temper," Camelia shook her head. She'd been wallowing in shame all week over rage quitting. "I didn't handle it well, and I regret it . . . well, let me clarify. I regret *how* I managed the situation, not that I quit. We were overdue for a breakup. And I'm sorry I didn't have a chance to give you a heads up. But when I went into that meeting, I honestly didn't know I was going to walk out like that. Things just kind of piled up on me when I was getting my butt chewed for the umpteenth time."

"I'm surprised you lasted as long as you did. He's really been a jerk lately." Cate gulped her tea.

"Ready to order?" the waitress interrupted.

The two women placed their food orders as a server refreshed their tea. Once they were alone again, Camelia leaned forward.

"You're right about Byron. He's been an outright asshole for months. Maybe his guilt over the affair with Sonia was eating at him, making him more surly than usual. Who knows?" Camelia waved her hair off her neck. Summer was already here. "But I've changed, too. When Auntie Freda died, it gave me pause. Then, when Josh Campbell died like he did, it was a lot to reconcile. I started thinking, is this how I want to spend my life? And Leon was in my ear about changing course because the Campbell thing really freaked him out.

I finally came to the realization, not that long ago, that even if Byron offered me partner on a platter, I didn't really want it."

"Seriously? Because you sure worked your butt off to qualify," Cate said.

"Well, I worked my butt off and Byron got the glory. And the profits. And yet, he was *still* being an asshole. And sleeping with Sonia? That's just a bridge too damn far."

"I agree. So disappointing. Trent's *furious* about all of it, by the way. You, Sonia, the end of the family law department." Cate sipped her tea. "But enough about them. Where will you go now? Have you reached out to anyone? You've got enough litigation experience you should be able to land a nice lateral partner position in any of the good firms, Cam."

"Maybe. But I'm going . . . in another direction." Camelia took a deep breath. "I've decided to start my own practice. And, I know it won't be a surprise that I would very much like you to come with me. You don't have to answer me now, but within a week or so, I'd like to know where you stand."

"Cam, you know I—"

"Wait. Don't answer yet. I just want to pose the question. Then I want you to go home, talk it over with Dave, and think it through. You can give me your answer next week," Camelia said. "For now, let's just enjoy our lunch."

"Okay, that's fair," Cate said.

They both paused as the waitress and server delivered their meals. Flatiron steak salad for Camelia, Dungeness crab salad for Cate. After grinding pepper on their salads, the waitress stepped away and Camelia continued.

"The real question is, can you *afford* to join me?" Camelia took another sip of tea and realized she needed to explain. "I ask because there's no way I can match the firm's benefit package. I can pay you the same salary and PTO, but there won't be a 401(k) or platinum level health insurance. If I'm lucky, there'll be covered parking and free coffee."

"Got it. And yes, I'll talk it over with the hubs, but I already know what he'll say." Cate smiled. "After everything that happened with Campbell, Dave thinks you're a goddess. He will one hundred percent support following you. And we're on his insurance anyway."

Camelia was equal parts relieved and terrified. It would be a huge weight off her shoulders to have Cate with her, taking charge of the administrative side of things. A familiar routine and a friendly face would be a boon for her new practice. But it was also scary. First, because she had no idea how she was going to pay her. And second, because Byron would no doubt interpret it as poaching. It would be a shot across the bow, and Camelia didn't need Byron as an enemy. Although given the way she'd quit, how much worse could it get?

"There's one other detail you should know. I won't be limiting my practice to family law," Camelia said. Could she really say it out loud? "I'm considering . . . I'm going to be offering investigative work. Not P.I. work, exactly. Just document review, internet searches, public records, things like that."

"Wow. That actually sounds like fun," Cate said. "A nice change of pace."

Camelia could see she was already hooked. But she had to tread lightly.

"I think so, too. But, again, you need to talk this over with Dave. And for the love of all that's holy do not breathe a word of it anywhere else, because it will take a while before I'm ready to open the doors. Hell, I'm still scrambling to figure out office space, malpractice insurance, and all the—"

Cate smiled. "Which is exactly why you need me now, not later."

"Yeah, but without any cash flow . . ." Camelia paused. "I'll just have to white knuckle it until I've got a couple of paying clients. But as soon as that happens, consider yourself hired."

Cate grabbed her purse and excused herself to the ladies' room. "Back in a second. Too much tea!"

While she was gone, Camelia's mind was churning over how she could afford to pay Cate her usual salary, and still have enough money left over for office build outs and furniture, along with a hundred other details she hadn't even bumped up against yet. Even if she cut the budget . . . what a joke. Her "budget" was the credit limit on her American Express card. Maybe she could borrow against her 401(k). She'd have to talk to her investment advisor and Leon about it. As she jotted a note to herself, Cate returned, flushed and breathless.

"Okay, it's all managed." She beamed at Camelia.

"Um . . . what's all managed?"

"Jesus, Cam. There's no way I could wait. I'm too damned excited." Cate grinned. "I called Dave from the bathroom. He's behind me, *and you*, one hundred percent. We've agreed I can accept the position with a 60-day deferred salary. But you have to make it up within a year. So, I have to give notice, but as of two weeks from today, I'm your new paralegal, office manager, and all around gopher."

Camelia dropped her fork, stunned into silence for a moment.

"Cate, you can't do that. I can't have you working for free, even for a couple of months," Camelia said.

"I never said I'd work for free. I said I would accept deferred compensation." She chewed a forkful of salad before continuing. "And it sure makes my mission today a lot easier, because I came to hit you up for a job. Even brought a fresh resume in case you were gonna approach someone like Sherman Wright."

Camelia was concerned that Cate was making a rash decision. "Is this a pity thing? Because you know I'll be fine, right?"

"Hey, I love ya, but this isn't about you, Cam. There's no way I'm gonna hang around and wait for Byron to change his mind and hire some creepy flake to take over the family law cases. Or worse, ask me to step into Sonia's shoes. Nope. Nuh uh. I'm outta there."

Camelia blinked back tears. Cate. Her steady as a rock, tough as nails, tender to the bone assistant was joining her, after all.

"Well, this is a really nice surprise, Cate. And you have no idea how much I appreciate it. And you." She took a sip of tea and swallowed her emotions. "But don't you have work to do? We can't be sitting around having long lunches on day one."

Cate laughed. "So. Business as usual, I see."

They clinked their tea glasses and toasted new beginnings. Camelia thought about ordering a round of drinks to celebrate, but then thought better of it. She'd been doing so well lately, no need to mess up her hard work now.

"First, we'll need office space," Camelia said.

"Yes, ma'am. Do you want to be near your house or near the court?" Cate pulled a notepad out of her purse. "And who do you like for phone service?"

Camelia laughed. This was going to be so much more fun than working with Byron.

62

ALTERNATE ROUTE

THURSDAY, APRIL 28

"Hi, Suzanne? It's Camelia." She swallowed. "I'm sorry to bother you, but wanted to check in to see how you are, and to give you an update."

After her long lunch with Cate, Camelia had driven back to the co-working space near her home knowing she had to start notifying colleagues and clients that she'd left the firm and was out on her own, now. And after all they'd been through together, one former client in particular should be the first.

"Oh hey, Camelia. Please tell me you're not calling with bad news," Suzanne laughed.

"No, it's good news. Last week, I decided to leave McCaffrey, Rhodes & Rodriguez. I just wanted you to know in case you called the office for something. This is now my official new business number," Camelia said.

"Oh wow. Congratulations! That's *very* good news! You're way too good for Byron's firm, Cam," Suzanne said. "It's their loss. So, where did you land?"

"I'm . . . I'm on my own, starting an investigative law practice, along with some select family law cases." Camelia felt a little whoosh of relief at finally having it out in the open.

"*Really?* Good for you, Cam. That sounds so interesting! Where's your new office?"

"For now, I'm in a co-working space on Seventh, north of Camelback, but I'm working on a more permanent solution. And Cate Sanchez, my assistant, is coming with me, so you'll have two familiar faces. In case you need a prenup," Camelia laughed.

Suzanne giggled in response. "Well, it hasn't come to that, yet. But you never know! I mean, if you had told me in December where I would be today, I would have laughed you right out of the room. Now look at me. I'm a rich widow with a hot young boyfriend, I just became a grandma, and I'm in the middle of packing for a trip to Montreal."

"What's in Montreal?"

"Nobody we know, which is just how we want it." Suzanne giggled again. "Dov and I are going for a month to sleep in and eat good food and do nothing. Life is looking up, if you ask me!"

"Sounds like it! And I hear the Sherman Wright deal went through."

"Yes, after a bit of wrangling. I had to give them a discount after all the bad press, but I still got a good price for my shares. And they're happy. They got a great deal *and* all the human capital, minus just four people," Suzanne said.

Aaron, Kaitlyn, Dov and . . . who else?

"Who's the fourth?" Camelia asked.

"Oh, I didn't tell you! I got a sweet card from Chris Fischer a couple of days ago," Suzanne said. "He's gone back to North Dakota. Waltzed right into a partner position at a firm in Bismarck. At least his experience with AndersLaw helped him land on his feet. Poor kid. He had it worse than any of us. I'm happy for him."

"Yeah, life didn't go easy on Chris Fischer these past few months, that's for sure. It's good to know he's okay," Camelia paused. "So, how is the . . . how are you feeling these days?"

"Honestly? Way better than I expected. That new doctor I found after I fired Rick Baum turned out to be a much better fit for me. I don't know if I told you, Dr. Kyle's a naturopathic oncologist. She's got me drinking some green smoothie crap for breakfast, an absolute ton of mushroom supplements, vitamin infusions, stuff like that. I don't mind, though, because I feel really good. Almost back to my old self. And . . ." Suzanne paused. "Drum roll please! Between the chemo and immunotherapy and her herbal cocktails, I just found out I'm in remission! No one knows how long it will last, but I'll take whatever I can get."

"Oh my god, Suzanne! That's the best news! I'm so glad to hear it!" Camelia felt relief wash over her. Suzanne deserved some goodness out of life. Especially after what Aaron had put her through. "As I've always said, living well is the best revenge."

"You know what, though? I never even wanted revenge. I just wanted some peace and quiet for whatever time I have left," Suzanne said. "Aaron was the one who always wanted revenge."

"Yeah, I noticed. What ever happened to make him that way?"

"I've asked myself the same question a hundred times, Cam. I mean, he wasn't always like that or I never would have married him. But over time . . . I blame the cutthroat lawyer culture. After a while, Aaron no longer valued the simple, easy, good things in life. It was all about the flash." Suzanne paused. "He was always trying to one-up, to prove his superiority, anything to win. But he just ended up cutting himself—and all of us close to him—on the sharp edges. Now that he's gone, I actually feel sorry for him. But I don't miss him. Not even a little."

"He seemed like a guy who was never content. Which is too bad, since he basically had it all." Camelia thought about all of Aaron Anders' over the top displays of wealth—the houses, the cars, the lifestyle—that in the end meant nothing. It didn't save him. "How are the kids managing?" She could picture their symmetrical faces. Perfect teeth. Perfect skin. Rich kid faces.

"Well, it's been pretty hard on Allison and they think that's why she delivered a couple of weeks early. Baby Erin is perfectly healthy and gorgeous, though, thank god. All three of them have had to face a lot of difficult, grown up stuff. But they seem to be coping." Suzanne sighed. "They've had Aaron cremated and interred, but they're holding off on the memorial services until the anniversary next year. We all thought, me included, that in light of all the other crap going on, services now would be . . . awkward. Poorly attended."

"Good point. Plus, you've all had so much to deal with," Camelia said, glancing at her watch. She'd love to spend all day talking with Suzanne, but she still had a long list of unchecked items staring at her. "Well, I've taken enough of your time. Give Dov my best and if he's ever looking for a job, I'd love to talk to him. As for you, just text me a selfie now and then, yeah?"

"You got it! And I'll pass the message along to Dov. He's enjoying the break, but I know how he is. He won't last long with nothing to do but feed me bonbons all day." She laughed. "Before you go, I just . . . thank you, Camelia. Through this whole mess, you've been such a help. Sometimes my therapist, sometimes my bulldog, but always on my side, and . . ." Her voice broke. "And I'm not going away for good, you know. Not yet, anyway! I'll call you when I get back, I promise."

Camelia hung up with a teary smile. It sounded like Suzanne's life was *finally* unfolding perfectly, with Dov at her side and her kids picking up the slack after Aaron's death. For once, a sort of happy ending. They were so rare in family law.

After completing another couple of client calls, Camelia briefly skimmed her inbox. It was almost five and still no email from her real estate agent. She'd paid for a month in the sleek co-working space, but feared she might be stuck here for a while, waiting for her agent to come up with an affordable lease offer.

She turned back to the list of tasks she'd brainstormed with Cate, trying to focus on something she could accomplish before heading home. There was one thing she'd been procrastinating: delivering the Sheridan exhibits to Sherman Wright, now that they'd taken over AndersLaw.

She still regretted how the case concluded—with a whimper, instead of the bang of a gavel—but maybe it was for the best. She shuddered to think what kind of hell Suzanne would have been subjected to if there had been a criminal indictment, then a protracted trial of Aaron Anders. Thankfully, Suzanne was spared that nightmare. Maybe there was something to karma after all.

Camelia couldn't put off returning the file any longer. She could take a detour downtown in the morning, drop off the file, close the circle. Camelia opened her rolling brief and pulled out the folder Skye had handed over to her as Saminski's attorney. She wasn't, really—he'd never formally retained her services—but she had given him advice. Close enough, under the ethical rules.

She emptied the folder on her desk and began typing a receipt for Sherman Wright. There was no way she was going to start this next chapter of her professional life with a loose end like this hanging over her head. And proof of delivery was necessary to ensure she'd closed the loop appropriately.

She entered the two items in a bulleted list:

- Traffic preemption device in padded envelope
- AndersLaw flash drive

Camelia picked up the flash drive and inspected the logo. Navy, cream, and gold. Very white shoe law firm. She'd have to come up with her own logo now. Something a little less staid. Maybe something more feminine?

Where was I again?

She needed to finish up and head home, take off her heels. As she turned the flash drive over in her fingers it occurred to her that its contents had never been disclosed. Had anyone even opened the drive? Surely Det. Luna would have inspected it? She popped the cap off and inserted it into a port on her laptop, clicking on the file manager. When the flash drive directory opened, there were a couple of Sheridan documents dating back to 2018, around the time the case first became active. But there was one other document file, titled Sheridan Gambit, dated March 19, 2023.

The same day Kaitlyn Fischer died.

Camelia's pulse quickened. It had already been accepted by everyone, at least informally, that Aaron Anders was behind Kaitlyn's crash. But with the case definitively closed when he died, did it even matter what was in this file?

Curiosity won and, despite her trepidation, she opened the document. It was a list, but she wasn't sure what she was looking at. A name, a phone number, a date, an intersection . . .

Tatum and Lincoln was where Kaitlyn Fischer died.

What the hell is this?

The document was dated March 19, but surely Anders' would have planned it all out far in advance of the AndersLaw annual party. Camelia clicked on the document properties and scanned the right side of the window.

Related Dates

Last Modified	2023-03-19 10:36 PM
Created	2023-01-26 7:27 AM
Manager	AndersLaw
Author	Kaitlyn Fischer

Last Modified By Christopher.Fischer@AndersLaw.com

Goosebumps rose on her arms when she saw the document history.

Camelia collapsed back into her chair. This couldn't be right.

The last person to touch this file was Chris Fischer, not Aaron Anders. And he did so on the night of the AndersLaw party, just about an hour before Kaitlyn died.

Camelia's mouth filled with the metallic tang of dread.

Fischer got away with murder.

He'd somehow pulled this whole thing off while everyone pointed the finger at Aaron.

So how could he have been so meticulous with all the other details, yet so careless as to leave this loose end dangling? Why didn't he just delete the file? Surely he would have known not to keep something like this around.

She needed to let Skye Samson know right away.

Camelia hit the X on the top of the document to close it. A dialog box popped up asking her to save the file. And she almost did. Her pinkie had already touched the enter button on her keyboard when she froze.

That's why Chris Fischer's name was on the file properties.

It was drilled into every lawyer's psyche to *constantly* save their work. Law firm lore was rife with cautionary tales of attorneys who lost entire appellate briefs—and months of work—by failing to hit *Save*. Based on the time stamp on Saminski's security footage, this document was saved while Fischer was at AndersLaw during the firm's annual party. He would have been in a hurry to get back. He wouldn't have thought twice. And just like Camelia, habit would have taken over. He probably didn't even realize he'd done it.

She tapped in Skye Samson's mobile number with shaking hands. When her friend answered, the words gushed from her mouth.

"Skye, holy shit, I just opened that flash drive that was in the Sheridan file you turned over to me. The one from AndersLaw. And I found something. I don't think it was Aaron. I think it was Chris Fischer. I think he arranged his wife's car accident. This list was saved by Chris on the day she died. We have to—"

Skye interrupted her tirade. "Hang on, slow down. You're not making any sense."

Camelia drew a deep breath. Of course she wasn't making sense. "Sorry, I'm freaking out over here. I found a document on the flash drive in the Sheridan folder. There's a list. Bullet points outlining the person, place, time, and payment for . . . something. A rendezvous. At Lincoln and Tatum on March 19 around midnight. That's where and when Kaitlyn died."

Skye sighed into the phone. "Okay? And?"

"It's all right here. I think these are *Fischer's notes,* his plan to set up the hit and run on Kaitlyn. And right now, he's thinking he pulled it off. Enjoying life as a law firm partner in Bismarck, North Dakota. So . . . does the case get reopened?"

Skye paused. "Cam, that's super interesting information, but I don't think it changes the overall case. We know Anders had the device the day after Kaitlyn died. One document on a flash drive without a chain of custody isn't going to sway the County Attorney. Anyone could have accessed that file. Like you just did."

"So Chris Fischer is gonna get away with felony murder or whatever this is?" Camelia couldn't believe how blasé Skye was being about what she considered a bombshell.

"Maybe. *If* he actually did it. But I have to tell you, there are holes in this a mile wide. Or at least big enough for a defense attorney to drive an acquittal through. Let's start with this. A list of things doesn't create a path from Chris to Kaitlyn. It's not A to B. It's one piece of a much bigger puzzle. Is it fascinating? You bet. Suspicious as hell? Yeah, to me and you. Clear and convincing evidence of wrongdoing? Not so much. And if I'm not convinced, a jury wouldn't be either," Skye said.

"I can't believe this. It seems pretty clear to me this note makes him guilty as hell." Camelia could feel her indignation gathering steam.

"I get it. But *pretty clear to me* isn't the same as *beyond a reasonable doubt*." Skye paused. "None of us like it and nobody wants to say it out loud, but you do know not every murder is prosecuted, right? We've got at least thirty-five percent a year in Maricopa County that are *never* solved. We don't even have a suspect in a lot of them. In this case, our primary suspect is dead and he took a lot of testimonial evidence with him. So even if Chris Fischer was actually behind his wife's death, we'll never be able to prove it. Unless he confesses."

Her phone dinged, interrupting her thoughts. Leon.

"Okay, but shouldn't we at least depose him?" Camelia said.

"On what grounds? And how do we pay for it? Because the cost of extradition would be on Maricopa County."

"And the County won't spend the money on something as nebulous as this," Camelia said.

"Bingo," Skye responded.

"That really sucks. But thanks for your honest assessment. I guess I need to start toughening up a bit if I'm going to be practicing in this area, huh?"

Skye laughed. "Girl, you need like four more layers of skin. But I'm glad to know you're out there paying attention."

Would she ever have skin thick enough to accept that murderers sometimes just walk away?

Camelia's phone dinged again.

"Okay, Leon's texting, so I gotta go, but let's get together in a couple of weeks." Camelia said goodbye and hung up.

She slammed her fist on the desk.

Goddammit.

It grated on her that poor, puppy-dog-eyes Fischer was not at all who she thought. How could she have been so naïve? Of course he would want Kaitlyn dead. She'd made a fool of him in front of everyone. And there's no punishment for being a cheating jerk, other than the very thing Kaitlyn wanted: a divorce. If Chris figured out how to get away with revenge, why wouldn't he take matters into his own hands?

And, if what Skye said was true, maybe there was a place for that kind of thing. Hell, maybe that kind of rough justice was just karma getting a helping hand.

But the way he'd been crying the night she'd driven him home from Durant's made it seem like he was genuinely devastated over Kaitlyn's death. In fact, he'd said more than once that it was a terrible accident. She replayed that night in her mind. The tears were real. So maybe he didn't actually *intend* for Kaitlyn to die? Maybe it really was . . . accidental?

Camelia glanced down at her phone where Leon's text message was waiting for a response. She couldn't devote any more time to Anders and Fischer. If either of them—or both—had a hand in Kaitlyn's death, karma would just have to take care of it. Like karma had already taken care of Anders.

Right now, Camelia had to concentrate on her new practice. And her marriage.

Leon had really stepped up these past few weeks, propping her up when she needed it, calming her down when she was frantically trying to manage the stress of every damn thing she'd been handed over the past four months. She mentally ticked off the list.

Auntie Freda's death and its messy aftermath.

Josh Campbell's suicide.

Byron sidelining her on the partner vote.

The roller coaster of the Anders divorce case.

Then Kaitlyn Fischer's death and its even messier aftermath.

Aaron's unexpected heart attack.

Suzanne's terrifying illness which was, thankfully, in remission.

Walking out on her job of seven years with exactly zero prospects.

But she'd survived, and here she was. Laying the groundwork to start her own investigative practice.

Maybe I'll name the new practice Legal Karma.

She laughed at her own joke and opened Leon's text message.

> New client wants me in Valencia for the launch. How does two weeks in Spain sound?

Camelia broke into a smile.

> I think a change will do us good.

THE END

Helpful Links

For help with alcohol and drug addiction:
Alcoholics Anonymous: https://www.aa.org/
Narcotics Anonymous is available here: https://www.na.org/

For information about warning signs of heart attack:
https://www.heart.org/en/health-topics/heart-attack/warning-signs-of-a-heart-attack

For information about warning signs of heart attack in women:
https://www.heart.org/en/health-topics/heart-attack/warning-signs-of-a-heart-attack/heart-attack-symptoms-in-women

For information about ovarian cancer:
https://www.mayoclinic.org/diseases-conditions/ovarian-cancer/symptoms-causes/syc-20375941

For help with anxiety, panic disorder, and other mental health issues:
In Canada: https://cpa.ca/public/findingapsychologist/
In the U.S.A.: https://www.findapsychologist.org/

For attorneys who need help with addiction and mental health issues:
In Canada: https://www.cba.org/Sections/Wellness-Subcommittee/Resources/Wellness-Links
In the U.S.A.:
https://www.americanbar.org/groups/lawyer_assistance/resources/covid-19--mental-health-resources/

If you are having suicidal thoughts, call 988 in the U.S.A. or Canada.

Author's Note

Finishing the second novel in the Camelia Belmont Mystery series has been an exercise in humility and patience. Just when I thought it was all wrapped up, my critique partners showed me the error of my ways: a massive plot hole. So, I put my head down and went to work. The result is—I assure you—so much better for it. Thanks are (always) in order, and here's my list. First up, the fam:

Brian Donison, my VP of IT, the best travel partner <u>ever</u>, a master of moka pot coffee and Spanish Breakfast, and the man who keeps me laughing at life.

Our daughter, **Stacie Elliott Donison**, and son-in-law, **Scott Elliott**.

Nadine (Watkins) Rayborn-Patton, aka Mama Nadine, who roped all her friends into buying my first book. Where's Waldo?

Joan (Peterson) Donison, my mother in law and voracious devourer of all kinds of books, including mine.

My critique partners (all *amazing* writers, by the way), without whom this book would be a hot mess.

Deepthi Atukarola
Martin Crosbie: https://martincrosbie.com/
Cormac O'Reilly
Leina Pauls
Brian Wyvill: https://www.brianwyvill.com/

The dearest cheerleaders a person could hope for (alphabetically). Thank you all for your encouragement, faith, tolerance, and commiserating!

Rhonda Berg	**Sharon Hansen**
Shannon Bradley	**Sarah Matheson**
Roxane Cappa	**Jennifer Near**
Karen Dodd	**Heather Pollock**
Barbara Evans-Levine	**Mark Szkoda**
Brooke Gaunt	**Allison Whiteside**
Jana Gill	**Sharon Yannarella**

Truth or fiction? Obviously, this is a work of fiction, but there are some real life people and places I want to acknowledge.

- Phoenix, Arizona, will forever be my professional home, the place I cut my lawyering teeth, and where I forged invaluable, lifelong friendships. The smell of the desert is something I will always crave.

- Maricopa County Superior Court is real, and I've spent way too many hours there over the course of my legal career; however, the attorneys, clients, and scenarios portrayed are fiction. Likewise, the law firms of McCaffrey, Rhodes & Rodriguez, AndersLaw, and Sherman Wright are all fictitious.

- The Arizona Women Lawyers Association, of which I am a past president, is a supportive home for women attorneys, particularly those who aspire to the bench.

- Paradise Valley Police Department is real; however, Det. Jose "Moony" Luna, Waylon "Tank" Sherman, and the circumstances portrayed are fiction.

- Durant's is a fabulous RatPack kinda place, popular with the legal community. I've enjoyed a lot of great steak dinners there and yes, you enter through the kitchen. The Henry has a wonderful, fresh-yet-homey feel and is the perfect spot for hanging out with colleagues and friends. El Chorro and The Hermosa Inn have two of my favorite patios for summer evenings lingering with friends. For takeaway, two of my faves are Pizza Heaven (the BBQ Chicken Pizza is making my mouth water just thinking about it) and Duck & Decanter (try the Creamy Herb Chicken Salad).

- Paradise Valley Country Club and Phoenix Country Club are both real golf clubs.

- Addiction, substance abuse, and mental illness are rampant within the legal profession. Coupled with the systemic misogyny in the field, women are even more severely impacted, both personally and professionally, by these challenges. My insights on this problem are here: https://bit.ly/DonisonOC

- None of the characters in this story are real people (even though some of these characters sure think they are!) and none of these events actually happened. However, two characters were influenced by real people. Dr. Carlos Chavez is inspired by the delightful, compassionate Arnold R. Lopez, LCSW. Cate Sanchez is inspired by the most talented, funny, brilliant legal assistants I've ever worked with: Mary Sanchez, Diana Garcia, and Cathy Skiles Chavez.

- As Suzanne Anders came to life on the page, real women were on my mind. Two sweet souls in my circle—a beloved friend from law school, and a dear client—died as a result of ovarian cancer. My sorrow over their loss drove me to spotlight that insidious disease as a message to my mystery loving sisters to not ignore the little warning signs. While Suzanne Anders isn't based on the tragically short lives of either woman, I like to think my memories and their beautiful spirits infused the fictional Suzanne with some of their grace and *joie de vivre*.

ABOUT THE AUTHOR

Pamela Donison, JD, has been a writer in one iteration or other her entire life. Currently a practicing attorney, she is a former award-winning military journalist and acquisitions manager for a division of Harcourt Brace. Her work has been published in numerous legal periodicals, as well as chapters in three legal anthologies.

Pamela writes under the pen name PJ Donison, because . . . bias exists. https://pudding.cool/2017/06/best-sellers/

Her first full-length novel, **Death Comes For Christmas**, is a soft-boiled murder mystery set in Regina, Saskatchewan, and the origin story for Camelia Belmont, an aspiring female investigative attorney. **Death At The Crossroads** is the second in the Camelia Belmont Mystery series. Pamela is currently working on **Death Of The Butcher**, set in Valencia, Spain, her current favorite city on Earth.

Her short fiction has been published by The Dillydoun Review, Drunk Monkeys, and the anthology Crime Wave 2: Women of a Certain Age, published by Sisters in Crime, Canada West Chapter. Her short story "Tontine Dream" will be in Crime Wave 3: Dangerous Games, coming in October, 2024.

Pamela is a member of Sisters in Crime and is the 2024 President of the Canada West Chapter. She is also a member of Crime Writers of Canada, Writers Guild of Alberta, and the Pacific Northwest Writers Association, as well as a member in good standing of the State Bar of Arizona. Pamela and her spouse, Brian, live most of the time in Lethbridge, Alberta, the traditional and unceded territory on the ancestral and traditional Indigenous territories of the Blackfoot and the Metis Nation of Alberta, Region III.

Email her at hello@pjdonison.com.

Enjoy this excerpt from
PJ Donison's next novel,

DEATH
OF THE
BUTCHER

A Camelia Belmont Mystery

1

FINIS MORS
THE END IS DEATH

SUNDAY, MARCH 10

Claudio Abarca methodically chopped bursting ripe tomatoes at his kitchen counter, tossing them into a shallow bowl as he went. A half kilometer away, El Micalet, the 485 year old bell at Catedral de Valencia, rang the hour: one o'clock. He crushed cloves of garlic with the flat of his blade, minced them, and stirred them into the tomatoes. He ground fresh sea salt over the mixture, maybe a bit too much. Finally, he drizzled his best olive oil, a gift from a wealthy parishioner's private olive press. Just as he pulled a fresh *barra de pan* from its paper bag, a rapid knock interrupted his meditative meal preparation.

He wasn't expecting anyone. Not today. Not on the Sabbath.

He wiped his hands on a faded dishcloth and slap-slap-slapped toward the door in his worn slippers. The only person who would show up like this . . .

"Enzo! I wasn't expecting you—" Claudio began.

Enzo pushed past him, agitated, twitchy. High on something.

This isn't a good idea.

"Yes, but I'm here, aren't I? I'm here and I want to dance. I want to eat a lot of food. And then I'll let you fuck me, padre." Enzo's cold smile revealed twisted teeth, one canine missing. He hummed an unfamiliar tune, ran his hand over his hair, and did a little shuffle. "Dance is over. I'm hungry."

Enzo was wound up and it scared Claudio to be alone, in the sanctuary of his home, with a drug addled freak.

"Where's Ivan? Does he know you're here?" Claudio was much more afraid of Enzo's dealer-pimp-boss than he was of Enzo.

Enzo shrugged. "He's at the beach with some of his Russki friends."

One less idiot to worry about.

"Why don't you shower while I finish making lunch?" Claudio extended his hand toward the bathroom. "By the time you're done, I'll have a feast ready."

Enzo sniffed an armpit. "Good idea. I smell like a *cabro*." He kicked off his boots, dropped his jacket on the couch, and headed toward the bathroom, just off the bedroom at the back of the apartment. "I won't be long."

By the time the bathroom door shut, Claudio's mind was spinning out of control. Enzo could be dangerously violent. He knew because the man had shown up more than once with bloodied fists and swollen, purple bruises on his face and body. His back bore a pale scar from the forty-six stitches required to close up a knife wound from a street fight.

With the thought of the knife, Claudio hustled to the kitchen as fast as his 76-year-old legs would carry him. He pulled open a drawer and extracted a long, thin boning knife, then scurried to the bedroom. He pulled up the corner of the mattress and tucked the knife in, blade first. Only the end of the handle was visible, which he deftly covered with the duvet.

Just in case.

He wiped the sheen of nervous sweat from his upper lip and hurried back to the kitchen. Claudio sliced the bread and chorizo, then scooped olives into a dish. The chicken roasting in the oven wouldn't be ready for another half hour. He set a second place at the table.

He glanced at his phone. Should he call someone? But who? Who on earth could a Canon of the Roman Catholic Archdiocese of Valencia call at one in the afternoon on a Sunday to complain about his current favorite prostitute showing up high and unannounced? Who would take that call?

No, Claudio was on his own.

He took a long sip of cold, crisp Verdejo. Maybe the shower would calm Enzo down, soothe whatever chemical beast was riding him today. He heard the water stop and braced himself. He poured a glass of wine for Enzo, and placed it on the table in front of the second plate. He ran thick hands over his broad face and down the back of his nearly-bald head.

Tranquilo, tranquilo.

Enzo—with his dark eyes and permanent smirk, curls slicked back, muscles taut under smooth brown skin—reminded Claudio of an otter as he strolled through to the dining area wrapped in a towel. He pulled out the chair opposite Claudio and plopped down, wriggling his pinky in one ear.

"The shower was just the thing, padre. I feel like a new man," Enzo grinned and held up his glass of wine. "And I know how you like a new man every now and then. Salud." He took two deep gulps, draining the glass.

Claudio chuckled and passed the bowl of tomatoes. "The chicken isn't ready, but we can start with the salad."

Throughout their meal, Enzo talked, rambling off into neighborhoods of slang unfamiliar to the old priest, but Claudio understood the gist of it. Enzo . . . well, actually, Ivan had been promoted, and his new role came with a new boss. A *ballena*, a big whale from St. Petersburg, higher up in the Tambovskaya than the last guy. They were expanding their reach, moving beyond the city, into the villages and small towns west, down the coast. And they needed names. Lots and lots of names. The type of names Claudio had already been passing along, but now they wanted them from more towns, all the way to Malaga and beyond. They wanted to own the Spanish coast. But they needed mourning relatives if their Pig Butchering operation was going to be a success.

Claudio nodded and listened as Enzo stuffed his face, washing mouthfuls down with a second bottle of wine. The man had an enormous capacity for food, yet barely an ounce of fat on his body. No doubt the meth helped. As he talked, his towel slipped away, and Claudio stole guilty glances at the dark puff between his legs. Finally, Enzo pushed his plate back and wiped his mouth on the faded cotton napkin.

"Gracias, padre," Enzo said.

He pulled the towel together and, grabbing a pack of cigarettes from his jacket, stepped onto the sunny balcony. Claudio tidied up the kitchen, watching through the window as smoke curled around Enzo's sharp face.

Enzo was a disgusting piece of shit who deserved his eternity in hell, but Claudio was almost as addicted to Enzo as Enzo was to everything else: nicotine, caffeine, alcohol, oxy, meth, sex. But today, Claudio felt a seismic shift in their dynamic. Enzo was no longer afraid. No longer in thrall to Claudio. This new boss, Alexsei Petrov, had given Enzo big ideas about moving up in his vile criminal business, and it could only mean trouble for Claudio. Potentially fatal trouble, if he didn't deliver.

And Claudio knew he couldn't. He was already mining the Diocese for every dead property holder he could find, and he had no authority or plausible reason to obtain that information from other dioceses. What excuse could he possibly give? The only thing he could do is what *anyone* could do: read the obituaries. He would be rendered useless. And useless people did not survive the harsh winter of Russian mafia discontent.

He could feel, already, the dry taste of the words in his mouth. The weak and helpless resistance he might try to offer. The steely grip of Ivan's meaty hands—

Claudio flinched as Enzo's arm fell across his shoulders.

"I'm clean, I'm full, I've already danced, and now . . ." Enzo whispered. "How about a little pleasure, then business."

Claudio heaved a sigh, despite his arousal. He wished he didn't want what he wanted so badly. He leaned into Enzo's shoulder.

"It will be our last time, Enzo. I'm going to Rome next week, like I told you. And I don't know exactly when I'll be back."

He followed Enzo to the bedroom, and their ritual began. First, the defrocking of the priest. Enzo stripped him down, methodically removing each layer of clothing. If this were olden times, the church would remove Claudio's vestments—those heavy, ornate robes that marked him as a holy person—just as Enzo was doing this afternoon.

Afterwards, curled into himself, Claudio's shame and self-loathing brought on waves of rage. He looked over at Enzo, already sleeping. Even though he was in his thirties, with his hair falling in soft curls around his face in the fading afternoon light, Enzo looked like a Renaissance boy. But he was no innocent *niño*. Enzo was an addict, a whore, a street-dwelling swindler, probably a sociopath. A dangerous piece of shit. There was only one clear way out of this mess.

Claudio rolled over and quietly slipped the blade out from between the mattress and bed frame. He clutched the handle with a prayer on his lips, rehearsing his actions in his mind. He would roll over and, without hesitation, shove the boning knife into Enzo's neck, slicing the artery. He would press his pillow over the wound to absorb the blood. He would wait for Enzo to expire. It wouldn't take long. He would call the police and report the home invasion, the struggle, the rape, the self defense.

He released a long, slow breath and rolled back towards Enzo, who was staring at him with a leering grin.

Claudio tried to hide the knife, but he was too late. Enzo laughed as he pried the knife from Claudio's knobby, arthritic hand.

"And what did you think you were going to do with this?"

"Nothing . . . I . . . it's for protection, when I'm alone. And I realized it was here, by the bed. I only meant to move it back to the kitchen, but I didn't want to wake you," he stammered.

"And what if I don't believe you?" Enzo ran the tip of the blade across Claudio's lower lip. "What if you're a liar, and you meant to cut me?"

"Why would I hurt you, Enzo? You're my darling, you know that."

Claudio started to rise, but Enzo pushed him back and rolled onto him, straddling him. He tossed the knife back and forth between his hands, laughing.

"Yes, but *what if* you're not really going to Rome? *What if* you're not really going anywhere?" Enzo stopped and glared into Claudio's eyes. "*What if* you actually want to kill me? To get rid of me? To show the new boss that you're the *real* boss?"

"What are you talking about? I don't know anything about your *boss*, and I'm not trying to get rid of you. And of course I'm going to Rome. The Vatican called us in for committee meetings. I'll be back when it's over. Three weeks. A month at most." Claudio's mouth was dry, and he struggled to swallow.

"What if I told you not to go?" Enzo's hands were on his hips, his face suddenly contorted into a mask of fury, his voice rising to a shriek. "Claudio! We need you here. I'm ordering you *not to go*!"

"Don't be a child. Of course I'm going. It's the Vatican. For the love of God, I can't tell them no."

"But you can tell *me* no? Your *darling*? Your *beloved*?" Enzo was leaning over Claudio, screaming into his face. "I'm the one who gives you every disgusting thing you want, but you will tell me no?"

"Enzo, I give you things as well—"

"Give me twenty five names and five thousand euros, you filthy *maricon*, and you'll never see me again." Enzo licked his lips. "Or take your chances with Ivan."

"You know I can't just come up with names out of thin air! I have to screen every family, make assurances, introduce them to Tomás, grease the wheels." Claudio tried to reason with him, but Enzo's dangerous mood was kicking off again. It was making Claudio anxious, but he wouldn't let on. "And I don't have five thousand just laying around. You know damn well I'd have to go to the bank for that kind of money. And get *off* me. You're too heavy to be sitting on me like a baby."

Claudio tried to push him off, but Enzo was too strong. He pinned Claudio's arms and leaned over him, screaming.

"*I'm not your fucking baby, padre!* I'm no one's baby. I'm a motherless bastard, and I'm the new fucking boss. You don't give me orders. Not now. *Not ever again!*" His face was red and his eyes were darting around as if shadows were chasing him.

Claudio froze in terror, squeezing his eyes shut as tears drained down his temples. They'd fought before, and it often got loud and physical, but nothing serious. They'd traded a few slaps, once or twice a forceful shove. But today felt different. There was a new, nihilistic edge to Enzo this afternoon.

Enzo's palm connected with Claudio's face in a stinging reminder.

It's the Sabbath, for the love of God.

But Claudio knew he deserved it. The older man began to cry, silent sobs racking his shoulders.

Then, without warning, in one swift movement, Enzo crushed his pillow onto Claudio's face.

"Stop fucking crying. Who's the baby now, huh? What's that Claudio? I can't hear you!"

Claudio kicked, he clawed, he tried to flip the younger man off him, but it was no use. He was pitifully weak compared to fighting-fit Enzo.

Claudio's last words were a torrent of muffled screams that no one heard. As he dragged in a mouthful of wet cotton and feathers, desperate for one breath of air, his heart spasmed from the oxygen deprivation. Claudio's life left the room on the afternoon breeze, rustling the curtains as he went.

Claudio was off to meet his maker. The only question was, which one?

# # #

The scent of sardines sizzling in olive oil and onions wafted through the vents, into the dim hallway of the building. But even the tantalizing stench of Señora Fernandez' mid-day meal couldn't mask the other smell sneaking out from under the door.

Death.

Fidel Lombardo fumbled with the mass of keys in his beefy paw, trembling with dread over what they would find in Father Claudio Abarca's modest apartment. He'd assumed Claudio was in Rome. The old priest had been bragging to anyone who would listen that the Vatican had called him in for something or other. Fidel tried to recall the last time he'd actually seen Father Claudio. Was it last week? No. It was a week ago Sunday. They'd passed at the front entry as the priest returned from mass. Nine days.

The two Policia Nacional officers at his elbows were crowding him, making it even more difficult to find the right key. Couldn't they see he was nothing more than an honest superintendent, trying to help? Couldn't they be more friendly in their inquiries?

Finally, he landed upon the right key. Fidel pushed it into the keyhole and turned the lock, then stepped back. Let them find the mess. Oh, he hadn't been inside, not yet. But Fidel had cleaned up more than one death in the building and he could well imagine what kind of oozing rot was on the other side of the thick, iron-sheathed door.

The short one pushed open the door. Fidel shuddered as the odor hit his nostrils. His hand flew to his face, covering his mouth and nose. He turned away, suppressing a gag.

The two officers paused, looked at each other, and the taller one spoke into his radio. An agreement had been reached. The shorter one pulled on a white paper mask and walked through, calling out "claro" as he inspected each of the home's rooms. Dining and living room, clear. Kitchen, clear. Bathroom, clear. Balcony, clear. All that remained was the bedroom, and Fidel could see from his station in the hall that the door was open and the bedclothes were unkempt.

The officer inside spoke into his radio as he walked back through the apartment, into the hall. He pulled the door shut. His eyes conveyed a silent message to his partner and they both turned to Fidel.

Speaking Valencian Spanish, the shorter one barked his instructions. "The man is deceased. You will come with us to give a statement. We need the keys to the flat, and no one else can enter until we are finished investigating." He glanced at his partner, who nodded. "Is there anything you need to do before we go?"

Fidel looked from one to the other and shook his head. His appetite for the lunch his wife had prepared was long gone, so he might just as well get this part over with. Besides, he couldn't very well call Enzo now, not with the cops breathing down his neck. But Fidel would most certainly have a chat with him later, because this sure as hell better not be Enzo's goddamn mess.

TO BE CONTINUED …

Be the first to know when

Death Of The Butcher

is released, and get deals, discounts,

and more when you join my mailing list.

CLICK HERE TO SIGN UP

Already a subscriber? Thanks so much!

pjdonison

26 Letters, Rearranged

www.ingramcontent.com/pod-product-compliance
Lightning Source LLC
Chambersburg PA
CBHW030536020726
47494CB00005B/1396

9 781778 038723